Look Into My Heart
By Iris Bolling

Siri Enterprises
Publishing Division
Richmond, Virginia

ISBN-13: 978-0-9801066-2-6
ISBN-10:   0-9801066-2-1

Cover and book design by: Judith R.E. Wansley

Published by:
Siri Enterprises
Richmond, Virginia 23222

The Heart Series
By Iris Bolling

Book One – Once You've Touched The Heart

Book Two – The Heart of Him

Book Three – Look Into My Heart

www.irisbolling.com

www.sirient.com

Acknowledgements

Thank you my heavenly father.

Raymond, Chris and Champaine, thank you for your love, support and patience.

Judith Wansley, thank you for the ability to "draw a little bit."

Linda Gordon and Kathy Six thank you for your time and knowledge.

Roz Terry, LaFonde Harris, and Gemma Mejias: the roots to my tree, thanks for always answering the telephone.

Valarie Johnson and Tanya Thompson, thank you for keeping it real.

Wiley "Devin" Franklin, thank you for sharing your knowledge.

To the beautiful people, Monica Jackson, Sakeitha Horton, Justin Wansley, Jason Wansley and Stephen Howell.
May God's blessings always be with you.

To my mom, Evelyn Lucas, my sister Helen McCant and brother Albert "Turkey" Doles, family is the strength that binds us forever and always.

To all of my readers, your wait is over. Enjoy book three of The Heart Series as the saga of JD and Tracy's journey towards the White House continues. Cynthia will capture your heart.

This book is dedicated to, Julia C. Nedrick, thanks for being there.

Prologue

Cynthia sat in her office at TNT Event Planning waiting for her late night caller to appear. It had been nearly two years since the two had met privately and she wondered—why now. What could he possibly want from her? If it wasn't for the fact that she knew him well enough to hear the distress in his voice, she would have simply said no when he asked to meet with her. But there was something urgent in his call and she couldn't turn her back on him. The man taught her the meaning of real love. He did not have those feelings for her, but he certainly loved his wife Carolyn Roth-Roberts with all her flaws, and she has plenty. Nevertheless, it was difficult for her not to appreciate and treasure the short period of time they spent together before he said, "I do."

She crossed her legs and sat back in the chair remembering how caring and attentive he was whenever he had free time, or Carolyn was out with one of her playmates. Governor Gavin W. Roberts knew about his wife's extra curriculum activities, but he loved her nonetheless. That realization did not come to light for Cynthia until the night of her friend, Tracy Harrison's wedding. Carolyn was distraught over JD Harrison, the now Attorney General of Virginia and a political powerhouse, choosing to marry

Tracy Washington, a virtual unknown over her. The
realization sent her running into Gavin's arms that night.
The way he held and consoled her, even though she was
crying over another man, let Cynthia know it was time to
step out. It was not in her nature to be the third wheel in
anyone's relationship. But she would be lying to herself if
she said Gavin did not touch her heart with his gentle ways
and caring manner.

"I always loved your legs in short dresses," Gavin said
from the doorway.

Looking up with a welcoming smile Cynthia simply stared
at the man who changed her life. He showed her that she
was worthy of the love of a good man. She just was having a
hard time finding *that* man. "Hello stranger. I would hug
you, but you and I know that would lead to something else,
and we are not going there." Frowning, she noticed the stress
she heard in his voice had reached his face. She could see
he needed to talk and of course she wondered if it was
Carolyn, but was too polite to ask. "So, what has you so
rattled that the strain is showing on that handsome face?"

The one thing he always loved about Cynthia Thornton
was she did not mince words. She was always straight with
him. He missed that. Taking a seat across from her desk
Gavin sighed heavily. "Before we get into serious things, tell
me what's been happening with you. I understand the Prince
of Emure has his eyes on you."

Placing her pen on the desk Cynthia stood, walked over
and sat in his lap. She kissed his forehead and smiled,
"Everyone is fine." She laid her head against his and smiled,
"And you know you don't give a damn about what's
happening with the Prince of Emure. But I don't like the
vibe I'm getting from you. So tell me what's wrong and how
I can help you fix it."

Gavin gathered his arms around her waist and held on
tight. How he wished he had fallen in love with her instead
of Carolyn. "I need to tell you about something that has

given someone control of my career." He reached into his pocket and gave her a blue velvet jewelry box. "I need you to keep this safe until it's needed. You'll know when and who to give it to."

Cynthia pulled away and looked down at him, "You're scaring me. Is something going to happen to you?"

"No," he smiled, "nothing like that."

As much as she wanted to, she didn't believe him. She took the box and opened it. Inside was a beautiful platinum heart shaped locket on a matching chain. When she opened the heart there was a small item that looked like a miniature compact disc. She closed the locket and replaced it inside the box. Moving from his lap, she retook her seat at her desk and placed the box inside her purse. "Tell me what's on your mind."

Outside the TNT building, the Governor's two bodyguards sat in the front seat of the black sedan, waiting for his return as instructed. "I'm not too crazy about this secret meeting. You stay here. I think I'll just take a look around to make sure the perimeter is clear," the man sitting in passenger seat stated.

"Make sure he doesn't see you. The man does not like his orders being disobeyed."

"It's for his safety." The man exited the vehicle and walked around the building. On the back side there was a light shining through the window. He assumed that's where the meeting was taking place. Being careful not to be seen he stood flushed against the outer wall and glanced through the window. A sly grin crossed his face when he saw the meeting was with Cynthia Thornton and she was sitting on the Governor's lap. "Playa, Playa." He whispered as he shook his head. No longer concerned with the meeting he was just about to walk away when he saw the exchange of the blue velvet box. "Damn," the expletive word escaped. Walking back towards the front of the building, he stop pulled out his cell-phone and pushed a button. Once the call was answered he informed the receiver, "I believe we have a problem. The information has been passed to a third party." The voice asked, "Who?"

"Cynthia Thornton, owner of TNT Event Planning." The man hung up the telephone and returned to the vehicle.

"Well?" the driver questioned.

"Here I was concerned for his safety and he's in there with a woman." The two men looked at each other and shared a knowing smile.

Donovan Tucker sat outside a club, watching his boss' teenage daughter which was proving to be more than he had bargained for. Man how he longed for the days of watching over Tracy, his boss little sister. Now she was easy. She spent most of her days in the library until she went off to college. Even then it wasn't difficult to make sure no harm came to her and to be honest, it was an honor to be given such a task. His boss, Al "Turk" day, entrusted the life of his little sister to him. To this day Tuck, as he was called by his men, believed he had a part in her becoming the person she was today—a beautiful strong black woman with her own multi-million dollar company, the wife of the Attorney General and now the mother of little JC Harrison. He couldn't help but smile at how her life had turned out after the rough start. It was good she had Turk around making sure she was happy. Then when Turk landed in prison, he gave Tucker the duty of watching over her. But his teenage daughter was nothing like Tracy that was for sure. His cell phone buzzed, interrupting his thoughts. "Make it good," he answered.

Listening intently to the information being given, he frowned. "The silent partner is making his move. He just put out a hit on the Governor's friend."

This was not good. Just when he thought things with Tracy was settled all hell was about to break lose. "Who has the contract?"

"The Latin Eagles."

"Damn, not them again. I'll handle it." Tucker disconnected the call. He immediately made another call.

"Thompson," the man answered.

"We have an issue. Meet me at Maxie's Club in an hour."

Chapter 1

The clock on the mantel indicated it was well after midnight. Cynthia glanced out of the window, a small smile crept onto her face; the snow had not begun. *With a little luck we can get out of here before the storm hit,* she thought. Well at the very least, she would let the catering staff leave within the hour. Stepping back into the grand ballroom of the mansion that was still filled with dignitaries, politicians and their wives, she looked around the room, a little angry with herself. Since her friend, Ashley's wedding, Cynthia Thornton promised herself she would no longer settle for just any man. She wanted the love of her life. No longer would she jump in bed with anyone other than whoever he may be. She was never one to believe in happily ever after or love at first sight. However, since her friends Tracy, Ashley and Rosaline had married the loves of their lives, she wanted the same, no matter how long it took him to come along. That was two years ago and the only prospect she had was Prince LaVere' Ashro of Emure. Yes, a true Prince and she still had doubts.

With all that said, she wanted to kick herself as she stood in the doorway looking around the room for the tall, ruggedly handsome man in a uniform who had been exchanging glances with her all night. She knew those glances—received them every time, yes, every time she walked into a room where the male population existed. All of her one hundred ten pounds, five feet six inch natural reddish brown hair, caramel skin, hazel eyes and voluptuous behind, made the *"you look good"* glances a norm in her life. But the glances from this man indicate he wanted to devour her in a very intimate way. That mere fact should have her running in the other direction, not trying to seek this man out. She could still feel the intensity of his glance in the pit of her stomach, which was inconveniently traveling to the area below her navel.

If this were any other client, she would let her assistants handle the closing and leave, before she would allow herself to forget about her promise to wait for Mr. Right. However, this was The Brooks. Avery and Gwendolyn Brooks was one of the most powerful political families in the country, in addition to being her friend Ashley's in-laws. With the potential for more business, there was no way she would not see this function to the end.

Cynthia put the man in the uniform and Prince LaVere' out her mind, put on her most professional smile and began to mix in with the crowd. Part of her job as an event planner was to ensure everyone was enjoying themselves and on this particular occasion, to keep the host, James and Ashley Brooks, abreast of the impending weather condition. It was early November and the prediction of a major snowstorm had some a little on edge.

Walking over to the mantel where the couple was standing in a virtual who's who in politics Cynthia could feel James' eyes on her as she whispered in Ashley's ear. She knew he was wondering what kind of trouble she was getting his wife into, now. Cynthia and her friends' husbands had a love hate relationship. Their wives loved her and they, in turn hated her. Always one to stir up trouble Cynthia stood and gave James a wicked wink just as Ashley began to walk away with her. James put his hands around her waist to delay her departure. "Where do you think you're going?" he whispered. "You know I like having you by my side."

Ashley kissed his cheek and smiled. "I'm going to check on the weather, handsome, I'll be right back."

"I'll go with you," James replied quickly.

"No, stay here and talk with LaVere'. I won't be gone long."

The man next to James smiled warmly at Cynthia, who, from what he could read in her face, was enjoying the banter going on between the couple. If he was not mistaken, she was deliberately egging James' anger on with her facial expressions. It was apparent the three were very close friends from the looks they shared. "Oh James, for goodness sake she is not going to break walking from here to the window. Get a grip." Cynthia said in a joking tone.

"Are you offering your neck?" James asked in a not too gentle tone.

Ashley put one hand on James chest and the other on Cynthia's shoulder and stepped between the two, "Okay, on the count of three, break and go to your opposing corners."

Prince LaVere' laughed and patted James on his shoulders, "James, my friend, I like your wife and her friend, whom, I have not had the pleasure of dancing with this evening."

Prince LaVere' remembered meeting the hazel eyed beauty at James and Ashley's wedding the previous summer. To this day, he had a difficult time forgetting the smooth silk feel of her skin when he held her hand. Nor could he forget the dazzling smile he received when he helped her up from a fall.

"You don't want to get that close—she is the devil's spawn," James replied with a curt smile.

"James!" Ashley exclaimed.

James took a sip of his drink, and gave Ashley a questioning glance. "Well she is, isn't she?"

Cynthia smiled, and then turned to the Prince, "Please forgive us. We both love Ashley, but have different opinions on her activities. I believe she is very capable of walking a mere ten feet to the window. While James believes she should not take any steps at all." She turned to Ashley, "Does he carry you to the bathroom and sit on the toilet with you?"

The Prince laughed along with Ashley and the other people standing around, however, it took a moment for James to see the humor in the comment. James smiled and threw up his hands, "I give up," he kissed Ashley before she walked away.

"James," LaVere' smiled at his college friend, "it's good to see you so happy. A good woman can do that for a man."

Shaking his head James smiled, "I never thought it could happen, but I am a happy man. Ashley and the twins make my life worth living."

"Spoken like a man in love." Hearing Cynthia laugh, LaVere' looked in the direction of the women who had gathered by the window on the opposite side of the room. He cleared his throat and turned to James. "Now would you extend the opportunity to your friend?" he asked as he pointed towards Cynthia.

James looked over at Cynthia, Ashley and their friend Rosaline who had joined them at the window and shook his head. "I don't want to jeopardize our friendship by doing that."

LaVere' smiled, "Something that exquisite cannot be that bad," he replied while watching every move Cynthia made.

James took another sip of his drink, "Believe me, it can," he mumbled to himself.

Ashley, Cynthia and Rosaline, looked out the window as the snow began to fall. "I have the kitchen clean and all the items packed in the vans. If we leave now everyone should make it home before the storm gets too bad," Rosaline stated. Cynthia could always depend on Rosaline handling the kitchen. Besides being business partners, they had been friends for years. The two worked together in one capacity or another since college. Cynthia handled organizing the parties while Rosaline Taylor-Marable handled the food and everything in the background. Then two years ago their friend, Tracy put together a business plan for them. Their company TNT Event Planning has been growing ever since.

"Well, I'll have the valet bring the guest vehicles around for departure. Is anyone staying the night?" Cynthia asked Ashley.

"LaVere' and his security staff will stay tonight," Ashley replied. "Oh, and you are welcome to stay if you like."

"We'll see. I want to make sure everyone is gone and the area is cleared out before I leave. But I'll let you know," Cynthia replied as she surveyed the room to determine the time it would take to clear things out.

"I'm sure LaVere' would be pleased if you stayed," Ashley smiled.

Rosaline looked from Ashley to Cynthia. "Who's LaVere'?"

Ashley turned Rosaline around by the shoulders until she was facing James and LaVere'.

"The man standing next to James, who has been asking about Cynthia since the wedding, is the one and only Prince LaVere' Ashro of Emure."

"Oh my, he's a prince?" Rosaline smiled.

"A damn good looking one at that," Ashley grinned.

Rosaline looked at Cynthia with a questioning eye. "He's about six feet tall, handsome and a prince and you haven't jumped on that?"

Cynthia looked over at the man standing next to James and smiled. "Actually, he is six-one, one hundred and ninety pounds, coal black eyes, third in line for the throne, has unlimited financial security and the look of royalty," she shrugged indifference and looked away. "However, I took a vow of celibacy, remember. If he is not offering marriage

I'm not interested." Ashley and Rosaline looked at each other and began to laugh so hard, you would have thought a comedian had just delivered the punch line to his best joke. With hands on hips, Cynthia turned to her to friends, and gave them a look that made both of them stand up straight. "I don't see anything funny about wanting to wait for the right man. You did," she pointed to Rosaline "and so did you," she said to Ashley. "Why is me waiting so funny?"

"Well maybe the fact that you have already slept with half of America. This is your chance to start on another country," Rosaline snickered.

"Are you calling me a whore?" Cynthia asked angrily.

"No," Rosaline replied quickly, "girl, you know I know better. But you have been around a stadium or two."

"Three, four, five, six of them at least and that's just counting the ball players," Ashley teased.

Raising her chin high, "Well, that was then, this is now," Cynthia replied. "I don't wish to live my life that way anymore. Can't a person change?"

"Sure they can," Rosaline sympathized with her friend.

"Of course," Ashley chimed in as she looked over at Rosaline who was shaking her head.

Cynthia caught the look, sighed and pointed her finger at them, "You know what? Both of you can kiss my natural ...."

"Ladies," James interrupted just before Cynthia could complete her statement. "I believe I lost my manners earlier. This is my friend Prince LaVere' Ashro. LaVere', allow me to introduce Rosaline Taylor-Marble and you remember Cynthia Thornton. She is the one that fell all over herself the first time you two met at the wedding."

"Prince Ashro," Rosaline extended her hand. Taking it, he kissed the back and turned his attention to Cynthia.

Cynthia smiled as she extended her hand. "It's a pleasure to see you again Prince Ashro."

"It's LaVere' and the pleasure is mine," he replied as his lips lingered on her hand.

Cynthia saw the look in his eyes and recognized it immediately, he wanted her, but she was no longer interested in the one nightstand game. She gently pulled her hand away and smile. "I hope you are enjoying your stay."

The action of Cynthia pulling her hand away did not get past LaVere'. "I'm enjoying it more with each moment I spend in your presence. Will you be staying the night?"

Eyebrows went up on every face, Rosaline, Ashley and James. They each turned to Cynthia. Who smiled sweetly, "Thank you for the compliment, but no I will be leaving with the other guest, which we need to see to." Addressing the group she smiled, "Would you excuse us?" She then turned to Rosaline, "Let's take care of the guest," she said as the two walked away.

"That was a rather hasty retreat," LaVere' smiled as he watched the two women walk away.

"Count it as a blessing," James murmured as he took a sip from the drink in his hand.

Ashley frowned at her husband then turned to LaVere'. "Cynthia has a lot on her mind this evening. She is concerned with getting everyone on their way and home safely before the storm hits."

"Thank you for trying to smooth my ego, but I am not deterred. I'm sure Ms. Thornton and I will see each other again—soon." He was going to make sure of it.

Prince LaVere' stood at the window where he watched Cynthia drive away earlier. He smiled at the audacity of the young beauty. *She is pretentious, that's for sure. Nevertheless, like all the rest she can be tamed.* He sat in a chair near the fireplace in the guest suite of the home of Avery and Gwendolyn Brooks. He attended Harvard graduate school with their son James and they became close friends. Over the past years James and LaVere' shared good times and bad in their individual lives. LaVere' was the reprieve for James during the time of his divorce and his brother's deception. James stayed in his country, Emure, until he was sure how he would go on with his life. Of course, those plans changed once he met Ashley.

As for LaVere', it was James who assisted him in negotiations that gained economic stability for his country. Now, he wondered if James would be willing to assist in a different type of negotiations. For some time now, his father has pushed for him and his brothers to marry and extend the royal family's bloodline. As the youngest of three sons and one daughter, the pressure was not as great, but it was unmistakably present. There was one thing LaVere' knew for sure. He did not want an arranged marriage. He wanted to select the woman that would become his wife. A woman his equal in intelligence and determination, but one that understood her place was to stand beside him and support him. In his mind, that woman was Cynthia Thornton.

LaVere' understood the women in America were different from the women in his county. Women from here were use to having their say, doing as they please, and going at will. While the women in his country knew their place, did not speak out of turn and did not go anywhere unaccompanied by a male. Women here did not have to have a man, and made sure men knew that. Women in his country were the property of men, and the men made sure everyone knew that.

Although he liked the customs of his country, LaVere' wanted to see progression in the area of acceptance. He knew, without a doubt his older brother, Aswan, who was next in line for the throne, would not take steps on his own to liberate all within his country. However, with a little persuasion, he was sure once his older brother became king, all social classes and women would become somewhat liberated.

LaVere' stood to refill his empty glass with the very smooth cognac, James had left with him. His mind returned to Cynthia. *She has the spirit to change a country*, he smiled. The self assurance she displayed each time he saw her, demonstrated she would be able to stand up to the scrutiny she was sure to encounter, whenever she attempted to do those things she was accustomed too. She had the right amount of spiciness, spirit and compassion. He laughed thinking how his compatriots would react to Cynthia and her antics.

There was a knock on the door. LaVere' continued to enjoy his drink as Charles, James's butler opened the door. James and Ashley stood there in what seemed to be a confrontation and looked as though Ashley was winning.

"LaVere' please excuse the interruption," James said as he entered the suite with Ashley closely in tow. "There's been an accident."

LaVere' sat his glass on the bar and walked towards the distraught couple. "What happened?"

Ashley did not give James an opportunity to respond, "Cynthia was in a car accident on her way home. We're on our way to the hospital to check on her."

"We regret having to leave you here alone but Ashley is determined to go," James explained as he looked over his shoulder at his wife's anxious retreat, and then turned back to LaVere'. He exhaled, "I love that woman but I swear she is going to be the death of me."

LaVere' nodded his head signifying his understanding, but at the moment, his concern was with Cynthia. "Allow me to tag along. I would like to know that she is alright."

"Sure, I asked Charles to have the car pulled around. Meet us downstairs in five minutes."

"I'm ready now," he said as he grabbed his coat from the closet.

James gave an exasperating look, "You are as bad as Ashley."

Chapter 2

There was a constant thumping or hammering going on. Not sure where it was coming from Cynthia moved her head in the direction she thought the sound was originating. The slight movement made it very clear, the pain and thumping was inside her head. Opening her eyes didn't help. She closed them hoping the spinning of the room would slow down. The stillness eased the pain slightly, but not completely. Fingers caressed the area on her forehead that was causing the pain. "Rest, Sleeping Beauty," a voice said, "You're not alone." The quiet voice had an immediate calming effect, an unexplainable sense of security from the gentle touch guided her deeper into the recesses of her mind and moments later she was lost in her dreams.

Hours later she cried out, "Turn the lights out." When the light remained, she slowly opened her eyes. At that point she realized it was the sun shining through the window. Looking around, somewhat disoriented, her eyes fell on a man sleeping in the chair by the door. He looked familiar, but she couldn't quiet focus on who he was. His long legs were stretched out and crossed at the ankle. *Nice shoes*, she thought as she continued her silent evaluation. She noticed the jeans fit his thighs rather well. Her eyes traveled up over the turtleneck sweater covering his expansive chest. That she remembered. As her scan reached his face, his eyes met hers. She could read the amusement in the coal black eyes as they stared back at her. Now, if she could just remember his name.

"LaVere'," he said as if reading her mind. "Good morning."

Cynthia looked around. She was certain he was not the man that brought her to the hospital. Nor was his the voice she heard during her sleep, but that was no reason to be rude. "Good morning," she mumbled as she attempted to sit up. The discomfort from the movement showed on her face. LaVere' went to her aide, lifted her as if she was a feather and gently sat her up in the bed. Holding her against his strong chest he positioned the pillows behind her and slowly laid her back down. He then pushed the button for a nurse.

"Is that better?" he asked concerned.

Amazed at how gentle he was, she smiled, "Yes, much. Thank you." She looked around the room, "Is Brian here?"

LaVere' put his hands in his pockets, "I'm not sure who Brian may be, but if he was the gentleman that was here when I arrived, he indicated there were issues he had to handle."

Cynthia frowned, "Describe him."

"Six two or three, light brown skin, close hair cut and rather mean looking."

Cynthia nodded her head without thinking of the pain it would cause and squinted, "Yeah, that's him." She grabbed a fist full of the sheet and squeezed as the pain literally shot through her head. The pain was so severe she thought she would throw up. Sliding down the pillow and her pain began to ease.

The nurse walked in and began to check her vital signs. "Good morning Ms. Thornton, how are you feeling?"

"As if my head was sandwiched between two Mack trucks going one hundred and twenty miles an hour before they slammed into each other."

The nurse chuckled, "That's quite descriptive."

"Is there something you could give her for the pain?" LaVere' asked.

She began to administer medication. "The doctor anticipated some discomfort and left instructions to give you this. It will help until he arrives."

"Any idea when that will be?"

The nurse looked at her watch, "He usually makes his rounds around eight. For now, you should rest." The nurse smiled and left the room.

"Keep your eyes closed and relax." LaVere' suggested. "Just relax." That was the last word Cynthia heard as she drifted back to a less painful place.

"Doesn't it seem like an awful long time for her to be asleep? Are you sure she was awake earlier?" Ashley asked LaVere'. The concern for her friend was very clear on her face.

"Yeah, are you sure Prince Ashro? I don't mean to question you, but Cynthia has never been a late sleeper. It's after ten in the morning. Surely, she should be awake by now." Tracy sighed from where she sat on the side of the bed holding her friends' hand as she slept.

Before LaVere' could respond, Rosaline who was on the other side of the bed exhaled. "I want to know where the damn doctor is. The nurse I spoke with said he would be here around nine, and that was an hour ago." She began to stand, "I need to go find her again."

"No!" the men in the room yelled in unison. They were desperate to keep Roz away from the nursing staff who had threatened to throw them all out if she returned to the desk.

"Roz, let's wait until she's awake. The doctor can't examine her until then anyway." JD suggested as he displayed that smile, which most people believe got him elected into office. "I'm sure the nurse understood our concern the first five times you told her."

"JD, you are the Attorney General of the State, can't you make them find the doctor or do something?" Rosaline pleaded.

"Yeah JD, can't you make them wake her up?" his sister Ashley questioned.

JD looked at the two women and wondered why they believed he would have any authority over the hospital. The court system in the state, yes, he has a say in that. The district attorney offices across the state, yes he also had a say in that. But to his knowledge nothing could move doctors to show up for rounds until they are ready to.

He was about to share that knowledge with them when his wife Tracy turned to him. "Sweetie, you are so good at convincing people to do things. Would you please ask the nurse to place a call to the doctor? I am so worried about her being like this."

All eyes went to JD as he melted from the beautiful brown eyes staring so sadly at him. There was nothing he could refuse Tracy. He turned to look at James who had nothing but a sympatric look for him. The bond between the two was more than brother-in-law to brother-in- law. It was one of mutual understanding. Neither of them could say no to their wives. Nevertheless, he also knew patience was what was needed in this situation. JD stepped over and kissed his wife's cheek. "I'll try babe."

Tracy rewarded him with a smile, "Thank you."

"JD, while you're out there, tell that nurse to bring some more of those really great drugs they gave me before." Cynthia said as she turned over on her side.

"Cyn," Rosaline cried out, "girl, how you feeling? Are you okay? Do you need anything? You want some water, or something to eat?"

Cynthia turned back towards them just as she saw Ashley run over to stand at the foot of her bed. "I feel like a sledge hammer is using my head for drums. No I'm not okay, but I don't think I'm dead, yet. Yes, I need that nurse with the really good drugs. No I don't want water or anything to eat."

"Okay babe," JD said to Tracy, "Cynthia is back to her normal bitchy self. Can we go home now?"

"Jeffrey," Tracy scolded. "She is just waking from a terrible ordeal. How else do you expect her to act?"

"Um, babe, I just had a traumatic ordeal also. I've been away from my wife, whom I love dearly, for two weeks. I have been a very patient man, waiting for the day I could come home and make love to my wife again. This is that day. And since she is neither dead nor dying, I will be damned if I am going to allow Cynthia to block that."

All eyes were once again on JD. He looked around at the expressions on his friends faces. "Oh, like you don't understand?" he said to James.

James chuckled, "I feel your pain. Been there, done it."

LaVere' smiled, "I haven't been there, but I feel your pain also."

Cynthia looked at embarrassment on Tracy's face and patted her hands. "Tracy, go home with JD. I think he needs you a lot more than I do right now."

Tracy was still looking at him in shock when Brian came into the room. He looked around at the silent faces and asked, "Okay, what did Tracy say this time?"

Rosaline and Ashley could not hold it in any longer and began laughing. James made an attempt to stand by JD and not join in with the women, but it did not last long.

JD shook Brian's hand, "Hey B."

"JD," Brian acknowledged as he continued to look around the room amused. "Tracy?"

Not at all ashamed by his statement, JD spoke up. "I was just explaining to my wife how much I was looking forward to staying in bed with her this morning. But since she insisted, and I, being the loving husband that I am, brought her here to see about Cynthia. Now that we know she is not on death's door, I was merely suggesting that we go home and resume the activities I had in mind."

Brian looked from his JD to Tracy and then back. "Hum, hum, in other words, you're horny."

"As hell!" JD replied.

"I see," Brian smiled and then looked at the group of women and smiled.

Tracy joined JD at the door and kissed his cheek. "I missed you too babe. And since you were kind enough to bring me here in the snow to see Cynthia, let's go home," she smiled up at him. "You can teach me that blow job thingy that Brian wouldn't show me." Ignoring the shocked look on her friends face, she turned to Cynthia. "I'll see you when you get home." She turned and walked out of the room.

JD cleared his throat, then smiled at his friends, "Check y'all latter." and took off behind Tracy.

"With that I believe it's safe for us to go home, also," James said to Ashley as he took her hand in his.

"What about Cynthia?"

"She is not going home with us," James ardently stated.

"I will take Cynthia home, just as soon as the doctor releases her. Which he indicated would be around noon."

"Thank you Brian," James smiled. "LaVere', we will see at the house." He then turned to Cynthia, "I do hope you feel better."

Ashley blew her a kiss, "I'll talk to you when you get home."

Cynthia smiled at LaVere' as he walked by to leave. "Thank you for staying with me."

"Anything for a princess," he nodded and left the room.

Once the room was clear, Brian gave her the clothes he brought from her house. "I thought you might need these."

"Thanks," she said as she eased her legs to the side of the bed. "Can you stop the room from spinning?"

He smiled, as he looked at the awful hospital gown she had on. "No, but once you get out of the prison getup, you will immediately feel better. Here, let me help you."

This was a constant in her life. Whenever she was in need, Brian was there to help her. Now that he had his own business, Thompson Protection Agency, she knew he was busy, but he still was there for her, just like when she was a little girl. He turned around and allowed her to balance against his back to get dressed. "Umm Brian," she said, "there was a man here last night. I think he was the man that helped me at the accident. Did you see him?"

Brian was sure she was referring to Samuel Lassiter, the man he had tailing her. Since the telephone call he received, he had assigned one of his new agents to trail her. He wasn't ready to tell her about the call until he checked things out. "When I left last night, LaVere' was here."

"Oh," she replied in a disappointed tone. Maybe it was just her imagination. The craziest thing was she was sure she recognized the face, the touch and the voice.

On the ride home, Cynthia was unusually quiet. Any other time she would have complained about his driving or something by now. Brian looked over at her. She was looking out the window. The look on her face bothered him—it always did when she was unhappy. "Are you okay over there?"

She slowly turned her head towards him and presented a sad smile. "Brian," she said in a sad voice that was very uncharacteristic of her, "is there a reason you and I never got together?"

Brian jerked his head towards her so quickly the vehicle veered into the next lane. He corrected the error quickly and took another quick look at her. Something warned him to tread lightly on this topic. "I am an asshole and you can be a little bitchy. It doesn't make for a good combination."

She stared at him, "You're right. You can be an ass." Then she turned and continued looking out the passenger side window. "And I can be a bitch." A few minutes went by before she continued, "At heart I think I'm a good person. I don't understand why no one loves me."

"What are you talking about? There was a room full of people at the hospital and each one of them loves you."

She slowly exhaled, "JD was there because he loves Tracy. James was there because he loves Ashley. Rosaline was there because," she hesitated "well she has just always been around. There was no one there for me."

"What about LaVere'?"

"He was there because of his friendship with James." Brian didn't believe for one minute the Prince was there for James. In fact when he left the hospital, it was LaVere' that indicated he would stay with her overnight. But sensing she simply needed to talk, he decided to just listen. "I get tired of being the third wheel and I'm sure you are too. When we are all out, you and I end up dancing together. And lately, even you have had someone there. Is there something wrong with me? Am I such a bad person that no one can love me?"

"You have a tendency to go after the wrong men for the wrong reasons. You haven't discovered that sex and love are two totally different animals, Tracy, Ashley and Rosaline have." He looked over at her, "When the time is right someone is going to see the beautiful heart you have and love you regardless how hard it is to look at your face."

A small smile creased her lips, "You believe someone will take the time to look into my heart."

"Yes, I do."

"Do you think you could send them soon? At the moment I feel terribly alone." She closed her eyes and dozed off for the remainder of the trip home.

Something in her voice worried him. Cynthia was always so spirited. Brian has known her since she was very young. He had never witness the type of despair he was seeing today. Nothing ever seemed to bring her down. Even when he knew she was hurting, he had seen her put on her makeup and smile. That smile never wavered, until now. Most of her friends thought it was just the way she was, nothing ever got to her. That was what she wanted them to believe. The truth was things touched her deeply, she had learned to mask the hurt, and keep smiling. Looking at her like this, he felt it was time for her to be happy. In his mind he began to wonder where to start. Does he start with the family that abandoned her? The man that he believed used her? Or should he begin a search for a man that will love her the way she deserves? He smirked, a man that will look into her heart and love her for her.

Chapter 3

Home was a gated community fit for a queen. Nothing but the best for Cynthia Thornton. That's how she was raised and what she was taught to expect in her life. The three level condominium was complete with a two car garage, four bedrooms, a dining room, state of the art kitchen, that she rarely used, four full baths, one connected to the room in the lower level, one connected to the spare room on the third level, one on the main level, a master bath that a normal house could fit into, not to mention the walk-in closets and full basement level family room. It didn't matter that she was alone in the place; it was the top of the line so she purchased it.

Night had fallen by the time Cynthia made it to her third floor bedroom. Her body and head felt as if they had gone through a spin cycle of a high-powered clothes dryer. Brian volunteered to stay in her guest room that night to make sure she was okay. It was the only way, JD, James or Marco, Rosaline's husband, would have their wives at home with them, for all three were making plans to stay with her for the next few days.

Just as she was about to doze off, Brian tapped lightly on the door. "Come in," she answered.

Brian smiled. "You okay?"

"Yeah," she replied slowly, "Just a little tired."

"Do you think you could give five minutes to The Prince? He stopped by to check on you."

She smiled lightly and sat up in the bed. "Sure," she replied. As Brian closed the door, she brushed her hair from her face. That motion never hurt before, but tonight it did.

"It seems every time I see you, there's a frown on your face. Is there something I can do to change that?" LaVere' smiled from the doorway.

"It's not personal, I promise."

"In that case, may I come in?"

"Sure."

"How are you feeling?"

"Like I went through the spin cycle of a clothes dryer."

He smiled, "I can imagine."

"What are you doing in Richmond?"

"I'm staying with James and Ashley until my home is ready."

She smiled, "You have a home near here?"

"Yes, in Hanover. "It's a small place for me to stay while I'm in the States." The drowsiness in her eyes signaled it was time to go. "Have you taken your medication for the night?"

"Hmm huh," she replied barely conscious.

He walked over to the side of the bed, gently pulled her into his arms placing her head on his shoulder and repositioned the pillows beneath her. Holding her head steady, he laid her back and found she was sound asleep. He pulled the comforter up to her shoulders and kissed her forehead, "Goodnight my princess," he said and slipped out of the room.

Brian walked LaVere' out, turned off the lights and locked the door. As he entered the guest room his cell phone buzzed. Earlier he turned off the ringers to all the telephones in the house to ensure Cynthia could sleep. He quickly grabbed the phone and answered, "Thompson."

"Hurricane here—how is sleeping beauty?"
"Sleeping probably tired from over exertion."
"Any word on the accident?"
"Nothing yet."
"Call if you need me."

For the first time since he was eighteen, Samuel was in his own home, preparing a meal in his custom built kitchen. As the oldest of twelve siblings, there were many days he would wake to his mother, Sally cooking breakfast in the kitchen for the rather large family. He would get up early and help her with whatever he could. Those moments became his one on one time with his mother. With twelve children and a husband to care for it wasn't often he had a chance to be with her alone.

He smiled as he remembered the cooking lessons and the many words of wisdom she would bestow upon him. His father, Joseph, would shake his head every time his mother would say, "Samuel you are going to impress some lucky woman with your cooking skills when you get older."

"Women will be impressed with a good strong body boy. Stick to the gym, that's how I got your mother," his father would say as the two exchanged knowing glances at each other.

It was those glances that gained him five brothers and six sisters, he later realized. Samuel admired both of his parents and the love they shared for each other and their family. He took the advice from both, he continued to cook in the mornings with his mother then would play football and hit the gym after school each day. When he joined the service, he gave up his passion for cooking, but continued his daily workout routine. At six-six, 220 pounds, he was lean and muscular, not an ounce of body fat on him.

Now that he was home, Samuel spent whatever free time he could in his state of the art kitchen. The house was completed only a month earlier. His mother and sisters decorated and furnished the four bedroom home, with a full basement containing an indoor gym, game room, basketball court and a security system that rival the system at the White House. From his past covert assignments, he understood the importance of a good security system.

Deciding his first meal would be a quiche', Samuel began pulling the ingredients from the refrigerator. "Good morning. Would you like some breakfast?" His friend and confidant, Rusty simply looked up." Rusty was a fully trained military dog that was given to Samuel as a parting gift when he left the military. The gentle chime of the telephone signified another interference with his carefully planned quiet Sunday of football. He ignored the call and thought about the interference from the night before. Was it an accident, or did someone tamper with the car? He replayed the scene in his mind.

At first he was a little angry to be put on this assignment. He didn't sign up to be a body man for a female with too many men. He didn't care that the woman's brother was some big time movie star, or that she was close friends with JD and Tracy Harrison or that his boss seemed to have a *close* relationship with her. He did not want to be guarding a woman! But that was before he saw her in the ballroom. From that moment, the only thing on his mind was how smooth her skin looked and what it must feel like to touch it. He closed his eyes and remembered every inch of the woman, from her delicately painted toenails, to the luscious curve of her hips, to the full rise of her breast, to the wholesome smile with the most adorable lips and her wonderful hazel eyes.

He cleared his mind from the memories to begin pulling out the ingredients for his meal. It had been a while since a woman had captured his attention. For the past fifteen years, he served in the Marine Corp as a Navy Seal. The thrill of the action and the idea of fighting for his country always meant the world to him. As a young man, his parents begged him not to join the Corp, but it was his dream. At the age of eighteen he followed that dream and never regretted it, until a little over a year ago. He met and fell in love with a woman during a covert operation. Never experiencing anything like it before, he asked the woman to marry him. He wanted to bring her back to America with him and start a family. Life had a different plan. He was a part of a covert operation which was intent on dismantling any military strong holds in her homeland. She shared that information with a member of her family when she told them of her plans to leave and start a life with Samuel in America. That information cost her life, and nearly cost his. When he returned from that tour of duty, he decided that was enough, it was time to let go. He placed a call to Brian Thompson, a former FBI agent and friend. A position was open in his protection agency and at the age of thirty-four Samuel accepted it without hesitation. Now, his job was to work on the personal protection detail of JD Harrison, the newly elected Attorney General of Virginia. Recent activity reports show a possible plot to harm the man most believed will someday be President of the United States. That's what he signed up for, not this. But some twist of fate apparently stepped in, and now he found himself babysitting who one of his sisters refer to as a spoiled brat of a woman.

Thinking back to the accident, he had just settled into the drive following the woman on Interstate 64 when he saw the brake lights go on, but the light colored Mercedes did not slow down. "That's not good," he remembered thinking, when the vehicle swerved into his lane then just as quickly sharply cut back towards the opposite side of the road. He heard the crash when it collided with something and slide into the ditch. He slammed on brakes, which caused his vehicle to swerve around on the highway. The vehicle behind him swerved to the right to avoid hitting him. Once in control again, Samuel turned the wheel of his vehicle, pulled over and parked on the side of the road. He turned on his emergency flashers and got out of the car. The Mercedes was off to the side of the road in a ditch with the airbag engaged and the alarm going off. He ran towards the vehicle to see if she was hurt. As she slowly opened the door, he could see there was a cut on her forehead and she appeared to be a little dazed. Samuel pushed the airbag aside as she unbuckled her seatbelt. She stepped out, leaned back against the car and looked up at him. "Are you okay?" he asked with a concerned look on his face.

Cynthia did not respond, she simply got out of the car and looked up at him as if she was dazed. Samuel grabbed her coat out of the car and wrapped it around her as she attempted to stand. He pulled out his cell and called the emergency number. After completing the call he turned to the woman, "Let's get you out of the snow."

"Thank you. But I'll sit here until someone comes. You can go on."

Samuel frowned, *Does she think I would leave her out here alone, in the snow on a highway with a storm ragging.* "You can wait for help inside the car, where it's warm. The emergency vehicles will be along soon." Samuel attempted to help her walk, but she pulled away.

"If you want to go wait in your car that's fine, but I'm staying here with my car."

The movement must have been too fast, for her knees buckled just as her eyes began to close. Samuel caught her before she hit the ground. Frustrated and cold at this point, he picked the woman up in his arms, and placed her on the back seat of his car.

The telephone chimed again, bringing him back to the present, he was sure the investigation was going to show someone tampered with the car. With his luck, he will be protecting her from some man's wife. Samuel pushed the button on the remote to activate the speaker to the telephone system. "How are you this morning mother?"

"I'm wonderful son. How about you? I heard you had a long night at the hospital. Is the woman alright?"

Knowing his sister Pearl, who was the press secretary for JD Harrison, must had mention the accident to his mother Samuel replied, "It was my understanding she would be released sometime this morning. She had a slight concussion, but was sleeping comfortably when I left."

"Well, it's a blessing you were there to help her that late at night. Did you contact her family?'

"No," he replied as he continued mixing the ingredients in a bowl. "Her family doesn't live here. Brian came to the hospital. He will make sure she gets home safely."

"Well, if her family is away, who is going to take care of her once she gets home?"

Samuel looked over at Rusty, who looked away as if he understood the conversation and his master's frustration. Sally Lassiter is about to take on another child. "Mother, you have twelve children, you don't need to take on another."

"Samuel Franklin Lassiter, I don't need you to remind me how many children I have. I was the one pushing each one of you out. I was just concerned for the woman, that's all. If something were to happen to one of my daughters I would surely hope some kind soul would look out for my child until I got to her."

Samuel knew that was his mother's guilt trip speech. He really wanted to enjoy his kitchen, watch NFL game day and just chill. "Mother, I'm sure she has friends that will check in on her."

"How do you know that Samuel? There was no one last night. The very least you could do is call to make sure she got home safely and was doing alright. I raised you to care about others."

"Yes, you did, that's why I called last night to check on her and she is doing fine," Samuel exhaled.

"You're a good man Samuel." Satisfied her son had done the right thing she turn to another subject. "How is my Rusty?"

"He's waiting for another pot roast," Samuel replied. At the mention of pot roast, Rusty head shot up and his ears were pointing on full alert. His tail waged once and hit the floor with a thump.

"Hello Rusty," she said through the telephone. Rusty replied with a happy bark. "Your pot roast will be waiting for you on next Sunday. Give him a good rub down for me Samuel."

"I will mother." Rusty put his head back down resting on his paws as Samuel disconnected the call.

"You know you are going to have to share that roast," Samuel raised an eyebrow to the 120 pound lean muscled German shepherd. He could have sworn Rusty replied, "Huh." As minutes passed Cynthia Thornton was still on his mind. As much as he wanted it to be a situation where she was just messing around with the wrong man, his gut told him it was something more. The people that gave Brian the information indicated this was a paid hit. Someone wanted this woman dead, the question was, why? He poured the mixture for the quiche' from the bowl into the pie shell on the marble counter top and placed the container in the oven. He made a mental note to call Brian later to get an update.

Chapter 4

Monday began with the smell of coffee penetrating the comfort of Cynthia's bedroom. Opening her eyes resulted in a dull pain versus the sharp pain of the day before. Turning over in the bed she found her body was sore. Muscles were hurting that she did not know she even had. A slow moan escaped her lips as she completed the turn in the bed.

"Is that your way of saying Good Morning now?" Gavin asked from the chair by the door.

Cynthia's head moved a little faster then she intended as she turned towards the familiar male voice. The smile on her face clearly expressed how pleased she was to see him. There was a time she could actually see herself married to the man. Seeing him now signified the very special bond the two formed during their involvement. He had to make a sacrifice to be here. If the press got wind of this visit, it could cause issues. If his wife finds out there will be hell to pay. It seemed none of that matters to him, because in her time of pain and suffering, which she truly was suffering, he was there with her. "Hello handsome," she groaned with a smile.

Gavin stood and walked over to sit on the bed next to her. "Hello beautiful," he smiled as he gently kissed her lips. He pushed her hair away from her face and frowned at the bruise on her temple. "How are you feeling?" he asked in a voice filled with concern.

"I feel like I was used as somebody's punching bag."

Nodding his understanding, he walked into the bathroom and turned the water on in the Jacuzzi tub. He knew the condominium very well, since he spent a number of nights there. Walking back into the bedroom he removed his suit jacket and tie. Turning to Cynthia he pulled back the comforter, "A warm sponge bath should help. Please, allow me the honor of bathing you." Her smile encouraged him to proceed. Gently he gathered her in his arms and carried her into the bathroom. Placing her on the side of the tub he checked the temperature of the water to make sure it was hot, but not to the point where it would be uncomfortable. He slowly began to remove her silk pajamas. The bruise on her smooth light brown skin clearly showed signs of trauma and it bothered him that he was not there to protect her.

Cynthia recognized the look of regret on Gavin's face as he saw the bruises. The look had become a norm during their short-lived relationship. During that time and now, there was nothing he could do to change the circumstances. Their relationship was not only sexual, but one of a deep caring and respect for one another. It was clear to her that if a man like Gavin could care about her; she had to have some redeeming qualities.

Cynthia kissed his hands and held them in between hers. "The bruises will go away. I'm going to be fine."

Gavin placed her in the tub. "Is the water too warm?" he asked without looking into her eyes.

"No, it's perfect," she replied as she reclined back in the tub and relaxed.

He took the sponge and after applying gel he began to gently bathe her. Special care was given to the bruise on her chest from the air bag. It took every ounce of his will power not to respond to her, when every fiber in his body wanted to pick her up, carry her back into the bedroom and make love to her. But he knew that it was best for her that he let her go. In his heart he knew there will never be a time that she will not continue to creep into his mind, whether they were together or not. There will never be a time that he did not care deeply for her. Seeing her bruised caused his heart to hurt. Although this visit to see her was going to cause an issue for him at home, there was no way he could stay away once he heard about the accident. He frowned, *was it an accident? It was too much of a coincident that it happened right after he gave the information to her. And he did not believe in coincidences.*

As if reading his mind, she held his eyes with hers, "This was an accident—nothing more. The roads were slippery and I slid into a ditch—an accident."

He pulled a towel from the warmer, opened it and extended a hand to assist her to stand. After wrapping her body in the towel he picked her up and carried her back into the bedroom. Taking his time, he dried her off then lotion her down. Hesitantly she put her robe on. Before either of them knew it, two hours had passed and their time together had to come to an end. If there was any doubt, Brian's knock on the door announcing Gavin's office was calling, sealed it. Brian gave Gavin the cell phone from his security man while passing a disapproving look her way, then walked back out of the room. It turned out to be his wife Carolyn on the other end of the line. Gavin put her on hold and turned to Cynthia. "I have to leave now. If you need anything, don't hesitate for a minute. You call me."

Cynthia tiptoed and kissed him on his cheek. "I won't call, but thank you for the thought."

He smiled, because he knew her well enough to know, she would not call. Gavin walked over to the door, looked back at her for a moment and walked out.

Cynthia was exhausted and a little depressed after Gavin's visit. *"You need to let that go Cynthia Antoinette. Your friends are there for you.* Not allowing the feeling to weigh her down, she decided to get dressed, which was a little more painful than she anticipated. Her head was still throbbing with a dull pain and her body was still sore, but better. She eased into a pair of sweat pants and a tee shirt then ventured into the kitchen. Sitting at her kitchen table she found Brian reading a file. Taking a look at the clock on her wall she wondered why he was still there. She thought for a moment—*yes, it's Monday.* "It's ten in the morning. Don't you have an office or something to go to?"

Brian turned at the sound of her voice. People can say a lot about Cynthia Thornton, but they could never say she was not a beautiful woman. "And good morning to you," he grunted over the cup of coffee in his hand. "I thought you would need me around, if for nothing more than to be your social secretary."

"One visitor does not warrant a social secretary," she countered entering the kitchen to get a glass of juice. As she reached up for a glass the pain in her chest stopped her motion. "Hmm" she groaned.

Brian stood, reached over her head and took a glass from the cabinet. "What do you want, water, juice or milk?"

"Juice," she replied while taking a seat at the breakfast bar.

"Where are your pain pills?" He asked while placing a glass of juice in front of her.

"On the nightstand," she replied as she placed her head into her hands. The body was not ready to do everyday things. The impact from the accident was more than she anticipated. Her head still hurt, just not as much. Her body was stiff and not ready for the movement her mind wanted it to do. So she sat. Brian returned and placed two pills in her hand. She conceded and took the pills. "Where's my car?" She asked as if she just remembered it was damaged.

"It's at Joe Harrison's shop. He called this morning, the front end was damaged, but it's repairable. You'll be without it for about ten days. I called your insurance agent. They are going over today to take a look at it and will arrange for a loaner. Joe will send the items out of the car over sometime today. Rosaline will bring your appointment book from the office so you can work from home for the rest of the week. She also asked Ashley to handle your accounts until you get back."

Cynthia sat there amazed at all he had taken care of in a short period of time. She always knew he was good at protecting people, but never realized how thorough he was. Base on the run down he just gave her, he had taken care of the car, the insurance company, her job and her finances. Now she wondered had he contacted her family.

"By the way, Ashley called your mother—brace yourself."

"Is she coming?" Cynthia asked as nonchalantly as she could.

Knowing the answer would hurt either way Brian shrugged his shoulders, "I'm not sure."

So much for that, she smiled to herself. "Is there anything else Mr. Secretary?"

Brian smirked at her from the dishwasher, where he placed the dishes from the breakfast she shared with Gavin. He turned to her, leaned back against the counter and folded his arms across his chest. "Yeah, since you asked. What's up with Gavin? I thought you let that mistake go."

No one knew the depth of her relationship with Gavin like Brian. He was assigned to Gavin's protection detail throughout the Governor's race and she was sure that had a little to do with him leaving the agency. The two men did not like one another. They each had a certain professional respect for the other, but that was where it ended. Brian was the one that kept things real with her early in her relationship with Gavin. But then, he was never one to bite his tongue, and neither was she. "That's Governor Roberts to you. And why do you care what's up with him?"

"It will always be Gavin to me," he glared down at her. "And in case you don't know, I don't give a damn about him; it's you that concerns me. You seem to have a weakness when it comes to him and I don't want to see you go back to playing seconds for him or anyone else. You deserve better."

That was the second time he had said that very thing to her. The first time was at JD and Tracy's wedding. That was the day she saw Gavin consoling Carolyn. The way he spoke to her and caressed her, made it clear he loved his fiancée more than he wanted to admit. "Why are you so sure I deserve better. You don't know me as well as you think you do Brian," she lashed out.

He took two steps and slammed his hands on the table in anger. "You forget who you are talking too. I was there every time you scraped your knee trying to ride that damn bicycle without training wheels to get your father's attention. I was there when you tried to get with JD just to please your mother. I was there when your family moved away to further your brother's career leaving you behind to fend for yourself. I've been through every holiday that you have spent traveling just to spend one day with them that left you feeling ignored the entire time. I have been there boyfriend after boyfriend, man after man. Don't tell me I don't know. Not only do I know you, I know and understand why you do the things you do."

"Oh really, why is that," she asked angrily.

"You are looking for what you think love is. But you are looking in the wrong places."

"Oh and this is coming from you, a man that is walking around pining after his best friends' wife? I think you need to take your judgmental behind and look in the mirror." The look on Brian's face let her know she had treaded into the wrong territory, but she did not care. He stepped over first. Yes, he had been there every time she had been hurt. Brian had always been the constant thing in her life. From when they first moved into the neighborhood, Ashley, JD, Brian and Calvin had been more like her family than her own. JD and Ashley's mom was the one she went to when she first got her monthly flow. It was Brian that talked to her about boys and how to handle them. It was Brian that stayed at her parents' house with her when they packed up and moved to Hollywood with her talented little brother, when she was nineteen. The house was a mini mansion and so big she was scared to stay there alone, during her summer break from college. It was Brian that helped her move into her condominium and closed up the big house. It was Brian that defended her with their friends when they found out about her relationship with Gavin. Brian had always been a big brother to her.

He stood and snatched the glass that was sitting in front of her. "I don't pine," he said as he turned to put the glass in the dishwasher. He sighed and turned back to her. For the life of him he could not understand why her family treated her the way they did. But he knew she didn't have anyone else to look out for her and he was not going to desert her like her family did. No matter how much she used that lethal mouth of hers against him, or how much she pissed him off with the truth. "So what did he want?"

"Don't you ever just give up?" She sighed.

"No, not on you."

She shook her head and smiled. Easing out of the chair, she walked over to him, put her arms around his waist and placed her head on his strong chest. When he wrapped his arms around her, she knew she had been forgiven for speaking the truth aloud. "He just wanted to make sure I was okay—that's all. I know you don't want to believe it, but Gavin was good for me. He finally made me see what I wanted. It's not a man that is committed to someone or something else. I want what Tracy, Ashley and Rosaline have, someone to love me, for me." A single tear dropped from her eyes.

Brian held her a little tighter as he kissed the top of her head. "I know. But you know God will put that person in your life when the time is right."

She looked up at him, "When did you become a man of religion?"

"I'm not," he frowned down at her. "It's something JD said. It sounded good so I tried it on you." She punched him in the chest as they shared a laugh. "Oh, by the way, the Prince called and those arrived while Gavin was here. He wanted to know if you had a peaceful night." Cynthia stepped away from him and looked at the flowers. "I checked him out. He seems like a decent guy."

She dialed Ashley's number and looked over at him, "Why did you do that?"

"Because he is interested in you."

"He's interested in sex with me. I'm not into that anymore. The next man I have sex with will be the man I am going to marry. I won't settle for anything less."

LaVere' listened attentively to the report from his secretary, Jamal, regarding the situation in his country. It concerned him that a small group of rebels had been discovered not far from his home. With his father and older brother, working diligently to bring about stability in another part of the region, his youngest brother, sister and mother were alone at the palace. The situations taking place in his country was inevitable and he had told his father that, earlier in the year. The only way to stabilize the situation was to bring about social change. His father believed the old way is the only way and Aswan was not strong enough to persuade him in another direction. LaVere' explained, with more and more of their countrymen being educated in America, they are bringing some of those ways home with them. The separation by class and status was not the way of the future. Their lands needed to become all inclusive. They need to allow everyone the freedom to pursue their dreams, regardless of who their ancestors may have been.   But his father looked at him as his youngest rebel son that received an education in the United States and was too willing to turn his back on his own country's customs.

"Excuse me Prince LaVere'." You have a call. Would you like for me to take a message?" Charles asked from the doorway.

"Who's calling Charles?"

"Ms. Cynthia Thornton."

"No, I'll take the call" LaVere' smiled. "Jamal, that will be all for now."

"Your Highness, we have several more correspondence to complete." Jamal replied clearly displeased with the interruption.

"Complete them we shall, but at a later time," LaVere' replied in an authoritative tone.   "You may now excuse yourself."

"Yes, your highness," Jamal replied as he bowed and exit the room.

LaVere' waited until the door closed before picking up the telephone. "Good Morning Ms. Thornton."

"Good morning, your highness. I don't mean to intrude, but Ashley insisted I speak with you."

"You are not intruding. How are you feeling today? Has the spin cycle ended?"

She smiled as she replied. "Somewhat. Thank you for asking. Your flowers arrived and they are beautiful. It was very thoughtful of you to send them. Thank you."

"You are a beautiful woman and should be surrounded with beautiful things."

"I keep trying to tell my friends that, but you know how friends can be."

LaVere' laughed at the presumptuous young woman. "You have friends that were very concerned for you. That can only mean they love you very much. It must be wonderful to be you."

What a funny thing to say, she thought. "Sometimes I like it and then there are times I don't. But you, you are a Prince, I'm sure you have many countrymen that love you for that reason alone. It must be nice to know you will always be loved by many."

"Well, that is true. I am honored by their love." He hesitated for a moment. "It is nice to know you are feeling better. Is there anything I may do to help you through this ordeal?"

"No, thank you. Brian has taken care of just about everything I can think off. Now it's just a matter of my body healing. That will take time," she sighed.

"Time heals most things, if you allow it."

"Do they teach philosophy in How to be a Prince 101?" she joked.

"No, they teach how to look behind the surface into the soul of a person," he replied.

"Is that what you are doing? Trying to look into my soul?"

"That and other things."

"That's what I thought. It's the other things that concern me."

"Why should that concern you? You are a woman of the world Cynthia Antoinette Thornton. You are not, nor can you ever pretend to be anything other than what you are. A woman that knows what she wants out of life and how to go about getting it. What should concern you is whether or not I am willing to give you what your heart desires."

Intrigued with the conversation, Cynthia could not resist. "What is it you think I desire, Prince LaVere' Ahmad Nassir Ashro of Emure."

Pleased she had not disappointed him, "To be treated like the queen that you are," he replied. "We will speak again soon. Good bye for now."

Cynthia looked at the telephone—*no he did not just dismiss me.* Her lips began to form into a smile when she looked into her mirror. He was right, she was a queen.

Armed with the knowledge that Cynthia was curious enough about him to check him out, he proceeded with his plan to seduce her into submission. Rather than going through Jamal, he decided to use his guard Edmond to assist him with his plans. He would allow thirty days to complete the task of preparing Cynthia Thornton to become his wife. He summoned Jamal back into the room to complete the correspondence and then placed a call to his family. His sister assured him all was well. With his mind clear, he began setting the ground work for his seduction.

Carolyn Roth-Roberts sat in the office of her home and re-read the report. Until now she was not concerned with Gavin's social calendar. But, seeing Cynthia Thornton's name appear twice in a short timeframe caused her to question why. Since they married under strained conditions, Carolyn stayed close to home, causing as little commotion as possible. The last thing she wanted to do was cause Gavin to doubt her commitment to him and their marriage. After all, he had given her the one thing she had longed for, the title of First Lady of Virginia. She owed him for that reason and more. She looked down at the report again. That in no way meant she was going to allow any woman to disrespect her or her marriage—especially not Cynthia Thornton.

Chapter 5

The next morning brought an array of surprises for Cynthia. The first was the arrival of her baby brother, Blake an actual movie star. Whenever the name Blake Thornton is mention, people know immediately whom you are talking about. If you happen to be at a grocery store, his picture is usually plastered on the cover of every magazine or newspaper in the rack. It has been that way for the last ten years of his life. At the age of twelve, he began acting professionally and his career has been non-stop. First there were commercials, then several TV shows, then came the movies and now at twenty-one he was considered the leading man to get. If Blake Thornton appeared in your movie for as little as ten minutes, you were guaranteed a hit. To have him in your movie your budget better have at least nine digits before the decimal point or Blake Thornton will not be appearing. His last movie grossed one hundred and forty-nine millions dollars the first weekend of its limited release.

To see his sister, Blake had to literally put on a disguise and use his private jet to get from Los Angeles, California to Virginia. From there, Brian picked him up and drove him directly to Cynthia's home. When she came out of her bedroom for breakfast, he was sitting at her table. She screamed at the sight of her baby brother. He was the one person in the world she felt was more beautiful than she.

Blake was six-two 200 pounds of breath taking manhood. His face was the color of light brown sugar, with a reddish overtone. For whatever reason he had grown, a mustache and beard which surrounded the most kissable shaped lips one have ever seen. With all of that, it was his eyes that drew women in. They were gray which turned as dark as charcoal when he was angry and as light as a sunburst when he was sexually aroused.

The sight of him brought tears to her eyes. It had literally been five years since she had seen him in person. Each time she went to California for a visit during the holidays, he had been on location.

"Blake," she cried as she hugged him. "I can't believe you are here."

"Hey big sis," he hugged her back. "It's so good to see you," he replied elated. "Man, it's been a long time."

"It took me being in an accident to get you home?"

"No, but it did give me an excuse." They both took a seat at the table and continued to catch up old times.

For the first time in years, Brian could hear the joy in Cynthia's laughter. People never took the time to see past the beauty and vainness to see she was actually a very sad woman. Yes, she had looks, money and talent, but she did not have a family or love. That simple fact became more evident in the past year, as each of her friends married their true love and two were beginning families. Of all the material things Cynthia craved for, she would give them up in a heartbeat for a family of her own. From day to day Brian would watch her smile and play the clown in front of her friends, all the while crying inside. When he called Blake, he explained his concern for her. To his pleasant surprise, her brother took the information serious enough to take time off to have an extended visit. Seeing the two together without the interference of their mother pleased Brian more than he would allow anyone to know. Hell, if anyone found out he actually cared about something or someone, he would never hear the end of it.

Now, he could go home, Brian thought as he walked toward the spare bedroom to pack up his things. Before he reached the room, the doorbell sounded. He change course and opened the door, it was a delivery man.

"I'm looking for a Cynthia Thornton."

"What do you need?" Brian asked.

"I have a vehicle delivery for her."

Brian turned and looked over his shoulder, "Cynthia, your rental car is here."

"Um, sir, it's not a rental."

Brian looked around the man and saw a service van and a beautiful white Mercedes. "Damn, that's a beauty."

"I'll say," the delivery man smiled. "I need you to sign here," he said as Cynthia reached the door.

She took the pen and signed for the vehicle. "Thank you," she smiled as he placed the keys in her hand. Never looking out the door, she turned and rejoined Blake at the table. Brian attempted to give the delivery man a tip, but he refused it, stating it was already taken care of. As the man walked away he stared at the vehicle, it was definitely not a rental from the insurance company, that's for sure. So where in the hell did it come from? Brian was not the type of man to just take things at face value. He went over to the window and stared at the late model luxury sedan a little harder. It was brand spanking new. For a moment he thought it may have come from Gavin, but for political reasons he wouldn't take such a risk. Then he walked into the kitchen where Blake and Cynthia were still talking. "Did you buy your sister a new car?"

Blake looked up and smiled, "No, but I will if she needs one."

Brian frowned and walked out of the room. Cynthia looked at Blake with eyebrows raised. They both stood at the same time and followed Brian to door. He opened the door as the two confused people stepped out. "Whose car?" Cynthia asked curiously.

"That's what you just signed for, without questions," Brian replied a little baffled.

Cynthia looked down at the keys in her hands, then to her brother and smiled.

He shook his head, "Don't look at me. I love you and would buy you anything in this world, but I can't take credit for that," he said smiling. "Whoever sent it has great taste. That's the top of the line."

Cynthia started to take steps toward it but Brian stopped her. "You don't go near it until we know where it came from."

"You are crazy if you think I'm not going to check that car out," she laughed and ran out.

Brian ran behind her, picked her up and carried her back into the house.

"Keep her in here until I get some answers," he ordered Blake. He took the keys from her, grabbed his jacket and went out to the car. Blake and Cynthia watched from the window as Brian circled the vehicle. He then slipped under it and for a few minutes did not reappear. When he did emerge, it was from the front end of the vehicle. Standing with hands on hips he then walked over to the driver's door, opened it and sat inside. He emerged from the vehicle and returned to the condo. Closing the door behind him and shaking off the cold, he gave an envelope to Cynthia. She looked at the envelope with a questioning eye. Slowly she opened the envelope with the two men looking on.

A smile creased her face. She moistened her lips with the tip of her tongue. She smiled brightly as she read the note.

"Okay, my curiosity has been peaked. Who is it from?" Blake asked.

"It's from LaVere'," she smiled. "He wanted to make sure I was not inconvenienced by the accident. He was sure whatever vehicle the insurance company sent over would not rival my beauty, therefore he sent something he was sure would."

"I believe that is my cue to go home. You now have two men to look out for you." Brian smiled.

As Brian left the room Blake turned to Cynthia and asked, "Who is LaVere'?"

Cynthia took a moment and told Blake about LaVere', how they met. Then she told him how LaVere' had cared for her since the accident.

Blake waited a moment before he spoke. He knew from what Brian mentioned that Cynthia was in a delicate place in her life. The last thing he wanted to do was upset her. His soul reason for being there was to support the big sister he rarely see. "You really don't know this man Cynthia. I don't think it's a good idea to accept this type of gift from him."

"I'm sure it's just a loaner until my car is repaired. I don't see why I should insult his generosity by refusing his gift."

"You should refuse it because you don't know what's attached to the gift."

"Why does something has to be attached to it Blake?"

Blake chuckled. "When a man gives a gift like that to a woman he barely knows, it's just to impress her long enough to get laid. It's that simple."

"That may not be the case. Don't you think it's possible a man like LaVere' could be interested in me?" she asked angrily.

Noticing her defenses were up; Blake decided to choose his words carefully. "I have no doubt, that this man could be interested in you. My God you are a beautiful woman, always have been. But I'm a man that has pulled this stunt a time or two and I recognize it for exactly what it is, game." He walked over and stood in front of her, "Cyn, I could be wrong about this, but I think you owe it to yourself to tell this man that your affections are not for sale. And if they were, it is definitely going to be more expensive than that vehicle."

She smiled at her brother, and then sighed. "Well, it was a nice thought. I can see myself in that car." She looked out the window. "You know, I could really make that car look good."

"You and me both sis," Blake joked as he yawned. "I'm going to catch a few winks; Jet lag is catching up with me. I'll talk to you later."

"Okay Blake. Are you going to be around for a while?"

"Yeah, at least a month." The smile showed her joy at this response. "I love you sis."

"Same here Blake."

A few minutes later Brian came down the stairs with his overnight bag on his shoulder. "I'm out. You know how to reach me if you need anything."

Cynthia walked over and hugged him. "Thanks for everything" she said and closed the door behind him. The thought of giving up the car was not sitting well with her, but what Blake said made sense. She knew she had no intentions of sleeping with LaVere' at this time. A gift such as the one parked in front of her home was only given if something was expected in return. A few months ago she would have jumped at it and paid the price, but now, she wanted more. As much as it hurt her, she picked up the telephone and called LaVere'. She thanked him for the gift, and suggested they talk about it over dinner. He accepted the invitation. Afterwards, she grabbed her coat and the keys, then drove the Mercedes into her garage.

Dressed in a long sleeved, scooped necked, fuchsia, form fitting dress that stopped just above her knees, a pair of sling back heels, her hair pinned up with a few curls strategically hanging down her neck, Cynthia opened the door for LaVere'. The man was impeccably dressed in a black silk suit that had to cost a few thousand dollars and must have been tailored made just for his body. His opened collar shirt was the only indication that this was a casual look for him. As they assessed each other, it was clear, both were pleased with what stood before them. His guard walked passed them and searched the condo. He nodded an all clear, then disappeared outside the door.

"Good evening Cynthia, your beauty is breathtaking."

She smiled, "Come inside LaVere'. Flattery will get you everywhere."

A laughed rumbled in his chest as he entered, "In that case, allow me to continue."

"Save it for after our conversation. If you decide you want to continue with the flattery after that, then by all means be my guest."

"Will our conversation be that serious?"

"I'm afraid so." She turned and walked up the steps past the kitchen, into the living room. "May I get you something to drink?

"Yes, cognac if you have it."

"I do," she smiled. She always kept cognac in the house. It was Gavin's favorite drink. She poured the cognac over two cubes of ice, out of habit, and then poured a glass of wine for herself. As she placed the glass in his hand, she sat on the sofa. "Please have a seat." LaVere' sat on the sofa next to her, leaving a comfortable distance and crossed his legs.

"You are uncomfortable with my gift," he asked after sipping his drink.

Cynthia nodded her head. "It's a beautiful car; however, I don't know you that well LaVere'. In this country a gift of that magnitude comes with attachments."

He nodded his head in agreement, "In my country as well."

She smiled and looked at him under her lashes. "LaVere', I am not one to bite my tongue. What I am about to say may be considered inappropriate to you but, here it is.

I do not intend to have sex with anyone other than the man I am going to marry. A few months ago, it would have been a different story. Now, I know what I want from a man and it's not a one night or week long affair. I want the happy ever after."

LaVere' placed his glass on the table and turned closer to her. "Allow me to be just as frank. I don't want you or any woman in my life just for sex. In my country, it is an honor to satisfy the sexual needs of the royal family. This is not about sex. I want a woman to be at my side as my wife— someone secure enough with themselves to support me in my efforts to bring unity to my countrymen. It was your beauty that caught my eye, but it was your feistiness that captured my attention." Watching her reaction closely as he spoke it did not appear that he had repulsed her and he continued. "I would like the opportunity to get to know you, Cynthia Antoinette, with every intention of you becoming my wife, not my sex toy. Do you think you could handle that?"

It was refreshing to have a man to be this upfront with what he wanted from her. She smiled then tilted her head to the side. "You are a prince. You can have any woman you chose, in this country or yours. Why me?"

He smiled, which caused his charcoal black eyes to glitter. "I love beautiful things. And Cynthia you are beautiful. Now, if it bothers you to hear that daily, then you may not want to become involved with me."

"Are you kidding? It will be nice to finally have someone else to see what I have known all my life and not be ashamed to admit it." She smiled.

He brought her hand to his mouth and kissed her fingers. "Good. Do we have an understanding, or do we need to discuss terms?"

"No, I believe we understand each other. However, if we do marry, there will be no satisfying of the royal husband, unless it's by the royal wife, in this country or yours. Do we have an understanding?" She asked raising her eyebrow.

"Will the royal wife be that satisfying, to keep the royal husband from wandering?"

Cynthia stood and placed her hands on her hips. "Only time will tell," she replied seductively and walked towards the dining room. She stopped and turned to make sure he was watching her walk away. Pleased with the expression on his face, she smiled. "Shall we have dinner now?"

The two sat down to dinner. LaVere' told her about his family and his home in Emure. She listened intently to the stories about the palace and his childhood there. It was clear that he loved his county and his family. Hearing the antics pulled off by his siblings seemed to pull her into what should have sounded like a fantasy life, but it did not. To her it sounded like the life of a normal everyday family. But she knew that the royal family was anything but normal. The fact that an armed guard was standing at her front door clearly indicated how abnormal they were.

After dinner, they sat in the living room before the fire and talked of what things he wanted to do for his countrymen. His love for his countrymen flowed just as deep as his love for his family. To know a man could care that deeply for others pleased her. Their understanding was not based on love, but the potential was there.

Cynthia walked him to the door when he stood to leave. They stopped before the door as he gathered her into his arms. He kissed her gently, parting her lips to allow his tongue entry. She complied and the kissed was enjoyable for both. LaVere' smiled as he held her in place. "Are you free for dinner tomorrow?"

"I'm not sure. I plan to go into the office tomorrow to catch up on things."

"You don't think it's too soon. It's only been three days," he stated concerned.

She smiled. "I'm feeling a lot better. Beside, Rosaline has been holding things down for the past few days. I should at least check in. If things are in order, I may be free for dinner."

"Then I will see you tomorrow evening." He gently kissed her lips again. "Thank you for a wonderful evening."

She smiled. "You are welcome."

She closed the door behind him and leaned against it. *The earth did not move, but not bad.* She thought, *not bad at all.*

The call from Joe Harrison caught Brian off guard, causing him to ask Joe to repeat what he said. "The brake line in the car you had towed here was cut."

"Are you sure Uncle Joe? Is it possible it could have simply broken on impact?"

"Yeah, anything's possible, it just not probable. But you believe what you want to believe, y'all young folks always do."

Sensing he had touched a nerve by questioning the man, Brian apologized. "I'm sorry Uncle Joe; I just don't understand why someone would deliberately cut Cynthia's brake line."

"That gal has been sleeping around all over town. It's a wonder some woman ain't did more than cut her brake line. You know what I mean."

It was more of a statement than a question, but Brian did not reply, his mind was now on who and why. "Thanks' Uncle Joe. I'll get back with you." He hung up the telephone before he heard the old man's reply. Sitting back in his chair he thought for a moment then placed a call to Samuel. "Anything happening on that end?"

"No it's quiet. Neither party has left the condo."

"Let's hope it stays that way. Joe Harrison just called, the break line was cut. We may need to beef up her security, especially now that the brother is here. "

"Where is his body man?"

"You're it."

"I'm not into the celebrities' man. They tend not to like it when I kill people."

Brian had to laugh. He recruited Samuel because he only wanted the best to join his staff as a part of JD's protection detail. He knew eventually his friend would be running for President of the United States. When that happened he did not want to depend solely on the Secret Service to keep JD and his family alive. He wanted men and women he knew he could trust with his life and theirs as well. Samuel Lassiter was one of those people. He thought about the conversation he had with JD regarding recruiting Samuel. *"Congrats man, I know you were recruiting him hard."*

"He's the only man I wouldn't want to come across in a dark alley. Hmm, except for his younger brother Joshua."Brian explained.

"I heard about him. Rumor is he can kill a man twelve different ways with his bare hands."

"Samuel, fifteen; Joshua you don't even want to know."

Brian knew this task was not what Samuel left the military for. "I know this is not what you signed up for. But I would take it as a personal favor if you would make sure nothing happens to her or her brother. I need some time to figure out why someone wants her dead."

"One good torture deserves another. Remember that." Brian smiled as the phone line went dead.

The security doors to the federal prison slide open as Tucker walked through the door. It was not the normal visitor's day; therefore the visiting room was relatively empty.

The guard at the desk was someone Tucker was more than vaguely familiar with. But this was the first time he had seen the one at the end of the room. Tucker took a seat in the middle of the room to ensure he was not overheard and waited for his boss. Al "Turk" Day walked into the visitor's room with the air of confidence most free men would have. The last two years in prison had not diminished his ability to command respect regardless of who he was around. Knowing his lieutenant was here on an emergency visit did not sit well with him. That meant one of his orders had gone astray or something was up with his baby sister Tracy. Either way, this was not going to be a good day for Tucker.

"What's up man?" Turk spoke as he and Tucker shared a pound and a shoulder bump.

"You pumping iron man. Keeping fit." Tucker said grinning at the six-one slim man he would give his life for.

"I got to do something to keep me focused. I see you cleaned up a little bit."

"Yeah, trying to handle your business while you away. I ain't going to lie, it feels good."

"I knew you could handle it."

"Turk, I appreciate your belief in me man. I ain't going to let you down."

"You earned it. What brought you here?"

"Little man is about to cross the line. How do you want me to handle it?"

"What else happened?"

"He tried to take the beauty queen out."

"Was Tracy with her?" Turk asked, concerned for his little sister.

"Not this time. But he's stupid and he will try again."

Turk sat back and ran his hand down his face. "Why now?"

"He wants to run for Mayor of Richmond. The dumb ass thinks he can control the city by eliminating people that know his history." He paused then continued, "You realize you're one of two on his list."

Turk waved the notion away, "I ain't worried about that."

"You know who he is going to target to flush you out."

"Yeah. If you see him going in that direction, take him out."

"He's controlling our distribution?"

"We can set up our own distribution." He looked at Tucker, "Have you taken your stuff legit like I told you?" Tucker nodded. "Good, pick your top two men. Put them on notice you're looking to step out. Turn this problem over to them. The one that handles it with the least bloodshed, that's the one you turn things over to. It shows he uses his brain power. In the meantime, keep your eye on the information. Get a message to Harrison that I need to see him in person."

"You going to tell him about the information and the beauty queen?"

"No, just like big man, I don't want to put him in that position."

"This was a stupid move on little man's part," Tucker said as he shook his head.

"Greed will do that to a man."

The two discussed a few other issues then prepared to part. Tucker stopped and turned to Turk before leaving, "You know my number one is a female.

"Hey, even our business has to be liberated at some point in time."

Brian walked through the rear door of his friends JD and Tracy's home. A security office had been set up in what was once the pool house of their home. JD was a prosecutor that did not believe in making deals. He had enemies that had gang connections. These enemies would pay handsomely to have JD in their pockets or eliminated from the land of the breathing.

In the past Brian came close to losing both JD and Tracy. Now that they have a son, JC, he was not taking any chances. The security office was equipped with surveillance cameras that covered every inch of the exterior of the house and was manned around the clock. At the moment, he and Magna Rivera were splitting twelve hour shifts. Once Samuel was free that would change to eight hour shifts for each of them. He knew he needed more staff, but for now this was it.

Knocking as he entered, he called out, "JD where are you?" He took the usual route directly to the office located on the first floor near the kitchen. "What are you doing home in the middle of the day on a Tuesday?"

"JC had a doctor's appointment," he then held up his hand and point to the telephone on the desk.

"Hey Brian," Calvin Johnson, the man on the other end of the call spoke.

"Calvin," Brian questioned. "What's up man?"

"I was just telling JD how to handle the Al Day situation."

"What situation?"

"Al has requested a meeting with me as soon as possible," JD explained.

"That's interesting. I came by to tell you about a call I received from Donovan Tucker." Brian replied as he took a seat in front of the desk.

"What did he want?" Calvin asked.

"Tucker never wants anything. He was giving us a heads up, just like he did with Tracy. Only this time it's Cynthia."

"Cynthia?" both Calvin and JD questioned.

"Why Cynthia?" JD asked.

"I have no idea. All he said was a contract was in place. Wait, there's more. I just talked to Uncle Joe. It seems the accident may have been a first attempt. He said Cynthia's break-line was cut."

"Where is Cynthia now?" Calvin asked.

"I have Samuel Lassiter on her."

"Does she have any idea who or why?" JD asked.

"I haven't told her yet."

"Why the hell not B?" JD frowned.

"Because it could be as simple as some man's wife trying to scare her. So Brian is playing her protector again," Calvin offered.

"That's true, but with Uncle Joe's findings I think it's more complicated than that."

JD sat forward, "If Tucker came—Al sent him. That means Al knows what's going on. Calvin political suicide or not, I have to see him."

"We can arrange it so no one will know. You can be in and out without anyone seeing you," Brian suggested.
"JD, if you are going to see Al be sure to talk to James first, just in case damage control is needed."

"Alright Calvin. I'll talk to James, you contact the warden. Brian you free to roll out?"

"Give me thirty minutes to set up coverage."

"Can I go?"

Both men turned to surprisingly see Tracy standing in the doorway. "You're talking about going to see Turk right? I'd like to go." The hopeful gleam in her eyes was not missed by either man.

"Um, Calvin, call me when it's set." JD disconnected the call then looked at Brian, "Give me a minute."

Nodding his head in understanding Brian stood and kissed Tracy on her cheek, "Hey Tracy."

"Brian," she smiled, and then looked expectantly at JD.

He waited until he heard the back door close then JD stood and walked over to the door where his wife stood with those adorable brown doe like eyes he loved so much and said, "No. You cannot go."

"Why Jeffrey?"

"It's not safe."

"You're going. And it's a prison. You can't get any safer than that. You know they have security fencing, and guards with guns." She said in a matter of fact tone.

JD smiled, "Yes baby, I know they have all of that. But it still is not safe for you to go." He walked by her going towards the kitchen. Once there he pulled a drink from the refrigerator and popped it open.

Tracy walked into the room and sat at the breakfast bar. "Jeffrey I try not to ask for much. But I haven't seen or talked to Turk in two years. He hasn't even seen JC, not as much as a picture," she smiled sadly and looked up at him.

"We are not taking JC to prison to see Turk or anyone else."

"Well you put him there Jeffrey," she angrily replied.

JD closed his eyes to stay calm. This was the first time his wife has brought this up. Speaking through clinched teeth he replied, "Turk's actions put him there, Tracy. All I did was uphold the law."

Realizing he took her statement the wrong way, she walked over to the counter, put her arms around his waist and placed her head on his chest. "I didn't mean it that way." When he did not put his arms around her like he normally would, she looked up at him. "You personally selected this facility for him to be in because you said it was close and one of the most secure facilities in the nation. I wasn't accusing you of anything Jeffrey. I'm sorry you took what I said that way."

It took a moment for him to let it go. He knew he took the only family she trusted from her. Not a day goes by that he don't think about all she has endured to be with him. He kissed the tip of her nose, "I'm sorry Tracy. I didn't mean to take that tone with you." He pushed her hair from her face that fell when she ducked her head down. "I would never do anything to hurt you. Taking you to see Turk could put your life in danger. I can't chance it." He tucked her head under his chin and hugged her. "I couldn't live if something happened to you. Please try to understand."

Tracy exhaled, "Okay Jeffrey, I'll try." She pulled out of his embrace, walked around the corner and up the stairs.

Watching her walk away a sense of pride engulfed him. She had given birth to his son and was still as beautiful and shapely as she was the first day his sister Ashley brought her home from college. And she was his. He believed she was a gift from God, for his life had changed the moment she entered it. He exhaled and walked into his office. There were a few certainties in JD's life. Number one was he loved his wife. Seeing the sadness in her eyes was killing him. At the moment he did not know how to change it other than giving in to her request. But doing that would certainly bring out the man that wants Turk dead. He knew, as others do, that the key to finding Turk was Tracy. The one thing he promised his brother in law was he would keep her safe. He had no intentions of going back on his word.

The telephone on his desk rang. Calvin had made contact with the warden.

He wasn't sure how, but Brian had a gut feeling the Al and Tucker contact was connected to Cynthia, the question was how. She wasn't involved in the case with Al Day. In fact there basically was no trail. Al pleaded guilty in return JD arranged for him to be placed in the facility under a fictitious name. Less than a hand full of people knew where Al was located. Shaking his head while thinking—*none of this has anything to do with Cynthia.*

The light on his dashboard of his SUV indicated a call was coming through. He pushed the button, "Thompson."

"We're set for seven o'clock tonight." JD hesitated, "I'm taking Tracy."

Brian exhaled, "Whew. Alright, we can make this work. I'll be at your place at six."

After dropping JC off with Ashley and listening to James lecture regarding political ramifications if anyone got wind of this little trip, they were on the road to visit Turk. It was hard for Tracy to contain her excitement. There were so many things she wanted to talk to Turk about, but knew the time was limited. In her mind she was trying to prioritize the subject based on importance. The first was to ask him to look out for JC while he's growing up. She did not doubt JD's ability to take care of their son, but Turk had a special knack for handling street situations. If his father could not handle a situation there was nothing wrong with having an uncle that could.

JD listened as Brian and Samuel discussed the situation with Cynthia while he watched the emotions playing across his wife's face. To him the disguise of overstuffed jeans, turtle neck shirt, man's leather jacket and a baseball cap did not cover enough. He could still see her curves in the clothes—he knew it was a woman under there. "Al is not going to tell us anything." JD responded to a statement made by Brian. "He never does. He will guide you. It's up to you to figure out what's actually happening."

"If he's willing to go that far, why not give you everything?" Samuel asked.

"Al's not a snitch. The only reason he gives us anything at all is to keep Tracy safe. Whatever he needs to tell me has a direct connection to her safety. If it didn't we would not be here."

Tracy smiled at her husband. "I know you think this is dangerous. But thank you for loving me enough to bring me."

He looked over at his wife and smiled. "Stop looking at me like that, we have children in the car."

Brian looked over his shoulder and smiled at the couple, then looked at Samuel in the passenger seat. "No one gets near that room. I don't care who they claim to be."

Samuel nodded, "I like exterminating people."

Tracy frowned at him then looked at JD. "He's not serious baby," JD shook his head.

The vehicle came to a stop at the gate where a guard checked their ID and allowed entrance. They pulled into a parking space at the first administration building. JD and Brian got out of the vehicle and met a man at the door.

Samuel turned to Tracy, "Mrs. Harrison, lay down on the seat until I tell you to sit up."

Tracy complied. "Mr. Lassiter, would you do me a favor?"

"If I can."

"Would you call me Tracy? Mrs. Harrison is Jeffrey's mother."

"I can do that, as long as you call me Samuel."

"Okay," she replied.

Samuel smiled.

JD opened the door and reached for Tracy's hand. "Tracy, there are camera's in the building. I don't want your picture captured on any of them. I need you to walk fast with your head down. Don't look up for any reason." She nodded and JD continued. "Samuel is going to be on one side of you and Brian on the other. A guard will be in front of you and I will be behind you. Do not speak until we are in the room and the doors are closed. You understand?"

The adrenaline was now flowing fast through her veins. "Yes," she replied with a little fear in her voice.

Sensing her fear, JD tried to comfort her. "I would kiss you right now, but I don't want the men to think I'm on the down-low out here kissing a man." She smiled up at him.

Damn, she could turn him on that easy. "Please don't smile at me any time while we are in this building."

She frowned, "Okay."

"Alright Brian, we're ready."

Samuel took one arm, while Brian took the other. To anyone looking on the men looked as if they were bringing a criminal into the building. Once inside they proceeded down the hallway until they reached the Warden's office. The guard knocked on the door and was ordered to come in. The guard opened the door and then stepped back.

"JD," the warden extended his hand. "Everything is set," he said as they shook hands. "You will be using my private conference room. There're two doors, this one leading from my office and one at the far end of the room leading to the opposite side of the building. I have two of my most trusted guards posted at each hallway leading to that room and four on the roof. You can position one of your men at each door while you visit."

"Thank you. Each of my men and I are armed." He felt Tracy shiver at his words.

"If anything goes down" the warden said, "my men will take the person down, not yours."

"You got it." JD agreed than looked at Brian, "Let's go."

They walked to the door of the conference room. Samuel and Brian entered and closed the door. While inside they examined every inch of the room and the hallway on the other side of the building. Samuel pulled out a small device and scanned the room for recording equipment.

Standing outside the door Tracy began to raise her head. "Don't look up and do not speak." JD cautioned.

She quickly put her head completely back down. The urge to take JD's hand was so overwhelming, but she held back. Suddenly the door was opened and JD pushed her inside. The door closed behind her but she waited until JD put his finger under her chin and pushed her head up. The minute she saw Turk in the corner of the room tears filled her eyes. She opened her arms and ran to her brother. Samuel stepped into the hallway and took up his post. Brian did the same at the other door. JD took a seat at the far end of the table, giving a little privacy and to wait. Nothing made him happier than seeing his wife eyes light up. He knew their time was limited, but he wanted to give this to her.

Sitting there he listened as she told her brother about JC, her home and about their mother marrying the senator. Then she told him some things JD did not know. She never told him how the people treated her during the campaign. This was the first he heard about members of his staff telling her she was a distraction. Then she told Turk how JD would not let her go back to work. He wondered if she realized he was right there in the room and could hear everything she was telling her brother.

"The next time I come I'll bring pictures of JC for you. This visit was a surprise. Jeffrey told me I couldn't come and then at the last minute he changed his mine. I think it's because he loves me."

Turk couldn't help but smile at his little sister. Even with the weak male disguise he could tell she was happy and that was all he wanted. Her life was so rough when she was growing up. Now she was all grown up with a family. "I think you're right, Sugie." That was his nickname for her. "Now tell me about your girlfriends. Whatever happened to the one who said you weren't good enough for Harrison?"

"Cynthia, she's good. Well, except for the accident she had last week. But now she's seeing a Prince. A real live prince, can you imagine. But you know I don't think its love. The few times I've been around them, I didn't see the sparks. You know what I mean. But who knows I could be wrong."

"So she is not with the Governor anymore?"

Tracy looked shocked, "How did you know about that?"

"Word travels," he laughed at her reaction.

"Man wait until I tell her people in prison know about that. She is going to trip."

"I don't think you should tell her that."

"Whew, you might be right." She shook her head. As if finally remembering she looked down the table. "Jeffrey didn't you want to visit with Turk."

Unable to resist, JD laughed. "This is a business visit, baby. You came with me, remember."

"I've taken up all your time." She looked at Turk, "I'm sorry, but I had so much to tell you. Oh, one more thing." She whispered something in Turks ear and he nodded his head in response.

"You didn't have to ask, it's done."

"Thank you Turk," she stood. "Jeffrey, you can have him now."

Turk couldn't help but laugh as JD stood. "Thank you baby." He knocked on the door and Brian opened it. "I want you to stand with Brian. Remember to keep your head down."

"I will." She turned around, "Bye Turk, see you next time."

"Bye Sugie." Turk waited for the door to close. "Have you lost your damn mind bringing her here?" He yelled. "Do you know how dangerous the man is that is looking for me? He will not, listen to me, will not hesitate using her or your son to get to me."

"Al what do you want from me? I can't stand to see sadness in her eyes."

Shaking his head, "Harrison, if anything happens to my sister I am not going to be as forgiving as I was the last time."

"I tell you what. You look in her eyes and tell her no." JD said angrily. "You're the man, Al. I want to see you tell her no. Look into her eyes and say no. When you do that—you will have my full respect, my brother."

"I'm not scared of Tracy. Bring her back in here. I'm gonna show you how it's done." Al stared JD down as he opened the door and motioned for Tracy to come back in.

"I'm so glad you let me back in. Turk I forgot to tell you about Ashley."

JD sat back in his chair, crossed his legs and watched as the big time, hard-hearted drug dealer melt in his sister's circle of love. He sat there wondering when Al was going to get around to telling Tracy she could not come back to see him. "I think that's it for real now," he heard Tracy say. She looked at Jeffrey, "Okay, did you need me for something?"

"Yeah, baby. Al has something he wants to tell you." JD stared at Al and waited.

Al looked into Tracy's eyes. "Look Tracy," he saw the happiness there and didn't have the heart to take that away. "I'm glad you came by to see me. Next time if JD says no, then it's no, okay."

"Okay Turk. Love you."

"I love you too." He smiled and waited until she was out the door.

"That's telling her Al." JD smirked then turned serious. "Don't threaten me when it comes to my wife. I will protect her and my son with my life." JD pulled his wallet out of his pocket, opened it and pushed it down the table to Al.

Still a little pissed, AL slowly reached for the wallet. It was opened to a picture of JD, Tracy and JC. Exhaling Al smiled, "He's a big boy." He longingly touched the picture. He turned to the next picture and then the next. "You are good for her."

JD walked down to the other end of the table and took a seat close to Al. Taking the wallet back he replaced it in his pocket. "You asked for this meeting. What's up Al?"

"I'm glad to see Lassiter on your security team. Do you have his brother on board?"

"No. You know Samuel?"

"Just by reputation. I feel good knowing he's around. Getting his brother will make me happier."

"I live to make you happy Al," JD replied sarcastically.

Al chucked than sat forward, "The hit on the beauty queen needs to be handled before it affects Tracy. It's a sign of desperation or greed you need to determine which."

"Is there a connection with you?"

"Look for the common denominator. Think of all the players, as you know them. Who is connected to you, me, Tracy, Cynthia?

JD thought, the realization showed on his face, "Gavin."

Brian walked in the door with Tracy, "We have a breach."

JD reached for Tracy and put her between him and the wall. He then pulled his weapon. Turk stood to the other side of Tracy blocking her from view, while Brian stood in front of all of them with weapons in both hands. A small commotion was heard outside the door, and then there was silence. It seemed like eternity, but a few minutes later, Samuel opened the door and looked in. "I think it's time we move."

Brian moved to the door and checked the hallway. Tracy tried to get up, but JD pushed her back down. Turk looked over at his brother-in-law holding a gun. "You know how to use that?"

"Someone comes through that door I don't recognize you'll find out."

"All clear," Brian nodded.

JD looked at Al as he holstered his weapon. "One question before we leave. Is the person we are looking for in the files?"

Al didn't answer, he turned to Tracy, "You cannot come back here until JD gives the okay."

Tracy hugged Turk, and then took JD's hand. He could tell from the look in her eyes she was frightened. Before leaving the room he took a moment to adjust her clothing and settle her nerves then he smiled down at her. "You ready to go home?"

"Yes," she nodded and walked out the room without looking back.

Once they were inside the vehicle and drove outside the gate, regular breathing fill the air. Until then everyone was on full alert. JD turned to Tracy and removed her baseball cap. "You don't need this anymore." She looked up at him with eyes as big as a saucer and as watery as the James River. He gathered her in his arms and held her tight. "It's okay; I won't let anything happen to you."

"Neither will I," Samuel added without turning around.

"I'm still thinking about it," Brian joked. He saw Tracy smile and put her head in JD's lap, "So what did you get?"

"We'll talk. In the meantime Samuel, stay close to our friend, real close." The last thing JD wanted was for Tracy to be worried about Cynthia.

Chapter 6

The date ritual was underway. First the long bath in
lavender scented salt beads, with the same scented
candles and her favorite CD, Moods by Will Downing. It
was time to make the tension of the day disappear. Stepping
into the luxury bath tub, Cynthia picked up her sponge. She
placed her head against her bath pillow and submerged into
the soothing comfort of the water. She closed her eyes when
her favorite song of all times began to play, *Inseparable*. A
small smile creased her face. LaVere' was slowly slipping
under her skin.

This was going to be her first real date with LaVere' and
she wanted him to definitely remember this night. Feeling
guilty about leaving her brother even for this one night after
he had come home just to be with her, she asked Brian to
take him out with the guys and make sure he had a good
time. Before leaving Blake told her a package had arrived
for her and he placed it on her bed. At the time she didn't
think much of it. Packages for events were always delivered
to her home if the office was closed. Since it was a Saturday,
she simply assumed it was for TNT. However, when she
entered her room the elegantly wrapped box was not from
UPS as she had assumed. She opened the box and inside
there was a beautiful indigo evening gown. She read the card

on top. "My dream for tomorrow is you, LaVere'." She picked up the gown and was stunned by the silky feel of the material. She hesitated for a moment, and then touched the cloth to her face. Anyone that knows Cynthia knows, she does not allow anyone or anything to touch her face. The material was soft and smooth. She removed the gown from her face and smiled. "I'm going to make you look fabulous."

After thirty minutes of relaxation Cynthia emerged refreshed and looking forward to seeing LaVere'. In the week she has known him, he has treated her the way she always wanted to be treated, like a queen. In addition, he believes she has something to contribute to this world and that alone inspires her. After placing lotion on her body she slipped the gown over her head. The feel against her skin was glorious. The reflection looking back at her was magnificent. The color against her skin tone was a match made in heaven. And that is exactly what she felt like in the dress, heavenly. The doorbell interrupted her assessment. She took one last look and went downstairs to answer the door.

Standing in the doorway was a man that was definitely comfortable with whom he was. There was a sense of power surrounding him. LaVere' stood there in a, tailor made for his body only, suit that probably cost more than any combination of items she had in her closet. If he was trying to impress her, he succeeded. "Please come in," she said stepping aside.

He kissed her gently on the lips and walked by as she closed the door. "The gown was made for you."

Turning to give him a full view, "It is wonderful. Thank you LaVere'," she hugged him.

He stepped back and looked her up and down. The look on his face was not quite what she expected. She knew the gown was on point. She reached up to touch her hair, self-consciously and that made her angry. The only person that was allowed to make her feel self-conscious about herself was Sophia, her mother. Placing her hands on her hips she stood a little straighter, "Is there a problem?" she asked raising an eyebrow.

He shook his head, "Not exactly a problem, but something is not quite right." He took her hand and guided her to the mirror. "Look for yourself," he said as he stood behind her looking into the mirror.

Cynthia looked at the reflection in the mirror. "I have no idea what you are referring to. I look damn good." She said placing her hands on her hips.

LaVere' smiled as he brought his hands around her neck and placed a sapphire and diamond choker there. "Now," he smiled, "Now, you are exquisite."

The necklace and the matching teardrop earrings that he placed in her hands had her speechless. She knew jewelry as well as she knew clothes and what she was holding in her hand had to be close to a million dollars in gems. Then she heard herself say something that she could not believe, "I can't accept these." She held the earrings to her heart. "They are beautiful, but too much, LaVere'."

He closed her hand around the earrings. "This is something you are going to have to get use too. This is just the beginning of our journey, Cynthia." He kissed her sensuously as he wrapped his arms around her waist bringing her closer to him. She put her arms around his neck and relaxed into the kiss. Slowly he pulled away and looked into her eyes, "I think we better go."

Cynthia grabbed her purse and they headed out the door. Edmund spoke as he opened the car door, "Good evening Ms. Thornton."

"Good evening," she smiled and turned to LaVere'.

"Edmond," he replied to her unspoken question.

"Good evening Edmond."

LaVere' and Edmond exchanged a brief nod. Once everyone was settled Edmond drove to the airport. Getting out of the late model sedan Cynthia saw that the plane appeared to be ready for takeoff. She turned to LaVere'. "I know you indicated we were going to dinner. Exactly where is the restaurant located?"

His lips curved slightly, "That remains to be seen. I promise you will be home in time for church tomorrow." He placed his hand in the small of her back and guided her toward the plane. The inside of the plane was regal, with leather seats to accommodate eight. There were four sections with two seats in each, facing each other with a table in-between. The pilot and stewardess greeted LaVere' in a manner that let her know they were very familiar with each other. LaVere' turned and introduced her to them and then they disappeared.

"Let's get you strapped in for safety," he smiled as he gestured towards the seats.

Cynthia took a seat trying very hard not to appear overwhelmed, but she was. Her brother had a private jet, but not like this. Yes, this was the life she wanted. She had to admit LaVere' was certainly making an impression on her.

"Are you trying to woo me, LaVere'?" she asked as he took his seat.

After he placed his seat belt on he looked up at her. "Is it working?"

Nervously, she crossed her legs at the knee and attempted to not reveal just how impressed she was and smiled. "Let's see what the remainder of the evening brings."

It was impossible not to notice the legs on the woman. LaVere' scanned her closely, from the French manicured toes to the upswing style of her hair. It was going to be a pleasure making love to her, he thought to himself. There was nothing undesirable about her and he was sure the same spirit she displayed in conversation will be tenfold in bed. He had made a good choice; she was beautiful, spirited and majestic. "I am going to enjoy having you as my wife," he stated with a smile.

She smiled, "A bit presumptuous aren't we? I don't recall agreeing to marry you."

As the plane took off he settled back into the seat and smiled, "That's just logistics you have to go through. I am at the finish line, you should join me."

"If I join you there now, it would take all the fun out of you trying to seduce me." She looked around and smiled. "I'll work through the logistics for the time being."

He laughed, "I'm sure you will."

The plane landed about an hour later in New York, where they received the royal treatment. There was a driver waiting for them at the terminal. Edmond joined him in the front seat of the vehicle, while they sat in the back and another vehicle followed closely behind. The first stop was the theater where they were ushered to their seats with Edmond clearing the way. Apparently LaVere' arrival was expected as additional security stood near the entrance of the box seats. Looking around Cynthia noticed there were other seats in the section; however no one was sitting in them. When she asked LaVere' about it, he stated the section was used for dignitaries. Settling back into her seat she smiled, "I think I could like this life."

He turned to her and kissed her on the cheek. "I know you can."

After the theater, they had dinner at a restaurant that seemed to sit in the sky of the city. The table was located in a private dining glass enclosed room. The view of the city was magnificent from where they sat. Cynthia remembered Ashley and her sister in law Nicole talking about the city and how glamorous it could be. Whenever he was filming in New York, Blake would tell her about the night life that he loved so much. But this was the first time she had ever been there and the virgin trip was worth the wait. She sighed as she feasted on the lobster tail appetizer; her family had experienced so much without her. It was as if she really did not exist to her parents.

At one moment LaVere' was getting the reaction to the evening he wanted, then for a fleeting moment it vanished. "Is everything okay?" he asked curiously.

Clearing her mind of the thought she smiled, "Everything is wonderful." And that quick the sadness disappeared. At this point in her life she was very experienced in masking her true feelings.

As promised she was back home in time to go to church the next morning. Before LaVere' left her doorstep she had to tell him, what a wonderful time she had. She attempted to give the necklace and earrings back because she assumed they were on loan to him. He gave a playful look of being offended and told her, "The set would never look the same on anyone else. Whether we marry or not, they were purchased exclusively for you. They are yours to keep." He kissed her good night and walked away.

After taking her shower and changing into her night clothes Cynthia picked up the necklace and fell asleep with it clutched to her heart. A few hours later she was awaken with a shock. The face that looked back at her in the short dream was not LaVere's, but the man with no name and it wasn't the first time. The face was not recognizable, but the voice certainly was. It was the same voice from the hospital. She frantically searched the bed and found the necklace tangled in the sheets. "Why in the hell do you keep creeping into my dreams?" she sat on her bed in wonder.

Samuel watched as the plane took off. His contacts were able to tell him where the destination was and he made arrangements to have someone keep a watchful eye on Cynthia while she was in New York. The fact that she was with Prince Ashro helped for he had a security detail of six traveling with him. Looking at the woman, he could not help but notice she was beautiful. She actually looked like a princess in that gown. Seeing her with the Prince was like being on the outside looking in. The lifestyle of the rich and famous was not something he could compete with.

The odd feeling of jealousy he was experiencing wasn't important. Figuring out why and who wanted her dead was. With that in mind he thought back to the meeting he had earlier in the day with Brian. There wasn't much to go on, but it was evident someone had tampered with the brakes on her car and there may be another attempt. Samuel sighed— the thought of someone causing her harm pissed him off. *Get a grip man, she is about the money and you don't need that in your life. Just do the job at hand and move on.* Resigned to what he had to do, Samuel drove home to get some rest until her return. Little did he know it would be the last good night sleep he would have for a while.

Chapter 7

Brian's continued attempts to ignore the telephone ended on the twentieth ring. In an effort to appease Cynthia, Brian did as she asked and made sure Blake had a good time. Now he was paying the price. What made him think he could hang out with a group of twenty-something year old people, he did not know. The one thing he did know was it would *not* happen again for they were nothing but trouble. The blame really didn't fall on them. It was his bright idea to take Blake to a nightclub. And since James Brooks, younger brother, Nicolas and his twin sister Nicole was in town visiting, it only made sense to get them together for some fun. They had a ball, but damn if he wasn't paying the price this morning.

The telephone finally stopped ringing. Placing his arm over his head he stared up at the ceiling he thought back to the night before. *How in the hell did last night go so wrong.* He called Douglas, a friend that went to high school with him, who owned the Renaissance Club. It was one of the most popular clubs in town and was known to be frequent by celebrities all the time. The security team there was top-notch and would be able to handle Blake being there. What he did not anticipate was the number of woman in the club who had a lack of self control.

Things were going well as a few people recognized Blake and just spoke and kept moving. With Nick, who was a multimillionaire sports agent with quite a reputation with the ladies, Brian thought Blake would have company. Nicole, who was usually in New York running her real estate business, decided she wanted to hang out as well. So to give her a little company Brian invited two of Samuel's sisters that were around the twins' age. Pearl, who was JD's press secretary and Diamond, joined them about an hour later.

The music was bumping, the atmosphere was relaxed and drinks were on the house courtesy of Blake. All was well. As the crowd began to grow, it became increasingly difficult for Brian to keep an eye on Blake. For that matter, having James' little brother and sister in the house meant he was spread a little thin when things began to go astray. First, there were the two females that decided to share Blake on the dance floor. Since Blake was a good six-two and the women were a little shorter, he could still be seen from where Brian stood. But then a few more women decided to join the group, so Brian decided to step in to remove Blake. The crowd was not pleased with that, although Blake was thankful. Now, if they had left then things would have been just fine, but no.....Brian took a look at his watch and thought it was still early, let them hang a little longer. He should have followed his first thought and left while the getting was easy.

Word of Blake's presence seemed to spread like wildfire. Women appeared out of nowhere wanting to touch the man. Blake took it all in stride. He smiled, took pictures, signed autographs and even danced with a few. Then suddenly, he disappeared. Brian walked through the club looking for him, but did not locate him before a ruckus started in the area where Nicole was. He made a u-turn. Apparently some guy asked Nicole to dance and she refused. The guy decided he was not going to take no for an answer and began pulling her to the dance floor. Brian arrived from one direction at the same time Douglas arrived. But before either could do anything, the guy was on the floor unable to get a sound out. Pearl had kneed him in the groin and the man was singing acappella. Brian and Douglas looked at each other, then at the ladies that were walking away. "I think the ladies can take care of themselves," Douglas laughed.

"It seems so. Have you seen Blake?"

"No, but I can check the monitors and locate him. The crowd is getting a little unruly, you got back up?"

"I'm it."

"Where are Blake's people?"

"He's on hiatus; his people don't know he's here."

Douglas looked around, "You came here with three multimillionaire celebrities and only you as their body man?"

"I kill people for a living. I can handle a few star-struck fans."

Douglas laughed, "No man, they're a breed all to themselves. Take my word on this, you better call in some back up. I'll check the monitor."

"He's right." Pearl said from behind him. When she saw the frown on Brian's face she continued. "Look, I'm not saying you can't handle this, but I called Samuel and he's on his way. If anything was to happen to Nick or Nicole you will have hell to pay trying to explain things to James Brooks. Do I have to tell you what you will be dealing with if anything went down with Blake?" She raised an eyebrow and waited for his response.

Before he could reply, another commotion began on the dance floor. This time it was Nick who was standing in front of the guy Pearl had taken down earlier and it seemed he brought in reinforcements. He was trying to be diplomatic with them as lawyers do sometimes, but they weren't hearing it. Nicole was standing behind her brother with Diamond next to her. Nick said something then turned with both women to walk away. The guy doing all the talking grabbed

Nick's shirt and this time it was Diamond who turned and accidently elbowed the man so hard Brian felt the pain from where he was. "Oh, I'm so sorry. Are you okay," Diamond bent down genuinely sorry to help the man up.

When the guy stood straight he swung up and back handed her. Pearl pushed through the crowd as Brian followed. Suddenly a body pushed past Brian and the next thing he knew the man who hit Diamond was up in the air flying, then landed against the wall. He turned back to see Samuel standing in the middle of the floor with two more of the friends. Before Brian could say anything, Samuel had banged their heads together. Brian watched as they crumpled to the floor. Samuel then stood there and quietly asked "anyone else?" Douglas' security team simply shook their heads at the giant of a man. "I think you cleared the floor. We'll take care of the clean-up"

Samuel turned to his little sister and began to check her out. Pearl and Nicole took her to the ladies room, while Brian and Nick attempted to explain things to a very angry Samuel.

Both men, who were a good size themselves, looked up at Samuel in awe. "Where in the hell did you come from?" Brian asked.

"Douglas Hylton," extended his hand to Samuel. "You looking for a job?"

"No, he is not looking for a job. He works for me." Brian replied aggravated. "You remember Samuel Lassiter. He played ball with us at Grant High."

"I thought you looked familiar."

A still angry Samuel shook Douglas hand. "I'll pay for any damages."

"Don't worry about it. You saved my security some action."

"You want to tell me what my sisters are doing here. And where the hell were you when Diamond was hit?"

"*Be happy to, but first we have to get these people out of here. This crowd is getting ugly.*"

"*I'll go look for Blake,*" *Nick offered.*

"*No.*" *Brian put a hand on his chest,* "*You're not going anywhere.*"

"*Blake Thornton is here?*" *Samuel asked fuming. Have you lost your mind? You can't bring him in here with no body man. Where the hell is he?*"

Brian looked at Douglas who was trying his hardest not to laugh at the astonished look on his friends' face. He had never known Brian to be at a loss for words. "*We were in the VIP section. Things just got a little out of hand. But since you mentioned it—you are now his body man. Find him and meet me at the door in ten.*" *He turned to Nick,* "*Let's go.*"

Douglas looked at Samuel and was certain he wanted to hit something, but he would be damned if it was going to be him—the man was too damn big. "*The monitors showed Blake in a booth in the back talking to a shorty.*"

For a minute Samuel did not move or say anything. He did not do celebrities. He looked at Douglas, "*Thank you for the tip,*" *he said and walked off.*

Samuel moved slowly through the room searching. Guarding Celebrities was not what he signed up for. They were temperamental and then you had to be nice to the idiots around them. Walking into the private area of the club he noticed a small group of men and a couple. "*This is not good,*" *he said as he moved closer.*

"*You're the pretty boy who gets the woman. But this ain't a movie. So show me what you got. Show me how you pulled this fine woman.*" *A man who apparently had a little too much to drink was showing off for his friends at Blake's expense.*

Blake put his hands up in a surrender motion, "*I'm just trying to have a drink with a lady in a quiet corner. You know how it is.*"

"This lady?" he slurred as he touched the woman's shoulder.

Blake looked at Monica, who turned out to be someone that knew his sister. The look on her face indicated she was about to go off. *"Yes, this lady."*

The man laughed, *"I want to have a conversation with the lady too."*

Doing his best to stay calm, Blake shook his head, *"This one is taken for the night."*

"I didn't hear her say that. Did you guys here her say that?" he asked his friends standing behind him.

"I'm taken for the night. Now do you mind?" Monica sneered.

"Actually I do. Come dance with me." The man replied.

"No thank you."

"Just one dance," the man took her arm.

She pulled away as Blake stood and positioned himself between the man and Monica, *"The lady said no."*

"All hell," Samuel mumbled as he stepped closer. *"Mr. Thornton, is there a problem?"*

Blake did not recognize the man, but he's been around enough protection details to recognize the stance. *"We're good,"* he said ready to take the man on.

"Who in the hell are you, his bodyguard or something?"

Ignoring the man Samuel turned to Blake, *"This way Mr. Thornton."*

Blake stepped away from the man and took Monica's hand, *"Let's go."*

"She stays," the man said reaching out to grab her arm.

Before he could touch her, Blake saw a movement go by his head and looked down. The man was on the floor out cold. *"Whoa,"* he heard one friend yell.

"Mr. Thornton, Miss," Samuel said as he gingerly moved them away from the scene.

Blake looked at the man on the floor with blood gushing from his nose then back up at Samuel whoes suit jacket was not even out of place. "Man, I need to hire you."

As they walked away, Samuel contacted Brian, "Celeb secure. Let's call it a night."

The telephone began to ring again bringing Brian back to the present. This time he decided not to ignore it. He sat up in the bed and picked up the cordless telephone. "Yeah," he all but yelled into the receiver.

"Brian, where in the hell have you been this morning. I've been calling you for the last hour." Rosaline yelled into the telephone.

"What's going on Roz?"

"Somebody broke into the office. I can't reach Cynthia and I need you to come and reset the alarm system."

Brian stood up. "Are you okay? Were you there?"

"Yes, I'm okay. I wasn't here when it happened."

"Is anything missing?"

"That's just it. Nothing is missing and the only room that was touched was Cynthia's office."

"I'll be right there."

Brian hung up the telephone and dialed Samuel's number. After filling him in, he jumped in the shower.

Brian and Samuel waited until the police were gone before they did their search of the place. It was determined the intruder came in through the window of Cynthia's office. The building was a three story old warehouse that was renovated into a beautiful facility with two ballrooms on the top floor, three offices, a state of the art kitchen and three meeting rooms where people usually held book club meetings and tutoring sessions. The basement was wall to wall shelves of boxes labeled for each holiday. Then from floor to ceiling there were boxes stored alphabetically with names and addresses showing on the outside.

Walking down the stairs leading to the basement Samuel could not help noticing the art collection mounted on the wall. It seemed to be the latest collection of a local artist Judith Wansley. He recognized a few of the pieces because his mother loved her work. There was one piece in particular, The Eye of the Sparrow, she wanted, that he planned to purchase and knew the original was expensive. All the canvas paintings appeared to be originals. Why would someone break in and not take at least one of the very expensive pieces. Walking further into the room he could see clear plastic containers were stacked neatly from floor to ceiling. There was a seven foot ladder off to the side. Long tables line the center of the huge room, with a desk and file cabinets to the right. Behind the desk was a set of double doors, with a fire extinguishing bolt next to it and the alarm system box on the other side. Checking the doors, he found them secured and bolted. The file cabinet had not been tampered with nor had anything on the desk been touched including what appeared to be a cash deposit bag.

Brian was sitting at Cynthia's desk sorting through the papers that were thrown aside when Samuel reappeared. "Whatever they were looking for was not money." He said as he threw the bag on the desk in front of Brian.

"Where was this?"

"On the desk downstairs in the open for anyone to see. Whoever did this knew this was her office. This was not a robbery."

"This is too close for comfort," Brian said as he leaned back in the chair behind the desk. "Leaving this office in shambles is a sign of someone getting desperate. I don't like desperate people. They get stupid."

Samuel looked around the room, "Do we have any idea what they are looking for? Or if they found it."

"No. But I get the impression that if they have to take her out to get it, whatever it is—they will."

"I think it's time you told her what's going on."

Brian nodded knowing Samuel was right. "Tell the officer out front not to move anything in this room. I want her to go through here before we have it cleaned up. As of now, I'm moving you in with her. I want you to cover her twenty-four seven. She's not going to accept this sitting down and will fight you and me all the way. But we have to protect her whether she wants it or not."

"You realize I kill people, I'm not good at babysitting," Samuel scowled.

"That's why you are the best man for the job. I don't want you to babysit her. I want you to keep her alive."

"What about the brother? Who is going to handle him?"

"For the time being I'll put Magna on him. I'll cover JD and Tracy Harrison until we clear up this situation."

Rosaline walked into the room and leaned back to stare up at Samuel again. "Damn. A person could break their neck looking at you."

"It's not that I'm tall. You're just short," he smiled.

She returned the smile, "So you got jokes, huh." She turned to Brian, I just got through to Cynthia and she wants to know why she is being told she cannot come over here."

"Tell her I'm on my way over," he replied refusing to take the telephone.

"Chicken," Roz teased as she put the phone back to her ear. "He doesn't want to talk to you right now." She held the telephone out so the men could hear Cynthia yelling. "Huh Honey, I think he hears you. He's on his way to you."

"Thanks friend," Brian said to Roz as he walked out the door.

Chapter 8

Being away from home on assignment was nothing new for Samuel. He knew how to travel light and prepared for just about anything. Before leaving, although he would be right in Richmond this tour, he always stopped by his parents' home to check in and let them know he may be out of commission for a while. This time he also wanted to check in on Diamond and Pearl, who had their own place on the North side of Richmond. His feathers were still a little ruffled about the events of the night before. Just as he walked through the crowd of people at the club he saw some guy hitting Diamond with the back of his hand. Asking questions was the furthest thing on his mind. For him there was no reason for a man to put his hands on a woman, especially one of his sisters. The anger at the site was still with him as he pushed the security button at their building.

The monitor came on and he saw Pearl looking into the camera. "Hey Sammy, come on up." The door buzzed open and he entered the building. Not bothering with the elevator, he took the stairs two at a time. The door was open when he arrived. Walking in he looked at Pearl who was standing in the kitchen with a cup in her hand and asked, "Where is Diamond?"

"I'm right here Sammy and I'm fine," she said coming out of her room. Ignoring the frown on his face she hugged him and kissed his cheek. "Just so you know I accidently hit him with my elbow. That's why the man hit me."

"You're under the misconception that I give a damn. No man is to put his hands on you—any of you in anger despite what you do to provoke him," he said as he looked at Pearl.

"Why are you looking at me? I didn't hit that man."

"No, you just knee the other one. That's what started the whole thing," Diamond stated.

Samuel looked from one sister to the other and shook his head. "Start from the beginning."

Pearl explained all that happened the night before. When she finished it was her belief that Brian was to blame for the entire evening. "If it hadn't been for him we would have been home looking at television or at the movies or something."

"That's true." Diamond added. "But then we would not have been partying with Blake Thornton. Man, how cool was that. Opal and Phire will lose their minds when we tell them about it at dinner this evening."

"Pearl you are twenty-eight years old. Blaming others for your decisions is a little farfetched. And I know for a fact that you don't really care about Blake Thornton. You were there to be around Brian."

Diamond smiled, "Really. He is kind of cute. I didn't know you had a thing for him. Why didn't you tell me?"

"Because I don't," she snarled at Samuel.

"Hum hum. Come here Diamond and let me take a look at your cheek." Looking at her face he frowned again. "That bastard cut your face."

"Well Sammy, you broke his back. I think you two are even," she smiled.

He glared at her, "I did not break his back, but as long as he is alive, we are not even."

"Sammy, you are beginning to sound like Joshua." Pearl shook her head and walked back into the kitchen.

Samuel hugged Diamond, "I'm sorry I didn't get there sooner."

"I'm okay Sammy," Diamond smiled.

"Alright, I have to run. I'll be on assignment and may not see you for a while.

Pearl came out of the kitchen, "On assignment? Why?" she frantically asked, "I thought you retired from government work."

"This is private."

"Protection detail for Brian?" Pearl asked.

"Yes."

"Who?"

"You really don't want to know." Samuel replied as he walked towards the door.

Curious now, Pearl walked towards him, "Who Sammy?"

Samuel paused; he knew she was going to find out anyway, it was better coming from him. "Cynthia Thornton."

Shock then anger appeared on Pearl's face. "You are joking." She said almost in a whisper. "You are joking," she said a little louder. "Tell me you're joking Samuel," she yelled.

"I'm not joking. Until we can solve this case I will be covering her and I expect you to behave." He said it in a very stern voice.

"Who's wife is trying to kill her?" Pearl asked.

Frowning, "I think it's a little more serious than that." As least he hoped it was. "You two try to stay out of trouble."

"We will Sammy," Diamond replied.

"I make no promises," Pearl smiled as she folded her arms across her chest.

When Samuel left the apartment Diamond turned to Pearl and asked, "Who is Cynthia Thornton? Is she related to Blake?"

"His sister and a whore from way back," Pearl replied as she turned and went into her room.

Pacing the floor in her kitchen Cynthia waited for Brian to explain why she could not leave her home. Her office had been broken into and no one was telling her anything. She looked up at the clock on the stove and then back at Blake who was reading a script. "Did Brian say anything at all about what's going on?"

"No. He just said I was not to let you out of this house until he got here. Then Blake looked up from his script. "He was very serious Cynthia and I am not going to piss Brian or his big man off."

"I don't care about pissing Brian off. I want to know what's going on. It's Sunday, my office was vandalized, I've missed church and dinner at Mama Harrison's house," she pouted.

Before Blake could reply he heard the front door open and was relieved to see Brian coming up the stairs that led to the second level of the house. Actually, he saw the head of Samuel before he saw Brian. When Brian reached the entrance to the kitchen Cynthia began with her questions. "You want to explain to me why I'm a prisoner in my own home? Or why I can't go to my office to see what has been taken? And where do you get off telling Blake not to let me out of the house?" All asked in one breathe with her back now to Samuel who just stood at the entrance.

"I'll be happy to answer all your questions, but first I want you to meet Samuel," Brian calmly replied as he took a coffee cup from the cabinet and filled it from the pot on the counter. "Is this fresh?"

"Yeah," Blake replied as he stood and extended his hand to Samuel. "Hey man."

"Blake."

Cynthia turned around to the voice almost stunned. That's the voice! That's the voice she heard in the hospital. It's the voice that creeps into her dreams. When she turned, she looked into his chest, and then followed up until she could see his face. He wasn't overly tall she thought, it just she was in flat slippers not her heels. Her neck began to strain from looking up so she took a step back. *Lord, talk about tall dark chocolate!* For a moment she actually wanted to lick her lips, but was certain that would be inappropriate, *but damn if he wasn't fine.*

Samuel was studying her just as hard as she was him. He had been following her for about a week, but this was the first time he had seen her face to face. And what a face she had. There was no make-up, her hair was in a ponytail flowing between her shoulder blades and she wore sweats low on her hips and a short sleeve tee shirt. There was always talk of her beauty, but the reality was still something to behold.

Blake and Brian stared at the two as silence filled the room. Then they looked at each other. Blake smiled and raised an eyebrow, it was the first time he had seen his sister rendered speechless. Brian cleared his throat, "Cynthia, Samuel is your new bodyguard."

She started to speak, but then turned to Brian, "My what?"

"I think he said your new body man," Blake explained.

"Why do I need a body man?" She yelled turning towards him with her hands on her hips. Then she heard a bark. Turning back towards Samuel, she looked up at him as if questioning if he had made the sound.

Samuel whistled and Rusty came up the stairs and sat next to his master. "This is Rusty."

Cynthia just stared at Samuel, then turned and placed an evil look at Brian then looked down at the dog. She ignored the man and smiled at the dog. "Hello Rusty, I'm Cynthia.

Do you know what's going on here, boy, because I sure as hell don't?"

Blake coughed attempting to cover his laugh. Brian frowned at him. "Samuel and Rusty are going to be staying with you for a while."

Hands across her chest she gave Brian a, *you have lost your mind look.* "Say what?"

"Have a seat. We need to talk."

She walked over to the cabinet near where Brian stood and pulled out a box of doggie treats that she kept for her neighbor's dog. She then walked back to where Rusty sat and pulled up a chair. She knew enough about dogs not to attempt to pat him so she simply held her hand out for him to take a sniff. The dog didn't move. Frustrated she looked up at the tree bark of a man standing next to the dog and frowned.

Samuel was tempted to play hard ball with her, but since he understood her frustration he looked at Rusty, who was now waiting for his command, and gave him a slight nod. Rusty took a step forward and smelled the back of Cynthia's hand. After rolling her eyes at the man, for his very presence was making her nervous, she sighed. "Which one of you is going to explain what in the hell is going on?" She asked as she rubbed Rusty's head and fed him a treat.

"That depends on how pissed you are?" Brian replied.

The look she gave him made Rusty whimper. She looked at the dog, smiled and decided to sit on the floor Indian style then patted her thigh for him to sit with her. Rusty looked up at Samuel. Cynthia then looked up at the man. From the floor it seemed he filled the room with his size. His nod was so slight she thought she had imagined it until Rusty laid down beside her and put his chin on her thigh. She began to pat him and sighed. That eased the tension in the room. "Why do I need a body guard?"

"Truthfully I don't know. But until I do, Samuel is going to be your shadow."

"You and I don't have secrets Brian. If I don't' know what you are protecting me from how will I know when I'm in danger?"

Hum, that actually made sense. Samuel thought as he watched how she continued to rub Rusty. He was stunned the dog allowed her to get that close to him so soon. For a moment he was a little jealous. Shaking the thought away he looked at Brian. "She has a point."

Brian sat forward and exhaled, "Uncle Joe thinks someone tapered with your car." She looked up from Rusty expectantly. Brian realized she was waiting for something more. "Then last night someone broke into your TNT building and did not take anything. The only room they touched was your office." He hesitated then continued, "About two week ago I received a tip indicating someone may have put a contract out on you. Not knowing if it was real or imagined, I asked Samuel to shadow you just to be on the safe side. The night of your accident, it was Samuel who took you to the hospital."

Blake and Cynthia both inhaled. "But why? Why would someone want to hurt Cynthia," Blake asked.

"We don't know. That's why we decided to talk to you," he looked at her. "Is there anything going on that you have not told me?"

"No," she replied softly.

"Have you had a run in with someone's wife or girlfriend lately?" Samuel asked.

The motion of her hand rubbing Rusty stopped as she frowned up at the man. "Are you insinuating something?"

"Not at all," he looked down at her. "I simply asked a question to get an idea of who wants to eliminate you from the land of the breathing."

"Cynthia," Brian spoke cautiously, "You have dated quite a few men. Some of whom were attached to other women. Is there a possibility that someone would be that angry with you to do something like this? I'm just asking?" He shrugged his shoulder.

"Am I missing something here?" Blake asked. "Someone is actually trying to kill my sister and you two want to question her dating habits."

Samuel removed his sunshades. "There are crazy people in this world. Some kill, because they can do it and get away with it. Other's kill if someone stepped on their sneakers. It is in the realm of possibility that a woman would kill over a man. At this point we need to question everything, just to get an idea of where to start." He looked down at Cynthia. "I don't know you. I only know what I've read and you have had a colorful record in the dating department. Currently you are dating Prince Ashro. Is there any chance his people may be involved?"

"Look," she sighed, "I just started dating LaVere' last week. If you got the tip two weeks ago I doubt it could be about him. It's not public knowledge that we are seeing each other." Just as the words left her mouth the door bell sounded. She stood to answer the door.

Brian grabbed her by the elbow, "Stay here."

She jerked away from him, "I'm not hiding in my own house. She stomped down the stairs with Rusty in tow and jerked the door open.

"What!" She was not able to complete her question. The vision at the door shocked her more than she would have ever expected, it was an older version of herself.

"Hello Cynthia Antoinette," her mother, Sofia said while walking up the stairs past her.

"Mother?" Blake called out as he jumped up from the table.

Cynthia was staring at her mother's back when her father walked through the door. "Brace yourself," he warned as he hugged her.

"Who is that man and why is he preventing me from coming into my daughter's home?" her mother said as she removed her coat.

Cynthia turned to see Samuel at the top of the steps with Rusty beside him blocking her mother's entrance. Rusty growled. Cynthia walked up the steps. "It's okay." When Sofia walked into the main floor of the house, she surveyed the area. Cynthia looked down at Rusty, "Next time don't let her in." Looking at Samuel now, without his shades on she could see he had the most wonderful brown eyes. She looked back down at Rusty and rubbed his head, "You can stay. She looked up at Samuel, "I'm not sure about you."

After surveying the main level of the house, Sofia walked back towards the kitchen and stopped in front of Samuel. "Aren't you one of those Lassisters?" she asked with a sneer.

"I am," was Samuel's salty reply.

"Hum, you look just like your father," she replied looking up at him.

"Thank you," he nodded.

"I didn't mean it as a compliment."

"I took it as one none-the-less," he replied and turned his attention back to Cynthia.

Sofia turned and looked at Brian, then walked away with an air of superiority and embraced her son. "Now, why are you here and not on location?" Sofia asked Blake.

"I received the call about Cynthia's accident. I wanted to make sure she was okay. When I arrived I thought we needed to spend some time together so I decided to stay for a while."

"You raised your son right, Sofia. He's looking out for his sister," her husband Jackson smiled as he extended his hand to Samuel. "It's nice to meet you son."

"Thank you sir," he replied.

"Brian," her father waved.

"Hello Mr. Thornton."

"Blake it may be wise for us to escape downstairs."

Knowing his father well, he knew that was a warning. "I'm right behind you dad."

Assuming her mother was here to visit with Blake; Cynthia turned to Samuel, "Okay, for that you can stay. But I still want an explanation." She looked at Brian and motioned for both men to follow her upstairs to her office. The trio walked into the living room to take the steps up to the third floor.

"Cynthia Antoinette," Sofia called out. "Come here," she said walking towards her. Cynthia froze where she was standing. It looked as if her mother was opening her arms to hug her. No, that can't .... The thought was interrupted when she felt her mother's arms circling her shoulders. Cynthia wasn't sure whose eyes were larger from the surprised show of affection, hers Brian's or Blake's. "Let me look at you." Sofia said taking a step back, but still holding her daughter at arm length. "It doesn't appear anything is broken. How are you feeling?"

Too stunned for words, Cynthia looked at her father, there were no answers there. She then turned to Blake, who shrugged his shoulders indicating he did not know what was going on.

Brian looked at Cynthia as shocked as she was at the show of affection from her mother. He turned to Samuel and the two continued on to her office to wait for her. He looked back just to make sure she was okay. Cynthia looked up at him with a strained look.

Waiting for a response Sofia shook her, "Cynthia?"

She stepped back and replied, "The accident was a week ago. I'm doing fine now."

"You should have called me when this happened. I would have been here to take care of you."

"Why? You never wanted to take care of me before."

That was Blake's cue. He looked at his father and they both walked down the stairs to the lower level of the house where the family room was located. Blake took a seat beside his father and turned on the remote to the fifty inch plasma on the wall. "So dad what's been popping?"

Jackson looked up the steps then slid a piece of paper across the seat. Blake looked at the article. It was printed from the internet, a paper in New York had a picture of LaVere' and Cynthia. Blake looked at his dad and shook his head. "This is not going to be pretty. It's a good thing I took a month off. This is going to hurt."

"She booked a flight out within minutes of reading that. She had the house re-opened before we came over here. I believe she plans on staying for a while. Your mother claims she is going to talk Cynthia into staying at the house, as a family should."

"You know Dad; I just don't see that happening. He knew he was the apple of his mother's eye—always had been. "When Cynthia realizes all the sudden attention is because of Prince LaVere', all hell is going to break lose." The men looked at each other and shut out the conversation taking place upstairs.

"Cynthia, I love both of my children. Blake's career dictated that I spend more time with him, you know that. You have never been a dependent child. You didn't need me like he did," Sofia explained as if she should have been understood.

"Is that what you told yourself at night?" Cynthia walked up the stairs and quickly closed the door to her office then looked at the two men sitting in the room. "Brian why is she here?"

Brian felt for her. He knew this was the last thing she needed right now. He was certain some way Sofia must have found out about LaVere' and the fact that he is a prince. Otherwise she would not be here. "I can't answer that. But Samuel will be staying here with you until further notice and if you ask him nicely I'm sure he can make her disappear."

She turned to Samuel with the saddest eyes he had ever seen, "Please make her disappear."

Samuel looked from her to Brian to see if they were joking—they weren't. "That's your mother. I'm sure you two will work out your differences."

Cynthia and Brian both replied, "Not!"

The two laughed. "Cynthia," Brian sobered, "What about Gavin? Has he told you anything that would cause this?"

She flinched for a moment, but recovered quickly, but not before Samuel picked up on the inflection in her face. "You are talking about the day after the accident?"

"Yes."

"No," she replied and looked away. It really wasn't a lie; he didn't give her anything that day. She thought of her purse. She never took the locket from Gavin out.

There was a knock on the door. They ignored it.

"I'm not going away and I'm only being polite by not just walking in."

Brian shook his head and motioned to Samuel. "That's my cue. Give me a call once you get settled in. Cynthia," he bent over and kissed her forehead, "Be nice to Samuel. He's here to help. I'll call you later."

Brian opened the door to find Sofia standing in the hallway. When Samuel stood so did Rusty and sat on his haunches. She sighed, "I guess that's my cue too." Samuel offered a hand to help her off the floor. The touch sent a sensation through her body. *Safe* was all she could think for a moment. As always she used humor to cover her uneasiness. Looking up with her head going further back she simply had to ask, "How is the air up there?" she raised up on her toes. "Hum," she said as she walked out the door.

"I'll take a walk around the premises. We'll talk later." Samuel smiled as he stepped into the hallway with Rusty following behind.

"Is that man going to be staying in this house with you?" Sofia questioned as Samuel walked by.

"Sleeping under the same roof to protect her from harm," Samuel smiled, put his shades on then walked away.

"Who is going to protect her from you?"

"Mother, this is my house. You have no say here." She walked to the double doors at the end of the hallway opened them, stepped inside and quietly closed the door behind her.

Sitting on her king size bed she dropped her head, closed her eyes and began to click her heels. "There's no place like home; there's no place like home." Praying the saying would transport her to another place; she held her head up and slowly opened her eyes—her mother was standing in the doorway. Cynthia cried out, "Damn, I must still be in Oz, the wicked witch of the east is still here."

Sofia stood in the door way and put her arms across her chest, "I don't find that very amusing."

"Neither did I," Cynthia replied with just as much venom as her mother dispensed. "It was a cry for help. It seems that cry is going unanswered the same as the ones did when I was a little girl."

Not thawed by Cynthia's response, Sofia stepped into the room and closed the door. She sat in the chair next to the door. "You are a grown woman. Therefore, I'm going to speak to you in that manner, straight up and to the point."

Cynthia raised an eyebrow and crossed her legs. "This should be interesting."

"I don't have to tell you this, because deep down you already know. You are a disappointment, always have been. When you were a beautiful young girl, you could have had the world at your feet. I knew you had the looks and the talent to be the queen of pageants, but you didn't want that and your father bent to your will. So don't begrudge the attention spent on Blake because he chose to embrace his talents. Let's not stop there. As you got older your beauty just matured with definition. I suggested you start dating JD Harrison. Do you remember that? I knew back then that boy was going places. Now look at him, Attorney General of Virginia and he's going to be president one day. Did you follow my instructions? No. You started sleeping with everyone else, except him. By the time you got around to him, he didn't want to have anything to do with you. You let that little meek thing that doesn't have half the looks you do take him away from you. Oh let's not disregard Gavin Roberts, the Governor. Don't look surprised, news travels. Of all the women in the state of Virginia, you lose him to the one that was a bigger whore than you, Carolyn Roth. So don't sit there like you are a victim. You made the decision to disregard your talent, not me." She stood and walked over to the bed and sat next to Cynthia who had tears streaming down her face. Her mother placed her hand under her chin and looked into her eyes. "Now is not the time to shed tears. I am here to help you get the life I always wanted for you. I only hope I arrived in time. I saw the picture of you and Prince Ashro on the internet. The media is asking questions about the young American woman that was on his arms at the theater. You two look good together." She dropped her hand and placed it over Cynthia's, which was folded in her lap. "But then you, my beautiful daughter, would make any man look good." She stood and walked over to the door. "It was a long trip and the time zone is playing havoc on my body. Your father and I opened the house. I want you to come by sometime tomorrow afternoon so we can talk about the Prince. Get some rest, dear. You don't need to have puffy eyes. What would the Prince think? Don't disappoint me again, I'll see you tomorrow." She turned, walked out and closed the door.

Cynthia wasn't sure how long she sat in that same spot on the bed. *Where was LaVere?* She could certainly use his calming presence right about now, she thought. Her feelings were so scrambled, she didn't know how to take what her mother said. It was no surprised that she had disappointed her family. Not a day went by without her knowing just how much of a disappointment she was. "Blake is doing this and Blake is doing that. What are you doing, nothing. You are not doing anything with your life." Yes, her mother words echoed in her mind. She called her a whore. That hurt deeply. Yes, she had slept around without a second thought. However technically she could not be a whore because she had never been married. She wondered if her mother remembered telling her to give her virginity to JD, that way he will never leave you. He's one of those boys that something like that would mean the world to him. Her mother's words were harsh. But, then she told her she was beautiful, and she wanted her to help her get the life she deserved. A life she believe a Prince could give me. Just the idea of her mother wanting to help her was a revelation. This could be an opportunity to make her mother proud of her. For once she would like to see her mother looking at her without the disappointment—just once.

Thinking he could offer some comfort, Cynthia picked up the telephone and called Ashley's home to speak to LaVere'. "Hello Charles, this is Cynthia may I speak with LaVere'?"

"Yes, Madame, please hold the line."

"This is Jamal, secretary for Prince Ashro. How may I assist you?"

There was something about Jamal, Cynthia did not like. She wasn't sure if it was the way he looked down his nose at her or the way he always made it seem as if she was an intruder when it came to LaVere'. Either way, she didn't like the man. "Good evening Jamal. I was holding to speak with LaVere'."

"Prince Ashro is not free at this time. Perhaps you may attempt your call at a later date."

"What exactly do you mean when you say he is not free?" she asked in a very agitated tone.

"In your language the interpretation would be he's busy."

Okay should I jump through the telephone and strangle him or send a hit man to take him out of his misery, she thought before replying. "Please advise LaVere' of this call." She stated before hanging up. That call only made her feel worst. She grabbed a pillow and wrapped her arms around it. She lay across the bed and did what she had done since she was eight years old. She cried herself asleep.

Samuel walked about the grounds of the complex of fifty condominiums to get a good feel of the layout. He spoke with the guard at the gate that seemed to have things under control at the time. After explaining why he was there the guard made a note of the situation in his log book. He also called his company to get another person to work at the gate until the situation changed. The guard explained Cynthia has a regular visitors list and gave a copy to Samuel.

Later that night Samuel and Blake talked about the family and why the strain was there. He liked Blake. The love he has for his sister was undaunted by his mother attempts to keep them apart. It also became very clear, the mother was jealous of her daughter. Blake surprisingly was not the "superstar" personality Samuel anticipated. He cared deeply for his family and believed he was the one person that could possibly bring them together. The vicious circle was a lot to put on the shoulders of a twenty-one year old. Sofia was angry with a little girl that only wanted to be "daddy's little girl." Jackson sacrificed his little girl to please his wife. Blake was used to fulfill his mother's dreams of grandeur. And Cynthia was just left out in the cold.

After talking with Blake, Samuel understood why Cynthia felt so alone. Being from a family of twelve, he could not understand being alone and not loved. The house was filled with love from his parents. And with five brothers and six sisters, there was never time to be alone or lonely.

Since Blake had the guest room adjacent to the family room, Samuel used the guest room on the third level across the hall from Cynthia's bedroom. After taking a shower, Samuel put on a pair of jeans and a tee shirt then walked down to the double doors where Rusty was lying. "You heard anything boy," he asked.

Rusty looked at him with sad eyes. "She's been crying?" Rusty laid his chin back on his front legs and looked up at him. Samuel knocked lightly on the door. When he received no response he slowly opened the door then stepped inside. He looked around making a note of the location of windows and the French balcony doors. Walking over he checked to make sure the doors were locked. He made a mental note to add another lock later. He had surveyed the private patio earlier so there was no need for him to go out the door. He then walked into the huge bathroom with a walk in closet that was the size of the bedroom he was using. "Damn," was all he could say.

Satisfied with his survey, he walked over to the bed that seemed to swallow her up. There was no denying she was a beautiful woman awake and a beauty asleep. He could see the tear stains on her pillow and instantly became angry at the cause. He knew of Sofia Thornton long before today, but he would put his feeling about the woman aside while on this case. The concentration was on keeping this woman safe. He then thought about the lie she told Brian today and wondered why and who was she protecting, Brian or Gavin. Was she involved with them in addition to the Prince? Those were questions that would need to be answered if he was to protect her. Reaching down, he removed her shoes, and placed the throw from the foot of her bed over her. She had taken the band that was holding her hair together off and her curls were covering her face, he gently pushed them aside. No one should be that sad in their sleep, he thought. "It's going to be all right," he whispered. For a moment he thought he saw her face relax at his words. He turned to walk away then stopped and looked back at her lying so still in the bed. "Who is going to protect me from you?" He asked, and walked out of the room.

That night her dream was different. There was no kissing, no touching, just words. *Be patient—love will come.*

Chapter 9

When she awoke the next morning, Cynthia was certain the dream meant for her to be patient with LaVere' and allow love to come later. Doing so would please her mother and make her the princess she was meant to be. With that mission in mind she showered, dressed and put a smile on her face. It was Monday, the beginning of a new week and a new lease on life for her. Today was going to be better. *Wrong.*

When she opened her door Rusty was sitting there with his tail wagging. "Good morning handsome," she placed her hand under his chin. "Did you sleep at my door all night?" Rusty responded by licking her cheek. "Well thank you for cleaning off my face," she laughed and Rusty barked. "Okay, come on." She walked down the steps and the aroma of coffee, and something more filled the air. From the bottom of the steps she could see Samuel in the kitchen at the stove. It was five thirty in the morning what was he doing up so early. Rusty ran by and sat in front of Samuel dressed in jeans and a pull over shirt that fit his body. It looked as if he belonged there, in her house, in her life. *Stop it,* she thought shaking her head. "Good morning," she said.

Turning to her he noticed she was dressed in sweats and sneakers. Battle number one was about to occur. "Good morning. Would you like some breakfast?"

"No thank you. I usually run in the morning," she replied while stretching her legs. "Why are you up so early?"

"I rise when you do," he turned and removed the food from the stove. "We need to adjust your habits."

She stopped stretching and looked over at him. "No, I don't. You have to find a way to keep up. Besides, who would know that I run at five thirty every morning?" she smirked.

Samuel put the food he was cooking into the dog plate and sat it on the floor in front of Rusty. Why do I have to convince people to let me protect them he wondered as he looked at her? "I know." He walked towards her, "You know how I know, hum?" He now stood towering over her with his arms folded against his chest. "Because I've been watching you. You leave the house at seven; arrive to work at seven-thirty except for Wednesdays. On Wednesdays you, Ashley Brooks, Tracy Harrison and Rosaline Marable meet for breakfast at Mama Mary's Sugar and Spice on Mechanicsville Turnpike. On Thursdays you and Rosaline go shopping for food and other supplies for the business. You leave work around five except on Fridays, when you close up at noon." His voice grew louder, "You want to know how I know this? I watch every step you take-the same as the people that are trying to kill you. They are watching for the most opportune time to take you out!"

With her head tilted back to see him, Cynthia stared at him in disbelief. How dare he try to frighten her. She wasn't some timid little thing that did not know how to take care of herself. She took karate classes and a self-defense class.

Not one to be out done, she pulled a chair from the kitchen table and stood in it. Now she was looking down on him. It wasn't by much, but it was enough for him to get her meaning. With hands on hips she proceeded to give him a piece of her mind. "It's your job to make sure they don't succeed. I have no intentions of altering my life to make your job easier." As she yelled she could have sworn she saw an amused twinkle in his eyes, but it disappeared as quickly as it appeared." And furthermore, I don't appreciate you yelling at me. My hearing is not impaired," she poked in his chest to emphasize her point. Stepping out of the chair, she calmly pushed it back in place. Seeing Rusty behind Samuel with his ears pointing up in high alert she spoke. "I'm sorry you had to hear me speak to your master that way. But that's the tone he took with me." She rolled her eyes and looked at Samuel. "Now, as I said before, I'm going out to run. I hope you can keep up." She turned and walked down the steps to the front door and opened it.

It was slammed shut before she could step out. Her body was thrown across his shoulders and carried up the steps to the guest bedroom he was using, while she pounded on his back. It didn't seem as if the attack fazed him, for he did not miss a step. He sat her on the bed in the room. "You will sit there until I'm dressed. Don't move." He pulled his shirt off, and then walked into the closet.

Getting up and leaving his behind in that room was exactly what she planned to do until her mind was cluttered with his wide chest and six-pack abs—or was it eight? She tilted her head to see. The way he put her over his shoulder, had her ready to fight. Now she knew why beating on his back didn't get any reaction. He probably never felt her fists. She peeked around the closet entrance, still stunned at his body. He walked out with sweat pants, a long sleeve body shirt and a pair of sneakers in his hand. Disappointed his body was covered she sat and watched as he put on his sneakers. He stood and pulled a matching sweat shirt over his head. "Let's go!" he demanded.

Still angry, she took her time standing, then walked by him in a huff. "Don't ever leave this house without me."

Looking over her shoulder she frowned. She did not like his commands, "How long do I have to put up with you?"

"Until I kill the person who wants you dead or they kill you. Whichever comes first."

The run was exuberating for both of them and it gave Rusty a good sprint. Tension was eased, ground rules had been established and it gave her a chance to think. He was there to protect her, Cynthia reasoned in her mind. She still wasn't sure why. Could it be the information Gavin gave her? There wasn't much to what he told her the night he gave her the locket. He never said who had information on him. Just that the man wanted him to support things as Governor, that he was not willing to do. The only legislation he mentioned was the one to make the mayor of Richmond an elected position. There was no reason to want to kill a person over that. Coming to that conclusion, she put Gavin as a reason for all of this out of her mind.

By the time they returned to the condo, the gates to hell had broken loose. It seemed the media had taken up residency in front of her home. As they turned the corner walking from the track, Cynthia's mouth fell open. The street was crowded with news trucks, cameramen and reporters. A few were actually knocking at the door.

"Oh hell," Samuel exclaimed as he pulled her back around the corner. He pulled out his cell and called the condo. "Blake, unlock the patio doors. We're coming through the back."

"Like hell I am. They are trespassing. Their behinds have to go!" Cynthia declared and took a step toward the front of her home.

Samuel grabbed her arm and looked down at her, "Don't test me." He pulled her along with him towards the back.

"It appears I've been discovered," Blake declared as they walked through the sliding doors.

"You don't seem to be bothered by it," Cynthia frowned.

"I'm immune to it Sis. How are you this morning?" He kissed her on the cheek.

"I was fine until he tried to stop me from running and the circus showed up out front."

"So I heard."

"I'm sorry Blake. Did we wake you?"

He nodded to Samuel who was on his cell phone. "I'm sure the entire neighborhood heard you."

"She turned to Samuel as he hung up his cell phone. "Well, what are you going to do about this?"

Raising an eyebrow, "I'm not doing anything. Brian will send someone over. Don't you need to get ready for work?"

Cynthia huffed and stomped up the steps. Blake looked on amused. Once she was up the stairs he turned to Samuel. "Well it seems you two are getting along just fine." Seeing the frown on Samuel's face he sat on the sofa, propped his feet on the table and grinned. "I can't wait to see what happens next."

Samuel walked up the steps mumbling, "I'm going to keep her alive even if it kills me."

Blake smiled and wondered if he was the only one that noticed the attraction between them.

Brian hung up the telephone, "This is not going to be a good day."

"It's not even seven yet," Pearl stretched in the bed beside him.

"Your brother is an early riser," he yawned while standing and walking over to the bathroom of his home.

The man had a nice body and knows exactly what to do with it, Pearl thought as she watched his naked body walk across the room. "That was Samuel?" she asked while getting out of the bed to find her clothes. The two were into a month long sexual release relationship only. Each was satisfied and clear on the parameters of their friendship with privileges relationship.

"Yeah, there's a situation at Cynthia's place."

"Isn't there always," she stated while pulling her dress down over her body.

Brian came to the doorway with his tooth brush in his hand and a quizzical look on his face. "What is it with you and her?"

Placing her panties inside her purse, she absentmindedly replied, "History." While sliding her shoes on, she looked up at him. "You're on your way over there?"

"Yeah," he said leaning against the door. He watched as she walked towards him. There was no doubt Pearl Lassiter was a sassy-sexy lady. Whenever she decides to allow someone in she is going to make someone a very happy man. She stopped in front of him. "We have to talk about Samuel." He exhaled, not sure how she was going to react to what he was about to do.

"I know," she kissed his lips. "It was one hell of a ride Thompson, but this is where it ends. We knew what this was about, so no bad feelings on my end. What about you?"

All Brian could do was smile. He could handle a drama free woman. "My relationship with your brother is important professionally. I don't want to jeopardize it."

"Are you trying to smooth over ruffled feathers?" She smiled up at him.

"Yeah."

"No need," she turned to walk out the room.
"Hey,"
Stopping mid step she turn back to him, "What?"
"You don't have no drawers on."
"Intriguing isn't it." She smiled and walked out of the room.

After taking his shower, Brian placed a call to Calvin to verify the time and place of their meeting. "Hey Calvin. Are we set for this morning?"

"Yes—my office at 9:00. Man this stinks to high heaven. Do you remember who was in that file from Al Day?"

"I remember Gavin was there." Brian replied with a little venom in his voice.

"That's true but the other person was Wilbert T. Munford."

Brian sat forward, paying a little closer attention. "The Chief of Police?"

"You got it. See you at 9:00," the call ended.

Brian sat back and wondered what Gavin and Munford could have in common. And how does it connect to Cynthia? Dismissing it for now, he picked up his jacket and left the apartment.

His first stop was to see Douglas. Samuel was going to need some back up. Checking his watch he noticed it was after eight. Douglas wouldn't be up after a busy weekend at the club. But as he pulled into the driveway he noticed Douglas was standing next to a car parked on the street. Walking towards him he noticed the person in the car was Karen Holt. "Good morning Karen," he smiled genuinely pleased to see her.

"Good Morning Brian. I'm running late and can't stay to talk. I'll see you later Douglas," she waived and pulled off.

"Man, she looks good." Brian commented.

"Yeah, she does."

It was hard not to notice the look of interest in his childhood friend's eyes. "You two hooking up?"

"Why are you here early in the morning getting in my business?"

"Not getting in your business. I'm just looking out for a friend. She went through some stuff man, and you know her ex-husband is crazy."

"I got this Dr. Phil," he laughed. "Why are you here?"

"We have a situation with Cynthia and I need your help. Samuel Lassiter is on detail with her, but now things have become more complicated. I need you to handle crowd control."

"I got you on this, but you need to hire more people. Brooks made sure finance wasn't an issue. What's the hold up?"

Brian hesitated, "The people I hire have to be at the top of their game." He hesitated then explained. "See, it's not just about who we have to protect today, but in the future as well. JD is going to eventually run for President of these United States. It's my responsibility to protect him and his family. I want people that I trust and know will have his back without question. So I'm taking my time and looking for only the best."

"You got any more like Lassiter," he laughed. "I wouldn't want to be on his bad side."

"He has a brother that's deadlier than he is."

"What?"

"Look I need you at Cynthia's like yesterday. Check in with Samuel when you get there. I have a meeting with JD and Calvin. I'll see you over there."

Brian reached Calvin's office just as JD took a seat. "Nice office Calvin. But why are we meeting here and not down the hall in your office," he asked JD.

"You don't like my office?" Calvin joked.

"It's nice, like I said, but JD's office is bigger, roomier, nicer."

JD laughed at his two friends that had been sparring with each other since high school.

"Why are you always the only one to complain?"

"I'm not complaining. I'm just asking a question."

"Will you two stop, we have business to handle," JD said.

"Alright, alright, one more question," Brian laughed. "Who's the honey sitting with Mrs. Langston?"

"I thought you were hanging with Pearl."

"I had to cut that short—Samuel is kind of big."

JD nodded, "Yes, I noticed that."

"I think he could take me," Brian nodded in wonder.

Calvin laughed, "Hell, I know he could."

"I know he would if he knew you what you are doing with his sister." JD offered.

"Then let's not tell him." The three friends laughed.

"Didn't you say he knows how to kill a man twelve different ways? And the other brother, Joshua knows fifteen ways?"

"That's right."

"Brian, if you knew that, why would you mess with one of his sisters?" Calvin asked.

Brian put his hands up in the air, "She couldn't resist all of this. She wanted a piece of the brother. I couldn't deny her."

Calvin shook his head laughing, "Man you need to stop."

"Umm, I distinctly remember you chasing after Pearl," JD stated.

Brian looked over at JD, "Now didn't nobody ask you to comment. Mr. I can't say no to my wife."

"Don't get mad at me because I speak the truth."

"Well, you can keep the truth to yourself. What's up with Al Day?"

"Oh, now you want to work," Calvin laughed.

"Yeah, this is a government office. We have business to discuss."

"You're not going to like the connection." JD said while shaking his head.

Brian looked from him to Calvin. "It's Gavin," he sighed. "I knew he was going to cause her problems. I knew it."

"Calm down Brian," Calvin warned. "We don't know all the facts."

"He's right Brian. I've given Calvin the thumbs up to begin an investigation on the people in the file. Because of my connection to Al, I can't be a part of any of this. That's why this meeting is taking place here instead of my office."

"An investigation is good and fine JD. But these people are after Cynthia now. They are not going to wait for you to complete an investigation."

"I agree. That's why I have an appointment to talk to Gavin tonight."

"Good, I'm going."

"No." Calvin and JD spoke simultaneously.

"Why the hell not?"

"You won't give the man a chance to talk," Calvin declared.

"Huh, I'm going."

Calvin looked at JD. "Don't take him with you."

JD stood, put his hands in his pockets and walked over to the window of Calvin's office. Looking out he began to think out loud. "The two people in that file have another person in common other than Al. They both have a connection to my father. The Chief was my father's partner when he was killed. Munford was Gavin's senior officer during his rookie year. Coincidently, it was the same time they both met Al Day. Something happened back then, that ties all of this together. Discover what that is and you will find the person trying to eliminate Cynthia."

Cynthia came downstairs dressed and ready for work then turned to Blake and Samuel in the kitchen. "I was wondering. How are we going to get past the crowd?"

Before either could answer some one began knocking on the door and ringing the bell as the same time. She raised an eyebrow. Angrily she started down the steps leading to the front door. Since it seemed neither of the idiots in the room knew how to get rid of people, she might as well try. Just like before, Samuel stopped her and carried her back to the first floor landing.

"Stay away from the door," Samuel growled.

"Then answer it and make them go away."

Samuel went back down the steps and jerked the door open.

Oh hell, Samuel thought, the crowd outside the door had grown. In the mix there was a petite blonde woman standing in the front. "I understand Blake Thornton is here."

"And," Samuel asked his arms folded.

The woman's vision traveled upward, "How tall are you?" She asked with a frown.

"Tall enough."

"That's an understatement. I'm expected," she stated and attempted to walk by him.

"And you are?" he asked as he block her passage.

She stepped back in frustration and sighed, "Shannon P, Blake Thornton's publicist."

Cameras began to flash and questions were being asked. "Come with me," he said.

Cynthia was still on the first floor landing, "Who are you?"

"I'm looking for Blake Thornton. Is he here?"

"Yes he is and you are," Cynthia replied with the attitude of a true big sister.

"Shannon P., his publicist. And you?" The blonde asked with just as much dignified attitude.

Seeing trouble brewing Samuel stepped to the side, "I'm going to make a few calls about your visitors outside."

Cynthia nodded her head and turned her attention back to the blonde, she placed her hands on her hips, "Cynthia T, the sister."

"Oh, so you're the one causing all of this," Shannon said and walked by. "Where is he?"

"Up stairs in the kitchen." How in the hell is someone that small going to handle the media, Cynthia thought as she began walking in the direction, but then another knock sounded against the door. Cynthia stopped mid-step and turn back to answer the door, before she reached the door, the telephone rang. She looked at the clock on the wall, it was not even eight o'clock you on Monday morning. To say her morning was not going well was be an understatement. Who would be calling? For that matter who would be knocking at her door. Picking up the cordless phone she looked at the caller id, it was LaVere' calling. Watching Samuel at the door, he stepped to the side to allow Magna Riviera, one of the agents that worked with Brian in. She pointed towards the kitchen as Magna did a motion for coffee.

Walking into the living room to hear better, she listened as LaVere' told her to expect the press to show up. "I think you are a little late. They are already here." She replied. He hung up stating he would be there within the hour.

Cynthia hung up the phone and dialed Roz number thinking this was not what she had in mind for her renewed life. "Roz, I have a situation over here I need you to come by before going to the office." Without a question Roz agreed. Now if the rest of her day would cooperate, she might live through it. She took a deep breath and walked into the kitchen.

Magna, whom she knew rather well, was leaning against the counter drinking a cup of coffee. Shannon, whom she did not know at all, was sitting in her chair eating her breakfast. "I need some caffeine. Do you have any real coffee in this house?"

"I do," Cynthia said placing her arms across her chest.

"Well, would you mind fixing some this is not going to do," Shannon pushed the cup on the table.

Cynthia and Magna looked at each other. Magna began to laugh as did Blake. Cynthia walked over to the cabinet, took out a can of coffee and slammed in on the table in front of Shannon. "You can fix it your damn self."

"Whoa, Whoa, chill out girl," she picked up the cup, walked over to the counter and began to pour the other coffee out. "Whatever happened to southern hospitality, this is Virginia isn't it?"

"It doesn't start until you hit Richmond, which is about five minutes south," Cynthia replied. She turned to look at Blake, who was failing miserably at concealing his laugh. "Who in the hell is this?"

"She's my publicist," he laughed.

"I already introduced myself to you at the door, don't you remember girl? I'm also the one that is going to save your ass, from this mess."

"I don't know what mess you are referring to, but, LaVere' is on his way over. I'm sure he can handle it."

"Good, I have a few things to say to him." She retook her seat at the table. "He's lived this all his life; he knew better then to take you to New York. I don't care how discrete it was, that city literally never sleeps. The media is 24/7, you can't hide there. Here, is a totally different story. That's why Blake was able to be here for this long without too much invasion. It's because of you that I have to be here. So like it or not you are going to deal with me."

Magna decided it was time for her to save the woman from whatever Cynthia was about to say. She extended her hand, "I'm Magna. I will be handling security on Blake for the remainder of his stay here."

"What exactly do you think you are going to do against that mob outside? Shoot them, it doesn't work. I've tried." She looked from Magna to Cynthia, "You two don't understand the media. They will eat both of you alive."

"If they are that bad, what makes you think you can handle them?" Cynthia asked.

"Because I can play just as dirty as any one of them, probably ten times better. The only stories and pictures that hit on your brother are the ones I plant. When one gets by me, the photographer and the rag that sells it, pays and they pay dearly. Don't let this petite body and blonde hair fool you."

Cynthia stepped up, placed her hands on her hips and towered over the short woman. "Don't you let this little Virginia girl fool you? The media here knows me, not you. Your LA ways will not work here."

Shannon stood and took the same stance. "You don't get it. It's not the media in Virginia you have to be concerned with. You are going out with a Prince. Not the Governor or the Attorney General of Virginia—a Prince. We are going to be dealing with the international media as well as the government. Therefore, missy, you need to take your fangs out of me and save them, because you are going to need them," she took a step back. "Now, where is your lavatory?" Cynthia stared at her for a minute startled, *did everybody know her business.* "Bathroom girl bathroom." Cynthia pointed down the hallway. "Thank you. While I'm gone, call your mother. I have a feeling she is behind all of this."

Magna looked at Cynthia, "Do you want me to shoot her? I do have two guns."

Blake laughed, "Please don't. I depend heavyly on her. She is good and she can handle what is about to happen. Let her do her job, you will reap the rewards."

"Okay, I won't shoot her, for now." She looked at Cynthia, "but, you tell me when and I will shoot her."

Cynthia laughed, "I know you will. But at the moment I have enough to deal with and don't' want to add a murder charge." She exhaled, "Do you think mother did this?"

"Yep," Blake replied as he stood, "I'm going to take a shower. We will probably be in front of the cameras soon. Oh, you may want to think about staying at the house until things die down. At least there's a gate to protect you."

Cynthia slummed down into the chair. "Magna how bad is it out there?"

Magna sat across from her, "Too many for Samuel to handle alone. Brian is bringing backup. I'm covering Blake until his body man arrives. Is Prince Ashro bringing anyone with him?"

"He usually travels with Edmond his body man and Jamal his secretary."

"You might want to give Pearl Lassiter a call. The Prince has his secretary to act on his behalf. Blake has Shannon. You are going to need someone to act in your best interest."

"Is all of this really necessary? Once they see Blake the crowd will disappear, won't they."

"Blake being here is the least of our concerns. You're dating a Prince. Any incident could have international implications."

"I'll call Ashley to see who she suggests."

"Cynthia!" A yell came from the front and was followed by a slammed door. Rosaline appeared in the kitchen. "What in the hell is going on? The street is covered with people with cameras, not to mention all those damn trucks.

"That's just the beast. I'll have them cleared out as soon as LaVere' and his entourage gets here." Shannon stated as she looked at Cynthia. "Don't you think you need to get dressed? And have you called your mother yet?"

"I am dressed and no I have not called her."

"Don't tell me you are scared of her too. Never mind, I'll handle Sofia, you need to change. You cannot appear with LaVere' dressed like you are going to work."

"She is supposed to be going to work," Rosaline said, still unclear what was happening.

Cynthia stood and turned Rosaline in the direction of her bedroom. "You come with me. I will explain everything." She turned back to Magna, "Would you call Ashley. Find out what you can and let me know how to precede." She turned to say something to Shannon, but she was on her telephone. Not taking her eyes off the woman Cynthia whispered to Magna, "If she makes a wrong move, shoot her."

Twenty minutes later Cynthia and Rosaline emerged from her bedroom. The first person Rosaline saw was the one person she wanted to avoid, Sofia Thornton. The woman had a way of belittling everyone and everything that crossed her path. Rosaline could handle it, but what she could not tolerate was the way the woman ignored her own daughter, then had the nerve to tell other people how to live their life. Rosaline ducked towards the front door, but did not make it out in time. "Rosaline, are you leaving this house without saying hello?"

"I was trying too." She whispered between clinched teeth. "Hello Mrs. Thornton."

"Isn't it exciting news about my Cynthia and the Prince?"

"Your Cynthia? Oh--now that you think she is involved with a Prince you can own her. I don't remember her being your Cynthia when you left her here to fend for herself."

Cynthia stepped between the two women. "Roz, be sure to contact Mrs. Sutton regarding Friday afternoon."

Rosaline nodded understanding Cynthia did not want a confrontation. "I'll take care of it."

"Rosaline before you leave, have they begun deportation on your husband yet?" Sofia questioned.

"That's enough," Cynthia shouted. "Roz, go. I will talk to you later. Rosaline rolled her eyes at the woman and walked out the door. "Mother, you have caused enough damage here."

"Well he only married her to get into this country. Besides, I'm only here to help you."

"Sofia, you never help anyone unless something is in it for you." Shannon stated, "So tell me, what it is this time? You have more money than the average person. Jackson has emerged as one of the best producers out. Blake is at the top of the A list. So what could it be?"

"You need to be careful how you speak to me. Your position with Blake is not completely secure," Sofia replied.

"That's where you are wrong. We have a new contract. It was signed last week before he came here. And if it wasn't it wouldn't matter much, because he still will not allow you to handle his affairs any longer. So deal with it."

Hearing enough Cynthia stepped in. "I don't know what's up with you two, but you will not use this situation to hash it out. The door opened and Cynthia was surprised to see Pearl Lassiter walked through. "It's a good thing I have a large home," she murmured. "What are you doing here? Is JD or Tracy coming here?"

"Good morning every one," Pearl smiled and then turned to Cynthia. "Ashley called Tracy and you know how it goes. Tracy called me and here I am. Samuel seemed relieved to see me and literally pushed me through the door." She put her portfolio on the table, as Cynthia made the introductions. "It's nice to meet you all," Pearl said and then turned back to Cynthia. "Is there some place we could speak in private?"

"Another Lassiter," Sofia sighed. "I guess it's to be expected. Your mother was breeding like a bitch in heat.

Well we are all in this together, no need for privacy at this point," Sofia stated.

Shannon rolled her eyes, "I don't like the idea, but I do agree with Sofia. When we address the media—we really should be on one accord."

A small smile creased Pearl's face as she looked at Sofia. "Don't ever mention my mother and bitch in the same sentence again. If you do I will demonstrate the true meaning of the word bitch." She turned to Shannon, "Your interest here, if I understand things correctly, is what's best for Blake." She looked at Sofia, "I have no honest idea what your interest may be. My interest is what is best for Cynthia. Once we have spoken and I am clear what her interests are, then and only then will we all be on one accord." She turned, "Cynthia, if you will lead the way."

Inwardly Cynthia smiled—finally someone is looking out for her, "This way." They walked up the stairs to her office. "Please, have a seat Pearl," she pointed to the chair and closed the door. "Thank you for coming."

"Cynthia, I feel it is important for you to know, I am not here for you per say. I am here because Tracy considers you a friend and loves you dearly. I'm not too fond of you as I'm sure you realize. With that said, I want you to know that nothing you and I discuss will be mentioned outside this door unless you wish it to be. I will ensure you are represented in the manner you wish. Knowing why I am here, do you want me to represent you?"

Taken back a minute by Pearl's bluntness Cynthia shrugged her shoulders. "I don't see where I have a choice. I have no idea how to deal with all of this. Yes, I need you to represent me."

"Very well then, let's have a seat. Tell me how you want to proceed. Do you want the media around or not?"

"Not like this." The women talked until Pearl had enough to properly represent Cynthia.

As the two walked down the hallway, LaVere' was walking up the steps. He walked over to Cynthia, kissed her gently and hugged her. "Please forgive me for this. I thought I had covered my bases in New York."

"There is no way you could have foreseen my mother's actions."

"Your mother? What does she have to do with all of this?"

"She took it upon herself to contact the media on her daughter's behalf," Shannon stated from the kitchen. "Hello Prince Ashro'," Shannon extended her hand, "I'm Shannon Payne, I represent Blake Thornton." LaVere' smiled and shook her hand.

Cynthia turned to Pearl, "LaVere', this is Pearl Lassiter. She is representing me in all of this."

"Ms. Lassiter, thank you for being here for her. Please make sure her personal interest is taken into account before any other issue."

Pearl bowed, "I will do my best, your highness."

"It's LaVere' and the pageantries are not necessary."

"Is Brian Thompson here yet? I hope you don't mind I requested protection for you until this situation is under control."

"Thank you, that was thoughtful. Samuel Lassiter was already on site. I'll fill you in on that later and Magna Rivera arrived earlier," Cynthia took his hand and walked into the living room. "LaVere', this is my mother Sofia Thornton and the cause of most of what you see."

LaVere' smiled and shook her hand. "It is a pleasure to meet you Mrs. Thornton. I would have preferred different circumstances."

"LaVere'," she smiled, "the pleasure is mind and may I say, your pictures do you no justice at all. You are a very handsome man. I can see why Cynthia is so taken with you."

"Thank you, but there will be plenty of time for you and I to get to know one another. At this moment my only interest is to get Cynthia out of this situation." He turned to Pearl. "Ms. Lassiter, this is my secretary Jamal. Would you two prepare a statement for the press.

"I'll join them," Shannon offered.

Jamal, who was standing off to the side taking notes immediately stepped forward, "Perhaps, a brief statement only indicating the two are friends and nothing more."

"Well that's a start," Pearl said as the two walked off into the kitchen.

LaVere' turned to Cynthia. "This will be over by noon. That's my promise to you. Where's Blake?" he asked looking around. "I need to apologize to him. I know he came here for solitude."

"He's on a conference call with a director, but no apology is needed, at least not to Blake. This is a bit much on top of everything else," Cynthia just shook her head. "I am so sorry about all of this."

Within the hour the news conference was scheduled at the Omni Hotel on Cary Street in Shockoe Bottom, downtown Richmond. To the media's delight and Cynthia's surprise the support in the room was a who's who. JD and Tracy Harrison, James and Ashley Brooks, Marco and Rosaline Marable were there for her. Of course Blake, Jackson and Sofia Thornton were there. At one point Shannon had to literally pull Sofia away from the press. The woman was exasperating to say the least.

Moving the news conference here was a relief for the Security Team as well as Cynthia's neighbors. Samuel made a mental note to speak with the guards at the front gate of the complex. There was no reasonable explanation of how the media was able to gather in front of her home. Earlier Brian and Samuel spoke privately with LaVere' explaining the presence of security for Cynthia. If anything was to go astray it could have international repercussions. To their surprise LaVere' was very understanding and thanked Samuel for his service. To relive some pressure off Brian's team, he offered to provide security whenever Cynthia was with him.

Blake, LaVere' and Cynthia stood center stage as Pearl read a brief statement. "Good afternoon everyone, I am Pearl Lassiter representative for Cynthia Thornton in this matter. I have a brief statement. Then you will hear from Prince Ashro and Shannon Pane, publicist for Blake Thornton. Prince LaVere' Ashro of Emure and Ms. Cynthia Thornton met a little over a year ago and have recently been seeing each other privately. Presently neither is willing to discuss details with the media. As with any new relationship, the two would like the opportunity to spend time with each other and not the world. At this time Prince Ashro would like to make a statement."

The moment Pearl stepped aside, the questions began. LaVere' smiled, "As Ms. Lassister stated, we are not ready to discuss our relationship with the public. In fact I would like to make a request of you. You see, while I am use to the media, Cynthia is not. I am trying to convince her that being involved with me will be a wonderful adventure." He pointed to the cameras and reporters, "Having a mob in front of her home was not such a good start. If you would give us breathing room, I promise the moment there is something to report; I will personally speak with each of you. All I request is a little time alone to get to know this very beautiful woman. Thank you all." He returned to Cynthia's side and kissed her on the cheek. The cameras began flashing.

Shannon stepped up. "Good afternoon. I'm the representative of Blake Thornton, Shannon Pane. Blake is home to visit his sister. He will be here for the remainder of the month, and then will return to the set to complete the filming of his next picture. Blake would like to make a statement."

Blake stepped up and flashed that million dollar smile. Reporter's clamored to get in position to take pictures.

Graciously Blake accommodated them; it was the least he could do to take some of this pressure off his sister. "It is wonderful to be home. I've been so busy over the last few years, that I have not had time to spend with my family. Just like any other brother, I am here to make sure this man is good enough for my sister." The crowd laughed. "So far, he's alright. I know this seems like a story, but unless you give them time, you will not have anything to report. Give them a chance by allowing them just a little privacy. In the meantime, I will be around and I promise to give you plenty to write about." With the crowd eating out his hands, he stepped back and stood next to his sister, then winked at her. Cameras flashed relentlessly at the threesome.

Pearl stepped back up to the podium. "Thank you everyone," she smiled at Blake. "This concludes the conference. Shannon Pane and I will be available for questions. And I believe Blake will remain for entertainment purposes only."

Back stage while LaVere' spoke to Brian, a beaming Sofia approached Cynthia, "I think that went well. The family unity would have been better with your father and I on stage too, but all's well that ends well I suppose."

"It certainly warms my heart that I could do something to please you. However, LaVere' and I would be immensely happy if you would stay away from the media."

"See, Cynthia Antoinette, that statement is the very reason I know you need me at this time. This is not the time to avoid the media. Just as they use you for profit, you can use them to build your popularity."

"That's just it mother, I don't want the popularity—you do"

Smiling wickedly she looked at her daughter. "I do look forward to both of my beautiful children gracing the covers of magazines and newspapers across the country. If we do this right you will be Princess Cynthia before the year is out." Jackson and Blake joined them with coats and gloves.

"Thank you darling," Sofia smiled up at her husband. "Cynthia I expect you and the Prince for dinner on Sunday. Come along dear, we have a lot to prepare for."

Jackson kissed her cheek then followed his wife. Blake just stared, "She just doesn't get it."

Cynthia looked at him, "Get what?"

"Living in the public's eye is not all it's cracked up to be. All any normal person needs is a decent living and a person that loves them unconditionally. Everything else is just show."

Reaching out she hugged her brother, "You've caught the blunt of her miss placed desire to be popular."

"Dad more so than me." He exhaled, "This life has its advantages. But there are other things in life that can give you just as much satisfaction." He looked down at her, "Like the way a man looks at you when you're not looking. Or the way you cause him to mumble under his breath because you simply drive him crazy." The frown on her face made him wonder if she got his meaning.

"You want a man looking at you like that?" she frowned.

"Not me—you sis." He laughed, "I see Samuel's frustration, you can be a little dense."

"Samuel?"

Chapter 10

Precisely at seven o'clock, JD, Brian and Samuel entered Gavin's residence. This was the first time in the Mansion for Brian since Gavin became Governor. Standing at the entrance he didn't look around at the grandeur of the home or the historical pictures on the wall. Instead he continuously counted to ten to keep his anger in check.

"Good evening Mr. Harrison, Governor and Mrs. Roberts are expecting you. May I take your coats?" The butler inquired.

JD complied while Brian and Samuel kept theirs. JD knew the jackets concealed their weapons. "Expecting trouble?" he jokingly asked the men.

"I always expect trouble when Gavin and Carolyn are around," Brian smirked.

"I might have to shoot him," Samuel smiled.

JD just shook his head at the two. "You realize if you harm him we will get no answers."

"No. but it will make me feel so much better."

"Hello JD," Carolyn smiled as she entered the room. "JD the only person you see?"

She exhaled and turned to Brian, "Having a successful protection agency hasn't changed your sunny disposition."

Then turning to Samuel, "You," she smiled, "must be Samuel Lassiter. Welcome to our home."

"Thank you."

She tiptoed in front of him, then put her hand through his arm and began walking forward. "My, are all of your brothers as tall and handsome as you?"

Use to the question, he smiled. "As tall, yes—not quite as handsome."

They walked into the library of the home where Gavin was finishing up a telephone call. "Would any of you like a drink?" Carolyn asked as each took a seat.

"No, thank you, we're fine," JD replied.

"Alright," she replied sensing this was not a social call, she looked over at Gavin. "He should be wrapping up shortly." Looking at JD, she asked, "How is the baby?"

Answering politely, "He's fine, looking more like his mother every day."

"I'm sure some of your handsome features are present as well."

"JD," Gavin said extending his hand. "Glad you could stop by. Brian," he nodded politely.

"Thanks for taking the time Gavin." JD turned, "This is Samuel Lassiter."

Samuel shook his hand, "Governor Roberts."

Walking over Carolyn kissed Gavin, "I'll leave you gentlemen to talk. It was good to see you JD and nice to meet you Samuel. Brian," she frowned and left the room.

"Well have a seat." Gavin offered. "Would any of you like something to drink?"

"No, we're good," JD replied. "Gavin we have a situation concerning Cynthia. That's why Brian and Samuel are here."

"Cynthia," he sat up. "What type of situation?"

"Someone has taken a contract out on her life," Brian stated through clinched teeth.

Gavin abruptly stood, "When did this happen?"

"The accident wasn't an accident. Then the other day someone ransacked her office at the TNT building. Any ideas who or why?"

Samuel silently observed Gavin's reactions to the conversation. It was clear he knew something.

Gavin turned and walked back to his desk.

The three men looked at each other. "Gavin anything you can tell us to protect her would be appreciated." JD encouraged.

Brian frowned at JD for taking the diplomatic approach. Frankly he would prefer beating the information out of Gavin.

"What in the hell have you gotten her into?" Brian yelled as Gavin sat back with a glass of cognac in hand.

"Brian, let him talk," JD spoke calmly. "Gavin, tell me about Munford."

"Or I could just beat it out of you," Brian stood.

JD put his hand up, "Brian, take a seat man." He then walked over to Gavin. "Cynthia's life is in danger. I know that's not what you want. Talk to me, what's going on?"

Gavin looked around the room, he trusted the men in the room, with the exception of Samuel, who he did not know. But he was there with JD and Brian, like it or not he had to trust the man. He hesitated then looked at JD. The man was his protégée and he was sure to surpass any office he has held. The admission from Munford let him know the man had gone too far. He had to be stopped and he believed JD could be the man to do that.

Taking a seat at his desk he sighed. "This goes back twenty years. I was Munford's rookie partner and I admired the man. He could do no wrong in my eyes."

"So much for the admiration society—what happened."

"Brian," JD tone was clear, "Continue Gavin."

"We had several domestic calls from the Washington household. "

"Tracy's family?" JD asked.

"Yeah. One of those calls turned into a DOA. Joan Day, sixteen year old daughter of Lena Washington died from an attempted rape. The assailant was listed as unknown, but we knew it was the step-father, Billy Washington. A few months later we were called there again this time the son, Al Day who was fourteen at the time had seriously injured Washington for touching his little sister, Tracy. It was never determined if what Day alleged was true or not because the little girl had been removed from the home and he refused to tell us where she was. Munford had the boy while I conducted the questioning of witnesses. EMT was called for Washington, but neither he nor his body made it to the hospital. Munford called me aside while I was taking statements and instructed me to write up the report as just another domestic call, nothing more. When I questioned him, he stated, *The man was trying to rape an eight year old child. You saw what happened with the sister, do you want that to happen to the little one too?* I saw how the older sister fought against the man that was attacking her and she still lost out. There was no way an eight year old would have stood a chance against the man. So I falsified the report. Little did I know that was only the beginning? For two years after that it was little omissions or a slight deviation from the facts. When I graduated from law school I joined the DA's office. From time to time he would give me information that closed major cases for me. After that he would call for little favors here and there. Nothing big, just support him on something he wanted passed or hire this person in a particular position. But lately he has become unmanageable, requesting things I could not support and when I refused the threats began. The Day investigation was given to you to pull him out. Munford knew Day's one weakness was his little sister. He decided to use her but you screwed him when you had Day's case sealed and placed under protected incarceration. Then to make things worst you married

Tracy, which made her untouchable. That pissed him off and you have been at the top of his list every since."

"Why does he need Al out of the way?" JD asked.

Gavin smirked, lowered his head and took another drink. "He wants to run for Mayor of Richmond."

"You've got to be shitting me," Brian exclaimed.

"No he's right," JD said as he took a glass off the table turned it up and pour the cognac inside. "He came by to see me before the vote on legislation to make the Mayor's seat an elected position. I told him I needed to take a closer look at the bill before I could make a decision. He wasn't happy with my reply."

"What does any of this have to do with Cynthia?" Samuel asked.

"A few months ago he asked me to come out publicly supporting the bill and him for Mayor and I refused. He became livid and made some threats. It was apparent to me that he was out of control and I needed to ensure the information I had on him was in a safe place. The next day I put a disc in a safe deposit box and gave the other to Cynthia with instructions to give it to JD if anything was to happen to me. When he called again I told him the threats would not work, if anything were to happen to me or Carolyn he would be exposed."

"Was she dispensable to you?" Samuel asked.

Gavin stood abruptly, "I would never put Cynthia's life in danger, never. She is the one person on this earth I trust with my life."

Samuel stood angrily towering over Gavin and ready to kill. "She can't say the same for you, now can she? You put her life in the hands of a man you said yourself was losing control. What in the hell did you think he would do—crawl in a hole because you gave someone the information. Hell no, you find and eliminate the threat. You put her life on the line to save your own ass. I can't help but notice no one has threatened your wife. There is no way a man would put the woman he cares about in harm's way. It's clear where your loyalties lie."

Tables seemed to have turned. Now it was Brian calming Samuel down. "Let's step outside," he suggested.

"Brian, hold up. There's more." Gavin looked at JD. "Cynthia only knows a little of this. She has no idea what is on that disk."

JD inhaled, "The problem with that, Gavin, is Munford doesn't know that. He probably thinks Cynthia knows everything."

"I need to speak to Brian alone."

"Say what," Brian raised an eyebrow looking at Gavin. "Give me a minute." He said to JD.

JD and Samuel shared a look, then stepped outside.

"This better be good to keep me from kicking your ass," Brian folded his arms across his chest.

"Munford confessed something to me you need to know. It will be up to you to share the information with JD or not. I would advise not to."

"What is it?" Brian asked impatiently.

"It was Munford that ordered James Harrison's death."

Relaxing his stance, Brian stared Gavin down. "JD's father was killed by a 14 year old gang banger."

"According to Munford, he controls the gangs, with the exception of Day's group. He ordered the killing."

"Why would he share this information with you?"

"To let me know he has no issues with taking out anyone. Including those in authority—more specifically, JD."

Samuel returned to Cynthia's home late. It was taking him a while to calm down from all that had taken place. It was difficult for him to understand the people in this her life. There was her mother whose only interest in life was to be noticed by the world. It never crossed her mind to put the interests of her daughter or son before her own greed and popularity. Then there's her father who don't have the balls to stand up to his wife when it's clear she's hurting his daughter. Then there was Gavin, a man she cares about, who is willing to jeopardized her life to save his career. Hell, the woman didn't have a choice but to have a hard shell. She wouldn't be able to survive any other way.

Getting out of his car he looked around, there was no guard; however, he did see a figure in the shadows of the management building. He decided to take a stroll around the complex to see what the person would do. He stopped at the corner to make sure he was seen, and then continued walking towards the park area of the complex. The person was following him at a safe distance. Whoever it was knew how to follow without being detected. The only reason Samuel knew the figure was there was to use a simple technique he learned as a Seal—listening. Sometimes it can be the best weapon in the world. He stopped again and waited until he heard the figure's footsteps stop as well. He began walking again, counting footsteps, stopped then listened and counted the followers footsteps. The routine went on for several sessions. It was clear the figure was not a threat, so he stopped, leaned against the fence surrounding the lake and waited. "What took you so long?" He asked when the figure stood within five feet of him.

"When did you pick me up?"

Surprised by the voice, but didn't let on. "At the front gate."

"Hum, here I thought I was being so quiet."

"Friend or foe?"

"Friend of a friend."

"Your meeting," Samuel stated never looking back.

"The security on this complex is piss poor at best. I count three on the grounds." The voice stated.

"Four, but I'm impressed."

"Who'd I miss?"

"Two by the entrance, one at the back gate, one with binoculars in the house on the corner."

"Oh, that fool is mine. Or he will be—he just doesn't know it yet. Got to go. Those fools from the Eagles have itchy fingers. They might miss you and hit me."

Samuel chucked, "You got a name?"

"Ryan."

"You're good Ryan. Next time don't wear the spike boots."

"Got to—that's my trade mark."

"Thanks for the info," Samuel smiled as he heard Ryan leave.

Life had a tendency of changing when you least expected it, Gavin thought as he enjoyed the smooth taste of a glass of cognac. Here he was, Governor of the Commonwealth of Virginia, married to the woman he loved and being threatened by the damn city of Richmond Police Chief. He sat the glass down on his desk and pulled out the photo that was under his mail on his desk. It was a picture of Cynthia coming out of her office building with one of Munford's men behind her. The note attached simply asked, "Where is Day?" There was a different question on Gavin's mind. "How could he protect Cynthia without causing a scandal?" There was no doubt in his mind that the picture was a threat against her life, if he did not cooperate. He stood walked over to the balcony doorway and looked out over the grounds of the mansion. It was a breathtaking view of the city that would calm his weary thoughts any other time, but not now. This situation was not one that diplomacy could get him out of. Munford had made this personal by involving Cynthia. He couldn't help but to wonder why. Since he became governor, Munford had laid low, not asking for much of anything. He seemed eager to close the doors to the past, which was fine with him. Gavin had too much to lose if his one indiscretion became public knowledge.

As Gavin stood, lost in his thoughts Carolyn walked into the office, saw the picture, and note on the desk. She heard most of the conversation with JD and knew her husband was concerned for Cynthia's safety. Lord knows she did not have the right to judge him, for she had definitely made her share of mistakes with men outside of her marriage. But now she was trying to be a good wife and a good wife did whatever she could to help her husband. "Gavin?" she captured his attention before she took a seat in front of the desk. When he turned and saw Carolyn taking a seat, his eyes went immediately to the picture and note on the desk. Carolyn waved the picture off. "No need to be concerned at this point."

Gavin exhaled and took a seat at his desk. "What do you need Carolyn?" he impatiently asked.

Dismissing his attitude she went directly to the point. "Have you asked yourself why Munford is pressing you now? Think about it. What you told JD happened years ago. What does he want from you so badly to make him use his trump card now?"

Gavin had long ago accepted the fact that his wife had the most cunning mind in the political arena. She has proven time and time again just how ingeniously devious she could be. There was a strong possibility that she may be able to turn this situation around. He sat up and opened the note. "Read this."

Carolyn took the note and read it. "What does he want with Tracy's brother?"

Sitting back in his seat Gavin exhaled. "Day and I are the only two that know what happened back then. If that information comes out now while he's pushing to become Mayor, it would be an end to his career and possibly mine."

Crossing her legs, Carolyn sighed, "Do you know where Day is?"

"No. JD has kept that information to himself. The only other person that may know would be Tracy."

Shaking her head Carolyn replied, "No, I don't think so. JD would not do anything to put Tracy in jeopardy. Telling her something like that when he knew someone wanted Day out of the picture would put her in danger. No, I think Brian would be a better bet."

Gavin pondered her statement, "You may be right. But either way I would not be in a position to get Day's location."

Carolyn sat up and pointed to the man in the picture behind Cynthia. "You may not be able to, but he could."

Gavin looked at the picture. "That's one of Munford's men. How would he get the information and if he could he would just give it to Munford."

"Why do you think he is one of Munford's men?"

"He works for Munford, I've seen him."

A frown creased her brow. Then her face began to ease into a very pleasant smile as she sat back in her seat. Gavin watched the transformation on his wife's face. "What?" he curiously asked.

"The government may be taking care of your problem for you. Joshua Lassiter is an operative for the CIA and the brother of the man you met tonight with JD. If he is working in Munford's office it's as an undercover agent, darling, not a paltry detective. If he or his brother is protecting your Cynthia you don't have to be concerned with her safety. That man can kill you just by looking at you."

"Are you sure?" Gavin asked perplexed by her response.

"Positive darling. Now, the question for you is, what can you do to help Joshua with his case against Munford?"

Clearing his throat, "You realize helping bring Munford down, could bring me down as well."

"You were once a District Attorney, make a deal?" She replied with a very sensuous smile. "Or, since you are now the Governor, you could ask questions to find out exactly what Joshua is working on." She hesitated, "Does Munford have anything else on you other than your connection to Billy Washington's disappearance?"

"No. It's the only thing I have in my past that could cause an issue. The thing is I have no regrets about it. If we had taken steps to stop him when the abuse was brought to us at first, a young girl would still be alive."

Curiosity got the best of her and she had to ask. "Was Tracy abused when she was young?"

Gavin knew there was no love in Carolyn's heart for Tracy. The man she planned to marry and live in the mansion with fell in love and married Tracy. He was not sure Carolyn would ever get over that. Telling her about Tracy's family may not be wise.

Carolyn could just about read her husband's mind. "I don't have any issues with Tracy. I am over JD. He was not the man for me. I know that now. But if you don't want to share, I understand."

He hesitated. She had been a good wife since they were married. It seemed she actually cared about him and their marriage, unlike the engagement. He had come to rely heavily on her and she on him. That was quite a change for them. "She wasn't as far as I know. I think that's why Al eliminated Billy. Lena however was a different story."

That caught Carolyn's attention. "What do you mean?"

"Let's just say momma dearest didn't have shit on Lena Washington. Tracy did not have a charmed childhood by any means." When she began to question him further, he put his hand up. "That's all I'm going to say about your new step-mother. Now my question is where do we start, Brian or your Lassiter?"

"Neither. We start with daddy."

Driving to her father's home, Carolyn was on a mission. This was an opportunity for her to prove her worthiness as a wife to her husband. They had a rocky start, but it was time to put that in the past. There was a time when the only thing she wanted in life was JD Harrison and the mansion. She may not have JD but it was Gavin that gave her the mansion. This situation gives her an opportunity to give him his career, worry free. Yes, she thought as she pulled into the garage, after this is over, she can began to prepare him for the Senate. Her father was talking about stepping down to spend more time with his new wife. That's a joke, but if he did, it would be easy for Gavin to take that seat. She was certain JD could be encouraged to support him, if they could get through this mess.

Carolyn put in the security code to the door of her father's home, but it did not work. She tried again, still nothing. Frustrated, she rang the bell. When the maid answered Carolyn frowned. "The code is not working on the door. Have someone check on it please." She stated while taking off her gloves and coat.

"The code in the door was changed Ms. Carolyn."

"Oh, well be sure to give me the code before I leave. Where's daddy?"

"We cannot give the code to anyone without Mrs. Roth's permission. As for your father, he was called to Washington this morning."

Carolyn stopped and turned back to the maid. "What did you say?"

"Your father was called to Washington this morning."

"No, not that. What did you say about the code?"

"Oh, Mrs. Roth instructed the staff not to give the code to anyone without her permission."

"Oh she did, did she! Where is she?" Carolyn demanded.

"In the solarium reading."

Carolyn turned and stomped off to the solarium. Why on earth her father married that witch she will never know. But this was her home and she will damn well have access to it. The woman from ghetto-ville was so beneath her father. It was clear she put some type of spell or something on him. Well, she was not as easily fooled.

"What is the code to the door?" she demanded as she entered the room. Lena looked up over her shoulder and turned back to her book. Not one to be ignored Carolyn walked further into the room and stood directly in front of the woman. "Did you not hear me? What is the code to the door?"

Lena exhaled, "I heard you Carolyn," she said not the least bit bothered by her step-daughter's presence or attitude. "It is customary to say hello, good morning, good afternoon, kiss my ass or something when you enter a person's home."

"You are so vulgar. No wonder Tracy is so socially deprived. She had to learn from the likes of you."

"Hum hum. I taught Tracy a few other things. Like how to whip ass. Would you like a lesson?" Lena looked up clearly ready to carry out her threat.

"Give me the code to the door."

"Why do you need it Carolyn," Lena asked returning to her book and turning the page.

"This is my home."

"No. You have two homes—the mansion and Gavin's house. This is not one of them." She continued reading.

"This is my father's house. I will not be locked out."

Lena closed her book, looked up and smiled. She wanted to witness the look on her step-daughters face when she heard the news. "See, that's where you are wrong."

"This is not just your father's house anymore. It belongs to both of us, literally and legally."

Frowning, not sure what Lena was eluding to Carolyn stared. Then smirked, "You're lying." When Lena continued to watch her with a satisfied smirk on her face, Carolyn shook her head. "I know you're lying. My father would never put your name on this house without talking with me first."

"Okay," Lena sighed and went back to her book.

Carolyn glared at the woman. Her father would not do this to her. Not wanting to be in the same room with this woman any longer she turned and walked out.

Lena exhaled, "I thought that would get you to leave."

Across town at Cynthia's home the morning was more relaxing then the previous. The first thing she did when she got out of bed was look out the window of her bedroom and was relieved to see there were no news trucks there. She was dressing to go for her run when her mother called, for no reason. She simply wanted to know how she was holding up after the hectic day she had yesterday. Sofia even went as far as saying she knew the public attention was something that was new to her and she would help her any way she could to deal with it. After she hung up the phone, Cynthia stood there staring at it, thinking someone was going to call back and yell, "Punked," but that didn't happen. When she opened her door, Rusty was there and looked up expectantly, she did not disappoint him. She bent down, rubbed him behind his ears as he licked her cheek. "Good morning Rusty. Come on boy, let's go for a run." He obediently followed.

When she reached the kitchen Samuel was dressed and ready to go. This morning he did not have a frown on his face. Maybe, just maybe this will be an uneventful day. *Not.*

They walked over to the track surrounding the lake and stretched. It was cold out and the weather man had called for snow flurries. But she wasn't concerned; she was dressed in layers and should be warm once she started running.

Samuel was throwing a ball down the track and Rusty was chasing after it. Smiling she looked up at Samuel, he was really a fine specimen of a man. She shook her head—where in the hell did that thought come from.

Samuel turned and saw the frown on her face. He stopped and walked towards her. When he stood directly in front of her he asked, "You okay?"

"Yeah," she said looking away.

"Look I know you had a rough day yesterday. If you need to talk, I'm a good listener."

Smiling, she shook her head, "I'm okay. Believe me I've dealt with worst. Let's get this show on the road." The pace was a slow trot at first. The two ran and carried on an easy conversation on the first round of the track. On the second, the pace was increased as the two concentrated. The third was a competition to see who would finish first. At the end they were both panting, but it was clear to her, he allowed her to keep up with him, for he was barely winded. "You're not even out of breath," she stammered out.

"Sure I am, don't you see me panting?

Walking around trying to catch her breath she laughed, "I see you faking it for my benefit." She bent down to catch her breath, that's when he heard the low whistle of a silencer, and so did Rusty. Samuel covered her body with his and rolled down the slight hill opposite from where the sound came. "What the hell?"

"Stay down," he tucked her head under him as he surveyed the area listening and waiting.

"What is it Samuel?" she asked.

"Shh,"

Getting angry, she pushed against his body to move him off her, but he did not budge. "Don't shh me. What's going?"

He put his hand over her mouth to keep her quiet. She began to wiggle under him trying to move. Then he heard Rusty bark. Looking around he did not see anywhere he could put her, but he did see Ryan near the bench. The nod was slight, but he understood. Cynthia was covered. "Stay here," he yelled while running towards Rusty's continued bark. When he reached the area Rusty was standing over a body on the ground, an AK-47 with a silencer attached next to him and a bullet hole in his head. Bending down he checked the pulse but knew before he touched him, he was dead. He looked around, no one was in sight, but someone had to pull the trigger that killed the assailant. He pulled out his cell phone and called Brian, "We have a situation." He turned at the sound of someone approaching and quickly blocked Cynthia's view. He looked at Rusty and the dog quickly positioned himself in front of the man on the ground.

"What happened Samuel?" she asked truly out of breath after running to him. She tried to walk around him, but he blocked her. "I told you to stay put!" he yelled.

"You took off running and so did Rusty, why?"

"Let's get you back to the house."

She stepped back and frowned, "No, I want to see what happened." She attempted to walk by him again, but this time found herself over his shoulder again heading back across the field. That's when she saw a man lying on the ground behind Rusty.

Samuel realized she had stopped fighting him when they reached the bench by the lake and he sat her down. The look in her eyes told him she saw the body. The fear and disbelief was in full force. "We have to stay until the police get here then I'm taking you back to the house." She didn't say anything. She just sat there looking down at her hands. He liked the feisty fighting Cynthia better. "Hey," he brought her eyes up to his. "I will not allow anyone to hurt you. Do you believe me?" Without saying a word she simply nodded and then looked back down at her hands.

An hour later they were back at her house answering questions for the police. Once Samuel's weapons were checked and it was evident he was not the shooter, the police concentrated on the crime scene area. Cynthia, Brian and Samuel sat in the kitchen after the officers left the house. "So this is real. It's not a bad dream," she said still looking down at her hands.

Brian was fighting his temper. He could not let her see he was rocked by the morning events. "Yes, it's real. Samuel was right there with you. He won't allow you to be hurt."

Looking up she faintly smiled. "Thank you Samuel." She stood up, "I'm going to get dressed for work."

Samuel and Brian looked at each other. "It may not be a good idea for you to go into the office."

Shaking her head, "It's the only way I can deal with all of this." She shrugged her shoulders, "Brian I haven't even had the chance to clean up my office from the break-in. The Policeman's ball is this weekend and Thanksgiving is next week. That's our busiest time of the year. If someone wants to kill me he's going to have to do it while I'm working." She went upstairs and left them in the kitchen.

The two men were silent for a moment, each collecting their thoughts. "Who shot the kid?" From the tattoos on the body it was determined the assailant was a member of the eagles gang.

"I'm thinking a friend of a friend."

Walking into her office an ominous cloud hung in the air. Clearly Rosaline had made an effort to clean up, but the evidence of someone searching the office was still apparent. When Rosaline looked up from the telephone and saw Cynthia in the doorway, she said into the receiver, "Mrs. Sutton, hold on. Ms. Thornton just walked in the door." She gave Cynthia an irritated look. "I am sure she will have the answers to your questions." Her finger was itching to push the hold button as the client continued to talk. "Hold, Hold on. Here she is."

Cynthia took the receiver from Rosaline. "Hello Mrs. Sutton." She listened to the woman's question. "Now, you know how I operate. You give me complete control and I guarantee the Policeman's Ball will be a huge success." She listened again, and then added. "TNT has provided event planning for several officials and to my knowledge has not received any complaints. We understand a number of dignitaries will be there. If I recall correctly, that is exactly why you hired us. You know our reputation for handling delicate situations. Please assure the Chief, he will not be disappointed." She politely ended the call and smiled at Rosaline.

Glad to have her partner back in the office, Rosaline returned the smile from the seat she took by the desk. "How are you feeling?" she asked sincerely concerned.

"I've been better, but I can't complain. Life is going according to plan." Cynthia replied as she sat in her queen style chair at her desk. Her friends were not aware of the threat on her life and she wanted it to stay that way.

"Good! If you have another accident or decided to die anytime soon, you better put someone else here to answer these telephones. I am not the one."

Cynthia laughed at her normally good natured friend and realized just how much she needed to be at work. "Anything urgent I need to address?"

"Other than Mrs. Sutton and the Policemen's Ball, no. Everyone else was very understanding and sent their concern for you."

"I'm sure the Chief is on her about the details. She really isn't the type to hover."

Nodding towards Samuel she asked. "Have they found out anything about the break-in?"

"Not yet. You didn't mention it to Ashley or Tracy, did you?"

"No, just Marco."

"Is he upset?"

"No. But he showed up yesterday and it would not surprise me if he makes an appearance today."

"I'm so sorry about all of this," Cynthia said.

"Hey, it's going to be okay," Roz comforted her friend who seemed a little shaken. Thinking she was upset about her office, she explained her cleanup effort. "You know I don't have your touch for decorating, but I did what I could putting this place back together."

"Oh, it's fine. I'll have this straight in no time," she said looking around at the damage

"Alright, I'm going back to my office. I'm working on the menu for Saturday. If you need me give me a holler."

"Will do." Cynthia inhaled and began repairing the damage to her office.

About an hour later Cynthia walked out of her office and was startled to see Samuel sitting outside her door. She was used to seeing him at her house, but here at work was something different. "You okay?" he asked seeing the look on her face.

Oddly enough, seeing him there and hearing his voice brought an inner peace. She felt safe with him around. "Yeah, I'm okay."

"It's been a crazy day. You don't have to play the super woman role with me. It's okay if you want to go home."

Smiling at how sensitive he was to her feelings, "I am super woman—didn't you know."

He put his head to the side and grinned at her. "I think you look more like a princess."

She jokingly punched him in the arm, "Ah shucks, you're going to make me blush."

"Yeah right. I'm sure you hear that all the time."

"I do. But it sounds nice coming from you."

The two simply stared at each other for a moment longer than necessary. "I was going into the kitchen to grab some lunch. You feel like being a guinea pig for Roz?"

"Can she cook?"

Shocked at the question, all Cynthia could say was, "Come with me."

Thirty minutes later Samuel was begging Roz to divorce Marco and marry him. "Look, I'm not one of those men that need a woman to cook. I know my way around a kitchen. But this was off the chain. You put your foot in this."

"Anyone could fix this dish, it's so simple," Roz boasted. "Even Cynthia."

"What do you mean even Cynthia? I can cook when I want to."

"Girl, I've known you since high school. I've never seen you at a stove."

"Are you kitchen illiterate?" Samuel joked.

Feeling a little defensive she lied. "No I am not. I can do a little something."

"Something that will be edible?" Roz asked.

"Yes. I mean I'm not Betty Crooker, but I can hang."

Roz looked at her with surprise at what she was hearing. Not only has her friend never cooked, she never showed any interest in trying to learn before now. "Really? Prove it. Cook a meal for Prince LaVere'. If he survives then I will never doubt you again."

"Cook for LaVere'?"

"Yeah. And I'm not talking about anything frozen and warmed up in the oven. I'll give you a simple meal plan and you will prepare everything from scratch."

"What do I get out of it?"

"Six months of catering from me whenever you want it. And maybe, just maybe a Prince in the boot. So, what do you say Ms. Thornton. You accept my challenge?"

Not one to step down from a challenge Cynthia agreed. On the way back to her office Samuel looked over at her. "Never touched an oven before, have you?"

"Not even in a dream."

He smiled and all of a sudden her world was right. The past two days with all the drama and gloom were a distant thought. "I'll help you."

"You will?"

"Yes, I will." He touched the tip of her nose with his finger.

"You will help me cook to impress LaVere', because I'm not really doing this for Roz."

"Well, you know they do say the way to a man's heart is through his stomach."

"Yeah, well, LaVere' isn't just any man. He's a prince. Let's pray he has a cast iron stomach and this does not backfire and cause an international incident."

The two laughed, but just as suddenly, Cynthia stopped and was staring over Samuel's shoulder. "May I see you in private for a moment," Carolyn Roth-Roberts asked while walking past them directly into Cynthia's office.

The sight of Carolyn Roth walking into her office immediately put Cynthia on alert. There has been too much drama in her life in the past two days to have to put up with her nonsense. Not only was Carolyn married to the man that would always have a special place in her heart, but she was also a person Cynthia never liked. Maybe it was because she always seemed to have the very things Cynthia wanted in life, money, recognition, family support and a man that loves her. Today, none of that matter. She was on her way to having all of that and more. Her relationship with LaVere' was on solid ground. That in turn had her mother smiling and happy. Yes, with the exception of someone wanting her dead, things were falling nicely into place. With all of that in mind, Cynthia was determined that the reason Carolyn Roth-Roberts was in her office was not going to get to her.

"I'll be right outside the door," Samuel cautioned.

Keeping a professional attitude, Cynthia entered her office. "Mrs. Roberts. What can I do for you today?"

"We need to discuss my husband," Carolyn crossed her legs and looked up.

Cynthia paused and looked at Carolyn with a questioning eye. She then continued walking past the woman to lean against her desk. "Why would we need to discuss The Governor?" she asked as gently as she could.

"He is planning on ruining his political career because of you. And I refuse to allow that happen."

"Because of me? I'm not sure I understand." Cynthia continued to stand, towering over the woman seated. As Carolyn assessed her from head to toe, she smiled inwardly. If there was ever a time she wanted to look good, it was here. The woman the man she thought she loved picked over her was checking her out, she loved it. "How would I impact his political career?"

"Shall we speak candidly?" Carolyn asked.

"Please," Cynthia replied as she sat on the edge of her desk.

"Apparently he feels you are in danger from one of his associates. The thought of something happening to you is a major concern for him." She paused. "Please save the look of surprise. I was well aware of your affair with my husband."

"You were not married during the time Gavin and I were seeing each other. He was not your husband."

Carolyn frowned, "We were engaged at the time."

"An engagement that apparently did not mean much to you, since you were getting busy with David Holt during that time." Cynthia replied as she crossed her arms across her chest. "Let's keep this real Carolyn. You and Gavin both had someone on the side. At least I did not attempt to rape anyone."

Carolyn stood, "Look I have not had a good day and the last thing I need is to play tit for tat with you. It seems you

are on someone's list to be eliminated. Frankly, I wouldn't
have a problem with you disappearing. Gavin, on the other
hand, feels the only way to keep you safe is to expose the
person and his connection to that person. Although he has
not done anything illegal, if his connection is exposed it
could raise an eye or two of potential campaign contributors.
As I'm sure you know, Gavin is planning a run for the senate
seat my father will be vacating. I am not going to allow a little
whore like you to interfere with our plans."

Apparently Carolyn knew a little more about this
situation than she did. If Gavin knew someone was trying to
kill her over the information he gave her, why didn't he tell
her. Cynthia eased off the desk and stood toe to toe with
Carolyn.

"Funny you should say our plans. Don't you mean your
plans? Unlike you, I listened to his wants and believe it or
not, the only thing he wants now is a family with you. Why
anyone would want you as a mother to their children, I have
yet to understand. You are and always have been a self
absorbed, high-class whore. Anyone that could get you
closer to what you wanted, you were theirs for the taking. I
can understand why Gavin hasn't touched you since the
wedding."

Without thinking Carolyn slapped Cynthia with the back
of her hand. Stumbling back from the impact, Cynthia
grabbed her face where the blow landed and looked at
Carolyn as if she had lost her mind. This was just too much.
Yesterday she had to deal with her mother, the media and
that damn Shannon. This morning a man tried to shoot her
near her own home. Now, here in her office the one person
she hated most in life had the nerve to slap her. Before she
could think clearly, Cynthia fist tightened at her side and in
an instant it was pounding continuously into Carolyn's face.
The next thing she knew, she was on the floor banging
Carolyn's head on it and Samuel was pulling at her. Where
Brian appeared from, she did not know, but he was standing

there with his arms around Carolyn holding her back as
Samuel put Cynthia over his shoulder and carried her into
another room. He put her in a chair and she immediately
tried to get up. "How dare that bitch? I don't know who in
the hell she thought she was hitting. But this whore hits
back." She jumped out of the chair and ran back into the
room where Carolyn was with Brian. Just before she
reached her Samuel grabbed Cynthia from behind. He held
her tightly around her waist.

Brian was on the telephone calling Gavin. This situation
could be bad on a normal day, but today it was lethal.
"Look, I'm at TNT, we have a situation here. You need to
be get over here before the press gets wind of this. And bring
a medical person with you." Brian hung up the telephone
and looked at Carolyn. "What in the hell are you doing
here?"

"Getting a well deserved ass whipping," Cynthia replied.

Brushing her hair out of her face with her hand, Carolyn
shimmied out of his hold. She walked over to Samuel and
attempted to reach for Cynthia. "Do you see what you did to
my face?" she yelled. Samuel stood between the two women
holding each at arm's length.

Brian stopped her progress by grabbing her hands and
pulling her back as the two woman passed insults between
each other. Rosaline came running into the room just as
Samuel began laughing and Brian began cursing. "You're
finding some humor in this?"

"Man, I have six sisters. This is a normal day for me. I've
just never seen anyone get beat so badly, so quickly." He
laughed, "I was sitting right outside the door. And I swear
they had not been in here five minutes before you walked
through the door."

Roz looked from Cynthia to Carolyn. "Damn girl" she
chuckled, "she really rocked your face. Here take this," she
grabbed some tissues off Cynthia's desk and gave them to
Carolyn.

Samuel sat Cynthia in another chair, "Don't you dare move!" He turned to look at Roz who was trying to gather herself, but was failing miserably.

"You are not helping." Brian stated trying hard not the laugh. He turned back to the ladies. "One of you wants to tell me what the hell is going on?" Both started talking at the same time pointing fingers at each other. "Wait! One at a time, Carolyn, you first. What are you doing here?"

"Why she get to go first?" Cynthia yelled.

Brian turned with little patience showing on his face. "Because I said so," he turned back. "Carolyn, I'm waiting."

"I came here to get her assistance with a personal matter with Gavin. I should have known better than to think she had an ounce of decency in her."

"Look bitch, let's get something straight. You didn't come here to help Gavin. You came here to help yourself. If you cared half as much about Gavin as he cared about you, you would have never got into bed with Holt."

"If you cared about Gavin, you would talk him out of what he is about to do."

"Okay," Brian exhaled, "let me get this right. This fight is over Gavin?"

"What in the hell? Carolyn?" Carolyn jumped up and ran into Gavin's arms. He held her as she cried on his shoulder. Gavin looked around stunned and saw Cynthia sitting in the chair behind Brian. He looked up to Brian. "What's going on?" he asked as he tried to console Carolyn.

Brian crossed his arms over his chest. "It seems they had a fight over you."

"It was not a fight over him." Cynthia stated as she walked over to her desk and pulled a mirror out of her purse. She prayed her face did not look as bad as Carolyn's. But then again she knew it couldn't. After the first slap, Carolyn never got a chance to hit her again.

Gavin turned to the woman behind him. He pushed Carolyn's hair from her face and took a good look at it. He tried to hide his smile as he looked up at Cynthia.

Cynthia put her hands on her hips and gave him the sister girl look. "What? She threw the first punch."

"Sweetheart it's not that bad," he lied. He turned to the guard that came inside with him. "Please take her in the other room and clean her up I'll be there in a moment."

Carolyn looked at Cynthia then at Gavin. "I truly did come here to help with your situation."

"I know. I'll handle this and be there in a minute."

Samuel and Brian stood back as Cynthia walked over to Gavin. "Your wife indicates you know someone is trying to kill me. She also believes it's because of what you told me. Is that true?"

He looked over her shoulder at Brian, who shook his head indicating he had not told her. He exhaled, "Yes."

She closed her eyes against the pain that shot through her. This is the man she would have protected to the end. "Please take your wife and get the hell out of my life."

The look on Gavin's face showed he was sorry and a little hurt. At that moment Carolyn came back into the office more upset then before. "Do you see my face? I'm pressing charges against her. That is not negotiable," Carolyn cried.

"That may not be a good idea, especially if you did indeed throw the first punch." Gavin replied as he escorted Carolyn out of the office. He looked at Cynthia. "I'll fix this." Then turned and walked out the door.

Brian looked at Samuel and Roz. "Would you two give us a minute?" Brian asked filled with concern for his friend. Once he was alone with Cynthia, he smiled. "I never knew you were related to Floyd Mayweather. Her face looked like hell."

"I would have done what she needed if she had approached me right."

"What would you have done?" Brian asked.

Cynthia exhaled. "I would have told him not to give in to protect me. But it never was about me. It was about his career."

"If it's any consolation, Gavin didn't know about the threat until JD and I told him."

Brian took her hand, pulled her into his arms and held her tight. "You know, Gavin is a person in the past. You have a decent man to look after you."

She looked up at him and smiled. "You know, you are right. I do have LaVere'." She picked up her purse. "Thank you Brian." She walked out to the room to Samuel.

"I'm going to see LaVere'."

Raising an eyebrow, Brian smiled as he watched the two walk out. He hadn't missed the way Samuel watched her. Or the anger in his voice when he spoke to Gavin about putting her in danger. Or the rage he demonstrated this morning when someone took a shot at her. "LaVere', wasn't who I had in mind."

LaVere' had moved into his home so the thirty-minute drive to Hanover was enough time for her to calm now. But to Samuel she seemed just as tensed as she was back at the office. He wanted to tell her how proud he was at the way she handled herself back there, but he was sure she would not appreciated it the way he intended. With all that she had been through in the last two days, she showed remarkable restraint against the governor's wife.

When they reach LaVere's home, Cynthia's already plucked nerves were tested to the limit even more. Jamal answered the door and literally refused to let her in. "Prince Ashro is not in. You may call him, I'm sure you have the telephone number."

Giving her best to be pleasant, since she knew Jamal was not the reason for her distress, she smiled. "May I come inside and wait for him?"

Looking at her bruised face Jamal smiled. "I see someone attempted to slap some decency into you. Did it work?"

That was her limit. She pushed past the miniature of a man and walked into the foyer. "I'm not in the mood for you Jamal."

Seeing the action from the car, Samuel got up and walked inside the open door. Jamal stood with his back to him in front of the seat Cynthia took near the staircase. "Since you are here and refuse to leave, allow me to take this opportunity to speak with you. May I have your permission to speak freely?"

Her mind was telling her to walk out, but her curiosity took over. "I can't imagine anything you would have to say to me that will hold my interest."

"If you care anything at all for the Prince, you will hear me out."

She placed her purse on the seat next to her and crossed her legs. "Let me warn you. I have not had a very good day, thus far. You may be taking your life into your hands if you say something that will piss me off. Do you still want to talk to me?"

"This must be said."

"Go for it."

"Your presence in the Prince life has cause turmoil not only with his family, but with his country as well. Several factions within the country are uprising against the royal family because of the Prince's choice for a wife. To date, there have been at least three violent attempts against the family. No one has been hurt, but it's only a matter of time. Rest assured the royal family will be protected at all cost. That means some of my countrymen will probably lose their lives because they feel so strongly about the Prince's choice."

"It is his choice."

Jamal put his hands behind his back and began to pace in front of her. "Not really. The Prince belongs to the people. What he does with his life directly affects them. They are not very accepting of outsiders, and you are an outsider. Let's put the people aside for a moment. The King is not pleased with this situation. He is on the verge of banishing his own son from the country if he continues to see you. Your relationship with the Prince has put a rift between the King and his Queen. That has only intensified his dislike for you. Can you sit there and tell me you care for the Prince and allow these things to happen? If you truly care, you would step aside and make way for someone that is worthy of him and his status."

There was no way in hell she was going to allow Jamal to see her cry. However, that was exactly what she was about to do. She picked up her purse and stood. "Would you tell LaVere' I came by?" Not waiting for a response she turned and saw Samuel standing at the door. Looking away from his face she walked out of the door.

Samuel stared at the sorry excuse of a man as she walked out. "If you ever speak to her in that tone again, it will be the last time you ever hear your own voice." He turned and joined Cynthia in the car. Without saying anything, he started the car and pulled off.

For a second back there she could have sworn she saw a smile on Jamal's face. But at the moment, that was the least of her concerns. LaVere' never mentioned the situation in his homeland. Why would he keep something so important from me? She looked around at the luxury vehicle. It had every upgrade available. Each day she received a gift from him, whether he was in town or not. This morning she received a dozen red roses. The message in the card read, *Only a princess could give this justice.* She opened the velvet box that accompanied the flowers and inside was a stunning swing drop diamond necklace from Tiffany of New

York. The day before it was a gown from Paris. He was keeping her mind off important issues by giving her material things. Placing her head back against the seat she looked out the window as the car moved down the highway. She sadly chuckled to herself, "Isn't that what I always wanted. Why does it feel so wrong?"

When they arrived home, Rusty greeted them at the door. "Hello boy," Cynthia rubbed his head and gave him a hug. "I'm going to bed," she said without looking back.

Samuel watched her climb the steps. She seemed so dejected. "Follow her boy," he said to Rusty. The dog ran up the steps behind her. Looking at his watch, it wasn't even six o'clock in the evening, but he understood. The last forty eight hours had been hell on her. At least the house was quiet, allowing her time to rest. Something had to give or he was going to kill the next person to hurt her.

Brian was reading the report from Calvin. The anger he was experiencing was unbearable. James Harrison was not his father, but he was an integral part of his life. It was because of him Brian wanted to be an FBI agent. When he would visit JD, his father would tell the most interesting stories about law enforcement. Never once did he say, "You can't be an agent, you're reaching too high." The day he received notification of acceptance, James Harrison was the first person he told. Brian knew if his feelings ran as deep as wanting to stop what he was doing to kill Munford, JD's would be worst.

Now the man had the audacity to want to take out Gavin, JD and Cynthia. He was either losing his mind or Munford had others in his pocket. What would make a simple Chief of Police think he could take out a Governor and an Attorney General? The answer to that question was too damn scary to contemplate, but there were two things Brian knew for sure, nothing was going to happen to JD with him around or Cynthia with Samuel around. He stood from his desk and walked over to the window. Looking through the buildings on Broad Street he could see the top of the Capitol where the Governor lived. How could he tell JD what he has found out—how could he not?

Sitting back at his desk he called Calvin. "I just finished the report. According to this what Munford confessed to Gavin is true. He had Mr. Harrison killed. How are we going to handle this?"

"We can't tell JD until we have everything we need to put Munford behind bars. Telling him any time prior to that, we will be asking for trouble."

"There's another problem. Cynthia doesn't know about Munford. TNT is handling the Policeman's ball this weekend. Munford is going to be there."

"You have to find a way to keep her from going."

"She has been through so much. Just bring him in."

"And charge him with what, Brian? He hasn't broken any laws we can prove. The man has covered his tracks. The only thing we can do is keep Cynthia protected."

After talking with Calvin, Brian decided to drive over to see how Cynthia was holding up. Tonight a simple telephone call would not do. He let himself in the house through the garage door; Rusty met him at the top of the steps leading into the kitchen. "Hey boy," he said as he walked into the kitchen. Samuel was sitting in the living room with a beer looking out the French doors into the night. He took off his jacket, went over to the refrigerator and pulled a beer out for himself then, walked into the living room and sat in the chair near the window.

Brian watched Samuel as he looked. He remembered the look he witnessed when he found Samuel at the hospital watching over Cynthia. Then a few other times he was sure he saw that look between the two of them. The same look he had seen a thousand times pass between JD and Tracy or James and Ashley. "You know, I generally mind my own business in affairs of the heart. But since at the moment you are in my employment, I have to ask, is there something between you and Cynthia that I need to be aware of?"

"Are you her personal aide or something?"

Brian smirked, "No, her big brother. I have notice the way you look at her. So my interest is twofold. I'm a little over protective when it comes to her and would have issues with someone getting involved with her for the wrong reasons. Sometimes she tends to disregard my advice, but that does not diminish my responsibility. I know better than most, she can be very distracting."

Samuel smiled, "She is a beautiful woman. But it's more than that. She is not what people think. She is so vulnerable and alone. I've been around this woman for over a week now. I cannot name one person that has her back. I mean really has her back. With everything that has happened to her, she has not called one person." He took a swallow of beer, then point, "No, I have to take that back. She went to see LaVere', but he wasn't there and this little prick of a man talked to her as if she was a nobody. Other than you and me, this woman is virtually alone."

"She has her brother."

"That's true, but let's be real—he can't help her with this."

"No he can't, but you can." Brian sat forward, "I don't think she should go to the Policeman's Ball. We know Munford is going to be there. It would be a perfect opportunity for him to have her disappear. She's beginning to trust you. Talk her out of going."

"Everyone seems to be asking her to give up something. For once, before this is over with, I would like to see someone, anyone give her something in return."

Brian smiled. "She's got you hook line and sinker."

"What the hell are you talking about?" Samuel said as he stood to get another beer.

"Look, I ain't mad at you. I'm just wondering how you're going to get past a Prince."

Later, after Brian left Samuel locked up the house and went up stairs. He lightly tapped on the door then walked in. She was lying in the bed looking at a movie with tears stains on her face. It dawned on him, this is the only room he had ever seen her cry in. She didn't cry during the shooting earlier that morning. She didn't cry during the confrontation with Carolyn, the words with Gavin or at the things Jamal said. This was the only room she allows herself to feel. He walked through the room and checked the locks on the windows. Walking over to the bed he took off his shoes and lay down beside her. He took the remote out of her hands and turned the television off. He gathered her in his arms and kissed her forehead. "It's going to end soon. I promise."

The moment his arms circled her all thoughts of LaVere', Gavin, Carolyn, Jamal, her mother and the shooter escaped her as she settled against his chest and closed her eyes. There was never a time in her life she had felt so protected, so secure, so at peace. That was the last thought she had before sleep took over.

The steady flow of her breath against his neck let him know she had drifted off to sleep. Unfortunately for him it also brought everything male in him to full attention. The silky feel of her hair against his cheek, the softness of her skin beneath his hand and the glorious mount of her breast that was rising and falling against his chest was playing havoc on his senses. And then the tips of her lips touched the side of his neck, every parcel in his body began throbbing. He saw a movement by the door and knew Rusty had settled in. He was able to relax his mind, now if he could just get the rest of his body to follow he could make it through the night. He kissed the top of the soft curls on the head of the woman lying in his arms and closed his eyes. Within minutes he had eased into a peaceful sleep.

Chapter 11

The sensation flowing through her body was a feeling she had never experienced before. Again and again, each time he entered her, the universe swirled above. His hands travel down to the small of her back bringing her body closer to his with a gentle force that made her explode out of control. Then he held her and whisper, "I love you into her ear." Never in her life had Cynthia felt so fulfilled than that moment. She reached to palm his face between her hands and looked into the cinnamon brown eyes of Samuel. She sat straight up in her bed. Perspiration was dripping between her breasts, not to mention the wetness that seemed to appear between her legs. She reached up and wiped the perspiration from her face and looked around the room to make sure no one was there with her. The covers were thrown to the side as she got out of the bed and hurried into the bathroom. She stripped out of her teddy and stood under the shower.

How could she have been dreaming of Samuel when she has committed herself to LaVere'? Why would she not dream of him? He was the one that held her last night when her tears would not stop, not LaVere'. Thinking of him she wondered why he did not call her last night. Had Jamal neglected to give him the message? Was he having second thoughts about them? A more important question was, is she having second thoughts. This wasn't good. She had to talk to Ashley about the turmoil that was called her life. She dressed quickly and ran downstairs. To her surprise sitting in her kitchen was Blake, not Samuel.

"Hey sis. Sleeping in late this morning I see."

"Hey Blake," she replied a little disoriented. "Where's Samuel?"

"He called and asked me to come over. Said he had to pay a visit to someone."

"At seven in the morning?"

"That's what he said."

"It's better he's not here. I need to talk to Ashley."

"I don't think you should be leaving the house until Samuel returns."

"Okay, I tell you what, you sit here and wait for Samuel. Tell him I'll be right back."

Blake beat her to the door. "I don't think so."

"Blake this is very important. I have to talk to Ashley this morning."

Seeing the determination in her face, he conceded. "Okay, but I'm driving."

Cynthia stopped at the door and looked back at him. "Do you know how to drive?"

Frowning he replied, "Of course I know how to drive."

"If you think about it, I've never seen you drive anything."

"Get in the car."

Fifteen minutes later she was knocking on Ashley's door.

Clara, the housekeeper answered the door. "Good Morning, Ms. Cynthia. You are out and about early."

"Good Morning Clara," she replied rushing passed her. "Where is Ashley, is she upstairs?" Cynthia called back from the steps.

"Yes ma'am, they are still in bed," Clara responded to a fleeting back.

Reaching the double doors of the bedroom suite at the top of the stairs, Cynthia knocked, "Ashley, I'm coming in."

"Cynthia," James said from under the comforter, "It better be your ghost in my bedroom at seven thirty in the morning."

"James, I need to talk to Ashley alone. Do you mind?"

James sat up and looked at Cynthia as if she had lost her mind. "You have exactly thirty seconds to get the hell out of this room, before I strangle you with my bare hands."

Cynthia walked around to the other side of the bed where Ashley had sat up. "I believe you tried with David Holt. Look where that got you. Ash, I'm in trouble," she cried ignoring James.

"What's going on?" Ashley asked in a concerned voice.

"I'm about to kill her," James said as he threw the comforter back to get out of bed.

He stood with no shirt and a pair of pajama bottoms. "Damn James, I didn't know you had all of that going on," Cynthia said as she eyed his half-naked body up and down.

Ashley looked at James, then to Cynthia. "Would you mind taking your eyes off my husband?"

"Oh, sorry about that, but Ashley," she said as she sat on the bed, "I need your advice."

James leaned over and kissed his wife. "Good Morning," he smiled at her. A smiled that disappeared once he looked towards Cynthia. "You would not have this problem if you did not go around sleeping in a bed with a man you are not committed too." He smiled and walked out of the room with Cynthia's mouth hanging open.

"Shut your mouth Cynthia, before something fly in. Now, what is this about a man and who is he?" Ashley asked.

Cynthia sighed, and laid her head on Ashley shoulders. "How did he find out about that?"

"I have no idea, but you can believe, if James knows so does LaVere'. Now, tell me what happened."

Cynthia sat up and exhaled. "His name is Samuel. He was the person that helped me the night of the accident." *The accident that really wasn't an accident,* she thought, but did not say anything. She stood up and walked over to the window. She pushed the drapes aside and looked out. "I don't know anything about this man except for the fact that since he's been around I feel safe and protected. I even find myself laughing with him. It's as if I lose sense of time. Time literally stands still when he is around. Ashley, I'm dreaming about him." She released the drapes and turned to Ashley. "I have committed myself to a relationship with LaVere' and to be honest, I'm so excited about it. Then I dream about Samuel and I don't understand why." She exhaled, "That's a lie. I do know why. I'm horny as hell. That's all it is."

Ashley laughed. "That may be true; however, it sounds like it could be a little more than horniness."

Cynthia shook her head, "It can't be."

"Why?" Ashley asked.

"Because I don't know him."

"But, you've slept with him. When and where?"

"Some things have been happening in my life and last night I sort of accidently fell asleep in his arms."

James walked in the room with a tray filled with fruit and hot tea for Ashley and coffee for Cynthia. "Is that what it's called these days' accidents?"

She frowned at James as he placed the tray on the table in the sitting area. "James, this is a private conversation."

"Cynthia, this is a private bedroom, mine."

"James, babe would you check on the twins, then give us a few minutes."

He looked at Cynthia then smile at his wife, "I'll be in the shower."

The ladies waited until the room was clear. "Cynthia," Ashley smiled, "has it occurred to you that you may have feelings for this man?'

"I'm developing feelings for LaVere". I have spent the last two weeks getting to know him and I like him. I don't know Samuel."

"Does LaVere' make time stop for you?"

The question took her by surprise. "I really like LaVere'. I have waited all of my life for a man that treats me like he does. I want him to be the one."

It did not escape Ashley that Cynthia did not answer the question. But from experience she knew she was going to have to reach the conclusion on her own. It took James just about a year to realize she had captured his heart. Cynthia was a tough cookie when it came to feelings. She was a pro at hiding her true feelings when she wanted to. "Well, ignore Samuel and concentrate on your relationship with LaVere'."

"Do you think that will work?"

"Ashley," she sighed. "For the first time in my life, my mother is proud of me. She is actually spending time with me and I like it. I like having her attention. If I mess up with LaVere', I'm going to lose that."

Ashley saw tears develop in Cynthia's eyes. Her heart went out to her friend. "You have to do what will make you happy, not what your mother wants. Frankly, if your mother's love and attention is only because LaVere' is in your life, then it will fade. It's not real love. You deserve real love. Not a love you settle for or that has terms attached. Don't settle Cynthia."

They finished their breakfast and Cynthia apologized to James for intruding. After she left James sat in the chair Cynthia vacated and placed Ashley's feet in his lap. "She is not in love with LaVere'. Nor is LaVere' in love with her."

"Do you know Samuel?"

He nodded, "Yeah, he's Pearl's oldest brother."

"Samuel Lassiter? Wow, He is such a serious man and so handsome. He doesn't appear to be the type to sleep in any woman's bed without meaning."

"He's not," James said raising an eyebrow.

Ashley smiled. "Cynthia said he makes time stand still."

"Hmm, so, where does that leave LaVere'?"

Whenever he was on an assignment Samuel usually did not make contact with his family. But this assignment was a little different; he was home and he was in need of advice. Holding Cynthia in his arms last night brought things to light. He was more than just a little attracted to her. That could cause a number of issues. Their family had a ritual, every member in the family made contact the week before Thanksgiving regardless of where in the world they were. The order of the calls determines who gets what duty for the holiday. He could knock out two stones at once.

Pulling out his cell phone, Samuel dialed the number and smiled instantly when he heard his mother's voice. "It's your oldest son, am I the first?"

"No, you missed by one, Joshua called around four am. You get game detail," she laughed.

"I'm pretty sure Joshua will not make it to dinner therefore he forfeits."

"Diamond believes she has the next bid on cake detail, because she helped with the shopping for Thanksgiving dinner. Nevertheless, I'll let you, Joshua and Diamond fight over that."

"Oh hell, Mommy you know Diamond doesn't play fair."

"You're the one that taught her how to negotiate," she laughed. "How's my baby?"

"I'm doing okay Mom. Is everyone going to make it Thursday?"

"Everyone except Joshua, but I'm not giving up hope on him yet. Your father has pulled out the football and chess set in anticipation of your arrival. I've picked up all the ingredients for your lasagna everyone is still raving about from last year."

"I'm looking forward to all of the festivities and more."

"Are you bringing someone with you this year? You know your father and I are not getting younger. We need grandchildren."

"You have twelve children. Grandchildren are the last thing you need."

"My baby is sixteen and in her last year of high school. I need babies. You are the oldest. It's your responsibility to lead the others."

"Lead them in what?" Samuel asked somewhat amused.

"In supplying me with a plethora of grandchildren," Sally replied in an *I thought you knew* kind of voice. "The Lord said, be fruitful and multiply."

"In the book of Samuel it reads, multiply and have children when you haveth a wife to care for them. I'm not Boo Boo the fool."

"I agree one hundred percent. You do need a wife. So do you have anyone in mind?"

That was such a smooth setup that he did not see it coming. She turned that conversation right in the direction she wanted it to go. For the past fifteen years he had dealt with spies, intelligence agents and secretaries of states. None of them has been able to twist his words. Yet it never failed with Sally.

Searching for the right words, Samuel cleared his throat. "Since you mentioned it there is someone that has captured my attention."

Sally inhaled with excitement. "Really? Is she nice?"

"Actually I think she's a little amazing."

Smiling, Sally sent up a silent pray. She wasn't sure Samuel would rebound from his last affair of the heart. She never met the woman, but he took her death very hard. Of her twelve children he was the one with the tough shell. Whoever slips in has love for a lifetime. "Will we get to meet her?"

He cleared his throat. "Umm, that's the thing. You already know her."

"Really, who is she?" Sally eagerly asked.

"Cynthia Thornton." Samuel waited. He knew the response was not going to be thrilling.

"Whew," Sally exhaled. "Your sister is not going to take this well, you do realize that, right?"

"I know Mom. But she seemed to handle things last week during the press conference."

"That was business baby, she had no choice." Hearing what sounded an awfully like despair in his voice Sally simply replied, "I love you Samuel. Whoever you chose to have in your life, I want them to be worthy of you. Only you can make that judgment. I trust your choice. If you believe this woman will make you happy, that is all that matters to me. If you can manage it bring her with you for Thanksgiving dinner."

"Thanks Mom. I love you."

"I love you too Samuel."

"Tell dad, I will see him on next Thursday."

"I will. Bye baby."

After the call, Samuel pulled his sweater over his head and walk towards the shower. "There is no way in hell I'm going to let anyone take her away from me. I don't give a damn who they may be." It was time to put Cynthia on notice.

It was nice to be in the office with no drama. Cynthia was able to get most of her paperwork done. Everything was set for the policemen ball on Saturday. Those homes that were decorated for the Christmas holiday by TNT each year schedules were in place, as well as the event schedules for December. Samuel crossed her mind. She missed him not being around this morning. She enjoyed having Blake around, but he wasn't Samuel. Why did he leave her alone? Shaking her head, she stopped herself. He was her bodyguard, she should be thinking about LaVere' and why she hadn't heard from him.

There was nothing in life that she wanted more than being loved. The problem was her definition of love. In the short time she has known LaVere', she has not wanted for anything materialistic. It was the inner satisfaction that she was not receiving and that was what was confusing. LaVere' was a Prince. The question was, is he her Prince Charming. Shaking her head she concluded, "Prince Charming does not exist. He was not going to rush in and save her from danger." Maybe LaVere' was as close as she was going to get.

Pushing the thoughts aside she began reviewing inventory for the ten house scheduled for holiday decorations on the Friday and Saturday after Thanksgiving. Her day was scheduled to began at seven a.m. and end at eleven p.m. To her staff it was hard work decorating homes for the holiday, but for Cynthia it was a labor of love. The look on her clients face once their homes were ready to ring in the holidays was wonderful to her, not to mention the twelve hundred per home she receives in compensation.

Looking up at one of the shelves in the inventory room she noticed the label on one of the boxes was turned backwards and she wasn't sure if it was a part of the order for one of the homes or not. The last thing she needed was to get to a house and not have everything on the truck to complete the job. The schedule was so tight there would be no time to return to the office. Not wanting to push the heavy ladder over to the location and then back, she took her heels off. Stepping on the bottom shelf, she reached up to turned the box around. Stretching up she still could not reach the box. She shook the stand to make sure it was sturdy. Believing it was strong enough to hold her she climbed to the next shelve and pushed the box around until she could see the label. She leaned back and the entire stand began leaning as if it was top heavy. "Oh shit," she screamed while holding on the rack for dear life. Just when she thought she was about to hit the floor, with the boxes tumbling on top of her, someone grabbed her by the waist. She balled into a fetal position and covered her head. After hearing one or two boxes fall, there was silence. She looked up to see Samuel balancing the shelves with one hand and holding her up with the other. "Whoa." She said as she clung to his thigh. Her eyes and hand were very close to a part of Samuel's anatomy that was triggering a reaction throughout her body.

The thought of boxes tumbling on top of his Cynthia propelled him into action. First he had to keep her from hitting the concrete floor, and then he had to prevent the boxes from falling on top of her. He made it across the span of the basement in three long steps. The racing of his heart began to slow down from the scare she had given him. He placed her on her feet, but could not release her completely. "I can't leave you alone for a minute. Holding her close to his side he pushed the heavy box back into its position. She reached up to try to help him, but he increased his hold on her. "Stay still." Holding the shelf in place with one hand and her at his side with the other, he turned and looked into her eyes. It was hard not to notice just how perfectly she fit against his body. "Am I going to have to keep you attached to my side to keep you safe from harm?"

Safe. That's exactly how she felt when he was around, just like she felt last night. But with Samuel there was more, a lot more. He listens when she talks, he laughs with her and he doesn't let her control him. Not to mention how aroused she gets around him. Safe and aroused, was what she felt almost to the point of distraction. Not able to pull her eyes from him, she held tightly to the muscular arm that was holding her. Just as if it was second nature her lips parted as she stared up at him. "You left me this morning?"

"I will never be far away."

Looking up with sad eyes she replied. "But I didn't know that. And you left me with Blake. He could have gotten hurt trying to protect me."

Smiling at her pouted lips he shook his head. "Rusty was there."

Neither moved as she absent mindedly rubbed his arm and he simply smiled.

"Please don't leave me again."

He could see how vulnerable she was. His daddy didn't raise any fools, he knew when an opportunity presented itself, you take full advantage, and he did. First he kissed her eyelids, "I won't leave you." Then he kissed the tip of her nose, "I promise to keep you safe." Then he kissed the top of her parted lips. "Cinnamon," he whispered before capturing her lips with his. He began a slow dance with the inside of her mouth, taking his time, enjoying the taste of her. The fact that his feelings for her were changing didn't mean hers were changing for him. He felt it was his duty to help her reach the conclusion. Slowly pulling away he captured her bottom lip between his lips then sucked and rolled his tongue across the smooth skin.

Lord, knows she needed to pull away, but he felt so good, so right. There with one arm around her, he was claiming her as his. No, her mind screamed and she pulled away. She felt the loss immediately. "Samuel," she shook her head. "we can't. I'm committed to LaVere'."

Making sure the boxes were secure he walked over to her. "Are you?" With his finger he lifted he chin to look into her eyes. When she opened them, he saw uncertainty. Realizing she was not ready he stepped back.

"Do you believe in the power of prayer?" he asked almost in a whisper.

Not sure why he asked the question, "Yes" she answered with beautiful wide eyes.

"I believe my prayer was answered on a snowy night just about a month ago."

Staring at him she could not believe how sure she was at that moment that her prayer was also answered. What confused her was which one was the answer, Samuel or LaVere'. In the past she had made one bad decision after another. She wanted to change that record. "We crossed a line Samuel and we have to step back." She turned away from him and picked up her shoes. Praying her body would stop trembling she stood once her shoes were on and surveyed the man standing before her. The man should be arrested for stealing someone else's manhood. She was sure it had to be against the law for any one man to look so totally manly. There was nothing about him that hinted at having a doubt about who he was and what he wanted. And from the look in his eye, she was on that list. No woman would ever go lacking with him as her man—that she was sure of. "If you don't stop looking at me like that I am going to give up my vow of celibacy." That's when she saw it; a smile that lit up the basement. He took a step toward her, "Stop, stop damn it. Don't come near me." She raised her hand. "I have made too many mistakes in my life and I don't want to make another one." She took a step back to give herself the space she needed to send him away. "I don't know where I'm supposed to be. A few weeks ago, I had no one in my life. Now there are two of you." She shook her head. "I know there's this sexual attraction between us. I've felt it for a while, but. I'm committed to making things work with LaVere'. With LaVere', I know what and who he is. I know what he wants from me."

Samuel slipped his hands into his pocket and nodded. "Okay, I'll wait.'

"Wait for what?"

He walked over to her and looked intently into her eyes. "Until you realize everything you want you will find in me." He inhaled and looked around the room. "Are you finished down here?

"Samuel,"

"You made your point. The conversation is over. I want you to do what feels right for you. Not me, not the prince and not your mother. But for you." He reached out to her, "Now, let's go upstairs. You're not safe down here by yourself."

Tucker sat in his office looking at the two people sitting in front of him. One was rambling to explain why he felt he had to shoot the Eagle. The other sat quietly shaking her head at the fool. "Now instead of one assignment we have three." Ryan stated.

"What the hell you talking about three. I got rid of an enemy. Huh, that one won't bother us anymore. That's for damn sure."

Sighing in frustration, Ryan looked at the fool. "Did it ever occur to you, that they would just send another person to handle the hit? The person doing the hit is not the one we want to bring now. We need the man at the top who ordered the hit. Now, we not only have to still bring down the man at the top, but the new hit man, and make no mistake there will be a new one, retaliation from the Eagles, the police and oh yes, keeping your dumb ass out of jail for murder."

"Where's the weapon?" Tucker asked.

"I broke it down, melted the pieces and distributed the contents in different lakes," Ryan explained.

"You hear that shit man, she ruined a perfectly good gun."

"She saved your neck, is what she did. That perfectly good gun is the only thing that could connect you to the murder."

"Ryan, you're working solo on this from here out. Tell them a professional is being brought in. He turned to the man sitting next to her. "Go anywhere near this situation and I will kill you myself."

Jamal sat patiently with his notepad and pen, waiting for LaVere's response to the report he had given. He was certain this would end the ridiculous notion about marrying this American woman. During their brief visit home, the King made his position on this matter clear, not only to LaVere', but to him as well. Unfortunately, LaVere' insisted that he alone would make the decision on whom he decided to marry. Jamal shook inwardly at the look the King gave LaVere'. It was good that Queen Nasheema was present. She kept the family discussion civil and did not allow the King nor LaVere's temper to get the best of them. "Shall I send your regrets for this evening?" He asked while beginning the note to the Thornton family. Cancelling this dinner would be a pleasant task for him. In his opinion the woman had no shame and was totally disrespectful of the prince's status.

While the report troubled him, it was not a reason to deter from his original plan. LaVere' knew his family would not be pleased with his decision. Their reaction was exactly what he anticipated. His father would be against it, Aswan, the successor to the throne would follow his father's lead, Raheem, the next in line would only want to know if she was beautiful, his sister, ZsaZsa would be elated at the prospects of having another female in the home and his mother would simply want his happiness. What seemed to bother him more was Jamal's betrayal. "Why did you bring a private investigator into this situation?" LaVere' asked the question as humanely as his temper would allow.

Taken back by his question, Jamal simply stared at him dumbfounded. "Your Highness, surely you can see that this is a common woman and is not worthy of you. It is my duty not only to my King, but to my country as well to protect them from your immature decisions."

Unable to remain seated, LaVere' stood and walked around to the front of the desk where Jamal sat. "You dare to question my loyalty to my country!" he roared.

"He did, my son. I clearly heard it as I came down the corridor," Nasheema smiled brightly. She walked over and kissed the shocked LaVere' on the cheek. "Good morning, my darling. I thought you may need your mother." She looked at Jamal with questioning eyes. "I can see I was right. Hello Jamal. It appears you have been the cause of disaccord within my family. Certainly you know that displeases me."

"Mother, when did you get here?" LaVere' asked pulling her attention away from Jamal.

"We just arrived. Edmund is showing ZsaZsa to a room as we speak."

"I am pleased to see you, however I am sure father is not happy," he smiled. "Come, have a seat. You look beautiful as always." As she sat, LaVere' turned to Jamal, "We will complete this discussion at a later time. For now you are dismissed."

Jamal stood to leave just as ZsaZsa floated into the room. "Jamal thank you so much for upsetting mother. I could never find a good reason to give father to allow me to come back to America, and you supplied me with it. Mother was so upset when you faxed that report to father that she wanted to come here and reprimand you personally. In fact that's all she talked about on the flight over." She turned from Jamal and ran into LaVere" arms. "Hello again, my unswerving brother. Boy is father upset with you, for pulling mother away. She was so angry at his reaction to Jamal's report that she immediately packed her bags to come and see what all the fuss was about. To this moment, I'm not sure she even knew I was on the plane with her."

LaVere' began to laugh. There was never a dull moment when ZsaZsa was around. She was a ball of energy at the sweet age of seventeen. He hugged her and enjoyed her giggles as he sat her back down on her feet. "I'm glad you are here. Leave it to you to put a full spin on all that has happen in the last two days."

She smiled, "Oh well, anything I can do to help you out. So where is she?"

"ZsaZsa please, give us a moment before you say anything more." Nasheema exhaled. Her daughter was the light of her eyes and she loved her dearly, but her energy sometimes was quiet overwhelming. She looked at LaVere'; "This is what happens when you have a child late in life. However, she is correct I came here to speak to you in person Jamal. So before you leave, I am going to have my say." She stood and walked over to him. "I do not allow anyone to come between the king and I, but you have. What possessed you to fax that report to Ahmed? You knew the harm it would cause LaVere's intentions. Have you forgotten your duty? You are his secretary. Your duty is to him first. My son's life was entrusted to you and this is how you protect him, by betraying his trust in you. I don't know what the game is you are playing, but you will not disrupt my family again. I took the liberty of contacting your mother. She is expecting a correspondence from you explaining your actions. Just so you know, I expressed my disappointment in you in no uncertain terms, and it is my wish that you be relieved of your duties immediately. But, since your family has been loyal servants to us for many decades, I'm hesitant to take that step at this moment. However, rest assured, given another opportunity and I will make certain that neither you nor any other member of your family serve the royal court again. Are there any questions?"

If he would not face being beheaded, Jamal could have slapped the woman for contacting his mother. The position his family has was one of honor and respect. He was a descendant of a long line of secretaries that has served the royal families. If he is relieved of his duties it would bring dishonor to his family. How dare she contact his mother on this issue? For a moment he thought to tell her he was only following the King's orders, but he thought better of it. He was certain if anything was to happen the King would protect him.

For a fleeting moment LaVere' felt for Jamal, however, that faded the moment he realized the same report he had just given him, was sent to his father earlier. "Jamal, the Queen is being very lenient on this matter, but I am not. As of this moment you are relieved of your duties. I will not formally dismiss you, but you will be reassigned. I cannot have someone on my staff that I cannot trust."

"LaVere'," Nasheema turned, "I promised his mother we would not take such actions. I know you have every say in this matter, however I ask you to please reconsider."

"Your Highness, my actions were to protect you. I may have overstepped my bounds."

"May have?" LaVere' questioned.

Jamal cleared his throat, "I overstepped my boundaries in an overzealous attempt to protect you. I assure you, it will not happen again."

Against his better judgment LaVere' conceded. "This is the only warning Jamal. Your actions will not go unpunished, you may leave now."

Jamal nodded, "Your Highness," and left the room.

ZsaZsa looked at her brother, "I don't know about you, but I did not believe one word of what he said."

LaVere' looked at his mother and smiled, "You've taught her well."

Her parent's home was in a whirlwind when Cynthia walked in. It was literally the first time she had been in the house since she moved out almost eight years ago. During that time it was not a gated community like it was now. But there was no denying the majestic feel of the house. The high cathedral like ceilings in the foyer to the, floor to ceiling windows with the regal drapery, to the marble floors that never seem to have a dull spot, it was her mini castle and she loved her home, when it was home. Looking in her rearview mirror she saw Samuel park behind her. *How do I explain him?* She sighed, got out of her car and approached him. "If anyone asks would you simply say you're here to assist with the media?"

"I could," he replied politely.

"Thank you," she said and turned to walk in the house. When he did not follow, she turned back and stared at him, "Aren't you coming inside?"

"I'll be fine here."

"It's cold out here and wouldn't you like some dinner?"

He smiled at her thoughtfulness. "Maybe later."

"Okay, I'll check back with you."

Memories of her childhood flooded her mind as she walked through the mudroom. Her memories were interrupted by the crash of glass and raised voices. She followed the sound. "Ah, Sofia at her finest," her father smiled as he walked into the kitchen behind her. "What she doesn't seem to understand is if she would only get out of the way, the people she pays good money to will be able to do their jobs."

"Jackson, don't you need to finish dressing?" Sofia raised a warning eyebrow.

Jackson looked down at his dress slacks and crisp collared shirt then back up at his wife. "I am dressed, for goodness sake, it is only LaVere', not the King himself."

"No," Sofia replied. "But the Queen will be here. Now go upstairs and finish dressing."

"What?" Cynthia exploded

"Yes sweetie. LaVere' just called. His mother and sister will be joining us for dinner. I of course told him that was not an issue, when in fact it is."

Cynthia heard Sofia rumbling on about something, but had lost interest. LaVere's mother was coming to dinner. This will be the first time she has met a man's mother. She shook her head, women tend not to like her. Most times, it was due to her bluntness, so she was going to have to control that for the evening. "Cynthia? Cynthia." She looked up; it seemed her mother was calling her. "Don't just stand there like a lost child, go upstairs and change."

"Change? What's wrong with what I have on?"

Exasperated Sofia walked over to her daughter. "You are your father's child. This is your future mother in law, who just happens to be a queen. You cannot meet her in that getup you have on." She examined her daughter, "While you're at it, put your hair up. You always looked like a princess with a few strands cascading around your face." She smiled, then slapped her hands, "Okay, hurry now, you have less than an hour before they arrive."

Precisely one hour later the buzzer from the front gate sounded throughout the house. Cynthia looked at herself one last time in the mirror and smiled. Her mother had selected a simple a-line black evening dress with a curved neckline, which contrasted against a low v-shape in the back. It was what some would call sexy elegant and it looked good on her. Sheer stockings and black pumps rounded out the outfit. No jewelry with the exception of diamond studs in her ears. Her hair, as her mother suggested, was pinned up with a few strands dangling around her face. Before leaving her room she looked out the window to see Samuel standing out by the gate talking to several other men. This was the right thing to do. LaVere' will be good for her. With her mind made up she took one last look in the mirror then left the room. She was walking down the staircase when her mother stopped her progression from below. "Don't you dare! Go back upstairs until I call you down. An entrance is everything."

Cynthia looked at her mother and exhaled. Turning she mumbled, "Have she forgotten that I'm twenty-eight years old and not a child."

"Apparently you have, since you are following her instructions." Blake laughed when she reached the top of the stairs. Cynthia rolled her eyes at him. "Hey, don't get mad at me, I'm twenty-one and she still does it to me too."

"How do you put up with her controlling nature?"

"You are the one that desperately wanted her attention. Well, you got it. I'm just thankful it's on you for a while and not me. I can actually breathe for a minute."

"I'm happy I could accommodate you. Now will you do something to get the attention back, please?"

He kissed his sister's cheek, "You look good."

She smiled, "It's in the genes."

"Cynthia," her mother purred sweetly, "LaVere' is here, dear."

Blake smirked, "You're on."

Cynthia poked her tongue out at him. "I'm coming mother," she replied.

She was walking down the stairs when Blake whispered, "I bet odds you will not make it through dinner without going off on her."

"Shh," Cynthia replied looking back at him.

As she came down the staircase, all agreed, she was beautiful. She looked the part of a princess even though she wasn't. Nasheema smiled as she watched her son beaming at the woman walking towards them. At the bottom step LaVere' reached out, captured her hands in his, and kissed her gently on the lips. "You look wonderful," he smiled.

"A small attempt to keep up with you," she whispered back.

"Cynthia, this is my mother, Queen Nasheema Farad Ashro and my sister Princess ZsaZsa Adannaya Ashro.

Pleasing her mother more than she could have imagined, Cynthia curtsy briefly then took the woman's extended hand.

"It is a pleasure to meet you Queen Ashro and Princess ZsaZsa, what a wonderful name," she smiled.

"Believe me, the pleasure is mine," Nasheema smiled. "Please Nasheema is fine. I always hoped my sons had impeccable taste, LaVere', has proven it. You are beautiful."

Cynthia smiled at the compliment as if she had never heard it before. "Thank you," she said as her mother and father looked on.

"I've set up the solarium for us to sit and talk before dinner. It's right this way," Sofia smiled and led the way.

Cynthia took LaVere's arm. "May we talk in private for a moment?"

He smiled at her, "Of course."

"Mother we will join you all shortly," Cynthia announced as she took LaVere' into her father's study. On her way home from Ashley's house she decided to be open with him about the events of the night before. If she was going to fully commit to this man, she was not going to keep secrets from him. Besides, she was sure there will be many occasions when she will do things he will not agree with. Now was as good of time as any to find out what his reactions would be.

Once they were alone inside the room, the conversation did not come as easily as Cynthia had hoped. She found she was nervous. What LaVere' thought of her was important and she knew her actions last night was not going to please him. She smiled as he stood near the window looking like the prince he was. It would be quiet easy to wake up to him every morning. He was a handsome man, very thoughtful and extremely generous, she thought as she began to speak. "I need to tell you about last night. This is going to be a little difficult for me, so please let me get it out before you say anything. Would you like to have a seat?"

It was clear whatever she wanted to say was making her very nervous, LaVere' thought as he watched her. He smiled, that indicates she at least care a little about him. If she didn't she would simply say what was needed and be done with it. "Alright," he exhaled and sat in the leather chair near the window, crossed his legs and listened.

Cynthia began to pace in front of him and told him everything about the previous night, including the kiss. For some reason she felt she had to protect Samuel. So she did not tell him it was Samuel. "I'm not a deceitful person LaVere'. Before we went any further, I needed to tell you about this. I don't think there is a place for secrets in a relationship." She stopped and waited for his reaction. And frankly she had no idea how he was going to take the information. But there it was.

He listened, but more importantly he watched her as she talked. The thought of her in another man's arms was distracting to say the least. But the fact that she told him the circumstances meant the world to him. He liked her honesty, but most of all he liked the fact that the events of the night before disturbed her enough to confide in him. What he adored was how she was now standing in front of him with a look of wonder on her face. She really did not know what to expect from him, but that did not stop her from being honest. He stood and walked over to her. She was posed for a fight, with hands on hips and a look that said, "Bring it on." Standing so close that he could kiss her without taking another step, LaVere' looked into her eyes. "Do you have feelings for this man?"

"I don't really know him."

"Hmm, what about Gavin, do you have feelings for him?"

"Of course I do. Our relationship meant a lot to him and to me. We will always be friends, regardless of how much of an ass he can be sometimes," she pouted and lowered her head a little.

LaVere' smiled and placed a finger under her chin to look into her eyes. "What about Brian?"

"Brian?" she frowned. "Brian is everyone's protector. He is the big brother I never had."

He smiled and allowed his competitiveness to get the best of him. "Do you plan to pursue this man?"

She was honest, but she wasn't a fool. There was no need to tell him the man was Samuel. "No."

"And if he seeks you out, what will you do."

"There is no reason for him to seek me out or vice versa. It was a kiss, that's all."

He leaned forward and gently kissed her lips, "Was it a kiss like this?"

The gentle, sweet kiss made her smile. She reached out and encircled his waist. "No, it was more like this." She tilted her head and pressed her lips against his forcing his lips to part. The kiss was filled with passion as he placed his arms around her to pull her closer. It was not long before he took over the controls and when it ended, it was clear to both there was some chemistry between them. *But not like Samuel,* her mind protested. *Stop that,* her brain replied.

"It was like that, hmm." He said as he held her and continued to kiss the side of her mouth. He looked at her, "Should I be concerned?"

"I don't think so." She laughed nervously enjoying his kisses as they continued down her neck. When she felt his body begin to respond to their closeness she started to pull away, but hesitated. If she was going to commit to this man, now was the time. She pressed her body even closer to his. His hands began to roam over her body as did hers. He returned to her lips and had just begun to deepen the kiss when a knock occurred and the door swung opened.

"Umm humm," They both turn their heads towards the opened door, but never released each other. "Your mother would like for the two of you to join us in the solarium," her father stated.

"It's a sunroom daddy," Cynthia beamed at him.

"Well to your mother it's a solarium."

LaVere' smiled at Cynthia, "Please tell her we will be there momentarily."

"Will do," her father said and closed the door.

"Thank you for telling me about last night." LaVere' smiled as he held her. "I realize you did not have to share that with me. You are a very beautiful woman. Men are going to be attracted to you. I am a very possessive man. Once you commit to me, you are mine and I don't like to share. I will allow you time to make sure I am the man you chose to be with." He ran a finger down her cheek. "Knowing that, would you make me one promise?"

"Anything," she smiled.

"If at any point you believe you have feelings for someone else, would you tell me first?"

She brushed a kiss across his lips. "I promise."

"Good. Now, let's go and see if ZsaZsa has talked everyone's head off."

On the ride home from the dinner Nasheema turned to her son. "I like your Cynthia; she is a breath of fresh air. Though I would be leery of this meal she plans to prepare for you with her own hands. Even her brother nearly choked at that announcement." They all laughed. "But, I must be honest son. I don't believe she would be happy in Emure. I believe our customs would suffocate her."

"I like her too LaVere'. She didn't treat me like a little girl and her brother—oh he is to die for. Do you think I could see some of his movies before we go home?"

LaVere' smiled at his little sister and realized, she really was not that little anymore. He was certain she was going to break some man's heart. "I'm sure I have one or two of them at the house you can see." He smiled. "I know she is very unconventional, that's what I like about her."

"There is chemistry between the two of you. But I don't see love. Do you love her LaVere'?"

"I could very easily love her."

Nasheema smiled, "What you are going to be asking her to do is going to take more than I could. It is going to take I love her beyond belief. You will be asking her to come into a hostile situation. It is going to take unbelievable patience on your part to help her through what our people will subject her too. Your father's and Jamal's reactions will be mild in comparison. Although, I believe your Cynthia could stand up to anyone she chose. She is a tough little lady."

"Yes, she is. But she cannot stand up to her mother."

Nasheema smirked, "Well, her mother is a very arrogant woman. She is determined to see her daughter marry well, whether it's you or not does not matter to her. Cynthia, on the other hand is looking to be loved. Can you do that LaVere'? Can you love her the way your father loves me? You don't have to answer to me. However, before you ask this woman to turn her back on her family and her country, you need to answer that question for yourself. Whatever you decide, you have my love and support."

The depth of his mothers' knowledge always amazed him. Even as a male child, he realized early in life that she was not just the woman his father married. There was a mutual respect between the two. He wanted a wife that would be his equal, just as his mother is with his father. He believed Cynthia could be that woman. Love may not be there at this moment, but time can change that. He leaned over and kissed his mothers' cheek, "Thank you for the unsolicited advice. I will take all that you have said under advisement."

"That's all I ask. In the meantime keep Jamal out of your relationship with her and for goodness sake watch him at all times. I'm not sure your father's trust in him is wise."

LaVere' nodded in agreement. "I have turned over most of his duties to Edmund. As soon as I can find a way to release him without hindering his family, he will be returned to Emure."

It was a difficult decision, but Cynthia believed she had
followed Samuel's advice and did what was best for her.
LaVere' was happy, her mother was happy and she was
happy. Then why did Samuel seeming so detached from her
displease her when they arrived back at her place.

"How did meeting the potential in-laws go?" He asked.
He could see she was uncomfortable around him.

"His mother and sister are very nice people. You would
actually love his little sister Zsa Zsa. She's very spirited and
full of life."

"She sounds like my little sister Phire."

"Phire?"

"It's short for Sapphire." The uncomfortable silence
continued. "You know your safety is my number one
concern. Everything else is secondary. What transpired
between us yesterday has you uncomfortable. And I don't
like that." She started to say something than stopped. "I'll get
Brian to take over. He won't know the reason why."

"I realize it didn't start this way, but in the last few weeks
you have become my savior. I depend on you for my safety
and sanity."

"I promised you I wouldn't leave and I'm not. You won't
see me, but I will be around and I won't let anything happen
to you. Do you believe me?"

"Yes, I do."

"Then whenever you need me just call."

Tears began to form in her eyes. She walked over and
put her arms around his waist. "Please stay my friend."

He hugged her and kissed the top of her head, "I will."
He exhaled, "Want some friendly advice?"

She looked up at him expectantly, "Yes."

"LaVere' is a sensible man. If this is what you want for
your life give him an opportunity to explain things for
himself. His servant stepped out of line when he told you

those things the other day. From what I heard today, I'm sure his days with LaVere' are numbered. I've met the King; he is a very reasonable man. He loves his family, but loves his country more. However, if he believed LaVere' was in love with you he would not object to the marriage." He pulled away, "It is my belief that you should only marry someone because that person makes the world right for you. No other reason. Not to progress a country, not to strengthen a family, not for any other reason than, that person makes the world right—just for you. Anything less than that you are short changing yourself." The words were spoken so sincerely, that they brought tears to her eyes. Suddenly his leaving was disturbing to her. He pulled out a card and a pen. Turning the card over he wrote down several numbers. "There will be several people with you at all times. You will not see them, but they will be there. If you need to talk, for any reason, give me a call." He turned to walk downstairs.

"You are a good man, Samuel Lassiter," she smiled.

The smiled was breathtaking. He wondered what in her life made her feel less than worthy of the very best. "Everyone deserves a life of love and happiness. A marriage of connivance does not grant either." He looked at her one last time, "Get some rest."

"I will," she said. She knew come morning he and Rusty would be gone.

It was time for Munford to know all the players in this game and Samuel was more than happy to oblige. If he was in Munford shoes the first thing he would do was eliminate a threat. Based on the information received, Gavin, Day and Cynthia would be on that list. He had to protect her.

Samuel sat back in the plush leather chair that was in the Chief of Police office as he took stock of his surroundings.

It was important to know all you could about the enemy. He looked at the pictures and awards on the wall, making a mental note of each organization named as the presenter. If he was going to play this game he had to know what was important to this man. The first thing to pop out was the many pictures of his daughter. Several were in ballerina outfits when she was younger and several in theatrical outfits as she became older. There was only one picture of the wife sitting on his desk. All of the pictures taken with different dignitaries included Wanda Jacobs, an administrative assistant in the department. "Hum," he sat in the seat behind the desk and waited.

Samuel heard Munford insert his key to come into his office. He turned the chair away from the door towards the window as the unsuspecting man entered. Munford was placing his briefcase on the desk when Samuel turned in the chair. "Good Morning Chief."

Startled the man who stood five ten and weight about two hundred and forty pounds went to pull his weapon. "Who in the hell are you?"

Showing no emotion, Samuel stared at the man who was now pointing his gun at him. "You don't know me Chief but I'm here to give you a heads up," he said as he slowly stood.

Munford sized the man up. He had to be at least six-six, two hundred ten solid pounds and he looked familiar. "I don't know you. You are an intruder in the Chief of Police office. Shooting you would be justified."

Samuel walked slowly around the desk as the Chief took a step back, "Then you would have to explain why a CIA operative was killed in your office.

"Only if they find your body, you see I believe in shooting first, asking questions later."

"Then shoot."

"You're a cocky mother-----I'm the one with the gun."

"What does that tell you Chief? You've dealt with people like me that don't give a damn about much of anything. The fact that you are holding the gun, in my estimation of things really means nothing. My presence here is to keep Cynthia Thornton alive without killing you. But just to be clear I don't have a problem killing you here and now, but it just so much red tape I would have to go through explaining you away. It can be a pain in the ass and who needs that aggravation."

Confused, the Chief frowned and shrugged his shoulders, "Who in the hell are you?"

Samuel took advantage of the confusion, in a split of a second he kicked the gun out of the chief's hand, knocked him to the floor and placed his booted foot in the man's throat.

"My name is Samuel Lassiter, that's two s's. I just happen to be the antagonist in the sad story of your life. As any good antagonist it has become my mission to make your life a living nightmare. Unlike others you have an opportunity to alter the ending to your story." Applying more pressure on the man's throat he bent down and leaned against his knee. He could see the color draining from the man's lily white skin. "Take Cynthia Thornton off your hit list. I'm going to let you up now. But I have to tell you this is the only warning you will get."

Samuel stood and extended his hand. Once he was standing Samuel adjusted the Chief's suit jacket and smiled. He could see the anger in his eyes. "If an accident, drive by, or any type of gang violence is in any way connected to a harmed strand of hair on Cynthia Thornton's head I will kill the person I believe to be responsible." He turned and walked out the door.

The moment Samuel walked out of the office Munford slammed his fist on the desk. "Damn," he walked over to his window as his chair rolled backwards from the action. The life he built for himself was beginning to unravel, he could feel it. Since JD Harrison came into the picture, Gavin had grown a conscience and was not as accommodating as he had been in the past. At one time, Gavin just looked the other way. Now, it had become increasingly difficult for him to get Gavin to follow his wishes. He thought telling him about James Harrison death, would let him know how far he would go to get what he wanted. But Gavin threaten to take him down. Now, he had Lassiter threatening him. He was getting sloppy. It was time to take a step back and tighten things up again. Then he would resume taking control of every aspect of city government. The Chief sat down at his desk, "What could he do that would affect both Gavin and Lassiter?" After thinking for a moment, a cynical grin appeared on his face. He buzzed his secretary. "Get Sanchez in here now. Then pull everything we have on a Samuel Lassiter." He sat back, who in the hell was this man that was bold enough to break into his office and threaten him. Didn't he know who he was? He was the most powerful man in Richmond, not Harrison and damn sure not Roberts, he was. If Lassiter didn't know that, he was about to learn it fast.

Chapter 12

Things with LaVere' and Cynthia had settled into a very comfortable routine. Their evenings together were spent usually at his estate in Hanover, which was about thirty minutes away down interstate 95. The best part of Cynthia was, she was no longer the third wheel, and that was worth her weight in gold. The only thing that seemed out of place was LaVere's Secretary, Jamal. He made her keenly aware that he did not care for her at all. Hell that was nothing new for her; she dealt with that all her life. There were times when LaVere' was not around that he made comments she did not appreciate and she let him know it in no uncertain terms. Once, he told her, "In my country you would be whipped into silence." Cynthia replied, "In my country I will shoot your ass if you put a hand on me," and walked away. There was another instance during the week when she heard him talking to someone on the telephone about LaVere' and his affections towards her. When he hung up, she asked him who he was talking to. He had a snide smile and walked past her without answering. She did not mention it to LaVere' because she felt if she was going to be a part of his life, she would have to learn to fend for herself in situations such as this. All in all things were good, but she did miss Samuel.

The past week her mother had talked with her every day, just to gage the progress with LaVere'. She was very pleased with the reports and offered advice when she felt it was needed. The transformation of her mother was amazing, now that Cynthia was doing something she wanted. Her mother actually told her she was proud of the way she was handling herself with LaVere'.

Now she prayed this meal she planned for him would score a few more points. When she and Rosaline shopped for the Policeman's Ball scheduled for the next day, they also pickup all the ingredients for her home cooked dinner for LaVere'. Surprisingly she was actually excited about the evening. Normally she would simply make a call and have the entire meal catered, but this one she was going to do with her own two hands. Of course she will receive step by step instructions from Roz, but hey, it's her first step.

The telephone rang as she walked into the kitchen, it was Marco. Roz sprained her ankle coming down the stairs and was ordered off her feet for the next twenty-four hours. Things for the ball were set, but she would not make it over to help with dinner for LaVere'. She talked to Roz for a few moments just to ensure she was okay and things for the ball were stable. But then when she hung up the telephone she realized her hopes for the evening were ruined. Desperate, Cynthia wasn't sure what to do and was about to give in and make a call to have the dinner delivered, when she heard the garage door open and Rusty's bark. She ran to the stairs and looked over the banister. Sure enough Samuel was walking up looking at her. It had only been a week, but she missed him being around. Between Brian and Magna, she was well protected, but it wasn't the same as having him around.

"Brian asked me to step in today, he has to leave town with JD and Magna is covering Tracy," he explained.

"It's okay," she said happy to see him. Rusty walked over to her and she bent down to hug him, "I've missed you boy," she heartily rubbed his back. She stood and looked at Samuel, "How have you been?"

"Good." He replied standing in the doorway of the kitchen. "What about you?"

"Things have been quiet. LaVere' and I have been spending a lot of time together. You know getting to know each other."

"And how is that going?" he smiled taking a seat at the breakfast bar, just enjoying being in her presence again.

"Good."

Silence filled the air as they just smiled at each other. "So, what's happening here?" He asked looking at the different things out on the counter top that was normally spotless.

"Well, I was suppose to prepare a home cooked meal for LaVere' tonight, but Roz sprained her ankle and can't make it. So I might have to cancel."

"You're trying to back out of your bet Roz." He joked.

"No, I was really excited about cooking for him, but with no instructions, I don't know."

"I'll help."

A light of excitement filled her eyes. "Really?"

"I promised I would remember."

Looking at him with a doubtful eye, "You'll help me cook a meal for LaVere'?"

Understanding her concern he stood and took off his jacket. "I wouldn't want you to cause an international incident by poisoning the Prince."

"Ha Ha, very funny."

"I thought so. What's on the menu?"

"Nothing major just prime rib roast with potatoes au gratin, broccoli and cauliflower."

"Sound simple enough."

"Well alright Mr. I know my way around the kitchen."

"Don't get it twisted. You're cooking, I'm just here to instruct."

It was Friday and after being in hiding for over a week while her bruises healed, Carolyn had things she needed to handle. Chief Wilbert Munford was first on her list. He has taken his blackmail efforts to the next level. An enveloped was delivered to her with pictures of Gavin and the wench, Cynthia Thornton with a note indicating the next installment would be sent to the news media. It wasn't clear if the pictures were meant to infuriate her, or threaten Gavin into conceding to his wishes. Either way it wasn't going to work. Gavin will never see the pictures or the note. They were going in her father's safe. While she was there, she might as well check out the mortgage papers to see if what the ghetto-queen said has any merit. Then she will take steps to protect her husband from Munford.

Carolyn knew her father and the witch would be out of town for the weekend. It was easy enough to get the code to the house. All she had to do was call the security company, give her name and they gave her the codes along with the passwords. This was the perfect opportunity for her to read the mortgage papers to see if her father really had lost his mind and put her step-mother's name on the house. She had to believe he would not give the only stable home she had ever known to that witch.

Standing in the foyer of the house she thought, where should she look first, the office safe or the bedroom? Since it had to do with the witch she turned and walked up the winding staircase to her father's bedroom. Walking through the sitting area of the bedroom, it was apparent that Lena had made some changes to the room. Shrugging her shoulder, Carolyn noticed no expense was spared on the new furnishings. "There was no accounting for taste," she thought as she past the fringy bedcovering. She turned to go into the expansive walk in closet when she suddenly stopped with her mouth gapped wide open. "No she didn't", she exclaimed as she came face to face with a stripper pole in the middle of her father's bedroom. She simply stared at the contraption for the longest time before she was able to move. Once she did she still had to look back several times to make sure that she did not imagine it. As hard as she tried she could not shake the mental picture the pole was creating. Shaking her head, "I have to get the hell out of here."

Walking in the closet she went to the very back wall which housed the shoes section. Applying pressure to the middle case, she stepped back and allowed the two selves to slide apart. She smiled as the safe appeared and prayed her father had not changed the code. She keyed in the code as she remembered it and then put her thumb on the keypad, the door clicked open. Pleased, she pulled out the bottom draw and took out the envelope that the mortgage papers were stored in. She began opening the brown envelope when another envelope at the bottom of the drawer caught her attention. She didn't remember anything being in that drawer. Picking up the envelope she noticed the outside indicated it came from a medical facility. In fact, it had her father's private doctor's name on the outside. Suddenly, she felt sick at her stomach. Her heart race increased and her palms became sweaty. Could something be medically wrong with her father? At first she thought to put the envelope back. If something was wrong with him medically, surely he would have told her—wouldn't he?

Standing there, stunned she was afraid to open it, but just as afraid not to. She put the mortgage envelope down, closed her eyes and said a prayer asking GOD to please let her father be well. Don't let it be cancer or Alzheimer's or worst. Then her eyes grew as big as a saucer, could that ghetto ho he married have given him AIDS. Now it was anger that began to consume her as she opened the envelope and pulled out the papers, "GOD please let him be hea---"the thought lingered as she read. "Establishment of Paternity," she read with confusion and wonder. "Paternity on who?" she continued to read. The findings confirmed specimen A is not the biological father of said child. The findings confirmed specimen B is, with 99.9% certainty the biological father of said child. "Who in the hell is specimen A?" she read on. Child in question: Tracy Alexandria Washington: Specimen A: William Alexander Washington: Specimen B: John Stephen Roth. Carolyn dropped the papers to the floor and slide down the wall until she reached the floor. She stared at the papers lying before her for a long while. There had to be some mistake. Picking the papers up again she looked to see the date on them. The test was taken a little over two years ago. Thinking back, that was before JD and Tracy were married or before Lena married her father. "That's it. This is the lie she used to get my father to marry her." She exhaled. "Daddy," she laughed silently. "You had me there for a minute." She stood, taking a moment to regroup. Beginning to understand all that had transpired over the last year Carolyn began to shake her head. "That woman would stoop that low to use her own daughter to get a husband." Putting the papers back into the envelope, she then opened the mortgage papers; sure enough there was Lena's name on there just as she had said. The woman was making a total fool out of her father and she was not going to allow it to continue. "Don't you worry daddy, I will have her charged with fraud before this is over with. She is going to wish she never heard the name Roth, when I'm through with her." Putting everything back in place, Carolyn closed the safe, pushed the button on the keypad and the shoe shelves slide back into place. Walking out of the closet, she stopped at the stripper pole, "You won't be here long," she said to the inanimate object and walked out to the room.

Chapter 13

With Roz on the telephone and Samuel in the kitchen with her, Cynthia was able to prepare a meal fit for a king—well in this case a prince. Samuel watched as she proudly placed the meat in the oven and closed the door.

He sat back in the chair at the breakfast bar with his arms crossed over his chest. It was good to see her accomplish this task. It was clear she was trying hard to impress the prince by cooking for him. Inside he was seething. The reason was confusing even to him. On the surface he felt it was because she was stepping outside of who she was to make an impression on the prince, who in his opinion should be willing to accept her for who she was. As a deeper thought filled his mind, he realized she really wanted this thing with the prince to work. She wanted to be accepted by the royal family and prove Jamal was wrong about her. Where did that leave him? The more time he spent around her the more he understood her. She wasn't the person his sister Pearl made her out to be. Nor was she the DIVA her friends thought she was.

"Well, let's see," she said looking around, "the wine is chilling, the table is set, the food is in the oven. Now, I just have to clean this kitchen."

"If you are anything like my sisters you have a date ritual. Why don't you get started on that while I take care of the kitchen?

Shaking her head, "I can't ask you to do that after you helped me prepare the meal."

"You didn't ask, I offered," he stood and walked around the counter and took the oven mitts off her hands. "Go make yourself gorgeous."

Smiling up at him, she shook her head; he was such a gentleman. His size and that frown on constant display is a contrast to the man he truly was. Unable to resist, she teased, by pushing her hair over her shoulders and saying, "I'm already gorgeous. I just need a minute to become irresistible." His eyes rolled up towards the heavens as he grunted. She sashayed out of the room laughing at his expression.

As Samuel cleaned the kitchen he thought more about the façade this woman known as *The Diva*, put's on. To her friends she is fiercely loyal--would put herself on the line for anyone of them. He thought about a night she threatened to beat a woman down for stepping between Tracy and JD. As for her brother, Blake, she acted as the protective older sister making sure his privacy was honored at all cost because she knew how valuable it was to him. The excuses she puts in place to protect her father's reputation when people speak badly about him not stopping her mother from moving the family and leaving her to fend for herself when she was only nineteen. Even defending her mother and doing all she could to please her by making this relationship with the prince workout. For some unknown reason she believes marrying the Prince will win her mother's love—a love that should have no conditions.

After finishing the kitchen, Samuel took a quick shower and changed into a suit with a silk tee shirt underneath. Since the prince was coming to dinner he wanted to be dressed appropriately so not to embarrass her. Now, standing in the living room, he lit the fireplace, giving the room a romantic aura.

He wasn't sure if it was a sound or he just sensed she was in the room, but something caused him to turn around. She was walking down the staircase with a stride that command attention. Every blood vessel within him began flowing profusely throughout his body causing his heart rate to jump.

Cynthia didn't know why but his reaction was important to her. This dress was purchased to dazzle LaVere', but Samuel's impression would let her know if she went overboard. As least that was what she was telling herself until she saw him rise to his full six-six height and began to silently caress her body with his eyes. His look rendered her speechless.

He was the first to recover with a curt nod of his head. "Well, if your intent was to be irresistibly alluring—mission accomplished."

A breathtaking smile appeared on her almost make-up free face as she came to the bottom of the steps and gave a compete turn for his viewing. "You like?" she asked while turning.

If the front of the flesh-toned dress was alluring, then the back was meant to drive a man insane, was his first thought. His second was, she could not be wearing anything under that dress. The third really worried him, he sincerely hoped he did not have to kill LaVere' tonight. "Is it too much?" she asked when he did not respond.

Realizing she was waiting for his response he attempted to answer, but then he noticed the bottom point of the diamond shape opening in the back of the dress stopped right at the curve of her full behind. He groaned inwardly and prayed she did not hear him. There was a single bow right below the nape of her neck that held the dress together—one single string and he was sure the entire dress would peel away from her luscious body. "If you are going for until death shall we part, that dress will do the trick."

"Thank you Samuel," she said as she turned and walked into the kitchen in her three-inch heel sandals that made her legs appear even longer under the knee length dress. "I'm going to take the meat out."

"Whew," he closed his eyes to try to gain some control over a certain part of his body that was raging out of control. "I already turned it down to simmer," he replied. *Just like I'm doing*, he thought.

As soon as she reached the kitchen the telephone rung. "I'll have to remember to turn this off. Nothing ruins a romantic evening like the ringing of a telephone." She joked as the answered the call. "Hello."

"Ms. Thornton, Prince LaVere' regrets he will not be available to meet with you this evening."

Frowning she asked, "Is he okay?"

"Why yes. Why wouldn't he be?" Jamal smirked.

Anger seeping through, she closed her eyes. "Let me speak with LaVere' Jamal."

"I'm afraid that is not possible at this time. Good night Ms. Thornton."

Cynthia frowned when she heard the dial tone. "You know I'm about sick of him." She hung up the telephone and dialed James number.

"Brooks' residence," Charles the butler answered.

Trying hard not to get upset, she sighed with relief. "Hello Charles. May I speak with James?"

"One moment."

The disappointment in her voice was very apparent. Only a few moments ago Samuel saw the pride beaming in her smile from her cooking accomplishments. Yet, here she was being dealt another blow. This one he had to admit he did not see it coming. The slump in her shoulders was a telling sign, she was defeated. "James, is everything okay with LaVere'?"

James exhaled before he replied. "He was summoned home by his father. It seemed word of his plans to marry an American has upset some fractions in his homeland."

"Why would that upset anyone?"

"There are some that feel the royal family should remain pure. His father is one of them."

"I see. Is his family safe?"

"I'm not certain Cynthia. Whatever is happening, LaVere' will handle it. Don't worry."

Cynthia wondered if it was the fact that she was American or her past that was causing the situation. "Thank you James," she sighed while hanging up the telephone.

She stood looking around the room. The dining room was breathtaking and the fire in the living room's fireplace set a very sensual ambiance to the room. Looking up at Samuel, who was leaning against the doorway, she smiled. "The fire is a nice touch, Thank you." Turning she walked over to the stove, took the meat out and turned the oven off. "Well it looks like we are going to have a lot of leftovers," she smiled. "You did a great job in here, but then again you always seem to know your way around a kitchen."

He watched and listened as she tried to play off the hurt and disappointment. She was walking around chattering about nothing as if she hadn't spent the day taking jabs from him and Roz about her cooking skills. Only to be disappointed by the Prince.

He walked over and placed his hands on the lower part of her back and gave her a little shove towards the dining room. "I think I would like to have dinner now."

Knowing what he was trying to do, she looked up at him shaking her head, "You don't have to do that.'

"Yes, I do. I'm hungry." The laugh was to relieve the tension he knew was there, but chose to ignore. "Hum, you're laughing and I'm serious. Here," he pulled the dining room chair out. "You sit your -*I look good enough to eat* self down. I'll bring the food over."

Once seated at the table the conversation was slow as he tried to draw her out. Eventually, like he knew would happen, she put a smile on her face covering the hurt, and began to relax. The conversation centered around his family mostly. When the laughter from his stories about growing up with a big family became real, he relaxed and just enjoyed the meal and her company.

"Shall we try the desert?" she asked with a genuine smile.

The smile radiated through him. He wanted to hold her and make things better. "Actually, I'd like to dance."

"Dance? You dance," she asked surprised.

Frowning at the jest, he stood, picked up the remote to the music system and hit the play button. Baby Face's Grown and Sexy began to play. He took her hand and swung her around as she stood. "Wow," she laughed. They danced a salsa to the smooth upbeat sound. The two merged into a sensual rhythm with each other, enjoying the easy way they fit. "You are surprisingly light on your feet Mr. Lassiter," Cynthia smiled as he twirled her and brought her back into his arms.

He dipped her and brought her back up to him. "In my profession I have to be quick and limber."

"Really, Please tell where did you learn the gracefulness?" She laughed at the appalled look he gave her.

"Football." Now he laughed at her look, and then brought her closer. "My mother is a dancer. Well she was until she gave it up for us."

The music changed to *Can't Stop Now*, "What type of dancer was she?" Cynthia asked as he smoothly fit her to him.

"Ballet"

Surprised she looked up at him, "She performed on stage"

Nodding he replied, "Broadway a few times."

The dazzling smile appeared. "Wow. My mother would be impressed." She placed her head on his chest.

"I doubt it. It doesn't seem a lot of things impress your mother, unless she's involved."

A soft giggle escaped, "You're beginning to know her so well."

"I know you put too much emphasis on trying to please her."

She stopped and looked up at him. Seeing it wasn't a criticism she put her head back down and continued to enjoy the warmth of his embrace. "Well, we humans try to get love where and however we can."

"It shouldn't be that hard, especially from your mother."

"We work with the cards we're dealt. I have a bad hand when it comes to people loving me."

He heard the despair in her voice and he did not like it. He stopped and looked down at her. "All one has to do is take the time to overlook the rough outer persona you have created as a defense mechanism and look into those amazingly beautiful hazel eyes to see your heart. Then they will know the person inside is a caring and unselfish woman who is just as beautiful as her exterior."

Surprised she looked up at him. "Do you see that Samuel? Can you see my heart?"

Their bodies stopped moving, as they stood in the middle of the floor staring into each other eyes. The tempo of the music, the crackling of the fire and the beat of their hearts touching breast to chest, stir every emotion in his body. "Every chamber." He continued to look into her eyes, holding her securely to him. "You want to know something else?" he asked in a deep sexually laced voice.

Not sure why but she seemed to have lost her voice. The way his hands felt on her back, right above the curve of her backside, the way their bodies touched, but more than anything, the look in his eyes rendered her speechless. All she could do was nod her head.

Taking his time, he lower his head until their lips were inches apart. "I love what I see."

She waited, but he didn't kiss her. The anticipation was more than she could take. As she looked into his eyes, she realized what he was waiting for. This would not be a kiss and nothing more. This was going to be the beginning of a commitment. Seeing the understanding form in her eyes he held her a little tighter. "I play for keeps Cynthia Antoinette."

It was a sign of anger whenever she heard her entire name called out by her mother. The way he said it was just the opposite. It was laced with love. "Kiss me Samuel."

And that's exactly what he did—slowly, methodically and thoroughly. When he finished making love to her—and he was going to make love to her, he wanted there to be no doubts to whom her heart belonged. This was the woman he wanted to brand as his.

Was she wrong to want this man? She committed herself to LaVere', but this man was stealing her senses with his lips, his tongue, his hands—big hands and oh so hard body. She realized she had clothes on, but the heat from his body was generating was consuming her. "Samuel," she barely whispered when his lips traveled down her throat.

Standing to his full height he pulled her body flushed with his, "Yes?" he answered in a raw sexual drawl. If she was about to tell him to stop, he would, because he wanted more than just her body. Nothing less than always and forever, would satisfy his soul as this point.

That's when she felt it, in all its hard core glory—the reaction of his body to hers. This man with the discipline of Ghandi and the patience of Job wanted her. May God help her—she wanted him just as bad. The vow to be celibate until she met the man she was going to marry suddenly became viable. This was the man for her. "Love me Samuel, love me."

Without another breath, he dropped to his knees and pulled the very essence of her to his lips. He inhaled her scent and kissed what will now belong to him—forever. The material of the dress did not protect her from the singe of his touch. She quivered at the touch and was forced to dig into his shoulders to keep from melting in the spot. Standing with her across his shoulders, he did not stop until he placed her body across her bed. Following her down, he covered her with his body and stared into her eyes. "Tonight you become my woman— heart," he kissed the right side of her lips, "body," he kissed the left side of her lips, "and soul," he devoured her mouth, leaving not an inch inside untouched. Her taste, texture of her tongue, her movements all seem to make him want more. Reluctantly leaving her mouth, he placed a trail of kisses down her throat until he reached the soft mounds of her breast. Definitely more than a mouth full, but not enough to fill his craving in one serving, he began to pace himself. He wanted to savor every morsel of her. Reaching behind her neck he release the single thread that held her dress together, then slowly lowered it down her body revealing a flawless, toned body. And as he suspected, there wasn't a stitch of anything underneath. Standing above her mesmerized by her beauty, it took him a moment to respond to her statement.

"One of us appears to be a little over dressed," she smiled at him praying that her nervousness to his response to her was not showing. This was a unique occurrence for her. There were a few things she was not confident about; her body was not one of them. But the way Samuel looked at her, made her want to be prefect and she, in this instance wasn't sure if she met his standard. When his eyes returned to hers, all doubt drifted away. With her hands over her head she watched as he removed his blazer dropping it to the floor. Then her breath caught when he removed his shirt, his chest was exactly as she remembered it, wide, strong, rippled. Kicking off his shoes and socks, she watched, committed to memory every muscle—from his arms, to his chest. Then he lowered his briefs and pants together and stood before her. Pulling a condom from his pocket, he ripped the packet open to protect them.

"Better," he asked raising an eyebrow.

Cynthia had never seen anything so exquisite in her life. She came up on her knees and ran her tongue over her bottom lip. Reaching out she touched the center of his chest with her index finger and ran the full length of his torso until she reached the most powerful member of his body. Par for the course, she continued down the length of him until she reached the tip. Sitting there on her knees, with her finger right on the tip of him, she looked up.

It took every ounce of discipline he could muster to not grab her and enter her in one powerful thrust. But there was more at stake than just this one night. So he held his patience—until she put the very finger that caused him to just about lose his mind into her mouth, never taking her eyes from his. That was it, the damn broke. All the tension, all the sexual crackling in the room burst as he lifted her into the air and brought her down onto him, fitting him so completely into her fold. She inhaled as her legs wrapped around his powerful back as she stared into his eyes, lips only a breath apart, holding on to his shoulders. He held her there with a single hand wrapped around her waist, while he used one hand to remove the comb to free her hair. Fanning her hair out, he watched the expressions as she adjusted to him, he wanted to make sure he did not hurt her.

There was more to this man that she anticipated; it never crossed her mind if he could hold her weight so easily in mid air. She felt more secure in his hands then she did on her own feet and to clear that glimmer of concern she saw in his eyes, she began to lower her body backwards while holding on to his arms until the back of her head touched the bed. With his hands at her waist he held her still and slowly withdrew from her and submerged himself into her again, and again, and again. Digging her nails into his arms she was amazed at his strength and knew, with him she never had to be afraid of anything. That was the last coherent thought she had as a scream began to escape from her. The intensity of the heat generating between them was explosive, there was no way she could hold back from the promise of fulfillment that was building inside. He eased his hand up her back and pulled her body back up flushed with his. Completely in his control, she wrapped her arms around his neck, "hold on baby," he said as he eased his hands down to her cheeks and squeezed them securely around him. The explosion rocked her body, as he held her and kissed her throat that was vibrating with her release. "Let it all flow. I want to feel all of you." He continued to stand there holding her as if she was the most precious item in the world. Her body rested limp against his, still reeling from the soft sensual release. How could this massive man be so tender, so giving, so loving?

With her head in the crock of his shoulder, it occurred to her that he did not explode with her. Her body tensed, she did not satisfy him—that was a first. All she could think to do was give him the same pleasure he had shared with her. They were still intimately entwined and the last thing she wanted to do was break the connection. She looked up with a questioning eye.

Having an idea of what she was thinking, he smiled, "You mentioned the celibacy thing. I thought you needed that one by yourself." They fell on the bed, "This one is for me."

The smile he generated flowed like a liquid flame throughout her body. Nothing could be more beautiful than his smile. "Bring it on big boy."

This man knew how to follow orders. He begin at the breast, rubbing each to the point of distraction, then taking them, one at a time into his mouth savoring the taste and her hard nipples between his lips. Still inside her, he lifted one side of her legs and placed it over his giving him a deeper penetration. Moving slowly in and out he began to feel all of the succulent offering surrounding him. Nothing felt this right, or so glorious. He pushed up on one hand and moved his lower body deeper inside her—pushing deeper and deeper, reaching for the glory that was waiting on the other side. The glory only she could give him. She lifted her body and pushed up to him, he growled. She did it again, the growl became deeper. Her pushing up to him, him pushing down into her over and over and over again until his growl became a howl. And he didn't stop, couldn't stop and continued until every last drop of his pleasure had flowed out of him. She held him tight, afraid to let go, afraid the feeling of contentment would disappear; afraid the feeling of being one with him would disappear, afraid she would never experience another moment like this one. But she was wrong; she felt it over and over throughout the night. For Samuel was determined to brand her his, and what a mark he left.

Sometime in the wee hours of the night Samuel went downstairs to clear the table and kitchen. Before returning upstairs he checked the window to ensure a bodyguard was watching over them—there was. Then he let Rusty upstairs to sleep by the door. He then crawled back into bed and wrapped his body around the woman that invaded his heart. As soon as their bodies connected, he became engorged again. He pulled her back to him and eased into her. Even in her sleep she responded to him with a soft moan. He moved his hand from her waist down to the warmth between her legs. While moving smoothly inside her he thumbed the crux of her womanhood and was promptly rewarded with her full release. His followed as he buried his head into her hair. His final thought being, this must be heaven, before falling asleep.

Chapter 14

Smiling with a sense of a life renewed, Cynthia stretched across the bed. She sat up suddenly finding herself alone. Did she dream it—again? No, his scent was still in the room. Her dreams were good, but not that good. The sun was just rising covering the room with the early morning light. Looking around, she saw her robe lying across the chair by the door. She promptly put it on and went in search of the man that rocked her world for eight straight hours. As soon as the door opened Rusty stood wagging his tail. "Hey boy," she patted him. She was about to ask where was Samuel, when she heard the shower in the guest bedroom running. She walked into the bathroom and leaned against the doorway leading to the shower stall. For a moment she wanted to laugh, he was almost too tall for the showerhead. But with his back to her, watching the water cascade over his muscled toned body stirred other thoughts. She dropped her robe and stepped inside.

"Did you enjoy the scenery?" he asked as she ran her hands from his shoulders down his back to his firm behind.

She placed a kiss between his shoulder blades, "Immensely." Her tongue trailed the center of his back until he turned, took her arms and pulled her to his lips. They were inches away from touching as the water cascade over both of them. He brushed the now soaked curls from her face and took her mouth with a hunger only she could fill. All she wanted to do at that moment was to show him just how much she wanted him. Pulling away, on tiptoes she kissed his neck, his shoulder, his nipples—that generated a moan and she smiled as she continued to follow the same path on the front that she did on his back. She ran her tongue between each of the indents from his six pack abs. Then she did something she had done for no other man, she took him between her lips and saluted his tip with her tongue. That was about all she could do, for there was no way she could take even a third of him in.

His knees buckled when her mouth closed around the tip of his manhood. The warmth of the enclosure, the texture of her tongue on him was sending him into overdrive. He pulled her up by her arms and placed her back against the shower wall and entered her with such a force he thought he may have hurt her. He froze to bring his emotions under control, but she wasn't having it.

Wrapping her legs around his waist and her arms around her neck, she brought him in deeper, she wanted to feel every inch of him inside her. With his body bracing her against the wall he held her face between his hands. "Open your eyes Cynthia Antoinette," he commanded in a husky voice. When she complied he could see the contentment in her eyes. But it was his job to protect her in all things. "You are not protected," he said not wanting to, but willing to withdraw from her.

It took a moment for her to clear her mind enough to comprehend what he was trying to tell her. Didn't he realize he robbed her of all sense of thinking the moment he entered her. She did not understand until he began to withdraw from her. She immediately clinched her thigh muscles tighter around him while simultaneously clinching her inner muscles to keep him right where he was. "I understand," she whispered against his lips.

He was doing all he could to keep from moving inside her, for he was sure he would explode any minute. "My father gave my mother twelve children, before he came up for breath." He stated while staring into her eyes.

She stared back still holding him tight. "Twelve?"

He nodded, "Hum hum, twelve," grinning at the look of wonder in her eyes.

"The bar has been set. I suggest you get to work, Samuel." She kissed against his lips.

He pushed up wards. "Say it again."

"Samuel," she repeated and kissed him again. He pushed up again, and she called his name again, and again and again, until they exploded together. Squeezing her inner muscles as tight as she could, the thought of capturing his seed and carrying his child thrilled her as he called out her name.

Leaving Cynthia in the shower, Samuel stepped out to get dress. He knew if he stayed any longer, they would not make it out of the house today. The doorbell rung as he reached the kitchen. He looked out the window and saw the limo parked out front. He checked the clock and it was barely eight in the morning. Why would Blake be there this early? Disarming the alarm, he pushed the button to open the front door. Standing over the railing in the kitchen he watched as Blake climbed the steps and then noticed Sofia was behind him.

"Good morning Samuel," he stated while giving a friendly shake.

"Morning Blake, Mrs. Thornton," Samuel replied.

"Where's Cynthia," Sofia asked without speaking.

When Samuel did not reply, Blake grinned and shook his head. His mother had finally met her match. "It's customary to say good morning especially when someone else speaks first." Samuel stated, looking down at the woman.

"It's also customary for hired help to be downstairs. Why are you up here?"

"Mother!" Cynthia chided as she walked into the room. "Don't speak to Samuel that way."

Blake took a seat at the breakfast bar and sighed as he watched the scene unfold. "Good morning Blake," she said as she continued into the kitchen. Samuel handed her the glass of juice he had prepared for her. "Thank you," she smiled looking up into his eyes."

"Morning sis," he replied to her. "See mother that's how it's done. Someone say good morning to you, and then you say good morning to them—or something."

Sofia frowned at her son as she continued to study this man that had her daughter smiling up at him.

"What are you two doing here?" Cynthia asked as she sat next to her brother and Samuel simply leaned back against the counter.

"Hate to have to tell you this, but I've been called back to the studio."

"How soon do you have to leave?"

"The studio sent their plane; I'm on my way to the airport as we speak."

Sadden by his news Cynthia closed her eyes. "I was hoping we could have a normal Thanksgiving meal this year, since everyone was home."

"We could still do that, with LaVere' at our home." Sofia stated, still watching the interaction between Cynthia and Samuel.

"LaVere' is out of the country."

"When is he going to return?" Sofia asked, now concentrating solely on her daughter.

"I don't know. I didn't know he was gone until Jamal told me last night."

"That would have been great, but from what Shannon is saying they will need me from now until next Friday." He hesitated, hearing the disappointment in her voice.

Cynthia stood there shaking her head in disbelief. Her family was abandoning her yet again. "I don't believe this. You're leaving now? Whatever happened to being here to make sure I don't make a mess of my life again?"

"I never said you made a mess of your life." Blake stated. "I came to make sure you were alright after your accident. And I stayed long enough to know you are in good hands with LaVere'." He said while glancing knowingly at Samuel

"See that's just it, I'm not sure I'm in good hands with LaVere'. He's not even here."

"Sis, I'm sorry, but I have to go. Think about flying out with mom and dad. I would love to have that family dinner you're talking about."

"I may not be flying out after all." Sofia stated. "I think I'll stay here with you for a while Cynthia Antoinette."

Somehow, her full name coming from her mother did not have the same effect as it did coming from Samuel. "No, I'm fine here. You and dad can leave with Blake."

"I wouldn't dream of leaving you here alone," Sofia said to Cynthia, but stared directly at Samuel.

"What's the difference from any other holiday?" Cynthia stated. She kissed Blake on the cheek. "Have a safe trip," she said then turned to Samuel. "I'll be ready to leave for the hotel in a few minutes." Then she walked out of the room.

"Hotel?" Sofia questioned as Cynthia continued up the stairs.

Blake turned to Samuel. "I know she is in good hands with you around."

"It's not the same as having her family," Samuel said as he poured the remaining coffee into the sink. "I realize this is business for you. Try to get back in time for the holidays if you can. She'll be okay."

Blake shook his hand. "Let's go mother."

"You go on to the car. I want to have a word with Cynthia before we leave." Sofia waited until Blake was outside then turned to Samuel. "What are you doing to my daughter?"

"Loving her Mrs. Thornton. What are you doing?"

"You do not have the means to love someone like my Cynthia. My child is destined for more than you will ever have in your life time. Don't think for a moment I will stand by and allow you to disrupt the life waiting for her with Prince LaVere'."

Samuel stared down at the woman that barely reached his chest. "Don't think for a moment that that's a decision for you to make."

Cynthia packed the things she needed to change into for the ball. More than likely she would not have a chance to return home to dress, so she was taking everything with her. She sat on the bed for a moment. When she woke this morning there was not one sad thought in her mind. Now it was flooded with them. What made her think this holiday would be any different than the rest? It looks as if she will be the extra wheel at the Harrison household again. She loved Martha Harrison like a mother. There was never a time that she did not feel welcomed in her home. It's just this year should not be like this. She should not have to depend on the open arms of her friends to get through the holiday. This year she is supposed to have a man. Not a married man, not a man that is living with someone else, her own man. Apparently, her man loved his country more than he loved her. Or does he love me. She walked over to the window and looked out. It was just beginning to snow. Leaning against the window sill she sighed. What was she thinking? LaVere' does not love her. He was very clear on what he needed from her. Why was she settling for something less than a man with a committed heart? "Hum," she sighed. She knew exactly why. The fear of being alone; growing old alone. Refusing to feel sorry for herself, she stepped away from the window and stumbled when she did. Samuel came to mind and she smiled. Butterflies began churning in her stomach as she thought about last night and this morning. The attraction between the two of them was sexual, that's all, she reminded herself. The past with Gavin taught her that was not the way to find true love. Then she thought more, sexual attraction never caused her to fall all over herself or to lose all sense of thought and time before. Samuel Lassiter touched her in a different way, in a deeper way. Then something her friend Tracy said on her wedding day came to mind, *"Once someone touches your heart; you'll know."* Samuel had touched her heart. She smiled, and then began to giggle. The sound startled her and she stopped. "What is wrong with me, I don't giggle." Was she falling in love with Samuel, a man as dangerous to her mind as he was to her body? Lord knows he was dangerous to her body, for just sitting here thinking about him made her long for another eight hour marathon.

Gathering her things with a smile, she was walking down the stairs as she heard her mother talking to Samuel. "LaVere' can give her a life filled with beautiful things, Samuel. What can you give her?" She hesitated then continued. "If you care for her, and I don't question that you do, wouldn't you want the best for her. Can you honestly think that you can give her the life LaVere' can? I don't think so."

"Everything you mentioned has only monetary value. What about that one simple thing that every person needs in their life—love? Do you even know what that means? It means accepting her for the beautiful person she is and not wanting to change one thing about her. See that's where I'm at with her"

"And what about her? Do you honestly believe she could be happy living with you and pushing out baby after baby like your mother did to your father, trapping him into a life of no possibilities," she snapped angrily.

"Don't," the deadly warning escaped before he could think.

Hearing the threat in his voice Cynthia called out, "Samuel could I get a hand with these bags?" She wasn't sure what the conversation entailed but it was enough to know it was about her.

Samuel held Sofia's gaze. "You should be gone when we come back downstairs."

Sofia returned the stare, "I will fight for the life my daughter deserves," she said then turned and walked out of the door.

Samuel walked up the first landing of the stairs where he met Cynthia. She could see the anger in his face. "I'm sorry my mother upset you."

"I'm not upset."

"Did you tell that to your jaw that's clinched tighter than my thighs were this morning?"

A slow smiled formed on his face from the memory. "That tight huh?"

She took a step down to him. "Yes," she kissed his temple. "I know I have a lot to sort out. But please know this. I don't regret nor would I change anything that happened last night."

He wondered if she knew that he was in love with her, that at that moment the one thing he wanted to do was to return to where they were last night. "Any chance of talking you into returning to that place and not leaving for a few days?"

She smiled and walked by him down the stairs. "No, I have the ball and I have to get ready for the day after Thanksgiving" She continued down to the lower level of the house. "That's the busiest day of the year for us. We have over fifty homes to decorate for the Christmas holiday on that weekend alone." She patted Rusty's head as she continued to chatter while walking into the garage. She waited for Samuel to set the alarm and placed the items inside her car. Before she got inside he pulled her close and kissed her. "Have Thanksgiving dinner with me and my family."

Her eyes grew as large as a saucer. "Samuel, you know I have to talk to LaVere'. I just can't not tell him what's going on."

"I understand. I still want you to meet my family."

"The whole family?"

He grinned, "The whole family."

"Hum."

Cynthia concentrated on the task at hand. She was in the Marriott Ball room, scanning the decorations and ensuring staff was in place. Roz was in the kitchen supervising the servers and the cooks, so she knew she did not have to check on them. She wanted to make sure the lighting was right, and the band was set up before she went upstairs to change.

She returned to the ballroom precisely at six to meet with Mrs. Sutton. They walked through inspecting everything from the flooring to the centerpieces. Everything was perfect and Mrs. Sutton told her so. She expressed her gratitude repeatedly. "The chief is going to be so pleased. I'm sure he is going to want to thank you in person."

"I'll be happy to meet with him if needed," Cynthia smiled. "Well, I say we are ready for business, how about you."

"We are definitely ready," she smiled back.

Apparently so were the guests. As soon as Cynthia opened the doors guest began to arrive. By eight o'clock the place was packed with officers in their dress blues and their wives and/or mistresses in their gowns. The top of the brass was in attendance. There was a rumor or two that The Governor, Gavin Roberts and JD Harrison were going to stop by. She wasn't sure about Gavin, but she knew for a fact JD was not going to be there. He was spending much needed downtime with his wife and son this weekend and left orders not to be disturbed.

As the guest arrived they checked in at the table, presented their tickets and were given a nametag and the table assignment. Most of the names on the list Cynthia recognized, but some she did not. There had recently been a number of changes within the different precincts. She distinctly remembered JD and Brian discussing them and did not seem too pleased with some of the Precinct Captain appointments. But then again JD and the Chief were not what you would call chummy. Actually, Chief Munford had been very vocal on some of the projects he had tried to implement and JD would not back him. He continually accused JD of forgetting where he came from. The truth of the matter was JD would not allow Chief Munford to control him, as Gavin did. Gavin was very instrumental in getting Chief Munford in place before he became Governor. He indicated to her that a number of favors were called in to get him appointed. It was strange that JD would not be closer to the Chief than Gavin; after all, the Chief was JD's father's partner at one time.

Cynthia put the thoughts aside as she continued to greet the late arrivals. She smiled as she greeted each person and directed them to their assigned table. One retired officer was being honored tonight came in and she decided to escort him to his table. Upon her return there was a bit of a line, so she pitched in to assist her staffer with the nametags. The line was down to two guests when Cynthia heard her staffer ask, "Name please?"

"Samuel Lassiter" the man replied. Her head snapped up and she was eye to eye with him.

"Mr. Lassiter, please allow me to escort you to your table." She placed her hand in the bend of his arm and walked into the ballroom. "What are you doing here?"

"Keeping an eye on you," he said as he took in her outfit. "You look good. Are you sure you can't skip this thing?"

"You know I can't."

She sat him at the bar. "Sit here and behave yourself."

"Are you going to fall into my arms tonight?"

She played it cool and replied, "You never know what the evening may bring," then walked away.

Samuel took his seat and watched as she walked away. Since she had to be here tonight, he wanted to make sure she was safe. Some of the men in this room carried badges, but they certainly did not represent the best of the very proud men and women that put their life on the line every day. These people were the ones that make the good officers' job more difficult. It's because of these people the good officers have a hard time getting the public to trust them. These officers are breaking more laws than the average dealer on the street. All for self-gain. The worst part to all of this was information is showing it may go all the way to the top. He did not have a problem bringing any bad cop down because he believed the system is only as good as the people running it. If there were dirty cops, it was his duty to bring them down.

For some reason, the possibility of her seeing him in a bad light bothered him. He was not sure what type of activity was taking place tonight, but he was sure the Chief's right hand men would be here tonight. With them and Cynthia in the same room, it would be the perfect opportunity for them to take her out. He may have to act out of his normal character and he did not want her to witness that.

He looked around to see the Chief was talking to a group of men near the podium. Probably discussing the presentations for the evening, he thought. Samuel was not sure why, but tonight there was something about the Chief that sent a chill down his spine. That's a feeling he did not like. Samuel recognized a few of the men in blue, Terrell Kane was standing behind the Chief, he knew that he and his partner Sanchez were dirty. He also knew they had been watching him. From what he had observed the group appeared to be cocky, as if they were untouchable. The only way they could be that comfortable was if someone high up had their back. Samuel believed that person was Chief Munford, but he had no proof.

"You looking mighty serious, Samuel. What's up?"

Samuel turned. Detective Donnell Williams was standing behind him. This was one cop he was sure was not dirty. In the past he and his brother Joshua had worked with Williams on undercover assignments with him as their backup. "Just checking out the scenery," he replied, slipping easily into the nonchalant role.

"Yeah, it seems to be the same crowd from last year" he said as he sat his drink on the bar and took the seat next to Samuel. "What are you working on?"

"I'm not on assignment."

"Bull." He smiled, "I can see the intensity of your look a mile away." He hesitated, then exhaled, "You're checking out the Chief, aren't you?"

Samuel never looked up. "What make you say that?"

Shrugging his shoulders, "I figured it was just a matter of time. Things haven't been right for a minute."

Knowing Williams was a man of few words, it concerned Samuel that he was talking now. "You covered man?"

"For now they keep a wide circle around me." He shook his head, "It's only a matter of time before I have to join in or be forced out."

Samuel turned to the bartender, "Two scotch please," then turned back to Williams. "You sitting here talking to me may expedite that. The Chief and I have declared war."

Detective Williams took the offered drink. "I'll take my chances with you."

They touched glasses, then both emptied the drink. "I'm working on private duty now. You think you might be interested?"

"Man, Harrison's camp and I don't get along."

"That was mentioned when I brought your name up. But you were wrong on the call. JD was not the shooter on the Eagles case."

"Never said he was. But he knows who took them out. As a DA, it's his duty to bring the culprit to justice." Samuel shrugged his shoulder as he continued to watch the room. "Besides, I would be too busy watching his wife."

"Yeah, it seems my boss has the same problem," Samuel laughed.

"Did you see the honey at the door? That's my take for the night." He leaned back into his seat as if it was a done deal.

Samuel looked out into the reception area. "Which one?" he asked coolly. The thought of him or any other man putting his hands on Cynthia was playing havoc with his mind. So he really hoped he was referring to the other young lady.

"The one in the red, with the body that look like she stepped right out of center page of Jet magazine."

He smirked and looked away from Donnell, "Looks like you're betting zero on woman?"

Donnell left eyebrow raised, "That's you?" he asked in a surprised tone.

Samuel looked over his shoulder at Cynthia. "Not yet. But it will before the night is over."

Donnell looked at him then gave him a pound, "I ain't mad at you brother."

Samuel saw the chief walking up. "Good evening," the Chief interrupted.

"Evening Chief," Donnell greeted. When nothing more was said, Donnell turned to see the Chief staring at Samuel.

Samuel stood out of respect for the man's position, but certainly not the man himself. "Good Evening Chief."

"This is a friend of yours Williams?"

"One of two men I know has my back for life," he replied.

"You should pick your friends more carefully," the Chief looked at Donnell and walked off.

Samuel watched the men that followed then turned to Donnell and cleared his throat. "You realize you are now a target."

He shrugged his shoulders. "I'll take my chances. Besides, I damn sure rather have you watching my back then Munford any day. You gonna need some backup tonight?"

Samuel smiled, "I appreciate that man. Just keep your eyes open."

"You got it."

After the presentations and dinner was served Cynthia was making her rounds through the crowd. This was the best part of her events. She was able to talk with people to get a feel for the service provided during the evening. People are genuinely honest once things are winding down. They are relaxed and usually speak freely. She stood at the table speaking with a group of women when suddenly she felt a wave of intense heat rising from the small of her back. Listening to the ladies she looked over her right shoulder, but did not see anything out of the ordinary. Then she quickly glanced over her left shoulder, turned back to the ladies then slowly turned her attention back to the left. Sitting at the bar with a drink in his hand was Samuel. His look was so intense she looked down to make sure she still had on clothes. He was looking as if he could see right through her dress. It was not her manner to be rude, and not giving someone talking to you your full attention is rude. She turned back to the woman and completed the conversation. When she was through she looked back towards the bar and he was gone. She shrugged her shoulders and walked through the tables heading in the direction of the kitchen.

The activity in the breezeway had slowed since dinner was served. Most of the staff was in the kitchen with Roz cleaning up. When she walked by the hallway that led to the balcony and several rooms, she thought she heard voices. However, the balcony was not in use. It was November and the weather was cold. No one in their right mind should be out there. She walked in the direction of the voices and was startled when a hand reached out from one of the openings and covered her mouth. Another hand circled around her waist and pulled her out of the walkway. Recognizing the touch, she relaxed as the man pinned her to his side. She turned to see it was Samuel. He looked at her and motion for her to be quiet. He looked over his shoulder and down the hallway to make sure they were not seen. He slowly removed his hand. "What are you doing?" she whispered loudly.

He placed a hand back over her mouth and gave her an agitated look. She mumbled something angrily, but it was muffled. He applied a little more pressure and turned his head back as if he was listening to something. She settled down and listened as well.

The conversation coming from the balcony became rather heated and the men seem to be attempting to keep their voices down. It took a minute but she recognized one of the voices. It was Gavin's and he was not pleased.

"This is the last opportunity I'm giving you to back me publicly. The choice is yours. Frankly if you don't come on board I'll find a way around you and Harrison."

"This is the last time I'm going to say this, you can't get around JD. He is too politically powerful. Without his backing, even if legislation makes the mayor seat an elected position, you will not win."

"Then I'll eliminate him in another way. There's nothing to it. It just has to be planned right," the man sneered. "Just like his daddy's."

There was silence as she saw Samuel close his eyes and exhaled. Looking into his eyes the realization of who they were talking about came to her. Her eyes grew as big as a saucer, "Are they---." Samuel quickly covered her mouth. Then Gavin began talking in a manner that sent a chill up her spine. "If what you previously insinuated is true—it's called murder. I will begin an investigation and if there is anything that connects you to James Harrison's death, I will crucify you."

"Neither you nor Harrison will live long enough to complete an investigation."

"If you go anywhere near JD or his family, I will have you taken out. If you go near Cynthia Thornton I will kill you myself."

They heard footsteps coming in their direction and Cynthia's heart leaped. "Don't you walk away from me Roberts!" the man yelled.

It sounded if Gavin stopped. "It's time for you to realize who I am. I'm no longer your rookie partner and you have crossed the line of friendship. From this moment on, it's Governor Roberts to you. Your telephone calls and demands to see me will go unanswered. You wanted me to choose sides—well the choice is made. I'm putting you and your department on notice," he said and continued in their direction. Samuel released his hands from her mouth and replaced it with his lips. Stunned, her eyes popped open as wide as a silver dollar. Slowly the softness of his lips awakened her senses.

His body pressed protectively against hers as he applied more pressure to her lips. Instinctively her lips parted and his tongue eased into the space where it seemed it belonged. His hands moved to cover her face as someone walked by. She wasn't sure if it was Gavin or the other man, for she was lost in the kiss. Moses himself could have been walking from the mountain top and she would not have cared less.

Samuel's first instinct was to ensure whoever was walking down that hallway did not see her, so he covered her body completely with his. As the steps continued down the hallway, he ended the kiss and listened. There were other voices that joined Munford on the balcony.

"Is everyone in place?" Munford asked.

"We have it covered. The woman will be handled tonight. I don't understand why you're going after her."

"It's not for you to understand. You simply follow my orders then report back to me tonight."

Footsteps sounded walking in a different direction. Samuel looked down as Cynthia who appeared dazed by all she was hearing. Another set of footsteps walked by and he kissed her again and covered her body with his. This time she knew why.

When he ended the kiss neither moved. He braced his forehead against hers and just held her. It was clear both of them needed a moment to regain their senses. She could feel his heart racing against her hand, so she began smoothly rubbing her hand up and down his back until the pace slowed. He in turned stroked her back to slow hers.

When she was able to speak she asked, "Were they talking about JD?"

For a moment she was not sure if he was going to answer. Nodding his head he swallowed hard and replied, "Yes."

Hesitantly she asked, "The women they are refereeing too would be Tracy and Carolyn?"

He looked into her eyes then brushed her curls away from her face, "No, you." He hesitated. "We have to leave here." He stepped out into the hallway to see if anyone was around. When it seemed clear, he pulled her towards the exit.

"Wait, there are still guest in the ballroom, I can't leave."

"You are leaving now."

"I am not," she pulled away.

It was then that a fast breeze went between them in the very spot she was previously standing. The sound and rush of air was so sudden, it took her by surprise.

Samuel knew exactly what it was when the bullet lodged into the wall behind them. He pulled out his weapon, grabbed her and pulled her out the exit door near the balcony. "Come on, now," he demanded. Once outside he went towards the back of the building that led across Marshall Street. He ducked in an alley between two buildings pinning her behind him. He reached into his pocket, retrieved his silencer and placed it on his gun. He then took off his jacket and placed it around her shoulders.

Breathing heavily, trying to catch her breath, she asked, "What in the hell is going on?"

"If I were to guess, we are being shot at, darling."

She hit him in the back, "Hell I know that, why and by who?" she demanded.

"Why? We overheard that conversation." he looked back at her. "The who would be Richmond's finest men in blue."

"The police," She looked at him as if he had lost his mind.

"Now listen, the office is only three blocks away. Do you think you can make it in those shoes?"

The look she gave him was a cross between are you crazy or are you crazy. "These are three and a half inch Prada. They are made to look good, but they are not made for walking." Before she could finish he covered her mouth, listened and began slowly pushing her back with his body shielding her behind him.

Samuel reached down to his cell phone on his hip and pushed the send button on his cell phone knowing it would dial the last number that came through. Just as the caller pickup a police scanner beeped.

"Anything on your end?" the person on the other end of the radio asked.

The person approaching them answered back, "Nothing. What's your location?"

"Third and Marshall just in case they try to get to the building."

"Who's on Fourth Street?"

"It's covered."

"Roger that. Go silent?"

The radio was turned off as footsteps came closer. Cynthia had a grip on his shirt so tight that her nails were digging into his skin, but he continued walking backwards pushing her further back into the dark alley at the same time watching and listening to the approaching steps. A car drove by when he felt a sudden jerk at his shirt. He turned to see Cynthia being grabbed from behind with her mouth covered and just as suddenly saw her body go limp. He raised his revolver and was about to pull the trigger when the person spoke. "Big brother if you shoot me I'm going to tell mom." He lowered his weapon and quickly stepped into the open back door to a vacant building. They waited until the footsteps of the man that was tracking them were in the far distance. The savior motioned for him to be silent, then pointed to a door on the front side of the building. Samuel nodded, took Cynthia from the savior's shoulder and gathered her in his arms. The two traveled soundlessly from the back of the building to the front and waited. Once the area seemed clear the savior pushed a button on a device inside his coat. The back door to a SUV parked at Fourth and Clay Street opened. Samuel slipped out of the building and placed Cynthia on the back seat. When he reached the driver side the door was open and the motor was running. He waited until the red light released and then pulled into oncoming traffic.

Fifteen minutes later Samuel pulled into the back of Brian's home. He looked back at Cynthia, she was still out. There was a moment in the alley when he thought she was going to witness just how brutal he could be and the thought bothered him. For some reason he did not want her to see that side of him. One thing was for certain, he was not going to allow anything to happen to her. He exhaled and stepped out of the vehicle, gathered her in his arms and used the side door to enter Brian's home. There was a keypad entrance, which only certain agents had the code.

As Samuel enter the room he normally met Brian in, he gently laid Cynthia on the sofa and took a seat in the chair next to the door. Staring at her he wanted to curse, she was so vulnerable. He stood and walked over to the bar behind the desk and poured himself a cognac. He turned back to her and his glazed went straight to her lips --the very lips that caused him to lose his concentration tonight. It was not his intent to kiss her, but doing so served two purposes: it shielded her from anyone that walked by and kept her quiet long enough to hear the exchange between Gavin and Munford. But it also caused him to lose count of the number of people on that balcony and that nearly cost her life.

The exchange, could he have heard right. Munford ordered the woman to be taken out. It was a stupid move. Munford thinks taking out the woman will make the men fall in line. He's wrong—it will make them want to kill him with their bare hands. Of that he was certain; it would be his reaction to anything happening to Cynthia. Samuel continued to think as he stared at the woman lying on the sofa still out. Munford had to know Cynthia and Tracy were being protected and he still tried to take them out. He set up suddenly remembering the question Cynthia asked him. Could he have been talking about the first lady too? "Damn," he pulled out his cell and called Brian. "Where are you?" he asked when the telephone was answered on the other end.

"I'm in downtown Richmond where an officer and another unknown was taken out. The perpetrator they are looking for sounds a lot like you. Care to comment?"

"Wasn't me, but you need to be home about now. On your way call Harrison but don't leave his family alone."

Ten minutes later Brian was walking through his door with haste. He stormed into the room where he normally met with Samuel. Seeing Cynthia on the sofa he went to her, "What happen?" he asked angrily of the man sitting next to the door.

"She's not hurt, just a sleep. It was easier to get her out that way. Samuel stood and poured two drinks; he refreshed his, gave one to Brian and sat the other on the bar.

"Who's that for?"

"Harrison, he's going to need it."

Brian sat at the end of the sofa, "Would you care to shed some light on this?"

Samuel relayed the events of the evening to Brian.

Brian lowered his head and exhaled. "Did she over hear the conversation between Munford and Gavin?"

"Yes."

"She distracted you?"

"Somewhat. But I'm staying on this case. No one will protect her like me."

So he was right. He sensed something happening with Samuel and Cynthia. He looked down the sofa at her, "Cynthia is like a little sister to me. She's a pain in the ass, but I will not stand for anyone hurting her. That, my friend includes you."

"I'm not asking for your permission to be in her life. I'm just letting you know how I feel."

Brian always appreciated a straightforward man. Moreover, he liked the idea that Samuel clearly does not seek approval for what he wants. "You realize she is high maintenance and I know what you make."

"I have faith in my skills."

Brian smiled, "It's going to take a little more than skills to keep that woman happy. Believe me I know. But if you are serious about her, go for it."

"Are you going to advise Harrison about the conversation between Gavin and Munford?"

"Not all. Calvin Johnson, JD's chief prosecutor has the information on Munford. We will not move until we have something concrete. This information creates new complex issues that could have political repercussions. How do you want to play it out with Munford?"

Samuel was not a man to drop the ball on anything. "I have a plan for him."

"No dead bodies?"

"I haven't left any thus far."

"Cynthia?"

"I'll tackle that when it becomes an issue."

"You are a better man than me," Brian said as he shook Samuel's hand. "Taking on a Prince, a Governor and Sofia—you have my respect."

A few minutes later JD arrived. Samuel did not contribute too much to the conversation He left it up to Brian how much of tonight's events he would share with JD. His thoughts now went to his brother. What was he doing in Richmond and how did he end up in that building?

After JD left, the two talked a while longer until Cynthia began to stir at which time Samuel explained how they got to Brian's home, leaving out the assistance from the savior. There was no need bringing him into the picture since she did not see him. She took a moment to call Roz to ensure her she was safe and that everything had closed out properly.

She then looked at Brian as tears rolled down her cheek. "Did he tell you Munford had Mr. Harrison killed?"

Brian nodded, "Yeah, he told me."

"How are we going to tell Ashley and JD?"

"We can't."

"What? We have too. Brian don't you remember what they went through?"

Samuel walked over to where she was standing, "Cynthia," she looked up at him with tears in her eyes. "We can't discuss the conversation we overheard with anyone until I can investigate further." He wiped the tears away with his thumb, and then held her until she cried out.

An hour later she was home tucked in bed with Samuel sitting in the chair by her door. Tears began to flow down her cheek as she thought of all that had taken place. Gavin was involved with Munford, the man that had Mr. Harrison killed. Replaying the conversation in her mind she remembered him threatening Munford if he tried to harm JD, she could still hear the anger in his voice. Then she thought about the conversation that night a few months ago. Was Munford the man Gavin was talking about? Did he have information that could ruin Gavin and if he did what was it. She sat straight up in bed, "the locket."

"Cynthia," Samuel called out to her as he approached the bed. He could see the tears stains on her face. Without asking he pulled his shoes off laid on top of her comforter and gathered her into his arms. "Whatever it is it can wait until the morning."

Samuel held her until he was certain she was asleep. Leaving the room with Rusty at guard he walked downstairs grabbed his jacket then stood outside the sliding doors of the family room and waited. It wasn't long before Ryan appeared. "Had a busy night here." She said with her hands in the pocket of her jacket.

"That's an understatement. How many came through?"

"Two were here scoping the place for possible entry. But here's the thing." She smirked and looked down, "I followed them when they left. Give you one guess where I ended up?"

"Police headquarters downtown." If she was surprised by his answer she did not show it.

"You need to move her. Cops can play a lot of games in different ways, especially if people don't know to suspect them."

"I need you to get in touch with Detective Donnell Williams. You can find him at the third precinct. Don't trust anyone else with the message. Have him meet me at The Renaissance Private Club at six in the morning."

"I know him. I'll take care of it personally. You should know Harrison's place had a few visitors tonight as well as the governors' place."

Well, that answered his question on which women Munford was targeting. "Is everyone safe?"

"Yeah, whatever happened downtown last night froze all action."

"Will your people allow you to see this through?"

"My boss wants this to end soon. It's interfering in our normal activities."

"Once this is over with, you and I are going to have a talk about those other activities," Samuel stated.

"We can talk, don't know if it will change anything," Ryan said as she strutted away.

Chapter 15

Sunday morning Cynthia awakened with a new goal in life: again. She wanted it back, not the way it was, but she wanted to be in control of her life again. It seemed, since Gavin gave her that information her life has slipped out of her control. First she was going to find out what is going on with LaVere'. Since they were supposed to have dinner on Friday, she had not spoken or heard anything about him. The one thing she did know was she could not marry him. She doesn't know when it happened or why it happened but she was in love with Samuel. It didn't matter if he could give her the world or not. At this point she simply wanted him, everyday without the craziness. Making that decision meant she was going to have to deal with her mother—and she will, when the time came. Then she wanted to meet with her girls. It seemed like forever since they had a get together just to talk. Then she was going to have to talk to Brian. She was tired of people running around trying to kill her—Cynthia! Enough was enough, either he was going to take care of Munford or she was. Hell the one thing Brian did teach her was how to shoot. And if Munford thought he was going to take her down without a fight he had better think again.

She showered and dressed for church then went in search of Samuel. Walking swiftly into the kitchen she came to an abrupt stop. A man was sitting at her breakfast bar drinking a cup of coffee and reading the paper. "Who are you?" she asked with a frown and ready to attack if she had to.

"I'm a friend of Samuel," he replied with a grin.

"Where is he?"

"He had to take care of a few things and asked me to watch over you until he returns."

"When will that be?"

"He didn't say."

She stared at him for a moment then walked over to the counter. Remembering her manners she turned back, "Good morning," she waited but he didn't say anything. "Do you have a name?" she asked raising an eyebrow.

"Yes," he replied and continued to drink his coffee.

Frustrated, she sighed, "Well what is it?"

"If I tell you I'll have to kill you and Samuel won't like that." She frowned at the response and continued to stare at the man. "You're safe with me," he smiled.

"I have to make a run out. Are you going with me?"

He looked at his watch. "You are going to someone's house at seven o'clock in the mooring?"

"You can try to stop me if you want too, but I must warn you I am not in the mood to be told what I can and cannot do today." She picked up her keys from the tray by the door and began walking down the stairs to the garage. "Are you coming?" she yelled back up the steps.

The man was tired, but he knew if anything happened to this woman, his ex-commander, Samuel was going to have his head. And if Samuel didn't then Joshua would. Of all the women in the world it would be just like Samuel to pick a stubborn one. "I'm right behind you." He finished his coffee and washed the cup. He knew she couldn't move her car because he had her distributor cap in his back pocket.

Concerned about the information Jamal relayed and not hearing from LaVere', Cynthia turned to the one person she knew would tell her the truth. "Hello Clair. Is James home?"

"Hello Ms. Thornton. Yes, come with me."

The laughter coming from the office reached Cynthia before entering the room. A slight smile creased her lips. Her friend was truly happy with that overbearing man. Upon entering the room Cynthia could not believe her eyes. "James, don't you think this is going a bit too far?"

James exhaled, "First things first, what are you doing in my house? And if it is not too much to ask what are you talking about?"

To stunned for words, she murmured, "A bed and a nursery in your office James? I mean my Lord, what are you going to do next move a toilet in here too?" She walked over to the bassinet containing two month old Jayda and Jayden. The twins were lying on their stomach and she had a hard time deciding which one she was going to pick up first.

"I have to work and I like to be near my wife and children. In addition to that, this is my house. If I want to kill someone here, I can and if you wake either of them—I will."

Ashley began to laugh at the monstrous look her husband was bestowing on her friend. "Girl, come over here and sit down before James literally kills you." Cynthia complied as she hugged Ashley then took a seat beside her on the day bed next to the window.

"Why are you here?" James asked frustrated, that she was interfering with his time with his wife and children.

"I need to talk to you." Cynthia exclaimed. "I'm concerned about LaVere'."

James chucked, "You're concerned with someone other than yourself?"

She exhaled, took a deep breath and continued. This was too important to let her pride interfere. "Do you know anything about the disturbances going on in Emure?"

James looked up from his desk and glanced at Ashley. She returned the glance then took her friends hand. Clearing his throat, James asked, "What disturbances are you referring to?"

"Is there more than one?"

"Emure is a progressing country, there are always differences taking place." James sat back in his chair and gave her his undivided attention.

She sat forward, "Is LaVere' and his family in danger?"

Detecting the fear in her question, James walked over and took a seat next to the daybed where Cynthia and his wife sat. LaVere' had not shared this information with Cynthia, although James thought she should have been told. LaVere' had come by the night before he left and told him he was returning to Emure, because his family may be in danger. It seems the idea of him marrying someone outside of the country was all the rebels needed to gather the strength to conduct attacks against the royal family. James advised him to confide in Cynthia, however, LaVere' thought it would be best to handle the situation in person, without involving her. "Have you spoken with him?"

"No," she shook her head. "I spoke with Jamal who indicated not only was the King upset about LaVere' and me, but so were his people. Is that true James? Is LaVere' and his family being attacked because of me?"

James glanced at Ashley for guidance. He understood LaVere' wanting to keep this from Cynthia. There were things James had kept from Ashley too, but in the end that had almost caused him to lose her. The situation with LaVere' and Cynthia was different. LaVere' was not in love with Cynthia. Nevertheless he was willing to do what he believe was needed to progress his country forward. That was what the people of Emure did not understand. Although his methods were questionable, LaVere's reasons were not selfish at all. He was sacrificing his life for his country. LaVere' truly believed Cynthia was the key to bringing his people, especially women, to a higher social and economic existence. "Tell me exactly what Jamal told you."

Cynthia stood and relayed the story to James as it had been told to her. As she paced back and forth, Ashley began to see a different side to Cynthia, she was concerned about LaVere' and his country. There was never a time when Cynthia did not put herself first. For the past month James had been trying to explain LaVere's reasons for picking Cynthia for such an honorable role in his life. She loved her friend, but until now Ashley did not clearly understand what made LaVere' think Cynthia was the woman he needed until now. What she saw and heard was a woman, not only concerned for the safety of LaVere', but that of his family and the people of his country. Who would have thought it?

When Cynthia completed the story, she retook her seat. "James, I'm afraid the very thing LaVere' believe to be best for his country, may tear it apart."

"LaVere' believes this will subside. That is why he went home. To ensure his family is safe and to speak to the people."

"He's in Emure? Is he safe? Why isn't Jamal with him?" She asked, concerned.

"Slow down. Yes he is in Emure and he is safe. He did not take Jamal with him because he does not believe Jamal is loyal to him."

Cynthia stood and shook her head. "I disagree. Jamal is fiercely loyal to LaVere' and his country."

"I believe Jamal is loyal to his country, I'm not sure if he is loyal to LaVere'."

Staring at James and frowning at his words she asked, "Aren't they one in the same?"

"No." James stood and approached her. What he was about to tell her was not going to go over well. "We believe, Jamal is connected to one of the cells that attempted to attack LaVere's family."

Shock and fear surged through Cynthia. She took a step back. "What! If you know that why hasn't LaVere' taken steps to stop him?"

James spoke softly and tried to reason with her. "Cynthia, we don't have any proof. We just know there has been contact from LaVere's house here to suspects in Emure."

"So, LaVere' is a prince. Can't the King have Jamal beheaded or something? Isn't that what Kings do when they don't like someone?"

He could not help but chuckle at her response. "It's not that simple."

"Hell yes it is that simple. You did it when Ashley was in danger. The only reason David Holt is in prison and not dead is because Brian stopped you. You were going to kill that man for touching Ashley, and you are not the King of anything. Surely, LaVere's father can have this man beheaded." The expression on James face clearly indicated he believed she had lost her mind. She grabbed her purse off the table and walked towards the door.

"Cynthia wait," James bellowed out as he walked over to block her exit. "Where are you going?"

She looked him up and down, "I'm going back to LaVere's house to beat the hell out of Jamal."

"Cynthia, you can't go there after what James just told you," Ashley stated as she stood to check on the babies.

Cynthia looked up at James and exhaled. "Tell me what to do, James."

"The first thing you need to do is talk to LaVere'. Stay away from Jamal, at all cost, until we know more."

"Fine, but I'm really tired of being told what I can and can't do," she pouted.

Sensing she was calmer James decided to put things back as they should be. "You mean the same way I'm tired of you being one of the first people I see in the morning."

"When you married Ashley you got all of us, Tracy, Roz and me."

"Then explain why you are the only one that continues to be in my house early in the mornings. Could it be they have something or someone occupying their time in the mornings, maybe you should try it."

"James," Ashley chastened him again, but doubted it would help. She turned to Cynthia. "I'm going to get the babies ready for church. Would you like to lend me a hand?"

"I was going to help you," James frowned.

"You're on punishment for the way you spoke to Cynthia. You can't help."

Cynthia looked at James and gave him a cynical smile. "I would love to help Ashley."

The Governor and First Lady were standing outside their church shaking hands after early service was over. Carolyn noticed the number of security men and women with them had increased. It also appeared to her they were on alert and she wondered why. When they were safely seated in the back of the sedan they arrived in she turned to Gavin. "What's happening?"

He waited until the vehicle was moving before he answered. "My meeting with Munford did not go well last night. He wanted me to take a stand and I did. Just not the side he wanted me to be on. I spoke with your father last night. He and Lena are back home I want you to stay with them for a while."

She waved him off, "I'm staying with my husband. Munford is the least of my concerns. I'm glad you finally stood up to him. He needs to know who you are." She stated emphatically. "He should have been grateful for the leniency you have afforded him thus far. But no, he has to be greedy. The ungrateful little rut," she huffed.

Gavin smiled at his wife. She could be fiercely loyal at times. He took her hand in his and kissed it. "I want you to be safe until I can bring charges against Munford."

Stunned but happy with the unusual show of emotions, Carolyn smiled. "I'm safe with you." She shook her head, "Besides if I stay with daddy I might kill his wife."

"What did she do now?" Gavin asked; glad to be thinking about something other than Munford.

"You are not going to believe this one. She actually had a DNA test done to show daddy was the father of her daughter, Tracy. Can you believe that? Now, I realize I can be devious, but to stoop that low at her age." She shook her head, "If I hadn't seen the papers with my own eyes I would have never believed it." She smirked and looked at Gavin who had turned his head looking out the window.

Okay, he was wrong. Munford would be easier to think about. "Gavin did you hear what I just said?"

He turned to her hoping his poker face was in place, "Yes. I did."

"Well?" she demanded.

Damn, she expected an answer. "I think you should leave it alone."

Feeling the wind taken from her sail at his response, she stared at him in disbelief. "You don't seem shocked at what I just revealed. Why is that Gavin?"

"I am shocked you saw that paper."

"But not shocked at the report itself?"

He squeezed her hand tightly, "I think you should talk with your father about what you saw."

"Gavin?"

"We will not speak on this again until after you have spoken with your father." He pushed the button on the door to open the privacy pane between them and the driver, "Take us to Senator Roth's home, please." He held her hand reassuringly as the vehicle turned in the direction of the highway.

It wasn't unusual for Douglas to get a call to open the Renaissance for a meeting. But when he saw who was in attendance, he was sure he needed a little extra security in the place. The least of his concern was Brian and Samuel. But when Donnell Williams walked in with of all people Donovan Tucker, he had second thoughts. The men that gathered in the JD Harrison room of The Chamber were a collection of sworn enemies.

Brian and Williams' bumped heads during the time the Eagles gang attacked Tracy. Williams' primary suspect in the shooting of the gang members was JD. A number of times while the investigation was being conducted, not only did JD and Williams go head to head, so did Brian and Williams. At the time Brian was an FBI agent and Williams was a detective, they should have been working on the case together to bring the person responsible for the shootings to justice. But, Brian was determined to protect JD at all cost and if that meant going up against one of his own, then that's what he did.

Tucker was a different story all together. He was Al Day's right hand man. Now that Day was behind bars, he was holding down the reigns until the next king was chosen. Tucker was the man that took over once Douglas stepped out—that's another story.

To keep the meeting as civil as possible Douglas had breakfast prepared and served before all parties arrived— there was one more expected. The irony of this group of individuals being in the same room would have been missed by most people, but not Douglas. He had been on both sides of the law and knew each of the attendees. All he could do was hope all remained calm. That hope died the moment the back door opened. At the crack of the door all weapons were drawn and pointed towards it. Only the person that entered had already moved behind them. "Who are you guys getting ready to shoot?" Joshua asked from the other side of the room.

The group turned to the voice. "You if you don't stop pulling stunts like that," Samuel stated then put his gun away as did the others and continued eating his breakfast.

Douglas stood in front of the man he knew could kill him several different ways. "You know the rules," he held his hand out.

"Did you collect from any of them?"

"None of them tear my place apart every time they set foot in the door like you. This is not negotiable. Pay up. If nothing gets broken you get it back."

Joshua reached inside his jacket, pulled out an envelope and placed it in Douglas hand. "You are going to have to forgive me at some point."

Douglas placed the envelope in his pocket. "At some point." He stared the man down. "We good?"

"Yeah, we're good." He waved Douglas off and took a seat next to his brother and began eating off his plate. "So, who's going to take him out?"

"No one is taking anyone out. We are going to gather the evidence and let the justice system do its job," Williams stated.

"He's not going to allow anyone to take him through an investigation Williams." Tucker stated. "His plan is to use whatever he has at his disposal to take out his enemies." He looked around the table. "Each of you has powerful connections and you may eventually get enough to take him down. But how many of your women do you want to lose in the meantime. Because that's who he is gunning for. He wants to hurt you where it counts."

"We have to find a way to at least end the current madness now. That cannot wait for an investigation to be completed," Samuel stated.

"You fouled his plans last night. That might slow him down for a minute," Williams stated.

"It just pissed him off," Joshua stated. "He called for a professional to take over the situation."

"What exactly is he asking the professional to do?" Brian spoke up for the first time.

"At first it was two targets, Al Day and Cynthia Thornton. Now, he has a growing list that includes Tracy Harrison, Carolyn Roth and to my surprise, you my brother," Joshua said as he looked at Samuel.

Samuel sat back, "Really."

"Yes, really," Joshua leaned back and duplicated his brothers' stance.

"What make him think he can get away with taking out the wife of a governor and state attorney general?" Brian asked, "He has to have more than the Eagles' in his pockets."

"He does," Detective Williams replied in a matter of fact tone and looked around the table.

"The most feared group known to man, whether you're on the right or wrong side of the law," Tucker responded, "He's got the men in blue."

The men around the table nodded, understanding the severity of the situation. "The question is how far up does it go?" Samuel asked.

"That my brother is the question that has my people concerned," Joshua stated.

All eyes went to him. "Why are you here?" Brian asked.

"I thought you would never ask. It seems your man Munford has made some serious connections with some unsavory characters from another country. What you are dealing with here on the local level is petty compared to our investigation. I suggest you join forces to do what is needed to protect your women. In the meantime, I'll put a stop to the current threat."

The meeting broke up an hour later after plans were formulated to ensure everyone was protected. Joshua disappeared after receiving his envelope back from Douglas, Williams left soon after that. Samuel, Tucker and Brian remained. "I need a word with you," Tucker motion Samuel.

They stepped to the side, "My person has been looking out for you and your lady. Now I need you to look out for her."

"What do you need?"

"I want Ryan off the streets. She is damn good at what she does and it's going to hurt me to lose her, but I want her to go legit and so does Williams. Your man needs good people. Put in a word for her is all I ask. She can carry it from there."

"I plan to talk to her about that very thing."

"Cool, I'm out." They shook and Tucker left the room.

"That went better than expected," Douglas stated.

"Everybody at the table has a stake in the outcome." Brian replied. "I'm concerned about Cynthia especially with LaVere' M.I.A. Gavin and JD have agents around them, she doesn't.

"I got her covered," Samuel stated a little more forcefully than he meant.

Brian threw his hands up, "I have no objections."

A smirk began to form on Douglas face. "She got you, doesn't she? It's not my business, but it's written all over you. That's how Munford knew where to strike. The question for you my friend is, what are you going to do about it?"

Samuel ran a hand down his face and sat forward in his chair. "I plan to marry her."

Brian and Douglas frowned, "And you plan to do what with LaVere'?" Douglas asked.

"LaVere' is not a concern of mine. He is an issue for Cynthia."

Laughing Brian shook his head. "Man you can't just set a Prince aside or fight your way through him."

"I don't plan too. As I said before, I don't have an issue with the Prince." He sat his glass on the table then continued. "Believe me, this was the last thing I was expecting in my life, but here it is. I would be a fool to let her slip away. Now, I have no idea what she plans to do with the prince and frankly I don't give a damn. I won't rush her. I'll give her time to get use to the idea of marrying me." He hesitated and then grinned. "She has until Thursday."

"That's giving her time." Brian smirked sarcastically. "Just out of curiosity what happens Thursday?"

"She meets the family and officially becomes my woman."

Douglas laughed, "Just like that?"

"Just like that," Samuel replied.

Brian watched the man sitting in front of him. He knew this was not a man to make trivial conversations. He was serious about marrying Cynthia. The question now was, is she going to recognize the love this man has for her. "Cynthia is not the tough woman she portrays to people. Contrary to what some may think, she has not had an easy life. If you truly love her, you are going to see through the facade and see the beautiful person she is on the inside. Do you love her the way she deserves to be loved? Do you love her from the heart?"

"I've known her for less than a month but I can tell you I can see into her heart and I will have it. I don't know any other way. I promised myself if I was ever blessed with loving someone again I would grab it and not waste a moment. Life is too short." He sat his drink down and picked up his trench coat as Brian stood. The two men faced each other. "There is nothing or anyone I would put before her. I know you care about her and I'm just as sure you know I would give my life to protect her."

It took Brian a moment, but he slowly extended his hand, "Welcome to the family, Sofia is going to love you," he stated raising an eyebrow.

Douglas extended his hand also. "I know you are going to be good for Cynthia, but you are not a prince. Sofia is not going to take you marrying her daughter well, so be ready."

Samuel smiled and replied, "Man I have fought against terror and came out on top. I'm sure I can handle a mother-in-law."

Brian shook his head as he opened the door. "Terrorists don't have nothing on Sofia. Good luck to you my brother. He turned to Douglas, "We're meeting everyone at the church for eleven o'clock service. Are you are coming?"

"I have to pass. Be sure to put in a word or two for me with the man."

"Will do," Brian replied. "Check with you later."

The Harrisons' favorite gathering place was church and then Martha's house afterwards. It was a Sunday routine everyone had come to anticipate each week. Today was no different. JD and Tracy entered with their six month old son JC and were immediately surrounded by people looking at one of the newest members. Not a person to deal well with crowds, it was a relief when Tracy saw Ashley and James walking up with the twins, one on each of their shoulders and Cynthia in the rear. The crowd just as quickly surrounded them as a chorus of oohs and ahs could be heard throughout. Soon Roz and Marco joined them in the vestibule. Martha Harrison soon stepped forward and parted the crowd. As she took JC in her arms, "Let's get these babies down to the nursery where they can breathe some fresh air. Come along Tracy." A grateful Tracy followed as did Roz, Ashley and Cynthia after taking Jayden from James. Not far behind was Magna, who would stay in the nursery with JC.

Once they reached the nursery, some parents were there also dropping off their children for church services. "Oh God," Martha whispered.

"Momma, stop calling the Lord's name in vain," Ashley whispered.

"I wasn't calling it in vain, baby. I was asking for his help to deal with your aunt."

Lillian, who was married to Martha's brother in law Joe, walked over. "Good morning all."

"Good morning Aunt Lillian," Ashley replied and kissed her cheek.

"How are the babies this morning," she smiled as the twins were placed in a bassinet together.

"They are wonderful," Cynthia replied.

"Hello Aunt Lillian," Tracy spoke.

"Tracy." She said then turned away and spoke to Martha and pointed to Magna. "Is it necessary for that woman to be here with that gun strapped to her hip like a slinger from the wild wild west?"

Martha frowned at the way Lillian had dismissed Tracy. "Yes. She is here to keep my grandbabies safe."

"Well, maybe your grandbaby should be somewhere other than in this nursery with other children."

Hearing the comment, Cynthia, Roz and Ashley turned. "If you have a problem with JC being here, you leave." Martha stated angrily.

"I'm thinking of all the children. And I'm sure I'm not the only parent that feels this way." Lillian replied rubbing her hands over her skirt and then folding them in front of her.

"Actually Mrs. Harrison," the young lady working the nursery spoke up. "I appreciate the extra hand that Ms. Rivera provides here during the service."

Lillian turned to the woman and rolled her eyes, "I don't' believe I was speaking to you."

"I don't think you were talking to anyone in this room Lillian Harrison." Cynthia stepped forward. "If I remember correctly, my donations built this nursery in this church. Any child is welcomed here. I suggest you go to the ladies room and release some of that pressure from your brain by loosening up that wig on your head."

"Cynthia, that was not nice," Tracy said as she turned to Lillian. "May I have a moment with you in person Aunt Lillian?"

If Lillian's look could have killed, Cynthia would be dead. Luckily, she was still standing, "Of course." She replied and stepped outside the room. Martha, Roz, Cynthia, Magna and Ashley watched through the window as the ladies talked. Well, as Tracy talked, because Lillian never had a chance to say anything before her hand flew to her mouth and she ran off. As Tracy came back into the room all eyes were on her. "What did you say to Aunt Lillian?" Ashley asked.

"I told her if she ever made a statement against my son again she will be barred from any functions we have at the Governor's mansion and at the White House. And in addition to that I will tell the world that she conceived her first child out of wedlock and had a shot-gun wedding."

The gasped went around the room. "No you didn't." Martha exclaimed.

"Yes I did and I meant it too." Tracy declared then continued. "That heifer had the nerve to say my baby should not be in here. If anyone should not be inside a church it would be her." She stopped then started again while putting a blanket over her son, "No, better yet makes sure she has a front row seat to Pastor's Smith sermon so he can cleanse her soul. Talking about where my baby should be. Huh,"

"Tracy honey," Ashley put an arm around her shoulder, "its okay, she's gone now. You can stop fussing."

"The hell she can. You have every right to be mad. How dare her!" Cynthia stated with hands on her hips. "I have a notion to go give her a piece of my mind."

"Okay four musketeers, calm down." Martha said. "Lillian is just being concerned for the children's safety."

"She didn't show a whole lot of concern for JC."

"Are you defending what Aunt Lillian said mother?" Ashley asked astonished

"Hell no," Martha replied. "Now you all have me cursing in church. All of us can use a little of the pastor's sermon."

Upstairs the men stood near the stairs leading from the basement. By this time, Brian and Samuel had joined JD, James, Marco and Calvin. Uncle Joe approached JD and pulled him aside. "Look, your wife, has upset my wife. And you know my life is miserable when my wife is upset. Will you please talk to your wife into apologizing to Lillian?"

JD frowned, "Tracy upset Aunt Lillian. Are you sure it wasn't the other way around?"

Uncle Joe shook his head, "Nope, in fact I'm sure Lillian said something she should not have. But she is saying we cannot go over to your mother's house after church unless your wife apologizes. Now you know that's the only peace of mind Lexi, Jonathan and I get on Sunday. Please JD, please ask your wife to apologize. I'm begging you."

"I'll see what I can do Uncle Joe," JD smiled and patted him on the back.

When the ladies joined them the first thing JD noticed was Tracy's face. She was frowning and that was not like his wife. The family walked in and took their normal seats on the right side of the pulpit. Martha sat on the front because she normally read the announcements. JD sat a few benches from the front with Tracy, James, Ashley, Roz, Marco, Cynthia, Calvin and Jackie. Brian called in a few favors and had a few off duty agents with them today. After the night before he was not taking any chances. Two men were covering the grounds on the outside, one on both side entrances at the front of the church while he and Samuel covered the main entrance.

A block away, several police cars were on standby. The officer on the phone was doing all he could to understand why he had been given the order to go inside a church to bring someone out. Not just any church, he was being ordered to go into a church and bring out a person that was a part of the Attorney Generals' security detail. His captain was checking the order all the way up to make sure this was correct. In an effort to build a stronger relationship with the communities this type of action was frowned upon. Why not wait until church was let out, and then take the man in for questioning. Before he took any action, regardless of who it was coming from, he was going to notify JD.

Captain Davis was JD's father's partner when he died. There was no way he was going to disrupt his family in this manner without a heads up. First JD's cell buzz, then Calvin's and last Brian. The message read the same on each, *Emergency.* JD and Calvin stood then walked along the outer wall in an attempt not to call attention to both of them leaving together. Brian stepped out the center door. In the vestibule of the church Captain Davis shook JD's hand. "Sorry to have to do this, but my men have been ordered to take in Samuel Lassiter and Cynthia Thornton for questioning."

"From inside the church?" JD questioned.

"That's the order from the Chief. I have the men on stand-down for the moment. "I don't know what the hell is going on. I received a called from Detective Williams and just arrived on the scene." Captain Davis explained.

"Questioning on what?" Calvin asked.

"The death of the officer from last night."

"He's trying to show his authority," Brian stated.

"How do you want to handle it JD," The Captain asked.

"Calvin, ask Samuel and Cynthia to step outside." As an afterthought, he said, "Bring James too." He turned to

Captain Davis, "Thank you for the call Captain. Would you take my word that I will have both of them in your office directly after church service is over?"

"I will, I'm not sure the men will."

"I understand, one of their own was killed. I would want answers too." JD stated.

James, Samuel and Cynthia stepped out into the vestibule. "JD, what's going on?" Cynthia asked.

"James I need you to act as Cynthia's and Samuel's attorney here."

"Alright," he replied just as ten officers came through the outer doors.

"Captain your authority here has been stripped and I have been instructed to take Cynthia Thornton and Samuel Lassiter into custody now." Detective Sanchez stated with a little too much enjoyment.

Samuel and James both took a step to block Cynthia from view. JD stepped in front of the officer. "Do you know who I am?"

"I know who you are," the detective replied as Detective Williams came into the church and walked over to where JD and Brian stood. JD saw the movement, but continued to focus on the defiant Detective Sanchez. "As the Attorney General of the State of Virginia I hereby reinstate Captain Davis' authority in this matter. Do you have an issue with that?"

"I don't, but I'm sure the Chief will."

"Calvin," JD called without taking his eyes from Detective Sanchez, "Give Governor Roberts a call. Advise him of the situation and the fact that our office is taking over the investigation of the deaths reported last night." He raised an eyebrow. "Captain Davis, no disrespect, but as of this moment you nor the men outside have any authority over this case. Please have your officers leave the property of the church."

The Captain smiled, "Will do sir." He looked at Williams. "Let's move them out Detective Williams."

"Be happy to Captain." Detective Williams stepped between JD and Sanchez. "Detective Sanchez, would you mine leaving the premises?"

Detective Sanchez stared Detective Williams down then turned and walked out of the church. Detective Williams turned and looked at JD. "Not bad Harrison. Not bad at all." He then followed his Captain out the door.

JD turned to Brian. "Do you think Munford knows who has the power now?" he asked.

Brian smiled. "Man you look like you enjoyed that."

JD smiled, "I did." He turned to Calvin. "How much trouble are we in?"

"If we can come up with a valid reason for taking over the case none, if not a lot."

"Then let's find a good reason."

"How about police corruption? I'm sure the two men that were killed were the two shooting at us last night," Samuel stated.

"Let's talk about it after church. We've had enough disruptions for today," JD stated as they all filled back to their seats.

Gavin and Carolyn were sitting in the family room of her father's house waiting for him to come home. Gavin felt this situation should be addressed by his father-in-law. John told him about the test results before he married Carolyn. But he did not want his daughter to know for several reasons and Gavin did not feel it was his place to tell her now. "Hello Gavin," Senator John Roth extended his hand as he walked into the room. He then turned to Carolyn and hugged her, "Hello baby girl. It's good to see you."

"Hello John. Lena." Gavin replied.

"Gavin and Carolyn. What a surprise." Lena spoke.

"Hello Daddy," Carolyn spoke. When she first saw that report she couldn't wait to tell her father but now, after Gavin's reaction, she was unsure about what she thought was a fake report. She looked to him for reassurance. "Lena, could you give us a moment?" Gavin asked.

"What's going on Gavin? John asked looking between him and Carolyn."

The fear of losing the one person that she knew loved her no matter what, that she had always kept hidden was threatening to surface. Standing there looking at her father and Lena together almost confirmed the results. Seeing her distress was a little more than Gavin could take. Her hands shook the entire ride over there. Now he wished there was something he could do to shield her from this blow she was about to receive. He walked over and took her hand in his.

"Whatever you need to say can't be that bad. Just spit it out," Lena said.

John looked at his wife, he had a renewed sense of life since marrying her a year ago. But he knew his wife and his daughter did not and would never get along. "Lena," he cautioned.

He walked over and stood in front of Carolyn. "Baby what is it?" He asked concerned.

"Daddy, are you Tracy's father?"

John took a step back as if he had been slapped in the face. He looked to Gavin with a quizzical stare. Gavin slightly shook his head. He then looked back at Carolyn. "I was putting some papers in the safe in your bedroom. I saw a medical envelope and I thought something was wrong with you and you weren't telling me. So I opened the envelope and read it. At first I thought it was something she used to get you to marry her. Now I don't know. So I'm asking you daddy. Are you Tracy's father?"

John closed his eyes and exhaled. He then turned to his wife, who did not know the results of the test, but there was no expression on her face. He turned back and reached for

Carolyn's hands. "Baby girl, you are my heart. You know that."

She pulled her hands from her father and took a step back, "You didn't answer my question." She shook her head not sure where to look or who to turn to. She just knew she couldn't look at him. Gavin went to gather her in his arms, but she put her hands up to stop him. "Answer my question Daddy," she yelled.

A stunned John stood there, not sure if he should lie or tell her the truth. "Lena and Gavin, leave us alone for a minute please."

Lena held her head high and walked out of the room. Gavin hesitated as he looked at Carolyn. "I'm here for you. I love you," He kissed her temple and walked out of the room.

Carolyn looked up at her father with tears gathering in her eyes and waited.

"Yes," John said.

The tears poured like a sink that reached its limit. Carolyn sat in the chair behind her, feeling her legs giving out on her. "Baby, I didn't know until JD came to me about a picture of me, Lena and his father. I didn't just meet Lena last year. I met her about twenty-five years earlier. We had a one night stand and Tracy was conceived."

"JD knows?"

"Yes he does."

"Gavin?"

"Yes."

"Tracy?" she asked angrily.

"No, she doesn't know."

She nodded her head. "All this time you said I was your only baby girl—your special gift from God. Not so special now, you have two of us. Are there any more?" she raised her voice. "Do I have a brother or two out there too Daddy?"

"Carolyn," he attempted to reason with her. "I know this is a shock and I did not want you to find out this way."

"Huh, you didn't want me to find out at all did you? If it wasn't for this crap going on with Gavin I would have never gone into your safe and I would have never seen the test results. Is this why Mother left you?"

"Carolyn."

"All this time you made Mother out to be the monster for leaving her child behind to have the good life her family could afford. Yet you left your child to grow up thinking another man was her father, she didn't have a good life Daddy living with that woman you now call your wife. Do you realize that?"

"What happened with your mother did not have anything to do with this. Your mother left for the life of luxury her family could give her that was not a lie. Baby girl," he sighed, "If you saw the report, you know when it was done. That's when I found out. But it doesn't matter, you are my baby girl and you always will be."

"Technically, that's not true Daddy." The anguish could be heard clearly in her voice, "See Daddy I'm older than Tracy. So technically, she is your baby girl—not me." She shook her head as tears streamed down her face. She picked up her purse and coat and walked out of the room. John ran behind her into the foyer, where Gavin and Lena stood. "Carolyn, don't do this Baby girl."

She turned and looked up at her father, "Don't ever call me that again." She swung the door opened and walked out.

Gavin looked at John, "I'll talk to her," he said and closed the door behind him when he left.

John stood there, not sure what to do. He then turned to his wife.

Lena looked at the man, who turned her world upside down a years ago. He may be sixty years old, but he was still a tall handsome man and she did love him. He kept this information from her for his own reasons that she was sure

of and they were going to have to deal with that. But for now
she had to find a way to help him with his daughter, Carolyn.
"We have two options here. We can continue to pretend
this information doesn't exist. Or we can tell your other
daughter the truth before Carolyn does." She walked over,
put her hands around her husband's waist and rested her
head on his chest. He held her tight, grateful she would give
him a reprieve for now. "Whatever you want to do I will
stand by you. But I will not allow Carolyn to hurt my
daughter because she is angry with you. Do you
understand?"

He looked down at his wife, "Thank you for not over
reacting to this."

She looked up at him. "Oh, that's coming, Carolyn is just
more important at the moment. But don't' get it twisted.
You will experience my wrath later."

"I have no doubt," he smiled at her. "I have to go to
Carolyn."

"No, she's not going to hear anything you have to say
right now. It's time for you to call her mother."

"Like hell," he said and pulled away.

"You made your bed. Now you lie in it."

James did not handle criminal law, but he knew his
brother Vernon was the best. He turned to his brother last
year when he nearly killed David Holt for attempting to rape
Ashley. That was who he called to handle this situation with
Samuel and Cynthia. Vernon took the private jet from
Northern Virginia to Richmond. It wasn't often his brother
called him for help. So dropping what he was doing on a
Sunday and flying to Richmond was what he did. He and
James were working hard to establish a better relationship.
Since he was responsible for most of the discord between

them, he took every opportunity to make things better. This was one of those times.

"Thank you," he said to his mother Gwendolyn Brooks who insisted on taking the short trip with him, using the excuse of seeing her grandbabies. He sipped the drink she offered and sat it on the table next to him.

"James didn't say what the problem was when he called?" She asked sounding a little concerned

"Yes he did mother," Vernon replied as he continued searching on his laptop. He stopped and looked up at her. "Don't ask because I'm not going to tell you."

A little disturbed by his response, Gwen looked out the window. "I'll find out when we get there."

He simply smiled, "I'm sure you will," and continued gathering all the information he could on Wilbert T. Munford.

Clair opened the door as the limo pulled up in front of the house. "Good afternoon Mrs. Brooks."

"Hello Clair. Where are my grandbabies?"

Returning the warm smile, Clair pointed, "With Ms. Ashley and her friends in the sunroom."

"Thank you Clair," Gwen replied and walked to the back of the house.

"Hello Mr. Brooks. Mr. James asked me to bring you to his office"

"Thank you Clair, I know the way." Vernon walked to the closed double doors and knocked.

"Come in," he heard his brother's response.

Standing in the doorway dressed in his dark blue Armani suit with a starched white shirt, silk pinstripe tie, with his six-one slim frame, was an imposing figure that was meant to intimidate. And in most instances he did, but not in this room. This room was filled with men just as or more intimidating than him. "I see we have a full house,' he commented as he shook his brother' hand. "Are they all being arrested?"

"Not at the moment," James replied, "However the day is still young."

"I see," Vernon replied as he looked around the room. "Mr. Attorney General," he shook JD's hand.

"Thank you for coming Vernon."

"Anytime. Brian, Calvin. And you must be Samuel Lassiter," he shook their hands.

"I am."

Vernon looked up at the man, "I would hate to run across you in a dark alley." He turned to take a seat and froze at the sight of two bassinets and a day bed in the corner of the room. He looked from the items to James then back to the beds. Brian and Calvin began to laugh at the exasperated look on Vernon's face.

"Say one word and I will knock you out," James hissed.

Vernon put his hands up in the air, "Hey, I'm remaining neutral until I hear Ashley's side to this display. He sat on the day bed and crossed his legs. "Where is Cynthia Thornton?"

"In the room with the women," James explained.

"Shouldn't she be in here?"

"There's a problem," Brian began. "Munford has a contract out on her life. If she or Samuel report to police headquarters, I'm afraid neither will come out alive."

Vernon sat up, "A contract, why?" He listened as the men explained what they knew.

In the sunroom the conversation was not about the happenings from the night before.

"Okay, let me make sure I have this right. The prince wants you to marry him to help with the situation in his country. You want to marry the prince because he can give you the world and make you the princess you have been trying to convince us you were since high school. He is not in love with you and you are not in love with him. Do I have this right so far?" Roz asked as she stood in front of Cynthia near the fireplace.

"I don't think it's quite that simple Roz," Tracy said. "Cynthia feels a little left out since all of us got married. Let's face it, we don't' spend half the time together like we use to. Most time Cynthia and Brian are alone. I'm sure LaVere' is nice and everything, but if you are going to marry someone you are not in love with why won't you just marry Brian? You love him and I'm sure he can make you happy in bed."

"Urrr, I rather stick with my brotherman," Cynthia frowned.

"Is Brian the one that looks like the Rock?" Gwen asked.

"Dwayne Johnson, the actor?" Ashley asked, "No, I mean Brian looks good and he may have the body, but, the Rock is fineeeeee." She and Cynthia gave a high five.

"With the raised eyebrow and all," Cynthia laughed.

"Yes he is fine? But he is not as fine as JD."

"I heard that, and he don't have nothing on my Marco-Polo, heyyy," Roz laughed.

"None of them have anything on James. Especially when he talks low and whispers," Ashley smiled, "Girls let me tell you, that man, he makes the earth move under my feet, he brings the sky tumbling down," she sang and began laughing.

"No ladies," Cynthia stood, "All of you been sleeping on the job, Samuel is the one. Haven't you notice those bedroom eyes that can see straight to your soul or the way he tries to be serious all the time, but that little crooked smile slips out on the left side of his mouth. Girl and the mouth, the way he use that mouth. Hmm, let's not leave out his hands; the man has hands that can take you to heaven and back. And ladies, I will tell you this, Mrs. Harrison said if you want to know what a man is packing check out his feet. Well, his size twelve feet did not lie, cause the man is packing and knows what to do with it."

No one said a word or moved an inch. They all were staring in awe at Cynthia, but she didn't notice, her mind was still on Samuel.

"My, I think I need to call my husband," Gwen groaned.

Cynthia looked around the room at the eyes staring at her, "I said a little too much didn't I?"

"A tad bit, I would say," Ashley smirked.

"Umm--Cynthia, did you have sex with Samuel?" Tracy asked.

The women all turned their heads to Tracy, "You think!" Roz questioned.

"Well at least you don't need your brotherman anymore," Tracy commented just as a knock sounded at the door.

Samuel walked in. All the women in the room eyes went down to his feet. He looked down to make sure his fly wasn't open or something then looked back up. "Is everything okay ladies?" He asked as he saw Gwen hand go to her chest, followed by her sitting down.

Ashley cleared her throat, "Yes Samuel, we're fine did you need something?"

He hesitated with a concerned look on his face, "Yes I need Cynthia."

"She needs you too," Tracy commented.

Roz fell out laughing as did Ashley, while Gwen tried to maintain a matronly decorum.

Cynthia walked over to him frowning at her friends' behavior, "Let's go Samuel."

As soon as the door closed behind them, Samuel looked down at Cynthia, "Were you ladies drinking?"

"No, talking about men." She looked up and saw Vernon in the foyer. "Hello Vernon."

"Cynthia. I can certainly see why LaVere' has snatched you up. Whew, you can take a man's breath away."

She could feel the tension building in Samuel at the statement, "So I've been told. You need to talk to me?"

"I do. You don't seem too upset about the prospect of being arrested."

"I'm not. Samuel said there is no way in hell he will allow me to be arrested. So I'm done with it."

Vernon looked at Samuel with a questioning eye, "Really?"

Samuel folded his arms across his chest and stared at Vernon, "Really!"

Vernon looked from Samuel to Cynthia and smiled. "So it's like that?"

"Just like that," Samuel replied.

"O---kay. Well, let's find a room to discuss how we are going to do exactly what you promised. He looked around, hopefully one without a bassinet in it."

Cynthia smiled, "See, she looked at Samuel. I said the same thing and James actually got upset with me."

"It's his house, if he wants bassinets in every room it's not our business," Samuel laughed.

They walked into the dining room and sat at the table as Vernon begin questioning them about the previous night.

In the meantime, the other men joined the woman in the sunroom. Clair served refreshments and everyone took a moment to breath. For a Sunday, it had turn out to be a very arduous day. The men ask the woman what they were talking about all except for Tracy went silent. "Well first we talked about you guys, and then we talked about Cynthia and Samuel's feet." Gwen almost choked on her water. Tracy turned to JD unaware of the reaction on the other women faces. "Babe, let me see your feet." Roz and Ashley laughed so hard they were about to cry. Gwen stood and walked over to the window and began to fan herself.

"Why do you need to see my feet, babe?" JD asked, lifting his feet up.

"I'm not really sure, but I will figure it out eventually. One thing for sure Cynthia doesn't need her brotherman anymore. She has Samuel now."

Roz and Ashley screamed as they fell off the sofa they were on.

"What in the hell is wrong with all of you?" Brian asked.

"I got to go." Roz said as she tried to get up off the floor. "Marco needs me at the restaurant."

"Liar," Ashley laughed.

"No really, I have to go," she sobered, "If I stay here a moment longer, I'm going to bust a gut." She looked at Tracy, "I love you girl. Don't you ever change. Give JC and the twins a kiss for me."

"I will," Tracy replied without an inkling of an idea why the women were laughing.

"You remember to look at Marco's feet when you get home," Ashley laughed.

James looked from Ashley to his mother, whom he could swear was blushing. "Which one of you started it?"

They both replied in unison, "Cynthia!"

A few minutes later Samuel and Cynthia joined the group in the room. James went in search of Vernon. When he walked into his office, Vernon was on the telephone.

"Neither of my clients will present themselves to headquarters." He listened and then replied to the person on the telephone. "Well you have a choice. You can speak with them on my terms or not speak with them at all. You have my numbers. Call me when you make a decision. In the meantime if either of my clients is harassed or even thinks they are being harassed by your officers, be prepared for the law suit of a lifetime. And make no mistake it will be played out in the media. So think carefully before you make your next move. Thank you for your time Chief Munford." Vernon then hung up the telephone.

James cleared his throat, "Is that going to hold him off?"

"Legally, but if this man is as dirty as you think, he won't be deterred by the law. He thinks he's above it. I would advise Samuel to be on guard."

"Samuel and his brother Joshua are dangerous men. They have been trained to kill people and ask questions later." James said as he took a seat in front of his desk. "Brian will not be able to restrain Samuel much longer."

"Especially if Cynthia is in danger," Vernon added. "This is a volatile situation you have here my brother. And what are you going to do about Samuel when LaVere' returns?"

"I'm staying the hell out of the way."

Vernon smiled, "Our mother did not raise any fools."

Carolyn had been dealt a blow and Gavin knew it was going to take his intervening to help her deal with the pain. Her father was the one thing she knew as stability and now she felt that had been pulled from under her. In the car on the ride home, she never made a sound. The only evidence of her pain was the silent tears that continuously fell from her eyes. The fight in her was gone and that worried Gavin. He knew once she came out of this all hell was going to break out. Of all the people in the world she had to share her father with the one woman that took away her dream of living in the Governor's mansion with JD Harrison. At one time it mattered that she did all she could to breakup Tracy and JD during the time he was seeing her. Gavin accepted the fact that he was her second choice. His love for her was enough to get them through, at least he hope it was. This situation will certainly be a test.

At the moment the only thing Gavin wanted to do was make Carolyn feel better. As they entered the house Carolyn went straight to their bedroom and closed the door. His heart went out to her and he would allow her a minute, but that was all. Taking off his coat, he placed a call to JD's cell phone. When he did not receive an answer he left a message. That was not going to be an easy conversation. JD was just as adamant about keeping this information from Tracy as John was about keeping it from Carolyn. Both men were going to catch hell from that decision.

Walking into the bedroom, he could see Carolyn sitting on the far side of the room staring out the window. He walked into the bathroom turned on the faucet in the marble encase Jacuzzi that sat in the center of the room. He put her favorite lavender scent in the water and returned to the bedroom. Taking off his tie and rolling up his sleeves, he went into the sitting area and picked his wife up in his arms. To his surprise she did not fight him or ask any questions. She simply put her arms around his neck and placed her head on his shoulders. He sat on the bed with her in his lap and undressed her. Taking a few combs from her vanity, he pinned her hair up, then carried her into the bathroom and placed her in the tub.

Carolyn slide down into the soothing water and allowed the pulsating water surround her body and began to relax. Gavin took a wash cloth, ran cold water over it than sat beside the tub and gently washed her face with the cool cloth. "I want you to look at me Carolyn," he said in a soothing tone. When she looked at him he saw the hurt and sadness in her beautiful green eyes. That was the first thing he noticed about her the first time he saw her with JD—those beautiful green eyes she inherited from her mother's side of the family. The family that could not accept the fact that her mother married and had a child by an African-American. It was her mother's side of the family that had the power, wealth and connections to make or break a political career. They were too righteous to outright deny the child as one of the mighty Worthington's, for she was the spitting image of her grandmother. Her skin tone was more olive than lily white, therefore, she was treated as an outcast grandchild. Her mother was eventually forced to make a choice between living the jet-set life of a Worthington or raising her mixed race child. Her choice was the life of the rich and famous, leaving John to raise his daughter on his own. To this day Carolyn had not wanted for anything. Gavin was going to have to find a way to remind her how very much her father loves her. "I love you more than life itself. If I could take this pain from you I would." He wiped a tear from her face, then took one of Carolyn's sponges and put some of the shower gel on it and began to bath her. "Love is a funny thing when you think about it. A person's heart is a small organ but it can carry a huge burden. It can be filled with happiness and sadness. Sometimes it feels as if it can burst from joy and hurt so much you feel as if you will die from the pain. We have to find a way to balance between the joy and pain by allowing another emotion called forgiveness." He continued to bathe her and talk. "This is the reason your father said he did not want you to know about the test. He could not stand the thought of you being hurt. That is the only reason he did not tell you about this. He was as shocked as you were tonight with the findings. I know it's going to take time, but for me please find room in your heart to forgive him. I've waited a long time to have your heart to myself. I don't want to share it with hatred for your father and Tracy. I want all of it." She closed her eyes. "Open your eyes Carolyn. I want you to see how much I need and love you." She reopened her eyes and stared at him. "Thank you," he smiled. "When you give birth to my son--" She raised her eyebrow at him. "That's right—my son," he smiled. "We are going to make a deal. There will be no secrets surrounding him. We will do all that is in our power to make sure he is loved and happy. We will not allow anything that is happening between us to interfere with his happiness. Do we have a deal?" he waited for her to reply. She nodded. He shook his head, "No, I need to hear you say it. I need to hear you say you promise to have enough room in your heart for me and our son."

Gavin had not made love to her in months. He made it clear on the day she tried to seduce him that their marriage will be for political appearance only. Carolyn knew she had pushed him to that point. She thought she had control of him, but Carolyn was wrong. She had misjudged Gavin and he had reached his point of tolerance with her. For a while, it did not bother Carolyn, she was getting whatever sexual satisfaction she needed from David Holt. But after a few

months and Gavin had made no attempts to make love to
her, she began to wonder why. Tonight she could not take
another disappointment. Tonight she needed to be loved.

As if he read her thoughts, Gavin ran the sponge between
her breast; across her stomach than down between her legs.
He pulled her leg up and washed her thigh; first one; then
the other. As he reapplied the body wash to the sponge, he
pulled her feet out of the water. He gently washed them;
going between each toe with precision. His touch was so
gentle, so caring, her body responded to every move. This
was what she needed. Once he had finished with the feet he
stood, then walked around the tub. This was where he
would leave her alone to deal with her father's deceit. In a
way Carolyn was thankful, the torture of his touch had
stopped. On the other hand she was sad and sorry for the
things she did to make Gavin walk away from their bed.

Gavin stood behind her and pushed her forward, "pull
your legs up," he said. Carolyn complied. She pulled her
legs up to her chest and laid her head on her knees. Gavin
used the sponge to wash her back. His touch was so gentle
and loving Carolyn got lost in it. The confession from her
father faded into the recesses of her mind as Gavin began to
sponge her shoulders and neck. "We have to make love for
us to have a son."

"Funny you should say that." He pulled a towel from the
warming tray and held it up. "Come make a son with me
Carolyn," he said.

Not sure what to expect, she stepped out. Gavin wrapped
the towel around her and left the room. Carolyn took the
towel and patted herself dry. She sat at her vanity dejected.
The bath was wonderful, but now she felt worst than she did
before. Gavin's touch had just reminded her of what she
was missing. It wasn't just a sexual touch but a caring touch
as well. He was showing her just how much he cared.
Carolyn stood to go into the bedroom and found Gavin

standing in the doorway. Carolyn wondered how long he had been there, but she did not ask.

He had pulled one of her teddies out of the draw and handed it to her. She dropped the towel and put the teddy over her head. The strap of the teddy caught on the combs in her hair and he smiled at the sight. He stepped to her and removed the comb from her hair. As her hair fell upon her shoulders, Gavin ran his finger down the center of her back. His touch was like a feather tickling her. She laid her head back against his chest. Gavin put his finger under her chin and pulled her face to him. He gently kissed her lips then pressed his other hand on her stomach pulling her closer to him. She could feel all of him against her hips. There was no mistaking the effect she was having on him. Then there was something in his touch that made her secure in what was about to happen. Gavin was not teasing her this time, he was making love to her. Gavin pulled Carolyn around to face him without breaking the kiss. She put her arms around his neck as the kiss became more intense. He gently pulled her closer to him and held her at the waist. He was pacing his self for the night. Carolyn was never one to need a lot of intimacy during sex, but tonight she not only needed it, but wanted it. She needed to feel loved tonight. Only a man that was in love with her could give that to her.

Gavin knew what Carolyn needed. He knew the revelation from her father cut her deep and he wanted to take that hurt away. He wanted to make love to his wife to let her know he was there for her through thick and thin until death they do part.

He ran his hand up her ribcage to her breast and caught one of her nipples between his fingers and squeezed it. She moaned at his touch. "Tell me Carolyn. Tell me you will make room in your heart."

He trailed kisses down her cheeks, around her neck to the other breast and gathered that nipple between his lips. "I will," she breathlessly agreed.

"You will what darling?" he asked dropping to his knees, pulling her body closer to his lips and kissing her navel.

"Make room in my heart," she whispered as her knees began to buckle.

His hands cupped her behind and squeezed firmly as he inhaled her womanly scent kissing the crease of her center. "For who?"

Her breath caught in her throat at the touch. "For you," she nearly cried.

His tongue snaked out and coated the core of her, "and?" he asked as he picked her up and carried her to the bed. He stood there staring at her as he removed his clothes. "Who Carolyn? Me and who?" he urgently asked as he went right back to the location he was sweetly torturing between her legs.

"Our son," she replied on the verge of exploding.

Before she finished answering, he covered her body with his and entered her with one mission in mind, to finally have the woman he loved to love him back.

No words were spoken between them throughout the night, but then none were needed. Gavin made love to Carolyn passionately all night and she responded to his every move; every touch; every kiss. With other men Carolyn always made them think they had complete control, even with JD. But tonight it was not a forced issue, Gavin had complete control and she was happy to follow. When Carolyn fell asleep in Gavin's arms for the first time in her life she felt loved by someone other than her father.

Chapter 16

Chief Munford was livid and that was putting it mildly, when he stormed into his office Monday morning. Not only had his orders not been followed, he also received a telephone call from a big shot attorney from Northern Virginia claiming to represent Lassiter and Thornton. He threw his briefcase on top of his desk and stared out the window overlooking downtown Richmond. They could not follow a simple order. Storm the church, bring Lassiter and Thornton to the station and make them simply disappear. He knew there were loop holes in the plan, but he didn't care. He wanted to send a message to Harrison that he controlled the streets of Richmond, VA. At the wave of a hand he could make his life a nightmare. Now he had Vernon Brooks to deal with. The damn Brooks money that stretched from Virginia to California and then overseas. All this bull started with that spineless Roberts giving the information to that woman. A knocked sounded at his door and he yelled enter.

Captain Davis stood in the door way, "You requested to see me Chief."

"Where in the hell do you get off counteracting my orders?"

Thirty years on the job and Captain Davis never thought of retiring until now. In the past he would see things happen and as long as it did not touch him or his men, he would turn and look the other way. In the last year or so it seemed the Chief was more blatant with his underhand dealings and frankly he was tired of it. "The order was so profound I did not believe it came from you. I've always known you to be an intelligent officer. This move was just damn stupid."

"One of our own was shot down in the street and those individuals inside that church were involved. Where is your loyalty to the men in blue?"

"You don't give a damn about the men. Save that bull for the media. Your purpose was to upstage JD Harrison. You couldn't do that with his father, and you damn sure are not going to do it to his son. I don't know why you hated James Harrison to a point of having him gunned down in the street. But you will reap what you sow the next time you step across the line with JD. And know this." he said as he took a step closer to the chief, "I'll be the one taking your ass down."

"If your loyalty to the Harrison family prevents you from carrying out your duties to the department, then turn in your papers."

"I wouldn't give you the satisfaction," Captain Davis replied as he turned to exit. "Send one of your men after me or anywhere near a member of my family and you will regret it." Captain Davis walked out and slammed the door behind him.

Chief Munford cursed then pick up his cell phone and dialed a number. "I want that information that Thornton has. Then I want Thornton and Roberts dead by the end of the week." He closed the cell phone then decided to spend the week of Thanksgiving with his family, just in case he needed an alibi.

For the next few days it was Samuel's intention to keep Cynthia under lock and key. Keeping a low profile for a few days he hoped would calm the situation down and give them a chance to counter Munford's next move. It wasn't to be. This being the week of Thanksgiving, TNT was scheduled to decorate ten homes on Wednesday and another twelve on the Friday. The staff was scheduled to be at the office by seven to layout the plans, box and pull decorations. There was no way Cynthia was going to stay home for a few days.

Not sure how far Munford would go, Samuel made sure Ryan was covering Cynthia's house during the day, while they were at the office. Dealing with the men in blue, there was no way of telling who was a good cop and who was on Munford's personal payroll, so driving was out of the question. They could get pulled over for the simplest thing and never be seen again. So for the time being a car service was transporting them back and forth to the office.

JD was having a different problem. He received a call from Senator Roth advising him of the situation with Carolyn. This was the last thing he wanted or needed to deal with. Those that knew Carolyn knew how vindictive she could be especially JD. He had been on the end of her antics more times than he cared to count. In addition to that, it was no secret that Carolyn hated his wife Tracy. Both the political and private circle knew it. Now he had to find a way to keep Carolyn from using this information against Tracy. On the same note, JD knew how much Carolyn's father meant to her and the fact that he has another child had to be devastating. To have that child to be Tracy of all people had to knock the wind out of her. He could hear the concern in Senator's Roth voice when he stated Carolyn has refused to see him or take any of his calls. What a mess this is turning out to be. JD was sure in addition to dealing with Carolyn; the senator also had to deal with his wife Lena who did not know the results of the test.

To think this all came about from an old picture his mother found when she was helping to pack his apartment to move into his home with Tracy. James Brooks recognize Lena Washington from the photo with Senator Roth and JD's father. Since JD and Tracy was about to be married and he was about to run for office they were doing an investigation into each of their backgrounds to counter act anything the opposition might attempt to use against them. During that investigation the question of Tracy's parentage came up. Lena explained she always thought Billy Washington was her father until an accident and Tracy hospitalization prove he was not. She was sleeping around with different men during that time, so other than Billy she had no idea who could have been the father. Needing an answer before marrying Tracy, James, JD and Senator Roth devised a plan to answer the question that altered all their lives.

It was a relief to find out JD's father was eliminated, but the test did reveal John Roth was indeed Tracy's father. The three men made a decision to keep the results confidential to protect Carolyn more than anything else. Now the one person that would be hurt more by this than any other knew the truth. The question for everyone involved was what Carolyn would do with the information.

JD attempted to call Gavin several times from his office, when that failed he finally gave up and went to their home. Only to be told the Roberts were not accepting visitors. JD left a message for Gavin to contact him and decided to go home instead of returning to the office. When he arrived Lena was there visiting with Tracy and JC. His heart skipped a beat as he watched them in the sunroom.

"Hey sweetie," Tracy beamed as she walked over and kissed him. "What are you doing home so early?"

JD hugged his wife and stared at Lena, who stared back, but did not indicate anything. He then looked down at his wife as she pulled back, but stayed in his arms. "I wasn't getting much done at the office so I decided to come home early."

A pleased Tracy smiled, "Well I'm taking full advantage of this. My husband is home early and my mother just happened to stop by to talk. The world as I know it is certainly changing. Why don't you two visit while I start dinner?"

"Tracy I can't stay. I just wanted to stop by to see how you were. I need to get back to John," Lena said as she put JC in his playpen. The baby immediately grabbed his rattle and drooled with a giggle.

JD smiled down at his son, then exhaled as he watched Lena. To this day he did not trust her. The money hungry woman he met a few years ago was always in the forefront of his mind when it came to her. He knew his wife had forgiven her mother for the things she did in the past, but JD was not convince she would not hurt Tracy again. To him, anyone that that might harm his wife stayed on his watch list. "Is the Senator okay, is he sick?" Tracy asked.

Lena shook her head as she picked up her purse, "No, he's just going through something with Carolyn."

"Huh, aren't we all. She called me earlier today, but Gavin came on the line and we never got a chance to talk." Tracy stepped away from JD, "It sounded like she was crying or maybe a little tipsy, if you know what I mean. I can't imagine why she would be calling me."

"Well, I wouldn't lose any sleep over it," Lena said as they walked towards the door. "JD, walk me to my car."

JD scowled at the request, but changed his facial expression quickly when Tracy turned to him. "Sure," he replied as he walked over and opened the front door. "I'll be right back, babe." He said to Tracy then walked out the door behind Lena.

"You didn't tell Tracy the truth when you found out," Lena huffed and shook her head. "You did everything you could to keep me from finding out."

"For obvious reason, shall I recite them to you?" JD angrily replied.

"No, but you better have your reason ready when Tracy finds out. And believe me Carolyn will make sure she knows. You better than anyone knows how much Tracy hates to be lied to."

"I didn't lie to her." He hesitated then continued. "For the first time in her life Tracy is surrounded by a loving family and that includes you. How did Carolyn react to the news?" Lena just looked away. "That's what I thought. How do you think it will affect Tracy? I think it will put a strain on what is a delicate rebuilding of a relationship between the two of you. I'm not sure I want to put her through that. I'm trying to protect her the best way I know how.

"No you were originally protecting your career and John's. There is no reason to withhold the truth from her now." Lena opened the door to her car. "JD," she exhaled, "I don't have any issues with you marrying Tracy. I know you love her just as much as you despise me. I'm asking you not for my sake but for your own. Tell Tracy the truth before, Carolyn gets to her." Lena started her car and pulled off.

When JD walked back into the house Tracy was waiting by the door with her eyebrows raised, "What was that all about?"

"What do you mean?" JD asked nonchalantly

Tracy stared at her husband. "My mother doesn't visit JD and you don't come home early. Then the two of you have what appeared to be a very intense conversation. I don't have to be a rocket scientist to know something is up."

JD held her stare for a moment. He eased his arms around her waist and pulled her close. "I can't' speak for your mother, but for me I just wanted to hold you." He said as he placed his chin on the top of her head and closed his eyes. He knew he had to tell her the truth before Carolyn or Lena, he just didn't know how. "I love you Tracy and I will tell you as soon as I think the time is right." He held her a little tighter and found comfort in her embrace. "You can't' blame a brother for wanting to hold his wife, can you?"

She hugged him back. Feeling the rapid beat of his heart, she knew something was wrong, but she didn't push. "No, just like you can't blame a wife for worrying about her husband." JC cried out and she pulled away. Walking towards the staircase she turned and looked at her husband "Whatever it is I trust you to tell me when you are ready."

He smiled as she walked out the room, "Thank you babe."

Waking up in Gavin's arms was a wonderful feeling and it would have healed all her worries if it had happened before Sunday. Now whenever he is with her, the hurt is dulled, but when he was not around the hurt was piercing. She felt as if someone was taking a sharp knife and continuously stabbing her in her heart. All her life the one person that was completely hers was her father. No matter what she did, no matter how much she spent, no matter who she hurt, her father was always, always there for her. Now, she had to share him—with Tracy. First she took JD from her. It was a foregone conclusion that JD was going to be governor of Virginia and possible President of the United States in eight years. The political world was swirling with conversations about the Attorney General of Virginia. Every time you turned on one of the national news channels and the networks wanted to get an opinion on the latest happenings in DC it was JD's face that appeared. The DNC was doing everything in their power to keep him in the center on national events.

Whenever he was invited to different social events, it was Tracy who was beside him and it's going to be Tracy that walks through the doors of the White House with him when the time comes. Tracy, Tracy, Tracy. To clear her mind she had to think and dig hard to determine why she was so angry. It wasn't that Tracy had JD. She was sure she was exactly where she was supposed to be, with Gavin. He loves her and to her surprise she loves him. It's the one thing that is keeping her from losing her mind. If this had come out two years ago, she would have lost it, for she was a lost person then. But now she was first lady of Virginia, wife of Gavin W. Roberts, Governor of Virginia. She has what she had always wanted, but what did it bring her. Nothing she thought it would.

The Worthington's still did not accept her as she thought they would. She was still the dark skinned daughter of one of their children and nothing more. It didn't matter how hard she tried to stay out of the sun when she was little to keep her skin from darkening, she was still not accepted. Even on inauguration night at one of the balls, her grandmother stated, "*You spent too much time in the sun, your skin is brown.*" Not, "*I'm so proud of you for finally putting a Worthington in the Governor's mansion.* Which was a feat they have wanted for years, none of their fair skinned granddaughters or grandsons accomplished that. But with her father, none of that was ever an issue. He loved her more than life itself.

She finished off the drink that was in her hand and poured another shot from the bottle of bourbon she had started an hour ago. First she lost her mother, then she lost JD, now she had to share her father with sweet little pathetic Tracy. Carolyn did not like her, nothing and no one was that innocent. Hell if her world was going to be turned upside down than so was Tracy's. She stood and picked up the telephone and dialed the Harrison's number. "Damn, if I'm going to be the only miserable one," she slurred into the telephone. "Tracy, this is Carolyn Roth-Roberts."

"Carolyn?" Gavin called from the doorway.

Carolyn turned and smiled at her husband, "Wait one minute sweetheart—I have to tell Tracy something."

Gavin rushed over and took the telephone from her. "Tracy, hi, it's Gavin. Look um, JD called earlier and I wasn't available. Would you tell him I returned the call."

"That's not what I was going to tell her Gavin," Carolyn said as she reached for the phone.

"Thank you Tracy. I'll talk to you soon." He hung up the telephone and turned to look at his wife. She was drunk, not a little tipsy, but drunk. She pulled away from him when he tried to take the glass from her hand.

"What are you doing?" she questioned as she stumbled back.

He looked around the room and saw the almost empty bottle on the table. "Carolyn, did you drink this whole bottle."

She smiled, "It was good," she nodded her head.

His wife was standing near the fireplace with hair pinned up, her pearls and cardigan sweater on as refined as ever and drunk. The sight would have been funny if the situation was different, but Gavin knew this could be a problem. "Give me the glass Carolyn." He held his hand out and walked over to her.

She tilted her head back swallowed the contents of the glass then gave it to him and smiled. "Are we going to make love again now?"

His smiled turned into a little chuckle at the way she was smiling up at him, like a little girl asking for another piece of candy. This was the first time in all the years he has known Carolyn that she looked so sweet, innocent and vulnerable. "No sweetheart. But I am going to put you to bed." He picked her up and she wrapped her arms around his shoulders then place her forehead on his, "You know what?"

"What?" He asked as he carried her up the steps.

"I love you."

He had heard her say the words before, but this was the first time he truly believed it. "I love you too Carolyn, very much."

"You want to know something else?"

"What?" he asked as he laid her on the bed and began to remove her shoes.

"I love my father too," she began to cry and turned away from him.

He turned her back over and looked into her eyes. "Your father loves you very much Carolyn. Don't ever doubt that."

"But now he's got Tracy, just like JD and that Cynthia woman's got you too. And I'm going to be all alone."

Wiping the tears from her face Gavin smiled, "The only woman that has me is you and I will never leave you alone." He touched her nose.

"Really?"

"Really."

"Gavin."

"Yes,"

"I think I dranked too much."

Laughing, "I think you did too. And you are going to have hell to pay in the morning." He sat there and watched as her eyes closed. Pulling the coverlet over her he just stared at her and thought. The last thirty minutes were probably the most honesty he had received from her since they had been married.

After she was asleep he asked her personal assistant to cancel any meetings she had for the rest of the week. Then he called her father who had called several times throughout the day. He promised John he would do what he could to get Carolyn to talk to him. He then called his office and found there were several calls from JD and Munford. He handled the state's business first then called JD. He informed him of the events surrounding him taking over the investigation of the shooting on Saturday. They both decided something had to be done with Munford. Gavin gave JD full control, wherever the pieces fall, they fall. They then discussed Carolyn and her telephone call to Tracy. They disagreed on the reasons, but it was imperative that they make a decision on how to proceed. If this information gets out it will not just be a personal matter, it would be a political issue as well. Senator Roth was a powerful man in the world of politics; the revelation could have an effect on not only his career, but JD's and Gavin's as well. That was what Gavin planned to use to get Carolyn to cooperate with whatever decision they made. When JD asked how Carolyn was taking the news, Gavin could only reply, "Hard."

Turk was surprised to hear he had a visitor. As he walked through the courtyard to the admin building where the visitor center was located he wondered what had gone astray. When he saw Tuck, a frown creased his brow. They shook, "Didn't expect to see you this soon."

"This situation calls for desperate measures," Tuck said and took a seat. Once Turk was seated he told him all that had taken place from the shooting Saturday, the meeting on Sunday morning and last but not least the order placed today.

"From what I was told the order was to take out the Governor. You and I know that kind of heat will hamper operations. And destroy our plans. Munford has to be stopped. Give me the word and I'll have him taken out."

Turk shook his head, "Naw, taking out a police chief will be just as costly. Besides, we don't kill people unless they are trying to kill us."

"What you think Munford is looking for you to do, give you a kiss?" Tuck asked angrily.

Turk chuckled, "Man, calm down. I told you the first line of handling business is to remain cool. You can't think straight when you're mad. Calm the hell down."

"This man is talking about taking you out and you want me to calm down," Tuck shook his head and sat back.

"Thanks for having my back man, but I'm not worried about Munford. He's into some shit now that is going to bring him down soon enough. What we need to do is give him a wakeup call to put a stop to this madness he has created." Turk sat up and motioned for Tuck to do the same. Head to head, Turk smirked, "You remember how we got Jazz out of town a few years back?"

Tuck nodded his head, "Yeah."

"Set it up," Turk nodded. You'll know when to move." Turk stood, gave Tuck a pound and left the room.

Chapter 17

At six in the evening, Thanksgiving eve, James watched as his wife slept on the bed in his home office. She was the most beautiful mother he had ever seen. Happy that she had finally conceded that helping her mother with Thanksgiving dinner with the twins was not an option this year, he sent Clair, his housekeeper instead. She had just gotten the babies asleep and decided she would lie down, but just for a moment. That moment had now turned into two hours and James was happy. The ringing of the telephone interrupted his thoughts. He answered it quickly so it would not wake Ashley.

"Hello Cynthia." James listened as he heard the concern in her voice. She wanted to talk about LaVere'. There was no way he was going to wake Ashley, so he took the position of counselor. For the second time in a week, he was surprised at the depth of her concern for his friend. It had been over a week since anyone heard from LaVere' or his brother and all, including the King was very concerned for their well-being. Then she said the one thing James would never had expected from her.

"I've been sitting here thinking about the last few weeks of my life. It seems like hell has broken lose on all fronts. Out of it all there is one thing I know for sure. I can't marry

LaVere', because I don't love him. Yes, he is a good man that could provide me with all the material things I could ever want or need. But, those things can't replace the fundamental need that every human has to be loved. I need that more than anything else. I hope my decision will not interfere with our relationship. Despite the way we stay at each other's throat, next to JD you are one of the best men that I know."

"Normally I would enjoy watching you stumbling around. But now that you have discovered what is important in life, I think you are ready to fall in the right direction. Samuel Lassiter is a damn good man. It's clear to anyone within two feet of the two of you that there is an attraction. I realize you have a commitment with LaVere' but you seem to have an infatuation with Samuel that needs to be clinched."

"Infatuation, hum. I'm afraid I may be a little past the infatuated point. I think I may be in love with him," she said timidly. "I don't know how to explain it to you, you know you are a man and unfortunately your capacity to understand woman's intuition is limited."

"I have a little experience in this area, try me."

She hesitated before continuing. "Well.... It's the feeling I get when he's around. I seem to fall all over myself and him every time he is in arms reach. And I do mean that literally. I feel safe when he's around. The night I met him after the accident, I felt him watching over me, to make sure I wasn't alone. I woke up during the night and he was there, as if he was waiting for me. I know that sounds a little crazy, because at the time I did not know the man. And to tell you the truth, I still don't know all that I want to know. It feels like....I'm home when he is with me. I don't want for anything or anybody—just him. I'm just beginning to realize he's touched my heart and I can't shake it."

"Stop trying to shake it; run with the feeling. Lord knows I ran from Ashley for damn near a year before I realized she was my life." Through the telephone he heard a knock at a door. Then he heard her open the door. "You want some dinner?" he heard Samuel ask.

"Yes, thank you." Cynthia's voice echoed through the telephone.

Smiling James replied, "I take it our truce is over."

"Yeah, I'll talk to you later."

James was still smiling when he hung up the telephone. "Lassiter is probably the only man in this hemisphere that could actually tame that woman."

"See you were doing really well until that comment," Ashley said from the sofa.

He looked in his wife's direction, "How much of that did you hear?"

"Enough to know, Cynthia and LaVere' will not be getting married. I think one of us owe Tracy some money."

Following him down the stairs Cynthia thought, *I have never seen a man with such a confident swagger.* It reminded her of every time Denzel walked into a scene of a movie, as if he was saying, "*I don't know about yall, but I got this.*"

They had spent the last three days together, at work and then at home, well at least her house. It felt right. It seem like it's always been this way. She thought about her conversation with James, she really didn't know Samuel that well. She knew he looked as good in an Armani suit as he did in a pair of jeans and a cardigan sweater as he wore tonight. She knew that he could cook, for the last two nights they had home cooked meals that he prepared as she watched. And she knew he made her feel like a million bucks whenever he was around. But could he save her from herself? Sofia had made one thing clear in life. If a man could not provide you with the lifestyle you deserved, you will eventually grow to hate him. Would that happen to them?

She bumped into him, not realizing he had stopped and turned. Catching her by the waist he held her tight. He had upheld his promise to keep his distance until she had a chance to talk to LaVere', but his discipline was wavering. In his entire life, Samuel could not remember anything feeling as right as her being in his arms. His military training on discipline and control drifted away the longer he stared into her eyes. It would be wise to remember technically she was not his woman; yet. At this moment she belonged to Prince LaVere'. Caution should prevail, but he found his arms pulling her closer. As he continued to stare into her eyes he saw something that caused him to proceed cautiously. What he saw in her eyes was fear.

There was nothing in her stance or in the words she spoke, but he knew fear when he saw it. Hell he was trained to produce it in others. This was the last person he wanted to fear him. Why would she be afraid of him, he thought from a moment, then realized, she wasn't afraid of him, the man. She was afraid of what he represented; love. "I always keep my word. Do you?"

Cynthia attempted to step back, stunned by his question. "I don't lie, cheat or steal," she replied indignantly. "Why would you ask me such a thing?"

Pulling her back close to his body, where she belong he exhaled, "You seem to be pulling away. Are you having second thoughts about LaVere'?"

She placed her head on his shoulder, not ready to completely concede to the truth. "I don't know you and the fact that you have such an effect on me scares the hell out of me."

So, of love, he realized. He held her tight and whispered in her ear. "Tell me a secret." She turned her face towards him with a questioning look. Her lips were so close to his, he could feel her breath on them. "Tell me something you have never told another person."

Seeing the intensity in his eyes, she thought hard, should she revealed her biggest fear to him. She hesitated, not sure if she could open up to him. He saw the hesitation in her eyes and whispered across her lips, "Tell me Cynthia."

Those were very tantalizing lips that spoke her name. Her eyes traveled from his lips back to his eyes. They had such depth and warmth; there was no way she could resist. "I'm afraid of growing poor, old and gray alone. His eyes never left hers, until she felt his lips gently touch hers.

"Then your fears end here." He kissed one corner of her mouth. "I have no intensions of going anywhere." He then kissed the other corner of her mouth.

Basking in the sensations his light kisses were causing, she parted her lips to speak. "Tell me a secret." She pressed her body closer to his and kissed the side of his lips. "Something you've never told another soul." She kissed the other side.

Mesmerized by her eyes he was tempted to tell her everything and anything, but he knew doing that would put her life in danger. But if he could he would tell her he did not like killing people. That was a strange place to be since he was a professional assassin for the government. He wanted to bear his soul to the warmth of her eyes. "I know you have a brand new brotherman to throw away." He replied pressing his midsection closer to her to ensure she know how she had stimulated him. He lowered his lips to hers, which parted willingly and began possessively stroking the inside of her mouth.

It took her a moment before she realized what he said. Laughter began to rise in his throat. She pushed him away and her hands landed on her hips. "How do you know about him?"

Samuel was just about buckling over laughing at her expression. Unable to resist, he pulled her into his arms and began to kiss her senseless.

Just before they reached the point of no return she reluctantly ended the kiss. "I'm not having sex with you."

Smiling he asked, "Are you trying to convince me or yourself?"

Inhaling deeply she replied, "Both," and dropped her head to his shoulder.

"In that case I think we better eat dinner and start your movie." She smiled, took his hand and walked into the kitchen. After dinner he cleared the table as she went downstairs to the family room to prepare for the movie. Walking down the stairs he looked around the cozy room and saw the snow gently falling outside the patio window, the wine bottle on the table with a single glass next to it and the lights turned down low. He stepped in and watched as she walked over to the bar and pulled out another glass. The setting could be lethal to someone trying to avoid a sexual encounter. "You may need to tell me what movie we are going to watch."

She walked over to the chaise lounge. "Take your shoes off and have a seat." He looked at her with one eyebrow raised, then complied with her request and settled in the seat. She gave him a glass of wine then took a seat between his muscular thighs. Placing his arm around her waist he adjusted her body cozily to his allowing her backside to collide with his arousal. "Perfect fit," he stated then kissed the top of her head.

Yes it is," she exhaled and pushed the play button.

To his relief when the movie began, it was *The Wizard of Oz.* Smiling he placed his hand possessively on her stomach. "You are full of surprises."

Laying her head back against his chest, she wondered if she would be able to surprise herself and not fall under the temptation of his touch, his kisses or those oh so powerful thighs his jeans were stretching across. From the feel of things brotherman would never be able to match up with what she felt against her behind. "Lord, help me through the night," she quietly whispered.

A guard at the federal prison sounded the alarm. A man was lying face down on the floor of his cell barely breathing. Help arrived and the man was taken to hospital. The doctor's examination indicated the man had what appeared to be an asthma attack, but with overnight breathing treatments, he should be fine. The man was placed in a room at the end of the hallway with a twenty-four hour guard. Right after the changing of the night hospital staff two men entered the room dressed in green scrubs to check the vitals on the prisoner. Approximately ten minutes later the two doctors left the room. The guard looked inside and saw the prisoner was apparently asleep facing the wall. Believing all was well the guard sat back down with his book and settled in for the night.

Wilbert Munford was in the comfort of his bed asleep, content with the thoughts that his path to controlling Richmond was within his reach. He turned over and was silently taken from his bed without arousing his wife who was asleep next to him. His eyes grew as wide as a saucer as the three men had him wrapped mummy style in a sheet and duck tape on his mouth so tight he could barely turn his head. Why in the hell won't his wife wake up? He wondered as the men carried him down the stairs. He was moaning like a calf in heat, but she did not move. Had they killed her? He attempted to struggle more, to no avail. They took him down to his office and stood him in front of his desk. Under his bare feet he could feel the cool sticky touch. He looked down and around the floor to see plastic covering over the carpet of the room, his eyes then narrowed at a man sitting in the chair behind his desk. The scene was eerily reminiscent of the visit from Samuel Lassiter. But when the man turned in the chair to face him, his knees would have buckled if he hadn't been wrapped so tightly.

"I hear you have been looking for me," Turk smiled. "Well here I am. Are you sure you wanted to find me?" Turk stared at the man who appeared to be near pissing on himself he was shaking so hard. "Now I bet you're wondering how I got out of the federal pen or how I got into your wonderfully secured home. I'll let you continue to think about that and this. I can get to you anywhere, anytime I choose to and have the perfect alibi." Turk smiled then waved his hand, "Relax man. I'm not gonna kill you.... tonight. But this is what you are going to do. You're going to call your people, cancel the contract on Roberts. Then place a call to Brian Thompson and make sure you convince him this is a done deal. If you don't I'm the last person you will have to worry about. That big man that is protecting the beauty queen will take your ass out. You understand what I'm saying?" Turk watched as Munford nodded. "Good, now, stay away from my sister, her friends and her husband. This is your only warning." Turk stood to walk out of the room, then stopped and turned to Munford, "Just in case you forgot, I control Richmond." Munford was knocked out cold with one punch.

"You want me to take him out?" Tuck asked.

Al shook his head at Tucker, "We are going legit. Man, we can't kill the Chief of Police."

"He's dirty Al, we can kill him."

Al laughed and shook his head, "No, we are not killing the man. We don't need the headache.

Let's get me back under lock and key." They left the men to put things back in order.

Twenty minutes later, the two doctors check vitals one last time for the night and then left the room. Al "Turk" Day was returned to the federal facility twenty four hours after his bout with asthma.

To say Munford was pissed when he awakened from his forced nap would definitely be an understatement. The man was beyond pissed. The Eagles of the past could handle a simple order. These new young bangers didn't know how to handle delicate situations. All they had to do was get the jewelry from the woman, eliminate her and move on. But they botched that job. Once Thompson put his man on the woman, it was damn near impossible to get near her. Before he went any further, he had to stop Sanchez. Then he had to figure out how in the hell Al Day got out of prison and into his house.

He dialed the number to his middle man and instructed him to contact Sanchez to stop the planned attack. And then Brian Thompson to call a truce. Always conscious of his position, he never gave direct orders to do anything. If any of his man ever had to take the stand against him none could say they received an order from him. After placing the call, he slouched back in his chair. How could Al Day get out of prison and into his house?

As he thought there was only one answer that came to him--JD. Harrison had to be involved. It was the only reasonable answer. He slammed his fist on the desk. How dare he interfere in his plans? He was sick of the so call Harrison's of the world being in power. They didn't know what to do with it—he did. It was his time to run things. Harrison was more of a hindrance than his father, the damn holier than thou pain in the ass. James Harrison knew too much and Munford knew eventually he was going to spill his guts. It was his damn honesty that got him killed, Munford reasoned as he sat behind his desk.

This time it wasn't an honest cop that was causing his problems, it was his own greed. Now he had to take a moment and think. Being Chief of Police granted him some power, but not enough for what he wanted out of life. The people he was now connected to could give him that and more. Becoming Mayor of Richmond would give him more access to the things his new partners would need. Having Gavin in his pocket would go a long way in getting the power he wanted. And everyone knows with power comes wealth. Eliminating JD Harrison would put Gavin right back in his pocket. It just had to be handled delicately.

He placed another call to his new partners. "We have a situation that needs to be eliminated before we can proceed."

"And that is?"

"JD Harrison."

Chapter 18

The next morning Cynthia was up and dressed well before seven. Samuel indicated he would be ready by eight. Her body was still reacting to falling asleep in Samuel's arms. For the first time in her life she believed in the power of love. She was willing to give up the material things and status a life with LaVere' would guarantee her, just to be with Samuel. The fact that he worked for Brian meant he would not be able to afford some of the things she wanted, but he would give her love for a lifetime, that she was certain of. And that's something you can't put a value on," she whispered as she checked her hair one last time, stopping to answer the ringing telephone. "Hello," she answered.

"You sound awfully happy this morning. What's up?" Brian asked.

"Hey you. Haven't heard from you in a few days. What have you been up to?"

"Work, what else," he replied. "What time are you going to the Harrison's?"

"It will be late, if I make it at all."

"I'm not going to let you sit at home on a holiday. Blake called. I know your people went back to LA."

"Yes, they did, but I won't be staying home. Samuel asked me to join his family for dinner today."

"Are you two a couple now?"

"I think we are more than just a couple. I'm in love with this man, Brian. I've been fighting it since the night we first met, but that has come to an end. I can't fight it any more, this is the man I want in my life for eternity." Cynthia giggled into the telephone. "Can you believe that?"

"The last time I heard you giggle was when I brought you that stupid movie for your tenth birthday." Brian laughed into the telephone.

"Hey, don't laugh, Samuel and I watched it last night."

"Cynthia, you know I love you and have your back no matter what. Listen to me on this. There are two sides to Samuel Lassiter and he is just as good in both. He's a damn good man. He loves his family and if he asked you to join them, than that means he loves you. I think you already know that and you could not be in better hands. He is also the ultimate professional. When the government is in need of someone with his skills, he is the first one they will call. There is no choice for him when the call comes; he has to serve his country. That mean you will be home alone, sometimes for long periods. Most of the time he will not be in a position to even call. How will you handle that?"

"Samuel told me a little about his work, but he never said exactly what he does when he has to go away. I trust him enough to know that when those times come; love will bring him back to me."

"LaVere' left with the impression that you were going to marry him. He's been gone all of a week and here you are talking about being with another man for eternity. So my question to you is simple, what's different with Samuel?"

"I'm not sure I know, but it is. LaVere' and I were together for the wrong reasons. I agreed to marry him because he made me feel worthy to be a princess. Samuel makes me feel worthy just to be me. He loves me from his heart and for no other reason than, I'm Cynthia. But what's more important is that I love him. Not for what he can give me or the status that comes with him, just because he is Samuel."

Brian waited before he replied. He had to be sure this was the real thing with Cynthia. If this went wrong, he would have to defend her against Samuel. That was something he wanted to avoid at all cost—he liked living. "I suppose this means I'm the only solo act in the crew now."

"I'm afraid so. But it won't be long. There is another Kaitlyn waiting for you."

Wow, that was a name from the past, Brian thought. It had been a while since he thought about the one woman that made his life worth living. She disappeared the week he graduated from college and he had not heard from her since. That was almost ten years ago and the memory was still vivid. "I won't hold my breath."

"Samuel is ready to leave, I have to run. I'll talk at you later." Cynthia hung up the telephone before he could finish his statement. Smiling, Brian hung up his telephone and shook his head. "She has come into her own, it's about time."

There has never been a time in her life that nerves have gotten the best of her, this morning was different. Her business puts her in the company of some of the most powerful people in the world. Hell, for the last month she had been spending time with royalty. But the thought of meeting the woman that gave Samuel life was wreaking havoc on her nerves.

Samuel could see she was nervous, but wasn't sure if he should try to reassure her or not. She was a proud woman that did not like to show her weakness. She was doing a good job of hiding it, but he made it a point to know her distress signs, like what she was doing at that moment; twirling a curl in her hair. The actions was so alluring to him, he was tempted to pull her into his arms and kiss her senseless. He parked the car and watched as her chest rose and fell heavily. He took her hand pulling it away from the curl that now dangled in her face and kissed her fingertips. "If you want to leave, we can."

She looked up from him kissing her fingers and prayed she was able to hide the sensation his lips sent through her body. "You would miss a holiday with your family for me."

"Yes."

She smiled and shook her head, "I can't let you do that. I would give anything to have a family that spent the holidays together." She turned to the two-story house with the snow neatly plowed away from the sidewalk and wondered how the twelve children and their parents could all fit.

"My family is going to love you. Just give them a chance."

His smile was so reassuring and just as irresistible. "I think my world is finally balanced. In the last twenty-four hours I have not tripped or fallen once. Do you think you can explain why?"

He leaned over to her. "Yes, you stopped fighting a losing battle. You fell in love with me in the hospital room the night of the accident."

"What make you think that?" she laughed.

"You told me," he seriously replied. "Then I told you to wait for me."

She sobered and asked, "Did I really say that?"

"Yes. Was it a lie?"

Glazing into his smothering eyes she replied, "I don't lie."

He gently kissed her lips then stepped out of the car to open her door. He then let Rusty out and watched him run to the back of the house.

Sally Lassiter was sitting in her kitchen kneading the dough for her dinner rolls when her oldest daughter, Ruby walked in the back door with a crock-pot in her hand. "Hey Mom," she said while placing the container on the table. She went back out the door as she heard her mother respond, "Hey baby." Walking back through the door with several bags in hand she placed them on the counter next to the crock-pot, then exhaled. "I would have asked Samuel to help me, but he seemed really engrossed in conversation with a woman in his car." She said raising a questioning eyebrow.

Sally paused and turned to her daughter, "He really brought her. Hum, must be serious. This is going to be an interesting day." She heard Rusty's bark and walked over and opened the door. "Hey Rusty," she hugged the tail wagging dog and scratched behind his ears. "You know where your ball is, go get it." The dog ran to the enclosed porch and grabbed his ball. Sally took the ball and threw it out the back door into the yard and enjoyed watching Rusty chase it down.

Hanging her coat in the hall closet, Ruby returned to the kitchen, "You knew about Samuel bringing a woman to dinner?"

"I sure hope there are no guns in the house." Sally replied as she washed her hands, and then wiped them on a towel.

Before Ruby could question the remark, Samuel walked through the door. Her mouth almost hit the counter it dropped open so wide. She closed it quickly and hoped no one noticed. *It can't be. There was no way in hell this woman was standing in this kitchen. Pearl was going to have a fit. Earlier this month Pearl had just mention the selfish heifer, um, woman.* Ruby quickly put a smile on her face when Samuel moved towards her. "Hey Sis, this is Cynthia, Cynthia this is my oldest sister Ruby." Pushing Samuel aside

Ruby extended her hand, "Hello, it's nice to meet you. Are you staying for dinner?"

"Of course she is," Sally commanded. "No one leaves this house on Thanksgiving without a full belly. Now, let me take your coat and gloves."

"Thank you," Cynthia replied as the soft-spoken woman took the items. She watched as Sally Lassiter walked from the room. It was inconceivable to believe a woman as attractive and petite as she could have twelve grown children. When Sally returned to the room Cynthia listened as the two oldest children and their mother discussed the activities for the day.

Sally Lassiter was all of five feet three inches tall with a short salt and pepper hair cut that was very becoming and weighted approximately one hundred twenty pounds. Looking at Samuel it was hard to believe a man his size came from this miniature of a woman. Turning to the sound of the back door opening, Cynthia saw five men walk through the door. All replicas of Samuel two a few inches shorter, and one that stood above them all, she assumed had to be his father. Since she had to hold her head back to see to the top of the man, she was certain he had to be close to seven feet tall.

"Well who do we have here?" One of the young men asked as he walked towards her with a mischievous smile on his face. Cynthia turned to Samuel and smiled from the seat she had taken at the breakfast bar.

"Cynthia these lumberjacks are my brothers, Mathew, Luke, Timothy and Adam. He stood next to his father and shook his hand. This is my father, Joseph Lassiter. Dad, this is my friend, Cynthia Thornton."

"Friend? Ha, now if I had a woman that looked like you, I certainly would not refer to you as a friend," Matt stated as he took a seat next to her.

Joseph grabbed the back of Matt's collared shirt and pulled him from the seat. He extended his hand, "Hello Cynthia. Welcome to our home."

It seemed Joseph Lassiter had the warmest eyes and the smoothest voice; it reminded her of Samuel and the way he talked to her. "Mr. and Mrs. Lassiter, I can certainly see where your sons get their good looks." She replied as she looked around the room at the men.

"She knows how to charm the men don't she?" Ruby whispered to her mother.

"Ruby, she is your brother's guest. Now, think about it, have you ever known him to bring a woman into this house?"

She thought for a minute, "No, I haven't," she replied startlingly.

"That fact tells me that this woman is special to him."

"Yeah, but is he special to her?"

Sally exhaled as she looked sideways at her daughter. She picked up the dishtowel and dried her hands. "Cynthia, I've been told you are a wonderful decorator. Could I impose on your talents to help me set up the dining room, while Samuel and Ruby finish planning the activities?"

"Of course," she replied as she looked in Samuel's direction for encouragement. He did not disappoint her as he winked and smiled.

The men watched as she walked from the room. Mathew was the first to speak. "How in the hell did you get a woman like that?"

"He's a Lassiter. There isn't a woman alive that can resist the Lassiter charm," Adam the youngest male of the clan at eighteen stated mockingly.

Luke who was twenty-two, in his last year of college turned to his little brother, and asked, "How would you know? Last I heard you were still using arm action."

The men laughed as Timothy, one of the twenty-year-old twins hit Adam lovingly on the shoulder. "He's graduated from one hand to two," then winked at his younger brother.

"Adam you haven't stepped over into manhood yet?" Mathew, the twenty-four year old high school basketball coach who has pledge his life to being a playa asked.

All eyes went to Adam, who wished he was any place other than in the room with his larger than life brothers. If he answers one way he will have to explain to his six-seven father. If he answers the other way he would have to deal with ribbing from Matt and Luke. Just when he was about to answer, the back door opened and his twin sister Jade walked in with Diamond and Timothy's twin Opal.

"Samuel," Diamond yelled with excitement and ran into the arms of her big brother, followed by Opal and Jade. The group almost sent him spiraling to the floor. "Is Joshua here too?" The sweet and sassy twenty-six year old Diamond asked.

"No. He hasn't made it yet," their father answered. Diamond frowned and went in search of her mother. Ruby walked over to Adam and whispered, "Jade's timing is impeccable. She saved you again."

Jade left Samuel's grasp and walked over to Adam. "What's going on?" she asked in her always-caring way.

"Nothing Sis, it's okay." Jade knew Adam was in turmoil regardless to what he said, she could feel it. They were both in their first year of college—she at Spellman, and he at Morehouse. Things were going very well for her, but not for her shy twin brother. She turned her attention to Luke, who she was certain had something to do with Adam's discomfort. Walking past him she kicked his shin.

"Ouch! Why did you do that?" He yelled.

"Reflex," she replied with a sly smiled and walked off.

"Where's Pearl?" Opal asked while sampling the biscuits Ruby made for breakfast.

"JD Harrison had a news conference this morning," her father replied. "She'll be here in time for the game.

"Good," Ruby said as she looked over to Samuel. "The game can start at ten."

Samuel heard his sister, but his mind was on the conversation between his mother and the woman he plan to make his wife.

Diamond ventured into the dining room where she saw her mother taking with a dazzling woman. By the tone of her mother's voice she knew not to interrupt. That was the fact-finding voice and she was not going to let the woman go until she had her answers.

"How did you end up with twelve children?" Cynthia asked while Sally watched her decorate the table.

"We had an overabundance of love to share with each other," Sally replied laughing. "Samuel came during our second year of marriage, Joshua in our fourth, Ruby in our sixth, Pearl in our eighth, then Diamond." She stopped as if thinking back, "Now that one was a godsend. Before she came along I was contemplating returning to work."

"Really, what type of work did you do?"

"I was a professional dancer."

"Samuel mentioned that, but I can see it as well," Cynthia absentmindedly nodded her head. "You have this graceful air surrounding you."

"Thank you," Sally beamed at the compliment she believed to be genuine. "Needless to say the decision was made for me and I did not return to the stage. Two years later Mathew was born and we moved into this house with six bedrooms. Of course we had to fill up the bedrooms." She laughed heartily. "Then the blessing really started to flow in. Our next two pregnancies ended up as twins, first Opal and Timothy, then Jade and Adam. We decided to give up trying to even the number out, but GOD had other plans. He sent us Sapphire."

Listening to Sally helped Cynthia to understand the love that flowed through the family. "What a wonderful story. It's quite evident you and Mr. Lassiter are still very much in love. It shows in the little glances between you."

"That's true. We love each other very much. I would not trade what we have for anything. Can you say the same about Samuel?"

"That was smooth the way you brought this to Samuel and I."

"Thank you. I inherited the trait from my mother." Sally replied smiling brightly.

She took Cynthia's hand in hers and looked into her eyes. "I can see you are in love with my son and he is in love with you. I felt it the moment the two of you walked in the room. But I also sense you are afraid of something. Will that fear keep you from committing to my son?"

How could a woman who has known her for less than an hour see so deep into her soul? How could she see her vulnerabilities when her own mother couldn't? Hesitating for a moment, Sally squeezed her hand to encourage her to continue. The warmth in her eyes and the sincerity of her concern prompted Cynthia to reply honestly. "Mrs. Lassiter, your son scares the hell out of me." She stopped and frowned. "Is it okay to say that?"

"You may speak freely here," Sally replied warmly."

She exhaled and continued, "I'm afraid to explore the depth of the feelings he has for me and I'm just as afraid not too. Does that make any sense?"

Sally reached her arm around Cynthia's shoulder and squeeze lightly. They began walking towards the kitchen. "Yes, it does. The love that Lassiter men have to offer is everlasting. They are quick to recognize what they want and will fight for it to the end. I have friends that were fortunate to find the kind of love that last an eternity. I hope that

Prince of yours has strong armor, because he is in for a battle."

Cynthia stopped abruptly, "Mrs. Lassiter I decided not to marry LaVere'. He's a wonderful man, but I need and want a little more than he was offering. I want a love for a lifetime, a love straight from the heart." The women continued walking into the kitchen.

Chapter 19

Once she realized the conversation in the dining room was meant to be private, Diamond walked back into the kitchen where her brothers and sisters were still planning the activities for the day. "Matt she is stunning. Where did you meet her?"

He looked up shaking his head as he finished his breakfast, "She's not mine."

"Oh," Diamond turned to her other brother, "Luke, she's with you?"

Not bothering to look up from his plate, he just shook his head.

Diamond frowned, "Thomas?" He shook his head no. "Okay, well the woman did not come here by herself and I'm certain she's not with Adam."

"What woman?" Pearl asked as she stepped in through the back door.

"It's about time you got here." Joseph smiled as he hugged his daughter. "I thought Harrison was going to keep you all day.

"Hey daddy," Pearl smiled and returned his hug. "Mrs. Harrison said to tell you and mommy hello." She began removing her coat and gloves when Ruby turned from the greens she was cooking, "We have a guest for dinner."

"We do? Who?" Pearl asked as Diamond took her coat to hang up in the closet.

"I hope you have better luck with that question than I did. I've been asking who she came with and haven't received an answer yet."

Samuel and Thomas came into the room with the equipment for the game. "Hey Sammy, I thought you would be working and wouldn't make dinner. Is Joshua here too?"

"No, but he did bring someone," Ruby replied.

"She's with you Samuel?" Diamond asked surprised. "Wow, she's gorgeous. What's her name?"

Sally walked through the door with their guest. "Pearl," her mother smiled and walked to her very stunned daughter and hugged her a little tighter than usual. "I'm glad you made it in time for the game." She knew this was going to be a defining moment for the day and wanted to do all she could to keep it positive for as long as possible.

Pearl's eyes never left the woman that seemed as shocked as she was, but that wasn't possible. This woman never left anything to chance. "Hi Mommy, Mrs. Harrison said hello," she said dryly. Then she noticed Samuel walked over and stood next to the woman. The past flashed through her mind. The senior prom when her date left her side to be with this same woman. She remember how all the girls at school wanted to hang out with this woman, it was like the rights to passage came with being her friend. She was after all the queen—the one that determined if you are in or out of the popular club.

The tension was instant and almost thick enough to cut with a knife, when Sapphire, the youngest child waltzed into the room full of energy. "Hey, Hey, the gangs all here. Are we ready for some football? She clapped her hands, cheered and wiggled her hips. Diamond, Jade and Opal joined in with the cheer which was a step routine regularly used at the high school. Knowing the cheer and wanting to cut the tension, Cynthia stepped over and joined them. The girls were surprised and delighted to see how she handled the steps with her three-inch heels on. When the cheer was over they all laughed while the men cheered them on.

Sally stood with her arms around Pearl's waist giving the little support that she could. She loved her daughter just as she loved all of her children. Her daughter was a very caring young woman, but carried scars from the past. Scars that the woman her son was in love with had a small part in causing. Although, she was sure Cynthia was not aware of her part in her daughter's broken heart or at least she hoped. "Well, it seems you ladies have something in common," Sally said in attempt to keep things calm.

"Excuse me," Pearl said and walked out of the room.

Ruby wiped her hands on the towel and started to follow her, but Samuel stopped her, "I'll go." He glanced at Cynthia and knew instantly she felt the tension in the room.

"What's up with her is it that time of the month again?" Luke asked jokingly. With a snap of the towel Ruby popped his arm and turned back to the stove. "Ouch. What is this, hit Luke day or something."

The girls who had paid no attention to the actions happening around them were busy chatting away with Cynthia. Sally looked to her husband for reassurance that things would be okay. He complied with a smiled and a curt nod of his head. Knowing his wife could handle things in the kitchen, he felt it would be wise to give his support to his Pearl. Yes, she was the one child that always needed him, even now that she was a grown woman and out on her own. Samuel was his first born, first son, the man he knew would take care of the family if anything was to happen to him. He stood at the doorway of the family room and saw the strongest member of his family and the most fragile. He was there to support both.

Pearl stood at the window, not sure if she could speak yet without emotions flowing through. Her parents raised her to be hospitable to anyone that came to their home.

Disrespecting a guest in their home was the same as disrespecting them and she couldn't do that. So she remained silent, as she had in the past.

Samuel hung his head when he saw the hurt in his sister's eyes. His father walked up behind him and gently pushed him forward into the room. He nodded, encouraging his son to talk to his sister. Regardless of how old he got the man he looked at would always tower over him, but never made him feel intimidated. Joe Lassiter and Samuel were both gentle giants, but when the woman they love hurt, so did they. It was impossible for them to rest until they were fairly certain all the woman in their lives were happy. For Samuel, the number of woman in his life that he loved had increased. He was in the middle of two, Pearl and Cynthia. For a moment he would rather be standing on the battlefield of Iraq, than having to choose between the two.

Knowing his father was there, quietly supporting from the back, Samuel walked over and stood next to Pearl. He could feel the anger radiating from her, but she would not let it out. Something inside of him urged him to force her to let it go. Folding his arms across his chest he decided to use the not so subtle approach. "I have a couple of punching bags in the basement of my new house. You are welcome to use them.....but not me. She exhaled but did not speak. Samuel waited a minute than continued. "My feelings for her are as much of a surprise to me as her being here is to you. I'm not asking you to love her, you don't have to even like her. All I'm asking is that you give her a chance. She is not the same as she was in high school. Hell, she's not even the same as what she was a month ago. I want her with me, but not at your expense. If you ask me we will leave."

With tears rolling silently down her cheeks, Pearl could not miss what Samuel was not saying. This brother did not mess around with woman. If he was with her it was because she meant something to him. Samuel wasn't like Luke or Matt, a different girlfriend each month. He and Adam were the sensitive ones. If Cynthia was here with him it was because he cared deeply for her. "Are you in love with her?"

"Yes."

Pearl closed her eyes, and exhaled. Another man for Cynthia to walk out on flashed through her mind. Why did women like her always seem to have it so easy? "She's engaged to another man Samuel, or has she forgotten?"

"No, but that is something for me to handle, not you."

"Samuel you don't know this woman like I do. She chews men up and spit them out. I don't want you to be one of them."

"I'm a big boy that knows how to take care of myself."

"Yeah, Lionel thought the same thing."

The idea of her comparing him to the worm of an ex-boyfriend of hers hurt, but this was not about him. This was about helping his sister deal with the past. "I know you are trying to protect me and I thank you for it. Please don't ever stop. But if I don't stumble and fall I will never know how to get up dust off my boots and move on."

"Huh, using my own words against me now?"

"Oh, you remember saying that to me? Refresh my memory, who were we talking about at the time."

She turned and playfully punched his bicep, "You're not funny," she smirked enough for him to see those dimples that garnered her the nickname, *Dimples.*

"Yes I am." He returned the smile, than became serious. "I love you Pearl, I would never do anything to hurt you. Cynthia is a part of my life now. I can skate around and not bring her to family functions to keep you comfortable. Doing that would not solve the problem. I want both of you in my life. Would you try to find a common ground with her for me?"

Looking up at her brother, she remember he was the one that consoled her for months when Lionel publicly broke up with her at the prom and declared his love for Cynthia. Samuel sat in the hospital with her day and night after the accident caused her to lose the child she was carrying. This was the brother that beat the crap out of Lionel a week after she was released from the hospital when he came by after Cynthia dumped him. Samuel and Ruby were the only siblings that knew of her ordeal and they both protected her. She could not deny him this one request. "I make no promises, but I'll try."

Lovingly he shoved her with his elbow, "That's all you can give me is I'll try." He asked jokingly.

Rolling her eyes at him and placing her hands on her hips she turned to him and said, "You're lucky you're getting that much."

That was his Pearl. He reached out and began to tickle her waist. "You can take your hands off your imagination, you don't scare me." She fell to the floor and he followed.

"Okay, okay. I give, I give," she giggled.

"You sure?" He asked before stopping.

"I'm sure, I'm sure. I give, I give."

"Okay," he said as he helped her up. "I love you Pearl," he said as he hugged her.

"I love you too."

"Well, now that that is settled, are you ready for some football?" Joe asked his two children.

Looking up at Samuel, Pearl asked, "Is the princess playing?"

Samuel frown inwardly, "No, the teams are even."

"No they are not. She can take Joshua spot on your team," Joe offered.

Liking the idea, Pearl formed a mischievous grin, "I'll go change my clothes."

As she ran from the room Samuel angrily looked to his father, "Thanks a lot dad."

"Hell son, she going to have to learn to fend for herself if she plans on being in this family."

The special thing about the Lassister' is if one is missing there are plenty others to take up the slack. Sapphire, who everyone called Phire, was definitely up to the task. Her nickname was a testimony to her personality. She was as lively as a spitfire and her spirit was just as warm. The moment Samuel left the room Phire kept Cynthia engrossed in her high school escapades. The two hit it off instantly. Their personalities were both electrifying. Phire was simply a younger version of Cynthia, without the flaw of being judgmental. However, all the activities and conversations taking place did not keep Cynthia's mind off Samuel's absence. It was apparent that Pearl was not pleased to see her. Which was not a surprise; Pearl never made it a secret that she did not care for her. It never occurred to her that she was Samuel's sister. Damn, it wasn't as if they did not already have enough to contend with. She still had to tell LaVere' about Samuel, and then she would have to deal with her family, well at least her mother. Closing her eyes to all the thoughts, she wondered if the feelings she had for Samuel were enough to make it though it all. She opened her eyes when laughter erupted in the room. Apparently Matt was the recipient of one of Diamond and Opal's take downs, for he was on the floor facedown with both sisters sitting on his back.

"Take that wrestling out of my kitchen while I'm cooking," Sally jokingly ordered.

"Save it for the football game," Joe added as he walked into the kitchen. Samuel was behind him, but Pearl was not. Cynthia looked to Samuel as he walked towards her. He took her hand, "Let's talk." She followed him out to the closed in porch as Matt teased, "Don't be closing any doors around here"

"Yeah and make sure both of you remain vertical while you're out there," Phire added. Samuel looked back at his siblings with a warning and closed the door.

Not sure how to read Samuel's mood Cynthia quickly offered, "I know how Pearl feels about me. I can leave. I'll call one of my friends to pick me up."

"If you want to leave I will take you, but I'm not asking you to go. I knew how Pearl felt before I brought you."

"Then why did you bring me here if you knew your sister didn't like me?"

"Because I like you."

Touched by his answer, she smiled and asked, "Why?"

He leaned back against the door and folded his arms across his chest. "You are a strong caring woman Cynthia Antoinette Thornton. You walk around making people think you are a selfish materialistic woman, when all you are doing is covering up your insecurities. You silently fight for your friends, but you don't want them to know how much you truly care for them, because you're afraid they will leave like your parents did. You voluntarily stand in the background while your brother earns the stardom that very easily could have been yours. Everything you touch becomes as beautiful as you are and you are very beautiful. From the golden curls that hang across your shoulders, to your perfectly shaped lips, to your exquisite body with a butt that don't need apple bottom jeans to look good, down to your tastefully painted toenails which I hope to gently kiss each before I partake in tasting other things when I get you home tonight."

She stood there staring into his eyes, with tears on the verge of flowing from hers. Damn if he didn't make a move on her heart. Afraid to move any closer to him, for fear she would strip him of every stitch of clothing and make love to him on his family's back porch, she blinked as a tear escaped down her cheek. "I was asking why Pearl doesn't like me, but I'll take what you said." She lowered her eyes to the ground, "You think my butt looks good, wait until you see the rest of me." She seductively looked up at him and smiled. "You think you know me so well. Tell me what I feel about you."

He unfolded his arms and took a step over to where she stood and slipped his hands into his pockets. "You are afraid of the love you have for me. You don't understand it because in your book it happened too quickly and you are afraid it's not real." He stood over her five-four frame and looked down into her eyes. He wiped away the single tear, "That's what's so remarkable about love, you never know when it will happened or with whom. The amazing part is we have the rest of our life to enjoy, if we grab hold and recognize how great a gift from GOD it is." He lowered his lips to hers and rendered the sweetest most sensuous kiss she had ever experienced.

This man plays dirty when they're on his turf, he goes straight for the heart. She had no choice but to surrender her heart to him. She moved her hands to touch him and he moaned. "I will not be responsible for my actions if you touch me. And I would hate to have to fight my father when he tries to stop me from taking you right here on this porch."

Taking a step back he looked at her and knew she was finally coming to grips with her feelings for him. "I want to talk to you about Pearl," he said as he took her hands into his. "You are on your own with her. The two of you will have to find a common ground, because I have no plans to spending the rest of my life playing referee between you."

"I will try. The problem is I have no idea what I've done to her. I'm use to woman disliking me without reason, and in the past I didn't care why. I guess now I have to take the time to find out."

"You will do that for me?" He asked with an enticing smile.

She contemplated that question for a moment then answered, "I would do anything for you."

He stepped closer and brushed his lips against hers, "Anything?"

"Anything."

A moment or two past before either spoke, "How about a game of football?"

Frowning she replied, "Football?"

"Yes, football. We are a man short since Joshua is not here. We need you to take his spot on our side."

"I'll be on the guy's side?"

"Yes."

"I can do that." She agreed feeling certain that the boys would beat the girls. Samuel smiled at the agreeable look she had on her face knowing exactly what she was thinking. He was not going to tell her that the girls had beaten them for the last two years.

"Okay, let's go."

It was inconceivable to Cynthia that families actually got together to do something like play a game together and enjoy it. The only family she ever really spent time with was the Harrisons. They did things together like cookouts, dinners and church. But this family played together like it was the most natural thing in the world to do. And they took it seriously. While she was upstairs in what was once Diamond and Opal's bedroom changing clothes, the girls were strategizing on plays all the while watching to make sure she was not picking up on what they were saying. All of them were just as intense as the other, Ruby and Pearl were the main two talking, and she was sure their plan of attack involved her. She wasn't worried, the guys had her back.

"Diamond thank you for the sweats and sneakers, they fit perfectly."

"You're welcome, but you are going down. I like you, I do, but you are on the enemy's team and I'm afraid we have no choice but to bring you down."

"I like you too," Phire added, "but you going down."

"This must be what they call intimidation. Well, let me tell you, better women have tried to bring me down, but I'm still standing," Cynthia replied courageously.

"You talk a good game sister. I hope there's enough of you left for Samuel to enjoy tonight," Jade taunted. "Let's do it." The women begin filing out of the room.

"Pearl," Cynthia called out. "May I have a moment?"

Ruby looked from Pearl to Cynthia, "You sure you want a moment alone with Pearl?"

Cynthia noticed the cold tone to her voice, "I wouldn't have asked if I didn't."

Ruby took an aggressive step in Cynthia's direction but Pearl stepped in. "This is on me Ruby, I'll meet you downstairs."

"Ruby is not someone you want to go up against," Pearl stated while staring at Ruby's retreating back.

"I don't want to go up against any of you. Look, I know you don't like me and that's okay. I'm sure you have your reasons and have shared that with your sisters. But I'm going to be around and we need to find a way to get along for Samuel's sake."

"For Samuel?" Pearl exclaimed sarcastically. "Let's talk about Samuel. The last time I was with you it was to handle a press conference regarding your relationship with Prince LaVere'. Now you are in my home with my brother. How do you expect me to react?"

"Pearl your dislike for me has nothing to do with LaVere' or Samuel. You made it clear long before either of those men came into my life that you did not like me. I'm not asking you why, because frankly I don't care. I know I have never harmed you in any way. Hell I didn't even know you before you started working for JD. I have lived with being disliked all my life, I'm use to it. I'm asking you to take steps for Samuel not for me."

"Why bother, you go through men like normal women go through a set of tampons: a new set every month. All I wonder is why Samuel. He's not what you usually go after since he doesn't own half the world. Why waste the time pretending to get along when this little fling might last all of one month." She turned to walk out of the room.

"Has it occurred to you that I might be in love with him?"

Pearl stopped at the door and turned back. "No. Women like you don't know how to love anything or anyone but themselves." She continued out the room and down the stairs.

In the snow-covered front yard the game began. Ruby, Pearl, Diamond, Opal, Jade and Phire were huddled at one end of the yard while Samuel, Cynthia, Matthew, Luke, Timothy and Adam stood at the other. Joe and Sally stood on the porch and watched as the first play of the game begun. It was obvious who the girls were targeting. Sally feared Samuel, as hard as he may try, would not be able to protect Cynthia. She slipped her hand into her husband's and whispered, "I hope for Samuel's sake she survives this game."

"Does she love him?" Joe asked.

"I believe she does."

"Then he won't let her fail. If he fights she will fight with him." Just as he finished his statement, Pearl, Ruby and Diamond rushed pass Samuel and tackled Cynthia, who had the ball to the ground with a thump. An imprint was left in the snow from the pile up. "Ouch, I could be wrong." Joe shuddered.

Cynthia waited for the pile of cement bricks, better known as Samuel's sisters, to move off her body, which was telling her to stay down. However, her mind was screaming at her to get up. Don't let them take this man from you. And that's what it was about. If she was not capable of handling this situation with his sisters, she did not have a chance at keeping this man. She had to fight to have what she was sure was the love of her life. When the last body was removed from her she opened her eyes and saw two pair of eyes close to her while four pair stared at her from a distance. "Are you okay?" Samuel asked.

She blinked back her body telling her to say no. "Yes. I'm good to go." She grabbed his hand and jumped up.

"Why didn't you throw the ball? I was wide open, Luke yelled.

"Don't yell at her. You didn't block off the line," Matt yelled back and pushed him.

They huddled again and Samuel took the lead, "Look it's clear they are aiming for Cynthia so let's take advantage of that. I'm going to pretend to give the ball to Luke but Adam, you're getting it. Run left then pass it off to Matt. The rest of us are going to hold the line."

"I think you should pretend to give it to me. While they are gunning for me Adam can take it in."

"You realize the girls aren't playing, they are coming at you," Matt stated.

"You're willing to take a hit for the team?" Samuel proudly asked.

"Yeah."

Samuel beamed, there was nothing she could have done or said that would have made him any prouder.

"What a woman," Timothy proclaimed.

"I agree," Matt smiled. "Luke, Timothy and I'll protect you. Adam, you're running behind Samuel. That ought to confuse them.

The play went off without a hitch. The girls went for Cynthia while Adam scored. After the boys helped Cynthia off the ground, they all ran to the other end and celebrated with Adam and Samuel. Sally kissed her husband and returned to the kitchen to setup for dinner. Joe smiled with the realization that his oldest son will be granting him another daughter. Not that he didn't have enough, but this will be the first of what he hoped to be a growing Lassiter family. He sat back and watched as the girls began to respect Cynthia and Pearl became more irritable. His Pearl was going to be a tough cookie, but something about the woman Samuel brought home made him think she could do it.

The men finally won the title back and they were not letting the girls forget it. Of course Diamond was the one to bring it all into focus for them. "You guys are forgetting one important fact about today's game. It was Cynthia, a woman that gave you the game changing play. So you guys may have won the game, but it was on the strength of a woman."

"Oh please, she is not all that. Give it a rest," Pearl said angrily and left the room.

"I don't know what the deal is between your girl and Pearl, but whatever it is it's not going to end well unless someone intervenes," Diamond exhaled to Samuel.

"They will work it out," he replied.

"I don't know Sammy," Jade dared to call him.

"Pearl is a very reasonable person. At least I always thought so. It's hard to see her so unforgiving," Opal added.

"To you. She is always rough on me," Phire sighed. "I think she likes me less than she does Cynthia, who I like a lot, Samuel. I hope you bring her around again," she smiled.

"Yeah she is real easy on the eyes, you know what I mean," Matt laughed while giving Timothy a pound.

"I like her too," Adam said. "She's a definite hottie. Does she have a younger sister?"

"No she doesn't. I'm afraid she is one of a kind and she is mine."

"Not a little possessive are you?" Luke laughed.

"A little, but you have to remember, I'm going up against a Prince. I can't waiver on my position."

"Wow, so she is involved with Prince LaVere' Ashro," Ruby stated. "I thought that was just a publicity stunt for her brother."

"Who's her brother?" Opal asked.

"Blake Thornton," Ruby replied.

"The actor Blake Thornton is her brother?" Opal and Jade screamed simultaneously.

"Is there any law against marrying the brother of a brother's wife?" Jade asked.

"It doesn't sound too kosher," Timothy laughed.

"What doesn't sound kosher?" Cynthia asked when she walked into the family room.

Samuel reached his hand out and she took it. He pulled her down to sit next to him on the sofa. She opted to sit between his legs on the floor.

"Jade was wondering if she could marry your brother," Matt stated.

"You and about a million other women around the world," Cynthia laughed. "Blakie works constantly I doubt if he has time to date anyone seriously."

"Would you introduce me to him?" Jade asked excitedly.

"Pearl and I already met him," Diamond said.

"When?" Jade questioned.

"A few weeks ago when Pearl's friend Brian took us all out.

"Well, now you have to introduce the rest of us, it's only fair," Jade continued to plead her case.

"Jade, give it a rest," Samuel cautioned.

"It's okay. I'll be happy to introduce you to him the next time he is home."

"Alright ladies, it's time to put the dinner on the table. Has everyone finished washing up?" Sally asked as she entered the room.

"Pearl is still upstairs. I'll go get her," Diamond offered.

Twenty minutes later as all the family sat at the dining room table Joe at one end and Sally at the other, each member of the siblings expressed what they were the most thankful for. Cynthia wasn't sure she would measure up until she heard Samuel's words. "As always I'm thankful to be here with my family. But in addition this year I am grateful to have parents that gave me the wisdom to recognize love when I found it." He looked to his right into Cynthia's eyes and continued, "I pray that person who has completely captured my heart will embrace and protect it from harm."

Everyone at the table watched as the two stared at each other without a thought of anyone surrounding them. The girls were in awe of the expression of love from the usually very private brother, while the men were waiting to see if he scored. Joe and Sally looked to each other while holding their breath and silently praying their son would not be disappointed.

Cynthia blinked back the tears she felt were about to escape. No one has ever put the care of their heart in her hands so sincerely, so lovingly. The room may have been filled with twelve other people, but it felt as if only the two of them existed. She knew he was waiting for her reply and her fears of expressing her love for the man next to her dissipated. A small smile creased Cynthia's lips. "I don't know what I've done to be granted such an honor. But I accept it and promise to protect your heart with every breath I take." She looked away from Samuel for fear she would throw herself into his arms and revealed in the love she knew awaited her. Looking around the table she declared. "I've never known what it was like to have a family. I'm thankful this year has granted me the pleasure of meeting yours. Thank you for having me."

Sally smiled and glanced at her husband with loving eyes. Joe gracefully nodded his acceptance and stated, "You are welcome into our family." He then looked around the table and smiled lovingly at his family. "Well, let's eat so these two can have the privacy it's very clear they need."

"I say let's clear the table and watch them go at it," Matt laughed. Opal smacked him on the head from one side as Ruby hit him from the other. "Ouch, Ouch... I just said what all of you were thinking."

"Yeah, that might be, but you were the only one stupid enough to speak it aloud," Timothy laughed as he reached for the macaroni and cheese. Everyone begin grabbing different entrees and piling their plates, with the exception of Samuel and Cynthia. They continued to stare at each other with the promise of what's to come.

Chapter 20

After spending a respectable amount of time after dinner, Samuel and Cynthia took their leave. As they walked to the car each was very aware of the eyes that were watching from the window. "Shall we give them something to really talk about?" Cynthia asked with a mischievously sensuous smile.

He was using all the discipline and control learned from the SEALS to keep his hands and lips from her since the speech at the table. But since she opened the door, why the hell not. He grabbed her around her waist and greedily captured her lips before she could catch her breath. Laughing she wrapped her arms around his neck and matched each stroke of his tongue until she could stand no more. When they pulled apart Samuel turned towards the house and in the window stood his siblings with signs with a score of 10 written on paper. Only Matt scored them an 8 and wrote a message "I'm better." Samuel and Cynthia laughed and got into the car.

It was only a fifteen-minute ride across town to Cynthia's condo, but it seemed like an eternity to the couple in the vehicle. Samuel was so preoccupied with the things he planned on doing with the woman sitting next to him, that he did not notice the Ford that was following at an unsuspicious distance behind them. Nor did he notice the black Chrysler Crossfire following the Ford. Samuel pulled into the garage and parked next to the Mercedes given to Cynthia by LaVere' and turned the lights out. He stepped out and opened the door for Cynthia. Taking the keys from her to open the door their hands touched. He could feel the heat from her radiating through the gloves covering her hands. They stared at each other for a moment before he turned and unlocked the door. Once the door closed behind them there was no hesitation. Samuel pulled her to him and continued the kiss he reluctantly brought to an end earlier.

The kiss was so intense Cynthia began unraveling her layers of outer clothing. The coat, hat, scarf and gloves were all at their feet, and their tongues were still intertwined. The heat between them flared to that of an inferno when Samuel's hands touched the skin under her sweater. There were still too many layers of clothing between them, she pushed his coat from his shoulder, and broke away long enough to pull his mocked turtle neck over his head. Her hands began to roam from his waist up to the muscled rippled chest. When she reached his nipple she gently kissed one and then the other, that's when she heard the low growl in his throat. He ran his hands through her hair and pulled her lips back to him. His reaction to her touch thrilled her in a way she could never explain in words. The feel of his bare chest against her body melted all thoughts of waiting any longer. She unbuttoned his jeans and pulled at his zipper brushing across the mountain of his arousal, which she could not resist squeezing. "Samuel," she whispered against his lips. He dropped to his knees leaving a trail of kisses from the crest of her breast down to her navel. His hands expanded around her waist and continued over the soft mound of her rear. He returned the lovable squeeze as he circle the inside of her belly button with his tongue. Suddenly he hunched back on his heels and stared at her body from her toes up to her eyes. There has never been a time when Cynthia was self-conscious about her body. But there was something in the way he was looking at her that made her think twice. The first time they made love was spontaneous. This time they both knew where this was leading and it gave her time to think. Was she attractive enough for this man? Does he like what he sees? Could she handle a rejection from him?

It was only there for a moment, but it bothered him to see fear in her eyes. He sat back on his heels looking up at the sexiest woman he had ever seen, with or without clothes. When her hands went up, it appeared she was trying to hide her body from him. Why would she need to do that? He'd seen her body before. There was no way in hell she could be ashamed of what stood before him; she was perfection. He reached out, ran his hands down her thigh, feeling the heat from her body through the jeans that remained on her topless body and unzipped her boots, one at a time then held her legs as she stepped out. He set the boots aside and pulled her down to the floor with him. Watching her reaction to his touch was enough to make him harder than a steel nail and he wanted her with an unexplainable hunger. Taking his time was the move to gain the optimal response he wanted and patience was needed. He pulled his hands away and caressed her with his stare.

"If there was a word to describe your worth, it would be priceless. If there was a word to describe your beauty, it would be exquisite. If there was a word to describe my love for you, it would be endless. There is nothing for you to fear from me other than being loved." He reached out, took her hand, and brought her fingers to his lips. "Will you take a life long journey with me Cynthia?" He asked as he succulently kissed the tips of her fingers. Putting each into his mouth and sucking them as a child would a lollipop. "Would you spend the rest of your life with a man you have known less than a month, but promises you a life of happiness?"

When he reached the thumb on her hand she breathlessly responded, "Yes." Placing her arms around his neck he slide her beneath him and began stringing kisses all over her body. Each touch of his lips claimed an ownership of her body that burned down to her soul. "Love me Samuel, love me now."

In reply to her plea he moved directly to her lips and proceeded to kiss every fear from the very soul of her. He wanted her to feel the depth of his love down to her toes. Rising he picked her up and carried her to the chase lounge where he gently placed her, followed by his more than ready body. Brushing her curls aside he glazed into her eyes he knew he would give his life for her. His manhood fit snuggly in her center. Although the jean material each of them wore was between them he could feel her drawing him to her, and that was just where he intended to go. It was at that moment he sensed another presence in the room.

Nothing or no one could have prepared her for the feeling stirring inside of her. It was more than the usual anticipation of having sex, it was the unfamiliar anticipation of making love to someone she suddenly found herself in love with. Unlike Gavin, whom she knew she had a connection with, this man had her entire body on fire, waiting for something she had never experienced before. As her hands continued to roam over the magnificent muscles in his back, she heard him ask, "Why are you here?" Confused by his question, she opened her eyes just as he tucked her body securely beneath his.

"Is that anyway to greet your brother?" Shocked to hear another person's voice in her home Cynthia attempted to escape the grasp Samuel had on her body to see who was there, but the struggle became useless.

Samuel exhaled sharply and kissed her lips, "Stay put, I'll take care of this." He then turned in the direction of the figure walking towards them. "That's close enough," he almost growled. "Grab my shirt by the door." He looked back to Cynthia with a gentleness that quickly covered the anger that laced his voice a second earlier. "Hold those thoughts, sleeping beauty."

Before she could answer a man that stood just as tall as Samuel with the same features of the other Lassiter men she met today, smiled down at her. If it was at all possible the man was more handsome than any of the others including Samuel. "I can see why it took my brother a moment to realize I was in the room. Your beauty would distract the hell out of a saint."

Returning his smile, she attempted to reach out to take the shirt he was holding out to her, when Samuel snatched it from his hands and demanded, "Turn around!"

The man smirked, "Sure," then turned his back to them. Samuel then sat up and hesitantly pulled the shirt over her head. He stopped at the crease between her breast and placed a kiss there, and then pulled the shirt completely down. Cynthia shook her head in an attempt to clear her mind. Her body expected to be quenched of it's thirst for him, but that was not to be. However, there were a few questions on her mind.

"How did you get into my house?"

The man turned and extended his hand to her as she sat beside a very disturbed Samuel. "Joshua Lassiter" he smiled as she slowly reached out and shook his hand. "It's all in a day's work."

"You break into people's homes for a living?"

"Sometimes," he smiled. "One day I'll explain, but at the moment you two have visitors outside your door."

Cynthia reached over towards the lamp on the table to turn on the light, but Samuel stopped her. "How many?" he asked as he stood and pulled a weapon from his boot and then walked over to the window.

"Two in the third vehicle down the street. I followed them and you from Momma's house. I wondered why you had not picked up on them while you were driving, but I can see why." He continued to smile at Cynthia, who remained seated on the sofa.

Samuel walked over and stood between them, "Do you like your teeth?"

"I do," Joshua replied.

"Stop smiling at her and I'll let you keep them. Where are you parked?"

"Out back. It's a clear path."

"Cynthia I need you to pack a bag."

"Wait a minute. Why?"

"I'll explain later. Right now I need you to pack a bag. You're staying at my place tonight."

She heard his reply but was not sure she wanted or could comply with his request. Looking from the serious look on Samuel's face to the amused look on Joshua's the reason for his request still was not clear. "Will your explanation include why your brother broke into my home?"

Raising an eyebrow at the woman that did not move as he commanded he replied, "Whether it does or does not isn't important. I need you to pack a bag now."

Placing her hands on her hips and giving him the look of death the staring match pursued. Joshua took a seat at the bar smiling, he really wanted to see who was going to win. The look on Samuel's face clearly showed he was losing his patience, so it was not a surprise when he bent over, picked her up over his shoulders and advanced towards the terrace door. Joshua opened the door then began to tie a bandana over Cynthia's mouth to cover the scream he was sure was about to escape. He then ran back to the front door, picked up both coats and followed his brother out the door.

Brian was enjoying the last of Martha Harrison's coconut cake when his cell chimed in. Shaking his head, he knew the peace of the day was too good to last, he answered the call. Listening attentively to the caller, he suddenly began laughing aloud. The others in the dining room turned in his direction just as he stood to leave the room. "I understand the anxiety you are experiencing. Women can be infuriating, but you wanted this one. Now that you have her, what are you going to do with her?"

"For the time being she will be at my place. I need you here with her until we can clean up the situation at her place," Samuel replied.

"We who?"

"Absolute is with me."

"You don't need backup." He placed his glass on the table to prepare to leave. "I'll be at your place in ten. Do me a favor; control him. The last time he was around, he blew up half the city." Brian placed his phone back into his pocket; he made his excuses and walked into the family room looking for James. He found him next to Ashley looking lovingly at his wife who was attempting to play twister with her younger cousins. He whispered in James ear and stood to find Ashley and Tracy staring at him. "What?"

"Did you saying something about Cynthia?" Ashley asked Before Brian could answer Tracy walked over and stood next to Ashley with a questioning look in her eye and JC in her arms.

"How in the hell could you have heard what I said from over there?"

"Our hearing is good," Tracy replied with an expression showing she was still waiting for a response.

Ashley shook her head disregarding the conversation. "Stop stalling. Is Cynthia okay? We've been worried about her all day. Why didn't she come over?"

"Yeah and where is she?" Tracy added.

"Cynthia is fine Ashley. Why don't you come have a seat for a while?" James requested.

"I don't need to sit down, James, I'm fine." Ashley replied with a wave of her hand. "Well where is she Brian?"

"Where is who?" JD asked as he walked into the room.

"Cynthia," Ashley and Tracy replied in unison.

"At the Lassiter's," he replied.

Surprised by his answer, Brian glanced in his direction. "How did you know that?"

"I spoke with Pearl earlier, she mentioned it."

Smiling at each other Ashley and Tracy shrugged their shoulders, "Okay." Tracy retook her seat and Ashley continued on her quest to win at Twister.

Pleased with the woman now off his back, Brian looked to JD. "James will fill you in. I'll be in touch."

By the time Cynthia walked into Samuel's home, she was furious and it was clear who that anger was directed at. Samuel had to secure her during the ride to his place which thoroughly entertained Joshua. Once inside with Cynthia on his shoulders, he turned to the right towards the bedroom as Joshua followed behind. "I don't think I have ever seen anyone this angry. I think you have done it this time, big brother."

Samuel turned and stopped, with Cynthia beating on his back. Would you mind taking a seat in there?" He pointed to the great room area.

"No, I don't mind. That's a nice piece of ass in those jeans, man. I'm just saying." Joshua threw his hands up in the air, turned and walked into the kitchen.

Entering the bedroom, Samuel closed the door behind him and set a fuming Cynthia on his bed. She immediately stood and reached for the object around her mouth. Before she could remove it, Samuel took her hands and held them gently behind her back, as he stood in front of her. He looked down into her eyes and spoke softly. "Cynthia, I am going to remove the scarf, but I need you to listen." She stomped on his foot with her spiked heel boots and he flinched. He then laid her across the bed and he followed, positioning himself on top of her and wrapping his legs around her to hold them in place. "Listen," he repeated a little more forcefully. She stopped wiggling beneath him and exhaled angrily. He waited for her to settle down. When she did he attempted to answer some of her questions. "I have to go back to your place to handle some business. I brought you here because I know you will be safe. I would not survive if anything was to happen to you. Loving someone more than I love myself is new to me and I'm going to make some mistakes. But know, I would never do anything to make you unhappy even for a moment. Will you forgive me?" He asked as he kissed the right side of her neck. He looked down into her eyes as he lifted his head. The anger was subsiding. She turned her head to give him access to the left side of her neck. He kissed it gently while releasing her hands he removed the scarf from her mouth. He kissed each side of her lips and then proceeded to dissipate her anger completely and meticulously.

Lovingly staring into his eyes, she asked, "What's happening Samuel? I thought this was over."

"I don't want you to worry about it. I will never allow anyone to harm you."

A loud knock came to the door. "Hurricane?"

"Hurricane?" she questioned.

"I'll explain one day." Samuel closed his eyes and dropped his head to her chest. Another knock sounded.

"Yeah, I'll be right there." He looked at her then stood and pulled her to her feet. "I'll be back."

Suddenly worried, but not quite sure why, Cynthia grabbed his hand as he walked away. "Are you going to be in danger?"

Shaking his head, "Not at all." He squeezed her hand, walked over and opened the door. She followed. They walked into the great room to find Brian standing at the window and Joshua in the kitchen eating. Samuel walked over and spoke quietly to Brian then turned to Joshua, "Let's go." He stopped at the door as Joshua walked out and turned to Cynthia. "Don't worry."

She went to him and kissed him, "I'm not." He walked out and closed the door behind him. Cynthia turned to Brian who was looking at her strangely. "Interesting outfit. That's a big shirt to fill, don't you think." She looked down at the long sleeve mock cashmere turtle neck that ended below her knees. "I think its fit for a queen," she smiled.

Samuel and Joshua returned to the complex Cynthia lived in. They parked outside the entrance and walked to the area Ryan used as a stake out. Behind the cover of the trees the three discussed the situation.

"What do we have?" Samuel asked

"A total of six," she replied as she looked at the brother in the suit, Kenneth Cole dress coat and boots.

Joshua appreciated being admired. "Like what you see?"

"Not particularly." Ryan replied. "I'm wondering how you are going to feel when your suit gets wrinkled?"

Samuel cleared his throat to cover his laugh. "Six of them—three of us. Seems a little lopsided," Ryan continued.

"Yeah, for them." Joshua said as he boldly walked over to the car where the men was watching the condo and knocked on the window.

"What the hell is he doing?" Ryan asked in an angry whispered.

"Evening out the numbers," Samuel smiled and walked around the back, knowing Joshua would handle the men out front. As he walked by he heard the painful moan of one of the men Joshua approached. Ryan went in the opposite direction towards the back of the condo and entered through the patio door.

The first man Samuel reached turned just as he approached. The first punch dazed the man, the second pushed his nose back towards his brain. Samuel wasn't sure if the man was dead or alive and didn't care, he wanted this ordeal over with. Satisfied, Samuel move on forward. He stepped over the body and proceeded to the next target. Reaching the corner of the condo, Samuel saw a lone figure standing just outside the door Ryan walked through. The man was about to fire his weapon, which was pointing at the back of Ryan's head. Samuel kicked him in the middle of his back with so much force, his spinal cord gave way. The man's yell caught Ryan's attention. She turned back and saw the man on the ground by the door and Samuel walking through. She looked up and nodded her appreciation then pointed up the stairs.

Following her lead, Samuel covered her from the back as she climbed the stairs to the next level. Once they reached the top he pointed to the right and then walked in the opposite direction through the kitchen.

They circled the room with weapons drawn to make sure the floor was clear. From there he could hear someone upstairs searching the rooms. The two met at the bottom of the steps leading to the third level of the home.

This time Samuel took the lead. They soundlessly walked slowly up the steps. At the top he peeped into the room he was using to make sure it was clear. Down the other end of the hallway he could see movement in Cynthia's room. Ryan looked to make sure there were no surprises. She tapped him on the back to signal all was clear. A quick look into the other room and bathroom indicated the predator was only in Cynthia's bedroom. Samuel put his gun in the back of his pants and simply walked into the room.

"Good evening," he said to the man searching the place.

"Don't do it," Ryan yelled at the man that went for his weapon.

"I'm a cop." The man said as he reached for his badge.

Two rounds left Ryan's gun before his hand made it to his pocket. He yelled, grabbed his knees and fell backwards in pain.

Samuel turned and gave her an exasperated look. "Why did you shoot?"

She didn't say anything as she walked by him to the man and pulled the gun from the inside pocket of his coat, broke it down with one hand and threw the pieces on the bed. "I know the butt of a gun when I see it."

"I'm impressed. But you are going to explain the blood stains on her white carpet."

Ryan looked at him and smiled, "Man you are so gone."

"And loving every minute of it," he replied standing over the man that was bleeding. He applied pressure to one leg by stepping on it. "Tell me what I need to know."

"I know you're going to jail for shooting a cop," he chuckled in pain.

The chuckle turned into a loud squall when Samuel stomped harder on the leg. "Give me a name."

"Well, well, well. What do we have here?" Officer Sanchez asked standing in the doorway with a gun in each hand. "Payday," he grinned as they turned towards him. "I get to please the Chief by taking in Lassiter and get to piss Detective Williams off by taking in his little sister. Hey Ryan," he looked her up and down. "You're still looking good." Taking a moment to survey the room, "You took out all my men. Don't matter—there's more where they came from. Now I saw you take out the men out back, but I missed the two in the car. Did you kill them too? I hope so, that's more time in the slammer. They are going to love a big boy like you in the pen" He smiled. Ryan smiled. "You glad to see me Ryan?"

"Not you—him." She replied with a nod of her head. She watched the man behind him leaning against the doorjamb checking her out from head to toe and wondered what he was waiting for.

"Sorry kid, I'm not falling for it. Break the gun down and throw it on the bed.

Ryan shrugged her shoulder, "Okay." She did and dropped the pieces to the floor.

Sanchez put one gun back into his holster then pulled out his handcuffs and threw them at her feet. "Cuff him."

She smiled then turned her back to him. Bending over slowly, the tight jean material stretched across her behind showing the curves of her body. Taking her time standing, she pushed her behind out for emphasis.

"Hmm you are packing girl." Sanchez moaned. "I think you and I are going to make a pit stop before I turn you in."

As soon as the words were out of his mouth Joshua took his Kenneth Cole booted foot and kicked Sanchez between the legs from the back.

Sanchez eyes bulged and mouth flew open. Not a sound escaped his throat when the point of Joshua boots connected with his jewels. Samuel grabbed the gun from his hand before he hit the floor.

"Nice move," Joshua smiled at Ryan.

"I thought you would enjoy that."

"You want me—don't you?" Joshua smirked.

"Keep dreaming," she replied and walked out of the room.

The sun was rising when Samuel returned home. The information they received from the two living perpetrators was more than they could have hoped. The two were taken in to protective custody by Joshua. Samuel hoped his brother understood it was his job to keep the two from further harm, even by him. Now he had the uncomfortable task of telling Brian the details of James Harrison's death and advised him, the justice for it will have to wait. It seems Chief Munford has more under his control then they knew.

Brian was stretched out in the chair in front of the patio doors with his weapon on the table and his coat over his body. Samuel tapped him on the shoulder as he sat in the chair opposite him and exhaled. He laid his head back and closed his eyes.

"Long night," Brian yawned. "I received an anonymous call stating the girl and governor were in the clear." He raised an eyebrow, "Interesting turn of events." He sat up, "What did you find?"

Samuel sat the overnight bag he was carrying on the floor next to his chair and sat up. He looked over at the man who had been his contact when he was undercover and saved his hide more than once. "You are not going to like what they told us."

"Still has to be said."

Nodding his head in agreement Samuel began. "It's going to take a minute. Let me get Sleeping Beauty situated."

He turned to walk towards the bedroom with the knowledge that the woman on the other side of the door will be his wife. Walking into his bedroom, a smile touched his lips. She was exactly where she was supposed to be, curled up in his bed. He walked over, set the overnight bag with her clothes inside next to the bed, and looked down at her. Her silky curly hair was spread out across the pillow and her arms were hugging the other. She appeared to be wearing his Alex Rodriquez jersey, his favorite Yankee. He sat on the bed next to her, and then kissed her cheek. "Wake up

Sleeping Beauty." He pushed her hair from her neck and gently kissed there.

Those were the lips she was waiting to feel and for a second she thought it were still a part of her dream. Then she felt his fingers touching her neck and the second kiss she knew was real. Secure in the knowledge he would not disappear she opened her eyes to him smiling down at her. "Good Morning," she smiled.

"Good morning," he replied with the sexiest smirked she had ever seen. "This nightmare is over and you are now free to roam. I stopped by your place and picked up some clothes and toiletries."

"That was very sweet for a tough guy," she replied as she stretched gracefully placing her arms around his neck and succulently kissed him.

"What were you dreaming about?" He teased her with kisses down her throat as he held her close.

"If I tell you, that Lassiter head of yours may not fit under your hat." Her cell phone sounded from within her purse. "Today is a busy day. I have to get that," she stated, but made no effort to move from his embrace. He reached down, picked up the purse and gave it to her as he continued to cover her in kisses. She reached inside the purse, withdrew the phone and answered it without looking at the number. "Hello," she purred into the phone. She jumped to her knees, "LaVere', are you alright. Where are you? I was worried sick about you."

Not sure he liked her reaction to the call, Samuel pulled away from their embrace. She reached out and held his arm begging him with her eyes not to leave. "I'm glad you're safe. You and I need to talk, this morning, if possible. Is it okay if I come by now?"

She completed her call and looked at the man she planned to spend the rest of her life with. "I have to do this before we can go any further." She placed her hand on his cheek, "Have no doubts, I'm coming back to you."

He kissed the inside of her palm. "Take care of your business." She smiled and climbed out of the bed. As she crossed the room to his bathroom Samuel could not help admiring his shirt. "A-Rod never looked so good."

Smiling she looked back over her shoulder, "You ain't seen nothing yet," then disappeared into the bathroom.

Samuel stood and walked over to the door. He stopped for a moment when he realized Cynthia had his heart in her hands. Looking at the door to the bathroom the memory of the night his last love that left him to talk with her family; she never returned. Shaking the thought from his head, he stepped out the room, different place, different time.

Chapter 21

LaVere' stood at the window savoring the warmth of his home and the peace in his homeland. The aftermath of the unrest created the perfect opportunity for him and his brother to travel the land and speak openly with their citizens. The very things he was crusading for with his family were foremost in the citizens' minds. It took their military a few days to stop and capture the resistors. Those who surrendered peacefully were granted an audience with the princes to voice their concerns. It was those concerns that the last few days were used to address.

What seemed to cause the once peaceful protest to escalate was the information received of his plan to marry an American and bring her in to lead the change. Several stated, if he was marrying for love, the woman would be accepted as his princess. But to bring someone into their country, who was not committed to their cause to lead them was not acceptable. Others simply expressed their discontent in being continuously oppressed, with no change in sight. Unrest is never a good thing; too many lives could be affected and lost. LaVere' chose to look at the positive only and use the negative to avoid future occurrences. The positive was clear. The King now understood the people of the land are willing to sacrifice their lives for equality. He agreed to allow his brother to institute changes within their educational system. Aswan, who is next in line for the throne, was impressed with the planning and execution of the unrest. As a clear sign of the change to come, he placed several leaders from the rebels in the military training program.

His father and brother had made concessions to control the issues in his homeland. Now LaVere' had to make the same sacrifice. The problem for him was simple; he never went back on his word. If Cynthia was not willing to release him from his pledge to marry her, then he would honor his commitment, but would not take her to Emure. The talk he had with a group of women whom supported the rebels played over in his mind. It never occurred to him just how deeply the citizens of the land cared about the well being of each of the royal family members, even though they disagree on politics. Each expressed a desire for the members to be happy. The women explained, when you marry someone for love, the devotion is deep. When difficult times come the one you love will fight harder for your cause than you will. If there is no love, the person will disappear at the very moment you need her most. They stated it was admirable of him to make such a sacrifice, but not necessary. They had plenty of daughters available and willing to be at his side, at which time they proceeded to provide pictures of each of them. Instead of providing an escape from the group of women that held him captive, Aswan participated in the selection of several daughters for him to court.

LaVere' smiled at the memory and stepped away from the window. He was taking his seat when Edmond walked in with Cynthia closely in tow. She ran by him right into LaVere's arms.

"Cynthia Thornton to see your highness," he stated with a smile in his eyes.

He returned the hug, "Thank you Edmond."

Once Edmond left the room LaVere' kissed the cheek of the woman who clung to him. "I'm fine," he reassured her. He held her at arm's length, "See, I'm in one piece," he said smiling.

"I was so worried about you LaVere'. I spoke with James and he told me what was happening in Emure. Are your family members okay? How are Zsa Zsa and Nasheema? Were they hurt?"

"Shh" he attempted to stop the questioning. "Everyone is fine."

She exhaled with relief then punched him in the stomach. He pretended to frown, but smiled instead. "I'm furious with you for not contacting me for almost a week. You don't do that to someone you care about."

"Will you accept my apology?" he asked sincerely.

"I will consider it, if you accept mine."

"Yours? You have no reason to apologize."

She placed her purse on his desk and removed her jacket and gloves. "I'm afraid I do," she exhaled. Standing in front of the huge picture window with the snow now falling, LaVere' looked to be the prince he truly was. Dark, tall and handsome was an understatement when describing him. But he wasn't Samuel. She sighed and began explaining. "While you were away I decided I can't marry you. You are a wonderful man and you do deserve me."

"Thank you," he raised an eyebrow.

"Well you do, but you also deserve love. I care about you deeply, but I'm not in love with you. I thought I could settle, but after this week I realized what I would be giving up. With all you have offered me, the jewels, the gowns, the lifestyle, it doesn't equal the joy true love brings."

"I see. I take it you and Samuel Lassiter have stopped running from each other."

She took a step back and glared at him, "How did you know about Samuel?"

"I'm sure you can figure that out."

"Jamal. That little ....."

He grabbed her hands and held them. "Hey, don't worry about him, he's unimportant now. Tell me about Samuel."

With warmth that reached the very core of her soul, she proudly told him about Samuel. Afterwards LaVere' hugged her, he was genuinely happy for her. "Samuel is a very lucky man to have you. I'm very fortunate as well. You have made what I had to do easy. Because of the situation in my homeland I to had to call off the pending marriage. It was going to be difficult because I respect and care for you very deeply. If it would have harmed your reputation in any way I would have honored my commitment. As life would have it, I now have the honor of calling you my friend. I must say, love apparently agrees with you. If it was at all possible you are more beautiful then you were before."

"You were going to break up with me?"

"Not without asking your permission first."

Cynthia tilted her head to the side, "You are such a prince. Some woman is going to be very lucky one day."

"As Samuel is today."

"You know I owe all of this to you. It was the way you treated me that made me realized that I was worthy of being a princess. I never thought a man would want me at his side for public viewing. I was always the one they kept secret. Samuel knows and accepts who I am and so does his family."

"You are worthy of that and so much more. I'm glad you decided not to settle for just me."

"A fine African Prince, you mean. A girl could do worst you know." She reached into her purse and pulled out the keys to the Mercedes. "I have to return these to you."

He closed her hands around them, "No, that was my gift to you. If Samuel does not mind, please keep it as a sign of our friendship."

"Are you sure?"

"Yes, I'm sure. But I believe I will return the private jet I ordered for you."

Cynthia's mouth dropped open surprised. "A private jet?"

"Yes."

"Wait a minute, let me reconsider this." She thought for a moment then smiled. "No, I think I'll keep Samuel."

LaVere' pulled her into his arms and kissed her cheek, "You are a special woman Cynthia Thornton."

"So are you," she hugged him tightly. "Thank you for understanding."

Outside on the terrace, Jamal stood watching the scene fuming. LaVere' had released him of his duties to be returned to his homeland in disgrace over this common woman. The anger radiated through the very core of him. There was no way in hell he was going to allow the heifer to reign over him or his people. Whether they deserved it or not it was clear he had handled this situation for his Prince, his King and his country. The woman had to be stopped.

Brian sat in the office working as the snow began to fall heavier. Magna, his second in command knocked on the opened door, "I think it would be wise to send the staff home before things get worst. You have any problem with that?"

He turned and looked out the window. "It looks like we are going to have some accumulation. No problem. Are you leaving too?"

"Not until later. I have the notes from Sanchez and on the Munford case. It's some interesting information there. Did you know Munford was connected to Al Day?"

Brian looked up. Then he remembered the meeting a few years ago with JD and Al. Al's right hand man Tuck gave him a folder with information on Gavin and Munford.

Al mentioned they were dirty, but did not offer any further information. "It had been mentioned before. Contact Calvin Johnson in the AG's office they have an investigation brewing over there. You might want to confer on that case." His cell phone chimed. He looked at it and recognized the number. "I have to take this. After you talk to Calvin, go home."

"Aye Aye Captain," she saluted.

"Hey, what's going on?" He said into the cell phone.

"Hey. You know I love you right," Cynthia declared.

Smiling he sat back in his chair, "Yeah I know you do, although you treat me like crap."

"That's because you are always riding my back about something."

"Probably due to your bad judgment."

"You're right."

Silence ensued. "Did you say I was right?"

"Yes, but you were wrong about Gavin. He was good for me. If it wasn't for him, I would have been blind to what Samuel was offering."

Hearing the happiness in her voice was all the assurance Brian needed. "Have you talked to LaVere'?"

"Yes, I'm leaving his house now. He was such a prince about all of this. I will always have a soft spot in my heart for him. I believe he is truly happy for Samuel and me."

"I'm happy I can finally get a break. With Samuel around I don't have to spend every waking hour trying to keep you out of trouble."

"You will always be the first person I call to get me out of trouble."

"Yeah, thanks a lot."

"I have to check on Rosaline and the crew. You know today is a busy day for us. I just wanted to let you know I love you."

"It's about time you recognize my value. Be careful out there, the weather is getting bad."

"Okay mother hen. I'll talk to you later."

Cynthia closed her cell and placed it on the console between the seats. Brian was right the snow was coming down a little heavier. But before she pulled off she needed to tell Samuel. The smile that lit her face at the thought of the man could warm a family of five for a year it was so bright. She dialed the number as an unexplainable peace settled over her. A higher power has decided she was worthy of love after all. She sent up a silent thank you as the voice she had come to love vibrated through. "Hello you," she blushed as she placed her head on the headrest.

"Hello beautiful. Where are you?"

"I'm just leaving LaVere's."

"How did it go?"

"Very well. I think both of us knew what we were about to do was not good for either of us. He is a prince in every since of the word and I'm glad I had the chance to get to know him." She hesitated then added. "I hope he finds someone that will love and appreciate all he has to offer."

There was a melancholy sound to her voice. "Are you okay?"

"I'm fine," she relied dismissing the unhappy feelings for LaVere'.

"That you are," Samuel replied with a low growl.

"Save that for later tonight," she teased in response.

"Tonight? How long are you going to be?"

Laughing she replied as she turned the key in the ignition. "My plan was to stop by to see how the decorating is going on some of my clients homes before going home. That way once we get started, there will be no interruptions."

"It's best that you handle your business now. Once I get my hands on you, you will not have the strength or inclination to do anything but lay your beautiful body in my arms."

Closing her eyes against the images his comments were stirring. She quietly whispered, "Promises, promises."

"No beautiful, fact. See you soon," Samuel replied and disconnected the call.

Cynthia exhaled as she hit the off button to the phone. She put her seatbelt on and pulled off towards Route 301 which was about two miles up the road. Halfway up the snow-covered road she admired the wooded area with snow covering the trees. It was picturesque, giving it the Christmas feel. If she had a camera she would capture the scene and share with the girls. Her thoughts went to her friends, Ashley, Rosaline and Tracy. Telling them about Samuel is going to blow their minds. For the first time in their relationship she has a man that loves her and wants a future with her. "And I love him back," she said aloud, "*God it feels good to say that.*"

In the flash of a moment the car hit something in the road causing a thump and the car to swerve. Instinctively she slammed on the brakes causing the car to go into a skid on the slippery road. Trying to remember what she was supposed to do during a skid she turned the wheel in the direction of the skid only to go barreling down the embankment. Colliding with several trees the air bag dispensed blocking any view and her ability to steer the wheel. The car collided with something and bounced backwards onto its side, then there was blackness.

Jamal stepped out from the other side of the road, looked over the embankment and smiled. "Better than I imagined." He picked up the simple garden tool that he used to wreak havoc, turned it over and pushed the snow around to cover the vehicle tracks. Turning back in the direction from which he came he walked backwards across the road covering his tracks. Once he was across the road he picked of the garden rake, put it over his shoulder and walked back to his vehicle whistling a happy tune.

Samuel was just pulling into his building as he answered a call from Brian. "Have you talked with Cynthia?"

"A few hours ago. She mentioned meeting up with Rosaline. Why?"

"No one has been able to reach her for the last hour."

Samuel looked at his watch, it was almost two. He spoke to her before noon; she should have been back in Richmond over an hour ago. "I'll call you back." He hung up and dialed her number. When there was no answer he called Joshua. "I need you to locate Cynthia. Her last known location was Prince LaVere' Ashro's home in Hanover around noon."

"Hold on." He came back to the line. "What is she driving?"

"CLK350."

"That has GPS capability," hold on.

"Her GPS service was deactivated at the beginning of the month. Her car is located in Richmond."

"Check under Prince Ashro."

"Hold on," Joshua came back to the line. "The signal is showing in Hanover approximately two miles from the house."

"Thanks, I'll get back with you." *Why would her car still be in Hanover?* Putting his SUV in reverse he then dialed Brian. "The car is still on Prince Astor's property in Hanover. I'm heading out there."

"Hold on," Brian said a bit concerned. He walked over to LaVere', who was in the room talking to JD and James. "Excuse me. LaVere', may I have a moment?"

"Of course," he replied and stepped out into the hallway.

"We are trying to locate Cynthia. Have you spoken with her?"

"Not since she left my home around noon. Is there a problem?"

"No one has been able to reach her in a while. The GPS on the vehicle she was driving is showing a signal about two miles from your house."

"There is only one road leading onto the property and I just used it to get here. Her car was not there."

Shaking his head, "Something's not right. "Where are you?" Brian spoke into the telephone.

"I-95 North, I'll be at his place in twenty minutes." Samuel hung up the telephone.

By this time JD, James and Calvin joined the conversation. "What's happening Brian?" JD asked.

"I'm not sure, but I don't have a good feeling about this."

"Details Brian," LaVere' commanded.

"We'll talk on the way to your place."

"You need backup?" JD and James asked.

The thought of the Attorney General being in the same room with an angry Samuel and an unpredictable Joshua was not ideal in Brian's opinion. "No JD. You stay here with James. Samuel is in route. Let's go LaVere'."

On the way down' LaVere' called his driver Edmond to meet them at the door. Looking at his watch, Brian exhaled. It was now after three in the afternoon. It would be dark in two hours and temperatures would be dropping. If Cynthia was in the element it could be a deadly situation.

"You are very concerned with this situation. Is there more to it then you have stated?" LaVere' questioned.

"Yes," was all Brian replied as he dialed Samuel's number. "Are you on site?"

"Pulling off the highway now. Joshua is on site."

"Has he found anything?"

"Negative. What's your ETA?"

"Twenty minutes. I have LaVere' with me. You have pre-eminence on his property."

"Ask him if anyone is on site."

"Only my secretary Jamal," LaVere' answered

"I got that," Samuel replied. "I'm on site. I'll get back with you."

Chapter 22

Samuel, Joshua and the pilot of the helicopter used to arrive at the site sat inside his vehicle surveying the twenty-acre property. The minicomputer Joshua was using indicated the vehicle last signal was within a two-mile radius. Satellite survey of the signal around noon showed the vehicle leaving the house and reaching the curve in the road, but never entering the highway. That information reduced the search area to the mile leading from the curve to the exit of the property.

The two brothers prepared themselves for the weather and possible retrieval gear as they discussed strategy. Samuel was going east through the woods, while Joshua tracked west. They would make contact every ten minutes. Not sure what they were up against, Munford's men or just a simple accident, the two armed themselves with weapons. The pilot would be handling the base equipment to keep track of their path.

As they stepped out of the vehicle they walked the road from the curve towards the highway first to see if anything stood out. Other then the tracks from their vehicles, nothing on the road indicated an accident of any kind. It took them less than ten minutes to walk the road before the property entrance came into view. The snow was intensifying, the day was darkening and Samuel's professionalism was slipping.

"Damn it, nothing. Are you sure we're in the right place?" he snapped.

Not allowing his brother's temperament to throw him off, Joshua turned and began walking slowly back in the direction they came from. This time he was shinning his light in the woods. "You know the strategy, start from the last sighting," he calmly replied.

Following his brother's lead, Samuel looked up towards the woods on the opposite side of the road. Taking small steps he flashed the light up and down the trees, looking for any sign of a mishap. The wooded area was dense, with tall trees that sole purpose was to keep the property secluded from outsiders. Most of them were older sturdy trees that a bulldozer would not have any luck bringing down, but there were a few that were less forbidding with broken limbs. Samuel took a few more steps then stopped. He flashed the light back to the broken limbs and walked closer to the embankment. "Joshua, over here." They both surveyed the area. "It looks like something came through here breaking a path down the embankment."

"Yeah it does. The question is," he said as he knelt down to see the area between the trees better, "when?"

"I'm going down," Samuel stated as he began descending the embankment.

Joshua followed suit as he yelled back. "We're going down an embankment on the east side of the road. Tell me what's down there."

The pilot put the co-ordinates from their tracking devices into the computer and waited. "The computer is showing trees, water and live stock, probably deer in the area.

"Copy," Joshua replied. The two moved slowly, following the broken limbs and marks on the trees. "The snow would have covered any signs of something coming through here in the last three hours."

"We may be in the wrong direction," Samuel stated fearfully.

"No. Something came through here--these nicks on the trees are fresh," Joshua replied. Joshua was a professional tracker. He could find people that took great steps to hide their tracks.

Samuel flashed his light back up the embankment. He, on the other hand, was the strategist. Thinking things through had put him ahead of people and incidents. Looking back up the embankment he followed the probable path of the car in his mind. Taking into consideration the stability of the trees and then if she was conscious and still attempting to steer the vehicle or if she had lost consciousness or if she was ..... he stopped his thoughts. That was an unacceptable notion.

Following the path of the trees the opening suggested a vehicle could fit through until approximately thirty feet from where Joshua stood. Then there was a cluster of trees that would have stopped the progress or boomer-ranged the vehicle. He looked to the right but the density of the trees would have stopped a car dead in its track. Going back to the cluster of trees and following the path to the right. "Joshua," he yelled and took off running down the hill.

The car was turned over on its side lodged between two trees. The front of the vehicle was severely damaged, the windshield broken and the airbag was deployed. Samuel climbed on the vehicle and noticed the window was rolled down. "Cynthia," he called out. No answer.

Joshua called in the location and raced over to Samuel just as he climbed off the vehicle. They pushed it right side up then frantically searched inside. "Is this her car?"

"Yeah. Her purse and cell phone are inside." Samuel replied dejected. "The good news is she is apparently alive and able to walk away from this. The bad news is she walked away from the car. Why would she do that?"

"I don't know. You're the one that fell for a city girl. Me, I want a good old country girl with enough common sense not to leave a communication device behind."

Samuel frowned and looked at Joshua. "A country girl wouldn't know what to do with a cell phone or me." He turned his flashlight back on and surveyed the area. Changing his mindset from what he would do to what Cynthia would do, he looked down and across the creek below. *Nope, the water would mess up her boots.* Looking along the creek, he turned the light off and placed it in his back pocket. "She would go back in the direction of the house."

Joshua looked in the direction, "I think you're right. I'll work from the house back to you."

"See you on the other side," Samuel replied as he put Cynthia's purse on his shoulder.

The sight froze Joshua in his tracks, "Goes well with your outfit."

The look from Samuel told him, his big brother was not in the teasing mood. "She will ask if I found her purse. You'll understand if you ever get a woman."

"Okay," Joshua chuckled as he began his climb up the embankment then mumbled. "I don't want a woman if I have to carry her purse."

"You have something to say?"

"Nope."

"I didn't think so."

When he reached the top of the embankment, Joshua was met by Brian, LaVere' and Edmond.

"What did you find?" Brian asked.

"The car flipped over down by the creek. Samuel is following the trail back towards the house. I'm taking it from the house forward. The temperature is dropping; we have to find her now."

The men jumped in the SUV and drove towards the house. "I'll go with you. Two sets of eyes are better than one."

"Make three sets of eyes. I'm joining you," LaVere' added as the vehicle stopped in front of the house. He extended his hand, "LaVere' Ashro." Joshua shook his hand but never gave his name. "I take it that's your helicopter I'm about to commandeer. Then you should at least know my name."

"Actually it belongs to the President of the United States."

LaVere' stepped out of the vehicle. "Better, tell him I have it," he said as he closed the door and ran into the house.

"Can he handle a chopper?"

"That and some more," Brian replied as they began their stride over towards the woods. "Your man at base said you have trackers on. You take the woods; I'll trail the property line. LaVere' will use the lights from the chopper once it really gets dark."

"Roger. Check in every ten minutes," Joshua called out as they went in separate directions. He pulled out his cell. "Sammy, Brian's on foot and LaVere' is going up in the chopper. Anything on your end?"

"Negative. I'm about a half a mile out from the clearing; nothing," he replied.

Joshua stood facing the woods and looked to his right; the woods extended for miles. He turned on his flashlight and waved it, "Do you see my light?"

"Affirmative."

Okay, we're talking about a woman. He thought. *What would a woman do?* "Go to your right. Follow the creek bed."

"It makes more sense to walk straight to the clearing. Turning would take her further into the wood," Samuel called back.

"Exactly, go to your right," Joshua shut off the phone and walked toward the woods.

Samuel looked around the area, the darkness had descended and his anxiety was increasing. His once regarded unbreakable control was about to shatter. Cynthia was somewhere out there, possibly hurt with the temperature dropping and no sign of the snow letting up. He flashed his light towards the clearing trying to decide if he should follow Joshua's advice. Cynthia's life could depend on it. The car was in bad shape; nine times out of ten she was injured. Nothing in front captured his attention. He turned towards the creek and flashed his light. *Listen to your heart* ran through his mind. Taking his own advice he turned and followed the creek. A half a mile in the area around the creek appeared to curve. A little further ahead a wooden bridge crossed the creek. He flashed his light under the bridge. His heart stopped at the sight, as he ran mindlessly through the woods praying and cursing until he reached the top of the incline. Climbing down the side he called out, "Cynthia." There she was curled up on a step under the bridge, unconscious with her coat wrapped around her. There was blood on her face, her clothes were ripped and she appeared to be frostbitten. Stunned, it took him a moment to gather his thoughts. Looking down at what appeared to be her lifeless body, an angry roar escaped his throat. She was his damn it, death was not going to take her away from him! Not now! He gently pushed her hair from her face and kissed her forehead, "I'm here Sleeping Beauty. Your prince is here to rescue you."

He pushed the button on his phone, "Joshua," he calmly spoke as he checked her vitals and then for broken bones. "We are about a half mile northeast from my last location under a bridge. She is unconscious, some broken ribs, a swollen foot and possible hypothermia. Get the chopper ready to take off as soon as we are clear of the woods. She's in bad shape."

Pushing all emotions aside, he continued to talk to her as he worked quickly, removing her wet outer clothing and wrapping her in an insulating blanket. From his backpack he pulled out items to create a makeshift harness which he quickly assembled. Stabilizing her fragile body and ensuring she was immobilized he placed her securely inside and carefully lifted her onto his back. Moving strategically up the slope, Samuel was careful not to lose his footing for fear of causing her more harm. Once he reached level ground, he proceeded in the direction of the house. Hearing the motor of the chopper he looked upward. The light from the chopper was sufficient to see his way through the now dark wooded area.

Joshua was at the edge of the woods giving directions to LaVere' on where the light was needed. LaVere' landed the chopper and jumped out as the actual pilot pulled up in Samuel's SUV, parked and took over. Brian, Joshua and LaVere' gently removed the harness from Samuel's back and placed it in the back of the chopper. Samuel and Joshua climbed into the chopper and were immediately lifted. Brian drove Samuel's SUV, while Edmond picked up LaVere' and headed to Richmond.

JD's cell phone sounded. Checking it, he recognized Brian's number. "Have you found her?"

"Yeah," he replied sadly. "We're on our way back in. Samuel and Joshua should be arriving soon by helicopter. I've placed a call to the administrators to advise them of their arrival. Her car swerved off the road down an embankment. She is alive, but unconscious."

JD took in the information as his wife, Tracy and Rosaline stood in the doorway staring at him. As soon as he hung up the call, Tracy walked over to him, "What's happened?" She asked in a fearful tone.

Not sure how to tell her without causing her pain, he simple reached out and pulled her into his arms. The action scared Rosaline sending her to the comfort of her husband's arms. They had all gathered at James and Ashley's home awaiting news. JD spoke calmly. "Apparently Cynthia's car swerved off the road and she was hurt. They found her near LaVere's home and are transporting her to the hospital."

"Is she alive?" Calvin asked.

"Yes, unconscious."

"I'm going to the emergency room," Tracy said.

"I'm going too," Rosaline joined her.

"I'll be there as soon as I tell James and Ashley what's going on," JD replied.

Chapter 23

The Intensive care unit of MCV hospital was no stranger to Tracy. She had been there as a patient and as a love one waiting, for JD to recover. It was not a place she wanted to be, but she could not bring herself to leave. The friends gathered in the waiting area for any word on Cynthia's condition. The only thing they knew thus far was she had suffered hypothermia, a concussion and a sprained ankle. The concussion was the concern at this point. The doctor could not explain why she was not regaining consciousness, and that worried all of them.

JD, Brian, LaVere' and Joshua stood on one side of the room, while Rosaline and Tracy paced back and forth. Neither could sit down with their friend hurt. Ashley walked into the room accompanied by James. "Ashley where are the babies?" JD questioned.

"The twins and JC are with Mommy and Gwen. Any word on Cynthia?" she asked looking to Tracy.

"Nothing yet," Tracy sadly replied.

"I don't understand what happened. I just spoke with her. There was nothing wrong with the car and the snow had not gotten that bad," Rosaline angrily stated. "Something doesn't feel right with this."

"I know what you mean," Ashley added. "When James told me Cynthia was missing, I immediately thought Jamal had done something to her."

LaVere' turned at the statement, "Why did you think Jamal had anything to do with this?"

"It was no secret he does not care very much for Cynthia. While you were away they had words that rattled her somewhat. You know that's not an easy thing to do." Ashley stated.

James shook his head, "That didn't stop her from threatening to do bodily harm to Jamal if he was involved with what happened to your family."

LaVere' smiled, "She is fiercely loyal to say the least."

"Tell me about it," Tracy smiled. "She threatened bodily harm to some woman that refused to take her hands of Jeffrey at the club one night."

"All she did was threatened? Huh, I watched her give a girl a serious beat down when she thought the girl had said something about me. Poor thing never knew what hit her." Rosaline said as she took a seat.

"She certainly gave me hell when it came to Tracy," JD added as he wrapped his arms around his wife. "At one time I thought I was going to have to fight her just to get to see you."

"I did have to fight her," Brian laughed. "When Kaitlyn disappeared and her best friend wouldn't tell me where she was, Cynthia drove up to campus, knocked on the girls door and proceeded to give her the beat down of a lifetime. I had to fight her to get her off the girl."

"Who's Kaitlyn?" Tracy asked.

JD, Ashley and Rosaline all turned to Brian. They knew that was an untouchable topic. In fact, JD was surprise to hear Brian mention Kaitlyn's name. However, before he could reply a commotion in the hallway took their attention. At the sound of a crash they all, with the exception of Ashley and Joshua ran to the hallway.

"What do you mean I can't see my daughter? I'm her mother and I demand to see her now."

Rosaline angrily went to Sofia and picked up the clipboard she had knocked out of the nurse hand. "For all that's holy, could you please think about your daughter and not yourself? You are in an intensive care unit at a hospital. Act like the sophisticated woman you claim to be."

Sofia turned on Rosaline with furious eyes, "Don't you speak to me in that manner Rosaline Taylor."

"Marable, Rosaline Taylor-Marable." Roz sneered back.

"Mrs. Thornton," JD interjected, before the scene escalated, "what's the problem? Maybe I can help."

"Hello JD," Sofia calmed a bit. "You can help. Tell this woman to let me in to see Cynthia."

JD looked to the nurse as the others watched the commotion. "Would you advise Mr. Lassiter that Cynthia's mother is here and would like to see her?'

"Yes Mr. Attorney General," the nurse replied as she gave Sofia a snide look and walked away.

"I'm sure Samuel will step out to allow you a visit with Cynthia." JD turned to step away but she stopped him.

"Who is Samuel Lassiter to be controlling who can and cannot see my daughter?"

From the doorway Joshua replied, "Her fiancée."

A frown marked her otherwise perfect appearance as she turned to LaVere', "What is he talking about?" she asked.

LaVere' looked to the small crowd that gathered in the hallway. "Perhaps we should step into the waiting room to discuss this." He said as he took Sofia's arm and guided her to the waiting room.

Sofia walked into the room with the regalness she possessed if only in her mind. "Ashley," she spoke as she turned back to LaVere'. "Someone want to tell me what's going on?"

"I'll be happy to, Mrs. Thornton." Samuel stated as he stepped into the room. "Cynthia and I planned to announce this to everyone together, but circumstances seem to have changed."

"What circumstances?" Sofia asked with sarcasms streaming from each word.

"I'm in love with your daughter and she is in love with me. I intend to marry her as soon as she recovers."

Sofia looked from Samuel to LaVere' and smiled sardonically, "The Lassister from the north side of town?" Laughing sarcastically, she looked at the people in the room, then back to LaVere' who had a somber look on his face. She stopped laughing, "You can't be serious. LaVere' tell me this is some type of joke."

Before anyone could stop him, Joshua stood in front of Sofia, so close she had to take a step back to look up at him. "What's the joke?" he asked angrily.

Not intimidated by his presence, "The fact that you believe I would allow my daughter to marry a Lassiter."

Samuel pulled Joshua back at her words and stood between the two. Angered by her holier than thou attitude, Ashley spoke from her seat. "Mrs. Thornton, you have not been privy to Cynthia's feelings for a while. I'm here to tell you, she is indeed in love with Samuel. Her plan is to be with him."

"Sofia," LaVere'," added, "I spoke with Cynthia and she informed me she does love Samuel and I released her from our commitment."

"Why in the hell would you do that, LaVere'? This man is not worthy of my daughter."

Knowing he would have to deal with this woman for the rest of his life as his mother-in-law, Samuel tried to hold his words. The attempt failed. "I believe it is you who is not worthy of your daughter. I don't know you very well Mrs. Thornton and I hoped your views on my family were vicious rumors from the past. I see now, they are not." He took a step closer, "Never the less, your grandchildren will be Lassisters and make no mistake, we plan to have quite a few.

Now if your intent for coming here was to see your daughter, you may do so now. If not, I am going back to her room because I don't ever want her to feel alone again."

"Sofia," her husband, Jackson spoke from the doorway. "We are here to see about Cynthia. Let's do that." Not satisfied with the command from her husband, she stomped past Samuel and the rest of the group. Jackson step over to Samuel and extended his hand, "I know your father. If you are half the man he is my daughter is in good hands."

The chill was still running down his back from the words spoken by Sofia, but the warmth of Jackson words began to seep through. "Thank you, sir." Jackson turned and walked out of the room.

Everyone seemed to exhale a sigh of relief. LaVere' walked over to Samuel and patted him on the back. "Good luck with that woman and thank you. You are a better man than I." He laughed as others joined in.

"I fail to see the humor in any of this," Joshua said as he picked up his computer and began reviewing satellite images again.

"You either have to laugh at Sofia or kill her." Brian stated, "If you kill her, which I have considered from time to time, there is the chance that she may resurrect and multiply. Therefore, I decided to leave well enough alone. Besides, Cynthia loves her mother, always has and therein lies the problem. If you want to be a part of Cynthia's life, Sofia comes with the deal."

Shaking his head Joshua laughed, "Ain't no woman alive that would make me want to put up with a mother-in-law like that."

"That's what you say now, but a woman will come into your life that will have you putting up with anything just to be with her," JD offered.

"Is that so?" Tracy smiled at her husband.

"Damn right," he replied smiling.

James turned to LaVere', "Do you have any idea what happened yesterday?"

"Yeah, Samuel is there anything you can tell us to help us understand." Rosaline asked, dismissing the whole scene that she had become accustomed to with Sofia.

Exhaling, Samuel stood next to Joshua. "From what we could uncover at the scene, it appears she simply ran off the road. She was wandering through the woods; I'm sure trying to find her way out."

"I don't believe in accidents without a cause," Joshua spoke without looking from the computer. "I'm with the one who asked what caused her to go off the road."

"I can't shake the feeling that Jamal was involved, But that may be just me." Ashley looked up at James. "I'm ready to go back to my babies now."

Tracy looked to JD, "Me too babe. I need to hold JC and tell him how much I love him. Brian, please call us if there is any change with Cynthia. Rosaline you have not slept all night. Why don't you go home and get some rest."

"Cynthia will never forgive me if I leave her here alone with that woman."

"You will be no good to Cynthia without rest. Come, I'm taking you home," Macro commanded. "I will bring you back first thing in the morning."

The women left the room' leaving LaVere', Brian, Joshua and Samuel to talk. "Could there be anything to what Ashley said about Jamal?" Brian asked.

"With what I gathered from home, it would not surprise me." LaVere' replied.

"Explain," Samuel stated.

"It seem Jamal was connected with the rebels that attempted to take over the palace in my homeland. He was to be sent back to Emure to answer to those charges."

"What would that have to do with Cynthia?" Samuel questioned further.

"Jamal believed my proposal would have a negative impact on the citizens of Emure, which unfortunately I found to be correct. He was rather vigorous in his attempt to keep that from happening."

"Was it to the extent to want to cause her harm?" Brian asked.

"Patriots have no sense of limitations to accomplish their goal," Joshua stated as he stood and looked at Samuel. He placed his laptop on the table. "Is that Jamal?" he asked LaVere'. The man came to where he stood and looked at the monitor.

"Yes it is," LaVere' replied with a confused look. "What is he doing?"

Joshua pushed the reverse button and then hit the play button, "Watch."

Using the satellite, Joshua found the feed beginning around noon and set the co-ordinance for the location of LaVere's property. Zooming in on the road the screen showed Jamal as he stepped out from the trees on the side of the road, looked over the embankment and smiled. He picked up the simple garden tool that he used to wreak havoc, turned it over and pushed the snow around to cover the vehicle tracks. Turned back in the direction from which he came he walked backwards across the road covering his tracks. Once he crossed the road he picked up the garden rake, put it over his shoulder and climbed into his vehicle.

Before the motions on the monitor completed Samuel was out the door. Brian and LaVere' ran out the door behind him, but he was nowhere to be found. The two returned to the room and found Joshua gone.

To no surprise Joshua's helicopter had already landed at the entrance of LaVere's property fifteen minutes before Samuel arrived. He anticipated his brother would arrive there before him to secure Jamal for his own protection.

However, Joshua was seated inside the chopper waiting for his arrival. Samuel pulled over long enough for Joshua to jump in. "He's in the back of the property putting luggage into a sedan. I believe he is attempting to leave."

"I'm here to help him with that," Samuel replied.

Getting his meaning Joshua cautioned. "You are now a normal citizen. You can't kill people without being charged with murder. I, on the other hand can."

"She's not your woman, she's mine. If anyone is going to take the little worm out it will be me." Samuel pulled the vehicle in front of the house and proceeded to get out.

Joshua walked around to the driver's side. "I can't let you do that big brother."

Samuel angrily turned on him, "Try to stop me and you will go down with him."

Looking at his brother, Joshua knew he could not take him, never could. But there was no way he was going to see Samuel behind bars. As Samuel turned to walk up the steps to the house Joshua pulled out a stun gun and sent several volts of electricity through his brother. He caught him before he hit the ground and placed him back into the vehicle. He shook his head, "That's going to hurt in the morning." Then thought of the beat down Samuel will give him the next time they saw each other. "The worm has to pay."

Joshua didn't bother to knock on the door. He reached into his coat pocket and pulled out a kit. With one of the tools he unlocked the door and walked in. In an inside pocket he pulled out a handheld computer and turned it on. The sensor showed heat in a room upstairs and a room in the back of the house. Following the flow plan on the monitor, he followed the heat sensor on the ground level. As he reached LaVere's office, he looked out the windows and saw the man his brother wanted to kill walking towards a sedan that was parked out back. The man saw him and began running towards the car.

Joshua ran out the front door just as the vehicle was turning onto the road. He jumped onto the hood of the vehicle with his weapon pulled and pointed it center chest through the windshield at Jamal. "I haven't killed anyone today, my trigger finger is itching. Give me a reason."

Jamal slammed on brakes causing Joshua to slide on the ground. Before he could think to pull off, Joshua was at the driver's window breaking the glass. He snatched the keys from the ignition and demanded Jamal to get out of the car.

He grabbed Jamal and slammed his head into the top of the hood. "That's for making me get my suit dirty." He watched as Jamal's body slithered to the ground. Picking his half-conscious body from the snowy ground, Joshua saw Brian's SUV coming down the road. He slammed him against the hood again, then stood over his unconscious body and yelled, "And that's for the ass kicking I'm going to get for keeping you alive."

Brian stood next to Joshua and asked, "Are you finished?"

Joshua looked at Brian and replied, "I reserve the right to kill him at a later date." He looked at LaVere'. "I suggest you have him on a plane bound for Emure before Samuel wakes up."

Brian looked around, "Where is Samuel?" Joshua walked over to the vehicle parked in front of the house and pointed. "What happened to him?"

"I stunned him."

"You stunned your own brother with electricity?"

"Have you ever tried to stop Samuel when he is angry? Well I have and it's not an easy task. It was the only way I could keep him from killing the son of a b....."

"It may not be a bad idea for you to take the plane ride with Jamal and I. That will guarantee his exchange will be handled by the proper authorities. And keep you safe from Samuel for a week," LaVere' stated as he walked towards the house. "After that, I'm afraid you're on your own."

"How long is he going to be under?" Brian asked.

"About an hour," Joshua replied.

Brian looked over his shoulder to LaVere'. "Anyway you could have your plane fueled and ready for takeoff in the next thirty minutes?"

An hour later, Sofia was bored from sitting in Cynthia's room. She ventured out into the hallway and was surprised to see Sally sitting in the waiting area. Sally was seated on the opposite side of the room flipping through a magazine. "Are you going to act as though you don't see me Sofia?" She asked without looking up.

"What are you doing here?"

Placing the magazine on the table and standing Sally smiled, "You are as beautiful as you were thirty years ago."

"I know."

Yes, I'm sure you do. But to answer your question, I'm here to see about Cynthia. Unlike you, your daughter has found her heart. She loves my Samuel very much and he loves her. I pray you allow them to be happy."

"If you think for one moment I will allow my daughter to marry any of your many boys, you are mistaken."

Sally exhaled and smiled. "Sofia when I turned down the part in the production, it wasn't because of your cruel words about my children. In fact I should thank you. It was those words that made me realized how much I loved my husband, my home and my children. I had several more after that, actually, a total of twelve, for the ballerina that could have taken your mediocre career away from you."

"You could never take anything away from me. You were never as talented as I and nor as beautiful. I proved that with Jackson, he is still with me."

Sally was so tempted to wipe the smudged look from Sofia's face by revealing it was her that turned Jackson away.

Instead, Sally picked up her purse. "Sofia, you know—beauty is only skin deep, but ugly is to the bone. You think about that one day when you are alone with your beautiful self. I will return to visit with Cynthia once she is awake." As she walked pass Sofia, Jackson was walking down the hallway.

"Hello Sally," he smiled warmly.

Sally looked at Sofia, and then back to the man everyone considered a catch back in the day. "Hello Jackson. It's wonderful to see you. Please know Cynthia is in Joe's and my prayers."

"Thank you Sally and please say hello to Joe."

"I'll do that," she replied and walked away.

Jackson walked over to Sofia who was fuming. "How dare you speak to that woman in my presences?"

"That was thirty years ago. You and I are now married with two children. Sally and Joe are happily married with twelve. What more proof do you need that nothing is happening between Sally and me? Let it go, your jealously is showing," he replied and walked back into Cynthia's room.

It was close to midnight when Samuel awakened in his own bed. It took a moment before his mind cleared and for him to remember what happened. "Joshua," he yelled.

"He can't hear you," his father replied.

Samuel sprung up. "I'm going to kill him."

"No you won't," his father laughed. "I actually think the whole situation is funny."

"Where is he?" His father raised an eyebrow at the tone Samuel had taken with him. Recognizing the look he took a breath. "Dad where is Joshua?" he asked calmly.

"He and Prince Ashro flew that little worm back to Emure so he could face charges."

Samuel relaxed and was about to lay back on the bed, but stood instead. "Cynthia, I have to get back to the hospital. I can't drive Dad, can you take me?"

"That's why I'm here. How long is it going to take for your nervous system to repair itself?"

"At least twenty four hours," Samuel replied as he put his shoes on.

"Well I left your mother at the hospital and I'm sure she has had enough of Sofia Thornton by now."

"It doesn't take long to get enough of her. Has Cynthia awakened?"

"Not that I'm aware of."

Shaking his head, "I have to talk to her. I need to tell her just how much I love and need her."

Joe smiled at his son that was the first time he had ever heard him say he needed anyone. "Let's get you over there." The two men walked out with a mission in mind.

Memories were flooding her mind. The problem was she couldn't distinguish what was real and what was not. There was a deer. No it wasn't a deer the tire hit something. The solider was there, the first time. No, he was there the second time. What was his name, Prince charming, that's who it was? No, it wasn't Prince charming, but it was Prince something. What is wrong with her, "Ashley," she called out. "Who is he, where is he?

"Cynthia open your eyes," Sofia ordered with no results.

That wasn't Ashley, she thought and retreated deeper into her mind. That was not a voice she wanted to hear. Moments later she saw him again, the man with voice, or was it the Prince. The confusion was getting to her and she begin to panic. "Roz call Brian, call Brian," she repeated.

Brian stood at the side of her bed as she thrashed back and forth. "Cynthia," he called out. "I need you to open your eyes and look at me."

"Where is he Brian? Why is he taking so long to find me?"

"Where is who Cyn?"

Tears began to run down her cheek, "Find him Brian, find him."

Frustrated Brian looked around and saw Samuel walking into the room. Then it dawned on him who she was searching for in her mind. "Cynthia, Samuel is here."

"Samuel," she cried out, "Samuel."

Gathering her gently in his arms, he held her and stroked her head. "I'm here Sleeping Beauty, I'm here." He felt her body relax in his embrace as she snuggled to get closer to him. "I'm here Cynthia." He kissed her head, "I'm here."

"I love you Samuel."

He had to blink to keep the emotions intact. "I love you too." Thinking she was a sleep again Samuel attempted to lay her back against the pillow, but her grasp was tight on his shirt and she was not letting go. "That's right baby, hold on tight and don't you ever let me go."

Around two in the morning, everyone had left to get some rest, but Samuel remained next to her bed waiting for her to open her eyes. He heard a sound and looked around. His sister Pearl stood in the doorway.

"I hear she's doing better."

He held his hand out towards her. She stepped forward and took it. "She's just sleeping now. Her body's' been through a lot in the last forty eight hours."

"Ruby said it may take her a minute, but she should be okay."

"That's what the doctors are saying," he smiled at her. "What are you doing here this time of night?"

Pearl shrugged her shoulders. "I wanted to tell you I love you and I want you to be happy. I said a prayer for her earlier tonight for her speedy recovery. I hear we have a wedding to plan."

"How do you feel about that?" he asked his little sister.

She kissed his cheek, "My feelings are for me to deal with, but thank you for caring so much. But your concern should be with the woman lying in that bed. You are a good brother Samuel Lassiter. I have to go. I'll talk to you in the morning."

He stood to walk her downstairs to the lobby, but she stopped him. "Your place is here." She turned and walked out of the room.

"You should walk her down; hospitals can be a scary place."

Samuel turned to see the eyes he had been longing to see for hours. "Hey you," he smiled as he sat next to her on the bed. "Will I ever get a chance to make love to you again?"

"You will have the rest of your life."

Epilogue

Cynthia sat at the vanity in the dressing room of her suite at the historic Jefferson Hotel in downtown Richmond. It was the perfect setting for the wedding of a princess with its majestic décor and elegant high vaulted ceilings. Surrounded by her friends, Roz, Ashley and Tracy, she was the last of the crew to finally say I do. It may have taken her longer, but the love she found was just as deep and profound as her friends. Samuel was everything she wanted and more.

After spending a week in the hospital, Samuel took her home—their home. When she was there before, she was taken under duress and left early the next morning and did not get a good look at his house. If she had, she would have known that Samuel was not a man without financial means as she thought. His home was nestled on a five acre estate, with a two level four bedroom Victorian home. The mile long circular drive way leading to the house was shaded with dogwood tress along the route. To say she was pleasantly surprised was an understatement, but the realization that she didn't care one way or another was the shocker. All she wanted was to spend the rest of her life with him. By the time she arrived, Samuel's family and her friends had moved all of her things into his house including some of her furniture to ensure she knew this was now her home.

With her head held down, while Ashley adjusted the veil on her head, the most serene smile appeared on her face. Looking through the mirror at her friend Ashley knew what the look was for. "Thinking about Samuel?" she asked.

Cynthia looked up into the mirror and nodded, "I'm thinking about the life we are going to have together and praying my first child will not be like Joshua."

The ladies in the room laughed, "I don't know, I like Joshua. I think he is hilarious," Roz replied laughing. "I can't believe what he did to Samuel."

"I'm glad he did. I believe Samuel would have killed Jamal," Tracy said as she chased after new to walking JC.

"I know he would have," Cynthia replied laughing at the giggling child. "Tracy let him run around. He's just having some fun."

Tracy stopped and looked at her friend, "Okay, but your ring bearer will be filthy by the time your pictures are taken."

There was a knock on the door. "I'll get it," Roz said as she walked out of the dressing room into the sitting area of the suite. Walking back she was followed by JD, James and Brian.

"I never thought I would say this, but you really are beautiful." JD complimented from the doorway, just before his son ran into his arms.

Cynthia turned and smiled at the men that were like family to her, "Thank you JD. Does this means we are not going to be at each other's throat from now on."

"No," JD shook his head, "Just until Samuel realize it's just the way you and I show how much we love each other. I would hate to be on his banded list."

The friends in the room laughed, "I like it. You know he told Sofia if she did not feel she could control what she says to you she is not to come within twenty feet of you today or he will kill her with his bare hands." Brian said with a smile, "And I think she took heed.

"Well we don't have to worry about that, she's not coming."

"What?" was echoed in unison from the women. Ashley touched her friend on the shoulder, "You're not serious?"

Tracy walked over to the vanity and looked down at Cynthia. "Your mother will be here. I don't mean to speak poorly of your mother, but she is too vain to miss out on all the publicity surrounding your wedding."

"She has a point there, Roz said as she looked out of the window. "There are literally tons of reporters outside the hotel and more inside. Between, Prince LaVere' and his family, James and the rest of the Brooks, JD and Blake, I don't think there is a reporter on earth that is not here. There is no way Sofia is going to let them put in their report that she was not present for her own daughter's wedding."

"Hey, look who we just rescued," Calvin said as he entered the room with Marco, Douglas and Blake. "There were so many women surrounding him in the lobby we decided to take pity on him."

"Didn't look like he was suffering to me," Douglas stated.

"Nor to me," Marco added with his Jamaican accent. "He seemed like a man in paradise."

Blake smiled. "Hey, I'm a twenty-one year old single man. I love being surrounded by women. Tall ones, short ones, brown ones, fat ones I love them all."

Then there was a burst of laugher coming through the door and everyone turned to see Samuel's sisters walk into the room.

Opal, Jade, Diamond and Ruby went over to talk to Cynthia, while Pearl hung back in the doorway. Phire stopped in front of Blake and gave him a good once over and approvingly shaking her head said, "Okay, I'll give it to you—you are fine. But you need to beef up a little. A girl needs some muscles to hold on to during those love making sessions you portray so well in the movies." She turned not aware of the open mouths or shocked looks on the faces of the people in the room. "Cynthia, Samuel asked me to give this to you." Phire said with a smile as she gave a gift box to Cynthia.

"You are ordered to open it now so that I can take pictures," Diamond said beaming with anticipation.

"I think that's our cue to leave." JD said as he kissed Tracy's cheek, "I'll take JC with me. We'll be with Samuel."

"Okay babe," Tracy replied as all the men piled out of the room with the exception of Brian.

He walked over to where Cynthia sat with the box in her hand, bent down and whispered in her ear. "Remember, I was the one that told you someone would come along that looked into your heart and loved you for you." He kissed her on the cheek. As he began to stand, she held his hand and pulled him back down to her. "You're next."

He stood up and frowned at her. "Don't wish that on me." He said as he stormed towards the doorway. He stopped and touched Pearl's shoulder. "Are you okay?" She nodded and he continued out of the door.

"Well, open the box," Pearl said from the doorway. "Samuel and I spent a lot of time designing this."

Cynthia smiled at Pearl, "You helped picking this out—is it a bomb?"

Pearl laughed as Cynthia shook the box, "Not this time."

All eyes watched as Cynthia opened the box then removed the card that was on top and read it. *To my one and only princess, Love always, Samuel.* Removing the layers of red tissue paper, she gasped in awe as she pulled out a diamond studded tiara. Holding it in her hand the woman in the room shouted with glee.

"Damn he's good," Phire shouted. Her sisters turned to her. "Hey you have to admit, that's a clincher. He's going to be getting some every night for the rest of his life."

Roz, Ashley and Tracy were laughing so hard tears were coming out of their eyes, as well as Cynthia's. But hers were tears of joy.

"Well," Pearl said as she walked over to Cynthia and took the box from her lap, "let's, remove the veil and crown the princess. A prince of a man is waiting for her downstairs."

The wedding party gathered at the top of the spiral staircase that led into the ballroom where the guests were seated. In the center of the room were her nine bridesmaids and groomsmen, which consisted of each of Samuel's sisters, Tracy, Ashley and her maid of honor, Roz, along with Samuel's brothers, Blake, JD, Calvin and Brian. All eyes fell on her as she entered the area. This was now her family, she would never be alone again and it was Samuel that made this all possible. In the short few months he had turned her life completely around. She was no longer looking for love, she had found it. The music signaled it was time to claim him.

Samuel stood at the front of the room with the pastor and his brother Joshua, who was smiling and profiling for all the females in the room. When the music began he watched as his mother walked in on the arm of one of the groomsmen and his father behind her. The pride in his father's eyes was evident as was the hope for grandchildren in his mother's eyes. Once they were seated, Sofia was escorted in with the air of superiority that only existed in her head. No one else seemed to recognize or acknowledge it. Not being a person of patience Samuel exhaled wondering how much longer was he going to have to wait until Cynthia walked through that door.

As couple after couple walked down and took their place his mind wondered to the bachelor party that was held in that very room the night before. James and JD teased about him taking Cynthia from a prince and a governor. Then asked if he was sure he wanted to marry this woman. "More than life itself," was his replied. For he knew she was marrying him for love. She had no idea just how well off he was. Financially he did not have to work another day in his life unless he wanted to. Being in the military he did not have to pay for living or travel expenses. His income was invested and it had paid off. The down turn in the recession had hit and it was hard, but it did not come close to breaking him. The home he lived in was a gift from a sheik whose daughter he had rescued from kidnappers. The yacht he owned was another gift from a family in Florida whose son he had saved from a drug lord and then personally saw to his rehabilitation.

The reason he worked for Brian was because he believed in JD Harrison. Once he announces he is running for President of the United Stated, Samuel wanted to be there to make sure he was well protected. When Cynthia realized financially she and Samuel were on equal footing the first thing she wanted to do was tell her mother. But he told her no. Her mother's love should not be based on how well her daughter married. If she could not give her love freely then it was not worth having. He promised to love her enough just for who she is, nothing more. And he would not change one thing about her. He didn't care about her history with other men, for they all simply prepared her for him.

As for Gavin, who was sitting among the guest, she had demonstrated her trust in Samuel when she gave him the locket. After reviewing the information on the disc inside the locket, he turned it over to Joshua. It seems Chief Munford had now expanded from just controlling the gangs to moving shipments of weapons along the east coast. Soon he would have more pressing things to deal with.

The music changed and Samuel looked up to see Cynthia standing at the end of the walkway looking like a majestic princess from a movie. And she was his. Joshua nudged him in the back, "You know if she had met me first, she would be mine."

Not taking his eyes from the vision walking towards him wearing the tiara he had given her, he simply replied in his gruff voice, "Get your own princess. This one is taken."

"You sound like you mean that."

He turned momentarily to Joshua just as Cynthia reached him. "I do."

Standing there with no veil to cover her face she smiled. "I do too."

Samuel put his hands around the slim waist pulled her close and kissed her. Joshua tapped the minister on his shoulder, "That train is pulling out of the station, I think you better hurry up."

The minister cleared his throat and announced, "At the couple's request this will be short and to the point." He to Cynthia smiled and said, "Do you?"

Cynthia replied, "I do."

Then he turned to Samuel and asked, "Do you?"

"I do," Samuel replied.

"Who gives this woman to this man?"

"Her Mother and I do," Jackson stated.

The minister smiled, "Then by the powers vested in me I now pronounce you husband and wife." He closed the bible he was holding and stated, "Now, this is how a wedding should be short and simple."

Sofia stood, "This is so improper."

Everyone turned to her and moaned. Jackson, who was still standing behind his daughter stepped over to Sofia and whispered. "If you don't sit your ass down and shut up I will divorce you before this day ends. Now smile pretty for the camera."

Cynthia wasn't sure what her father said to her mother, but Sofia looked flushed then sat down and smiled. Jackson turned to the minister. "You can finish now."

The minister nodded his head and said, "You may kiss your bride."

Samuel did not have to be told twice, he captured Cynthia's lips with his leaving no doubt she was now his queen.

The reception that followed lasted a lot longer than the wedding. As Samuel and Cynthia danced Brian actually smiled. Cynthia was happy and that was all he could ask for. Pearl walked over to him, "We have a situation in the lobby. You better come with me."

He looked down at her then in the direction of the lobby where he saw Gavin standing to the side. Looking around the room, he checked to make sure his people were in place. Ryan, who had just joined them as part of his security team was covering Blake. Her brother, Donnell Williams was covering Prince LaVere' and his family. Looking to his right he noticed JD and James had both stood and was walking towards the lobby. "Don't tell me Munford is at it again," he mumbled.

"Munford would be a piece of cake compared to this," Pearl said as he followed her out the door. If anyone had ever told him there would be a day when he saw Carolyn Roth-Roberts drunk in public, he would have took odds and knew he would become rich. But there she was drunker than a sailor on weekend liberty, being refrained by Gavin, or at least he was trying.

"What in the hell?" was all he could say.

"My thoughts exactly, but with the media around, I don't have time to find out." Pearl explained, "I have a room available let's try to move this circus in there."

"You got it." Brian moved swiftly, walking past Gavin and pitched the slurring Carolyn across his shoulders then just as quickly followed Pearl. The screaming Carolyn kicked him several times, a little too close to his jewels and he smacked her behind as the doors were closed behind them. Brian placed her on one of the soft leather chairs then turned to Gavin. "What in the hell are you doing here, with her?"

Gavin exhaled and ran his hand down his face. "I didn't bring her."

"She's drunk Gavin," Brian stated.

"She's been like this for the last few weeks," he said as he sat down beside her.

"Why? I thought now that Cynthia is married you two would be in wedded bliss."

"Don't talk about me like I'm not here. If you want to know why I'm here I'll tell." She stood uneasily and walked over to JD. "I want to talk to Tracy," she pointed what once was a perfectly manicured fingernail into his chest.

JD took her hands and held them in front of her, "You don't want to do that Carolyn."

"On hell yes I do. Your little angel," she slurred, "has ruined my life. Now I'm going to ruin hers. You didn't tell her did you JD." She snatched away and almost fell as Gavin steadied her. "What you think she going to do after she finds out you been keeping secrets from her?"

James looked at Gavin and questioned. "You told her about Tracy?"

Shaking his head filled with concern for her wife, "No."

"No, my husband didn't tell me. Neither did my father." The word came out as a choke and tears began to flow down her cheeks.

Gavin gathered her into his arms as he looked at Pearl who stood by the door. "Find us a back way out of here. The press has the front covered."

"How did she get in without being seen?" Pearl asked.

Carolyn laughed, "I was good." She pointed at them smirking, "I got by all your so call security, hah."

Gavin and Brian turned their heads as the brandy laced breath filled the room. "There's a privacy tunnel that's used for dignitaries when staying at the hotel." Brian stated. "I'll carry her, you make sure the way is clear," he said to Pearl.

Brian looked down at Carolyn and exhaled. "Look, I know you are angry, but I also know you love Gavin and you would not do anything to publicly humiliate him."

Carolyn looked at Gavin with caring tear-filled eyes. "I'm sorry. You've been so good to me. I love you." She cried.

"I know," he consoled her and looked at Brian. "Let's get her home."

Pearl looked at them, "I have an idea. Give me one minute." She left the room. Less than five minutes later she walked back in with her father, two brothers, Mathew and Luke. They were each all six-four and taller. With Carolyn in the center, no one would be able to see her.

Brian liked the plan. The men gathered around Carolyn and Gavin and walked out into the lobby. "Your driver moved the car to the Cary street side of the hotel," Pearl explained. Once they were in the lobby JD and James walked in the opposite direction to go back into the ballroom where the reception was taking place.

Suddenly, the doors opened and out stepped Tracy and Ashley with little JC. "Jeffrey, there you are. JC needs to go to the little boys' room."

Hearing the voice Carolyn turned and pushed through the men surrounding her. Gavin grabbed her, but she pulled away. "Tracy, I want to talk to you."

Tracy and Ashley looked at each other and frowned.

"Babe, let's take care of JC. You can talk to Carolyn another time." JD said as he attempted to turn Tracy back towards the ballroom.

"Tracy looked up at her husband and whispered, "Is Carolyn drunk?"

Anxious to get Tracy away from Carolyn, he nodded, "a little babe," he replied and tried to turn her away.

Tracy looked back and stopped. "Here babe, take JC," she pushed the child into his father's arms. "I need to go help her." She walked towards Carolyn whom, Gavin seemed to be pulling back.

"I don't need your help," Carolyn snapped angrily. "I'm a true Roth, through and through. It will be a cold day in hell when I have to get help from the likes of you—my father's bastard child." Everyone seemed to have frozen in place—no one seemed to even breathe.

"What?" Ashley asked as James pulled her close. She looked up at him with questioning eyes.

JD put JC up on his shoulder and grabbed Tracy's waist.

Tracy frowned. "Carolyn what are talking about?"

"Ask your husband and your brother-in-law. They know." She stood her ground. "Tell her JD. Tell her who her real father is."

Tracy looked to Jeffrey then back to Carolyn. She then looked at all the faces standing around in the lobby. This was not the place for whatever Carolyn was blabbering about. Turning to Pearl, "Find a room we can take her."

"Actually babe, Gavin is taking Carolyn home." JD said, still trying to prevent his wife from being hurt.

Ashley looked at her brother then at her husband. Now Tracy may not have paid attention to what Carolyn said, but Ashley certainly did. "Carolyn, repeat what you said."

"You heard me. Tracy is my father's bastard child."

Tracy looked from Jeffrey, to James to Ashley then back to Carolyn and asked. "Tracy who?"

Once You've Touched the Heart

ISBN 978-0-9801066-0-2

The Heart of Him

ISBN-13: 978-0-9801066-1-9
ISBN-10: 0-9801066-1-3

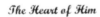

Available at
www.irisbolling.com
www.sirient.com
www.myspace.com/irisbolling
www.amazon.com

Made in the USA
Middletown, DE
19 December 2017